CHASING DAYLIGHT

A STEALTH OPS NOVEL

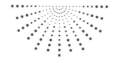

BRITTNEY SAHIN

EMKO MEDIA, LLC

Chasing Daylight

By: Brittney Sahin

Published by: EmKo Media, LLC

Copyright © 2020 EmKo Media, LLC

This book is an original publication of Brittney Sahin.

Chief Editor: Deb Markanton

Editor: Arielle Brubaker

Proofreader: Judy Zweifel, Judy's Proofreading

Cover Design: LJ, Mayhem Cover Creations

Photography: Eric Battershell Photography

Ebook ISBN: 9781947717251

Paperback ISBN: 9798664235401

❀ Created with Vellum

For all the list-makers in the world like Anastasia and me ...
this one is for you!

PLAYLIST

Lil Nas X, *Old Town Road* (Chapter 2)

Brett Young - *In Case You Didn't Know* (Chapter 7)

Blake Shelton and Gwen Stefani - *Nobody But You* (Chapter 12)

P!nk, Khalid - *Hurts 2B Human* (Chapter 19)

Thomas Rhett, Reba McEntire - *Be A Light* (Chapter 21)

The Avett Brothers - *Ain't No Man* (Chapter 23-24)

Luke Bryan - *What She Wants Tonight* (Chapter 25)

Blake Shelton - *Hell Right* (Chapter 25)

Lee Brice - *I don't Dance* (Chapter 25)

Regard - *Ride It* (Chapter 26)

Kelly Clarkson - *I Dare You* (Chapter 33)

Andra Day - *Rise Up* (Chapter 36)

Blanco Brown - *The Git Up* (Chapter 38)

Keith Urban - *Somebody Like You* (Chapter 38)

Luke Bryan - *Knockin' Boots* (Epilogue)

Spotify Playlist - Chasing Daylight, Brittney Sahin

CHAPTER ONE

JUST OUTSIDE BIRMINGHAM, ALABAMA

"THEY'VE GOT ME SURROUNDED." ROMAN'S DEEP VOICE remained calm despite his statement as he spoke over comms. "Need an assist."

A.J. quickly took cover behind a thick oak probably older than his granddaddy. "What's your grid?" he asked urgently, slightly out of breath and regretting the big breakfast he'd eaten. But when it came to grits and sausage, he had no self-control.

"The safe house," Roman shouted as the crack of enemy fire erupted in the background.

"Help is on the way," A.J. confirmed. "Hold your position."

"Seriously? Like I have somewhere else to go? You think I want to get my ass nailed?" Roman snorted. "Don't you dare respond to that."

A.J. bit back a laugh. They needed Roman intact. Out of the five of them, he was the guy on Echo with a virtual Wikipedia app inside his head. Swinging his weapon around

1

from where it hung off his shoulder, A.J. snuck out from behind the tree.

"Shit, Wyatt's down," Roman announced. "We need that backup and now."

A.J. maneuvered through the woods toward the safe house that wasn't all that safe at the moment, considering Roman was surrounded, and now they were out their best sniper.

"Hang tight," Owen's voice broke in. As the only pilot on Bravo and Echo Teams, Bravo Two was their secret weapon today. Well, the bird he was flying in on, at least.

The tree branches erupted and birds took flight at the *chuff chuff chuff* of helo rotors beating the hot, heavy air hanging above the treetops.

"The guys are fast-roping to you," Owen alerted over comms, and A.J. advanced to the prearranged spot to wait for Chris and Finn. Echo Three and Five, respectively, had won the Rock Paper Scissor challenge for the privilege of making a dramatic entrance.

Owen was flying a bird that belonged to one of A.J.'s friends, who was currently overseas doing some sort of clandestine shit in the Air Force. A.J. had called in a favor, and while it wasn't a Chinook, the Sikorsky his friend had modified to allow for such an occasion as jumping out of it worked for what they needed today. With no place to land, Chris and Finn entered the forest by way of a thick, braided rope dangling from the chopper.

"They got Wyatt, huh?" Chris's booted feet hit the ground, and he detached from the rope. Finn next.

A.J. nodded. "But Roman's now at the safe house. Old Man Shaw's place." A boarded-up dilapidated cabin that'd sat empty ever since Shaw's wife passed away, and Shaw claimed she haunted the place. Swore he heard banging pots and pans. Floorboards popping up and smacking him in the head like in a Roadrunner cartoon.

You know better than to go play hide-and-seek on Shaw's property, his mom used to yell at him and his brothers when they'd head to the cabin in an attempt to spot the ghost.

A smile crossed A.J.'s lips at the childhood memory. They never did see Mrs. Shaw, but the spine-tingling creeps that hit A.J. whenever he got within a hundred yards of the place inched over his skin even now as he was fixin' to rescue Echo Four.

"You sure you're alone in there?" A.J. prompted over comms. "Not seeing ghosts or anything?"

"You're hilarious," Roman responded as a *snap! snap! snap!* rang out in the background. "Paranormal phenomena is a cultural creation not supported by science."

A.J. grinned. "Yeah, but you got the heebie-jeebies, don't ya?"

"You seriously trying to creep Echo Four out right now?" Chris shook his head while clutching his gun. Mission-focused and ready to kick some ass.

"Trust me, if you'd ever been inside that cabin—"

"I can still hear you," Roman cut off A.J., and he practically heard the eye-roll accompanying his words loud and clear.

"Mmhm. We're moving out." A.J. pumped his fist in the direction they needed to go, and they fell into formation, using the cover of trees to approach the property. Once in view of the cabin, they stopped behind a bank of oak trees. "We need to neutralize the threat on the south side first."

"Roger," the guys replied in unison.

A.J. broke through the line of trees as carefully as when he'd gone outside the wire in Afghanistan and had to avoid stepping on an IED.

3

IEDs had been everywhere in Afghanistan. *Literally* everywhere. No place, no speck of ground was safe. His world had once been defined by the territory that had been cleared of devices and areas still at risk.

He was pretty sure Old Man Shaw hadn't set any booby traps out there, but it was still a possibility. "Watch your step," he warned the guys.

"Got a live one," Chris commented. "He looks like he's preparing to make a run for it," A.J. followed Chris's gaze to an enemy crouched behind an oak thirty yards away on the perimeter of Shaw's property.

A.J. readied his Spyder .68 but halted with a grunt when something pegged him in the arm. *Where the hell are you?* He backed up and ducked behind the closest tree, weapon still drawn as he eyed his surroundings for a possible hunting tree stand where the opposition may have been perched. "I took one in the arm," he informed Echo Team.

"Doesn't count. It's not a head shot or center mass. Keep moving." A snap followed Chris's order. "Got him. You're clear to pursue."

"Who'd you nail?" A.J. shifted out from behind the tree and crossed over a pile of rocks.

"Brian," Chris replied, his tone far too blasé.

"Damn it, Chris, I had dibs on Brian," A.J. grumbled.

Brian was marrying A.J.'s sister, Ella, on the Fourth of July, and maybe he was looking to instill a little fear into the man first. Brian needed to know what he was signing up for when he joined the Hawkins family.

As far as A.J. was concerned, he was taking it easy on Brian by using paintball guns today. Of course, they weren't standard-issued models used for recreational games. They were the kind utilized in battle simulation training. Paintball guns were more effective than laser tag when prepping for missions. The physical force of getting struck by a paintball or two was a dose of reality and served to hit home the consequences of a failed real-life op.

As Chris began his approach toward Brian to zip-tie his prisoner, Finn shouted, "It's a trap!"

Chris dodged the paintball bullet using his lightning-fast reflexes, and in a smooth maneuver, dropped to a knee, spun around, and took the shot. "The enemy team is down to two from what I can tell," he announced. "Looks like one of them is up on the cabin roof preparing to breach."

"Old Man Shaw will lose his shit over a hole in that roof, even if the place is already falling apart. Hell, Mrs. Shaw might even make an appearance." A.J. aimed his weapon toward the opposition, currently doing a little shimmy on the shingles, who also happened to be one of his best friends growing up.

Jesse was the kid who'd encouraged A.J. to sneak into Shaw's cabin and search for ghosts.

The one to "borrow" A.J.'s dad's farm tractor and ride into town to spy on the girls at the ice cream parlor at thirteen.

And he was also the kid that jumped in front of another guy who'd been about to punch A.J.'s brother in the face, taking the punch instead.

But today, Jesse was on the enemy's team, and A.J. had no problem dropping his buddy.

"At least the paint all over the cabin brightens up that shitty-looking place. Maybe Shaw won't notice a hole in the roof," Finn said over comms.

"Maybe not, but I bet Mrs. Shaw would fly off the handle. We can give Roman that scientific proof he needs that ghosts are real." A.J. kept his head low and inched toward the cabin to get a closer shot.

"Since when do you believe in ghosts?" Chris asked.

"We were in a Russian ghost town not too long ago, or have you forgotten?" A.J. reminded him. "You didn't have to walk through those deserted children's nurseries like I did. Damn, it was creepy. Seeing little shoes lined up against the wall." As if on cue, his body sprouted a coating of goose bumps on his arms and right down his legs beneath his cargo pants.

"Yeah, well—"

"A.J.!" Finn hollered, interrupting whatever Roman was about to say, no doubt in protest to their talk of the supernatural.

Shit. A.J. should have known better. Jesse had lured them into a trap. He'd gone on the roof to divert A.J.'s attention. Dangled himself like candy. Jesse used to pull similar moves when they played war games as kids.

A.J.'s older brother Beckett, also on Jesse's team along with his other brothers Caleb and Shep, had a red dot laser-focused on A.J.'s chest. Beckett took the shot before A.J. had a chance to move or return fire.

The paintball hit A.J. a bit harder than expected, and he stumbled over a gnarly tree root—probably Mrs. Shaw's doing. He lost his footing and fell backward, the back of his head connecting with something hard. That random pile of rocks he'd encountered moments ago, maybe?

A.J. blinked a few times, trying to regain his focus amid the sunlight shining down between two branches that swayed overhead.

A.J. closed his eyes, sealing out the light. Attempting to gain his bearings. Shake off the knock on the head.

"You good?"

The voice was familiar. Not any of his Echo teammates, though. Not Jesse or one of his brothers.

"A.J., you hit your head?"

A.J. allowed his mind to wander, trying to place that voice, to understand what or who he was hearing.

Forcing his eyes open, he sat upright while cradling the back of his head where a throbbing pain made his skull feel as though it were splitting open. The migraine of all migraines.

"Where am I?" A.J. dropped his gaze to his legs. Desert digital camo clothed his body. A short-barrel M4 carbine lay off to his left. The blades of a CH-47 Chinook were chopping the air in the distance. Flames and black smoke off to his right engulfed an old Land Cruiser.

"Yo, man, you good? You lost your helmet."

That voice. Deep. A slight hint of an accent.

Am I good? A.J. lowered his hand to his lap and shifted his attention to the outstretched hand gripping a ballistic helmet by the strap. A drop of blood fell as if in slow motion capturing that one moment in freeze-frame.

It was too bright. Too *everything* to be in the woods in Alabama.

"You must've hit your head harder than I thought." The man moved closer, maintaining hold of the helmet and squatted, revealing his face.

A hand reached out and firmly gripped A.J.'s shoulder. A hand he hadn't seen in years. "We gotta get the hell out of here before we get our asses blown up. Can you move?" His teammate cocked his head, his dark eyes focused on A.J. with concern.

"What's going on?" A.J. implored. "What happened?"

"A.J.!" Loud clapping sounds had him blinking to find Chris bending down and smacking his palms together to get his attention.

A.J. released a sharp breath and flung a hand over Chris's wrist.

"The back of your head is bleeding," Finn told him. "You banged the back of that thick skull of yours on a shitty pile of rocks."

"Damn, I didn't expect you'd go and fall and hit your head." It was his older brother Beckett. He and Chris helped A.J. stand, but . . .

"I need to see him again." A.J.'s mouth felt like it was stuffed with cotton. The words hard to get out, but he managed to push through, to speak. "I need to talk to him. There's so much to say. I never even said goodbye."

Chris shifted his face shield up. "What are you talking about?"

A.J. peered around at the men surrounding him. Worried expressions on their faces. He attempted to stand on his own but decided it was a bad idea when a sharp jolt of pain shot through his head. Suddenly there were too many hands reaching for him, and it was as if he was moving through a turnstile of arms as they tried to keep him on his feet.

His head hurt like something fierce. But his heart hurt even more.

"I'm fine," A.J. responded at the realization they were on the verge of having Owen medevac him out of there on the chopper after hearing a few grumbled words from his older brother: *concussion, helo,* and *hospital.* "I promise." He added a nod, hoping to come across as confident.

"Maybe don't tell Mom about this," Beckett said once A.J. was mostly steady on his feet, still a bit off-kilter.

A.J. forced a smile before his lips flatlined at the sight of someone walking away in the distance wearing a full kit of eighty or so pounds of gear. Helmet on.

"Wait!" A.J. called out as emotion choked him up.

"What? Who?" Chris twisted around to follow A.J.'s outstretched arm.

"*El se fue.*" A.J. swallowed and stumbled back a step. "He's gone," he repeated in English this time, growing nauseous and dizzy. Beckett grabbed hold of A.J.'s arm before he lost his footing again. "He's just gone."

CHAPTER TWO

A.J. SMOOTHED A HAND UP AND DOWN HIS ABDOMEN, checking to see if he still had a six-pack after all the food he'd eaten an hour ago—catfish, okra, green tomatoes. You name it, his mom fried it. Oh, and the homemade pecan pies . . . yup, he was stuffed.

He'd told himself he needed that second slice of pie to help absorb all the ibuprofen he'd popped to get rid of that nasty headache. The throbbing in his head had finally tapered off enough that he was beginning to feel like himself again. Plus, being at his parents' house earlier had helped put his mind and body at ease. But something still gnawed at his subconscious. *I did not see a ghost today. It was a figment of my imagination.* Those words had rotated round and round like he was on the spinning teacups at Disney World his brothers used to force him to go on even though they knew it made him dizzy.

"Our mom swears people come all the way from Montgomery to attend our little church just to try her pies she serves after service." A.J.'s brother Caleb, the youngest of the four brothers, announced to the table inside The Drunk Gator, one of only two bars in their town. They were short three men right now. Owen's wife called earlier with the news that their son had come down with a virus, so he decided to fly home early. Jesse was outside on the phone. And the groom-to-be was somewhere else in the bar, preferring not to hang with them.

A.J. briefly peered around the bar and found Brian talking with a brunette by the jukebox, the sounds of Lil Nas X's *Old Town Road* playing. Thank God the bartender upgraded the jukebox from when A.J. used to live there. Not that A.J. had anything against some of the greats, like Elvis.

"I might need to come all the way down from D.C. for her pies." Wyatt, who served as team leader of Echo Team, leaned back on the chair next to A.J., laced his fingers behind his back, and stretched. "And don't get me started on that catfish."

"Nothing beats Mom's cooking." A.J. eyed his brother Beckett sitting across the narrow table from him as the bartender set down a tray of shot glasses and a bottle of bourbon.

"Maybe if you came home more often, you wouldn't miss it so much." Beckett's statement wasn't a surprise. He was constantly trying to convince A.J. to move back to Alabama.

"I came home at Christmas," A.J. reminded him as the bartender filled their glasses.

"And for some crazy reason, McKenna seems to like you the most even though you're not around." It was his brother Caleb giving him a hard time now. "Always hanging on to your every word. Begging for stories."

"I lead an interesting life, what can I say?" A.J. offered the usual answer he gave Caleb. The guy sounded like a broken record, reciting the same lines whenever they saw each other.

McKenna was Beckett's eleven-year-old daughter and one of A.J.'s favorite people on the planet. A ray of sunshine. When Beckett became a single dad, he moved back home to be near family to help raise her.

A.J. knew his brother Shep would chime in, too. He wouldn't be able to help himself. *And in three, two, one.*

"Nah. That's not the case. McKenna probably likes A.J. the most because he's *not* around all that often." Shep, only two years younger than A.J., threw out his two cents on the matter.

"Every time I come home, I get grilled by y'all, and yet you wonder why I don't make the trip more often," A.J. teased, warily eying the shot of top-shelf bourbon, not sure if he should drink given the knot on his head and the ibuprofen. But they were at a bachelor party, and no one liked the sober guy at such an event.

"Such a city slicker." Shep lifted his shot glass and examined it with scrutiny as if the bartender had poured a Cosmo or Sex on the Beach. "You lost whatever Bama you had in you spending all that time in New York City."

"Oh, trust me, he didn't. A.J. becomes as Southern as Southern can get when he's in the South." Chris served as Echo Three when the boys weren't running around shooting paintballs in the woods. He was the youngest on Echo Team, but not by much. He'd be hitting thirty-seven this year. They were all getting up there in age.

"I've noticed," Wyatt began. "I was fixin' to do this, and I reckon y'all better do that." Wyatt's imitation of A.J.'s Alabama drawl had A.J. lightly elbowing him in the shoulder. Of course, A.J. always gave Wyatt hell about his British accent becoming thicker whenever they traveled outside the U.S., so maybe it was Wyatt's turn to heckle him.

"Well, can you blame me when I'm around these

knuckleheads?" A.J. lifted his shot glass in the direction of his brothers, still not prepared to gulp it down.

"Maybe one of you single guys should go chat up that pretty brunette instead of the guy who's marrying your sister," Chris announced, which had the men shifting their attention toward the jukebox just as the brunette set a hand on Brian's chest.

I knew it, damn it. Not good enough for his sister.

"I nominate A.J. for the job of going to rescue that woman from a taken man." Chris leaned back in his chair with a satisfied grin. A.J. wanted to smack the smile right off Echo Three's face. That damn *knowing* smile of his. "Ah, that's right, you won't." One eye closed for a second as if Chris were focusing on reading an eye chart to check his vision. "Because your heart belongs to a woman who doesn't even know it."

Shep waved a finger A.J.'s way, momentarily distracted from the girl talking to Brian. "And who is he talking about?"

A.J. grunted, finally tossed back his shot, then coughed out, "No one." But Chris was right. He'd been unable to get his mind off the smoking hot FBI agent he'd met in Charlotte last year. Literally unable to stop thinking about her to the point he was beginning to worry if there was something wrong with him. Gorgeous women had hit on him, and he'd not had even the slightest stir in his pants. The fucker was asleep. He'd call his dick Sleeping Beauty if his niece didn't watch Disney movies like it was a sport.

"Well, does this woman have a name?" Shep pressed. He wasn't going to let this go, and if the man wanted to tangle, well, A.J. knew his brother's hot buttons and had no problem applying a little pressure.

"Anastasia Quinn. Redhead. Brilliant. FBI agent." Damn Echo Five. Now Shep would prompt Beckett to do a little recon on her and tap into his law enforcement resources for some dirt since Beckett was sheriff of their small town. A town A.J. hated to admit he did miss. But if he confessed to missing home, he'd have to reexamine his life on the go, and he wasn't ready to stop operating. The world needed Bravo and Echo Teams. "A.J. believes in ghosts and love at first sight, so it would seem," Finn added, and A.J. made a mental note to kick his ass the next time they sparred at the gym back in New York.

"She goes by Ana," A.J. blurted as his attention moved back to Brian, who was still chatting up the brunette.

"That with one *n* or two?" Roman asked, and A.J. wasn't sure if Roman was kidding or not.

"I don't know." What A.J. did know was that he needed this conversation moving in a different direction. He twisted on his chair to better observe his future brother-in-law. "Does she know Brian is marrying our sis?"

"The question should be, does Brian remember he's no longer single?" Jesse asked, returning to the table at the right moment—when Brian was two seconds away from getting chewed out by a bunch of protective guys.

Brian turned as if Jesse's intense stare had morphed into something he could physically feel. His expression said it all —he'd been caught flirting. A dip of the brows. A white slash for a mouth. Brian nodded at the woman, then left her alone at the jukebox, returning to their table.

"Who were you talking to?" Shep quickly asked Jesse as if sensing a potential brawl was on the horizon. Jesse had never liked anyone Ella dated in high school, same as A.J. and his brothers—they were all protective of her. And if Jesse thought for one minute Brian was even thinking about cheating on Ella . . .

Jesse tore his light blue eyes to Shep. "My sister. She showed up in town tonight for a surprise visit."

"Rory is practically one of the guys. You should invite her to Caleb's later for part three of this party," Shep insisted, which drew a caveman-like grunt from Brian.

"She should come," Caleb agreed, clearly to piss off Brian.

"I'll ask her. She does miss y'all." Jesse settled onto the chair opposite Finn next to Roman.

"How's Rory?" Beckett asked. "She didn't come home at Christmas."

A.J. wanted to hear more about Rory, but he was annoyed Brian was given a reprieve from the boys interrogating him about the girl at the jukebox.

"You know Rory. Always flitting about the world chasing artifacts, treasure, or whatever you want to call it." The lip of the shot glass hovered near Jesse's mouth as if he wanted to say more but wasn't sure how much to divulge. "She did tell me she's considering putting down some roots in New Orleans. Maybe even pursuing her other passion." Something in his eyes said, *God, I hope so.*

"You mean canine training?" A.J. remembered Rory had spent all her free time volunteering at some big animal shelter in Birmingham every summer growing up, rehabbing dogs to help with adoption.

"Yeah, I mean, she's practically an animal whisperer," Jesse answered.

"Well, I hope she does settle down," Beckett said, worry in his voice. Typical father.

Rory was Rory—a carefree spirit who hated being tied down. If she ever decided to get hitched, the boys would step up and ensure the man was worthy of someone like her. She was practically a sister to A.J. And as for Ella, he had to make sure Brian was the right match for her, which was basically why he'd recruited his buddies to create the mission earlier. Of course, things had gone a bit south after he whacked his head on what he was now calling a small-sized boulder to make himself feel better about it.

"You call this a bachelor party weekend?" Brian slapped his hands together, forcing a change in conversation, one centered back on him. Bull's-eye.

Brian. Damn, damn Brian.

He was a banker from Mobile. VP of some fancy place, the kind that had put many of the mom-and-pop banking operations out of business, which had drawn the Hawkins brothers' immediate distaste. Brian had a tall, lean frame. Not much in the way of muscles. Black glasses perched on a wide nose. Dark hair closely cropped. Clean-shaven when clearly beards were supposed to be "in" from what A.J.'s niece declared, pointing to A.J.'s beard at breakfast while reading *Vogue. And why was Beckett letting her read that?*

"What are you getting at?" Wyatt spoke up before anyone else could, but A.J. was certain they were all thinking the same thing.

"First, we ate breakfast with your family," Brian said as if that were a damn crime. "Like more grits and sausage than a man can tolerate. Then, y'all staged some sort of military-type battle—to what—scare the hell out of me from marrying Ella Mae? Then, we spent an hour while you all tried to convince A.J. to see a doctor when it's clear he's a stubborn ass and won't. Then back to the Hawkins house for dinner. Who does all that for a bachelor party?" He gathered a breath after cataloging their day's events as if the guys had partaken in the activities but were currently suffering from amnesia. Okay, given A.J.'s head bump, maybe that was fair. "And now we're at the local tavern where the ratio between male to female is pathetic. Where are the strippers?"

Beckett abruptly stood from the table, his chair falling over, but Finn was quick and positioned it back upright. "Say what?"

"I'm kidding. Relax." Brian held his palms open and patted the air as Beckett hovered at his side. The sheriff appeared grumpier than his normal grumpy self.

"No worries. We'll be heading to my place soon to party," Caleb said while standing, trying to diffuse the situation. "But no strippers. You're marrying our baby sister, so you won't be stuffing bills, or anything for that matter, in, on, or near any woman."

Beckett leaned in closer to Brian. "*Ever* again." He left off the *Am I clear?* but it was heard loud and clear.

And based on the daggers Jesse was now shooting Brian's way, A.J. wouldn't be surprised if Brian faked a headache and hopped in his car to head back to his home in Mobile.

Brian swallowed. "Understood."

Beckett sat back down, and Caleb hesitantly returned to his seat as well. The tension was still palpable, and from what A.J. could tell, "Perfect Brian," as his mom called him, was far from perfect.

Beckett had warned everyone Brian wasn't right for Ella even before A.J. had returned for Christmas. But Beckett didn't like anyone.

However, when A.J. had come home only to have Brian steal Ella away on CHRISTMAS DAY to take her to Tahiti . . . A.J. realized Beckett was right.

But damn it, Ella was happy. And if Ella was happy, A.J. wanted to be happy for her, too.

But Brian? Fucking Brian? A.J. doubted the guy would be brave enough to even kill a spider, let alone protect Ella from any trouble. The cocky attitude A.J. had witnessed all day had been backed by bullshit.

"So, um, how is it that we Southern boys managed to school a bunch of former SEALs today?" Brian asked as if trying to lighten the mood, but did the man not know better than to poke a bear? "If you ask me, you guys don't look all that rough and tough."

A devious, all-too-familiar smirk traveled over Chris's lips. "We're more of the triathlete variety than the bodybuilding type. And if you're not satisfied with the turn of events today, we'd be happy to challenge you to something else."

A.J. removed his cowboy hat and pressed the heel of his hand to the back of his head where the bandage was taped.

Refusing to go to the doctor. Typical Teamguy, his sister had yelled at him over the phone after Caleb narced on Beckett for shooting him.

"We really do need to liven this night up, though," Brian said after a few more awkward moments passed during which Chris and Finn made a few jokes about the paintball fight today. They'd purposely discussed maneuvers that had gone right over Perfect Brian's head. "I mean, the bachelor party my best man threw me in Vegas last weekend was—" Brian let go of his words, squeezing his eyes closed as if shocked he'd outed himself. "I mean, the work conference I had to attend that sort of turned into a bachelor thing . . ."

"Come again?" Jesse asked, slowly placing his palms on the table, readying to stand as Shep extended an arm to block him. It was clear Shep knew Jesse was itching to throw down with Brian. A.J. had his reasons for not liking Brian, which were mostly based on his gut, but he had a feeling Jesse knew a bit more, especially since he'd initiated the "let's get to know the real Brian" bachelor party weekend.

The base of Brian's neck grew a touch red as everyone at the table stared at him like he was an enemy combatant with an RPG in hand they needed to take down.

"That's why your best man and other friends declined our invitation to join us this weekend? It's because they threw you another party already?" A.J. had forgotten all about the knot on the back of his head now. Maybe he'd even join Jesse in fighting Brian. He preferred his gun to hand-to-hand combat, but he'd make an exception in this case.

It'd been weeks since he'd shot someone, why not Perfect Brian?

He could bury the body out back at Caleb's place, and no one would know.

"It wasn't planned. I work with my best friends, and we were all in Vegas for work, so we decided—why not have some fun?" An attempt at smiling loosened the scared-shitless expression from Brian's face.

"*Hangover* movie kind of fun?" Caleb asked, and he and Shep were on their feet, no longer the guys trying to calm the crowd.

"I swear," Brian started, "I would never cheat on your sister." His hand went to his heart. "Nothing happened."

"What hotel were you at?" A.J. asked.

"What?" Brian gulped. "Why?"

"So I can pull the surveillance and ensure you were a good boy." A.J. smiled, the bourbon and his ghost-memory encounter earlier taking a back seat to his sudden desire to wipe the nervous grin from the man's face.

Tahiti. Who goes to Tahiti on Christmas? Men named Brian, that's who. Okay, so maybe he was letting this Brian give every other Brian on the planet a bad rap, but A.J. had felt there was something off about him from the beginning. Hence the request for the assist from the guys on his team.

And had the rest of Bravo been available, he would've recruited their help as well.

"You know, Wyatt here is getting married in July, too." Roman pointed toward Echo One. A.J. took a deep breath, unsure whether to be thankful or not for Roman's effort to calm everyone down and prevent the exchange of blows. Roman hadn't been around the Hawkins brothers long enough to know if they were all hot-tempered or not, but Roman knew A.J., so . . .

"Congrats," Brian said, his eyes widening in a silent thank-you for the help. Not too many friendly faces at the table. "And what kind of bachelor party are you having? Not like this, I bet," Brian remarked, inching back into the territory of clueless and stupid instead of afraid.

"Not having one," Wyatt quickly replied.

"Let's hope work doesn't get in the way of Wyatt's wedding," Chris joked, and the blood nearly drained from Wyatt's face as he pivoted toward Chris.

"You did not just say that." Wyatt scowled. "You probably just jinxed us."

"That's like saying it's quiet while working a shift on patrol on the streets of L.A.," Beckett said with a grimace.

"Did you work in L.A. before here?" Chris asked in surprise as if not expecting the Alabama sheriff to have ever worked in Los Angeles.

"Yeah, but that's a story for another day," Beckett answered, his tone gravelly.

"If I don't get to marry Natasha on time because we have to spin up," Wyatt said, dead serious, "I'm gonna kill you."

CHAPTER THREE

A.J. SCRUTINIZED HIS REFLECTION IN THE MIRROR ABOVE THE sink in Caleb's guest bathroom. Hands braced on the cool tile counter, he took a moment to stare into his light green eyes as the day's events played over in his mind. When his gaze slipped down to his denim shirt, the top two buttons undone, the sleeves rolled to the elbows, he shook his head. What had he been thinking wearing something so hot during summer in the South? Was it the bump on his head that had him off? That had him seeing his long-lost friend as clear as moonshine on a summer day?

"Get a grip." He turned on the faucet, splashed some water on his face, and expelled a deep breath before using a white hand towel with a crimson letter A embroidered on the center. His family bled the University of Alabama colors. His mom had preemptively stitched baby onesies long before McKenna was born in red and white with "Roll Tide" or "Crimson Tide" printed on them. She had a whole stack waiting for when the rest of her children chose to procreate. At the rate they were all going, Beckett might have offered their mom the one and only grandbaby.

"Maybe Ella was right? I should've gone to see the doc."
He twisted to the side to glimpse the bandage in the mirror.
Still intact. "And am I talking to myself?"

There was a knock at the door, followed by a soft voice
asking, "You okay?"

A.J. opened the door and scooped Rory into his arms for
a hug.

"Aren't you a sight for sore eyes?" She squeaked as A.J.
tightened his embrace.

"It's been too long." He set Rory down and leaned against
the interior frame of the bathroom door while she remained in
the hallway.

"You know me. Always chasing the next big adventure."
Rory pushed the wisps of light blonde hair that had fallen
from her ponytail behind her ears before tucking her hands in
the back pockets of her frayed jean shorts.

"Where were you last?"

"Somewhere in the Caribbean." She gave him a bold
smile that said it all. He needed more details, but he also
knew Rory wasn't going to divulge much more.

And if he pressed her, she'd push right back about his life.
It had become a balancing act between them over the years.

Rory's smile stretched, her eyes glinting as if reading his
thoughts. "So, how's private security treating you? Eight and
a half years with that agency now, right?" And this was her
opening, her way to remind him he had secrets, too.

His parents had practically begged him to leave his
"civilian" job and move back home to help on the family
ranch. Follow in his father's footsteps. Neither his mom nor
his dad understood the work he did, and how could they? A.J.
had lied to them for eight and a half years. Besides, they had
Caleb and Shep for help. Did they really need A.J.?

"I'm still in one piece," he said with a half smile.

He grabbed his hat from the bathroom counter before they walked down the hall to the big open kitchen. A.J.'s mom had used her design skills to create a plan for Caleb's house whether he wanted her help or not. His brother now lived on the pages of some Southern home magazine.

"And what happened to your head today?" She pointed to the bandage on his head, which was a reminder to put his hat back on.

"A rock. No big deal." Only maybe it was because he saw a dead man near Shaw's haunted cabin, and then he'd puked in the privacy of the forest without the guys knowing shortly before they helped patch his head.

They stood in front of the sliding glass doors that overlooked the patio and pool area out back. A few of the guys were in Caleb's pool, including Perfect Brian, whose hair was no longer perfectly styled, but the wet strands were sticking every which way from what A.J. could tell.

"You boys play too rough." Her Southern drawl hadn't been lost during all her worldly travels. "And what are they doing to that poor guy?" Rory lifted her gaze to A.J.'s for a moment, humor shining in her pretty hazel eyes before she focused back on Chris, who'd just cannonballed into the pool missing Brian by a fraction of an inch.

He didn't want to talk about Brian, even if that was why they were there. "I hear you're thinking of moving to New Orleans. You consider changing your line of work? You always loved working with animals."

"One last gig, and maybe I'll switch gears." She lifted her shoulders, not too convincing. She was a thrill-seeker, that was for sure, and it was something he understood. "I did speak to a few people about possibly helping out with training police dogs."

He pointed to Chris, who was now on the diving board

about to do a backflip into the deep end. "Captain America over there wants a canine for the team. Maybe you can help us."

An amused chuckle left her lips. "Well, if y'all have any questions or need anything when the time comes, look me up. You know where to find me."

"Actually, I don't. You're on the go as much as me."

"Life is short. Gotta live it up while you can, I suppose." She reached up and fixed his hat. "Ella says you're still single."

"Yup." A.J. had been burned before, and maybe that was why he'd been too afraid to take the plunge and call Anastasia.

Rory knew all about A.J.'s past since A.J.'s long-time relationship back in his twenties had been with one of Rory and Ella's best friends. But maybe burned was the wrong choice of words. That damn fire Caleb had going back behind the pool, the flames shooting a bit too high, was screwing with his thoughts.

A reminder of Afghanistan. The burning Land Cruiser.

Shep was on approach to the firepit, most likely planning on giving Caleb some fire safety tips like he loved to do as a firefighter—he just couldn't help himself.

"Brooke's single." Was Rory really trying to play matchmaker?

"I don't live here anymore, and you know Brooke and I were just never good for each other. We tried the long-distance thing." He'd been wrapping up his first deployment when they split in his twenties. God, that felt like an eternity ago. Would he be single forever? Of course, Wyatt was turning forty this year, and he found love . . .

And do I want love? I really did hit my head today, didn't I? Or was I possessed by Mrs. Shaw's spirit? There'd been some paranormal shit going on out in that forest. Either that or he'd been hallucinating.

"Well, we all miss you. Especially your brothers, even if those Hawkins boys won't admit it." Rory may have been a globe-trotter, but from the sounds of it, she was better at keeping in touch with everyone back at home than he was. A.J. needed to make more of an effort. His friends and family deserved better. Bravo and Echo fought to make the world a safer place, but all too often, he forgot to enjoy life in that world.

"Caleb told me Grant let you borrow his helicopter. How is he? I haven't seen Grant in a long time."

His buddy Grant had been the one to offer Owen use of his chopper even though he was out of town. "He's good. Just had a new place built on thirty-plus acres."

Grant had texted him image after image during construction, an attempt to get A.J. to visit, not that Grant's schedule ever matched up with A.J.'s since they were both doing covert shit all the time.

"Of course, Grant won't ever use it since he's never home," Rory pointed out. "He's as mysterious with his work as you are."

"And apparently as mysterious as you, Miss Treasure Hunter."

She rolled her eyes. "That's not exactly what I do."

"And what is it that you do?" he challenged, knowing damn well the woman wasn't about to answer. And yup, he got a shrug and wink, that was it.

He patted the air a few times, motioning for her to get outside. "You're letting all the good air out, leaving that door open like that."

"Now you sound like my mama." She threw a smirk over her shoulder before stepping out onto the patio.

"And I sound like mine, too." As soon as A.J. pulled the door closed, they were met with a sopping wet Chris, standing so close in his star-spangled-banner swim trunks that water dripped onto Rory's nude-colored sandals.

Echo Three stared at her totally dumbstruck. "Hi. You must be Jesse's off-limits sister." He stuck out his hand, and Rory chuckled.

"Yeah." Rory took his palm. "He loves to introduce me that way. Sorry about that."

"No worries." Chris waved his hand between them. "If I had a sister, I'd, um . . ."

"Torture her fiancé like y'all are doing to poor Brian?" She tipped her head toward the pool where Brian was attempting to escape. Unlike Chris, he was in his jeans and a tee, totally drenched once he made it out of the pool, only to have Wyatt plow him right back in the water in a playful (not really) way.

"Yeah, that guy is a pretty boy. Borderline douchey from what I saw today." Chris eyed A.J. once his palm was free from Rory's.

"Oh, he can't be that bad." Rory folded her arms, her gaze on the pool where Wyatt, Roman, and Finn appeared to be putting Brian through their own version of a SEAL training exercise. "But Jesse did want my opinion, so he asked me to crash the party. No man will be good enough for Ella as far as Jesse is concerned. I swear that man is almost more protective of Ella than he is of me."

"I doubt that," Chris said, never taking his eyes off Rory. Spellbound. Yeah, Rory probably had that effect on most men she met.

Anastasia Quinn certainly had that effect on A.J. when they'd first met, so he could relate to how Chris may be feeling at the moment. The wind knocked out of your lungs. Hard to gather a deep breath. Time standing still.

"It is strange my sister has never introduced you to Brian before tonight." Ella and Rory had been best friends growing up, and they still remained close despite Rory's travels.

"In all fairness, I'm never home," she countered.

Still, A.J. wondered if that was the only reason.

"Well, that fool challenged me to a race on a John Deere later." Chris swiped the beads of water from his hair, his eyes taking a slow journey up the length of Rory's legs before meeting her face. "Does he seriously want to race lawnmowers?" He grinned. "No cow tipping? Wrangling bulls or something?"

"Is that what you Northern boys think we do down here?" Rory's hand went to her hip as if she were about to challenge him to something herself, or maybe throw a *Bless your heart,* his way.

"What makes you think I'm a Northerner?" Chris stepped closer to her, a teasing smile plastered on his face. A.J. knew that look . . . Echo Three was preparing to move in and amp up his flirting game.

"I detect a Boston accent you appear to be working hard to disguise," Rory answered.

Chris full-on grinned now and peered at A.J. "Who is this girl?"

"Someone you don't want to mess with, remember?" She returned his flirty smile, then started for the firepit, a little bit of sass in her step. Chris slapped a hand to the back of his head and turned to watch her walk away.

"And she's good with animals? Holy hell." Chris pressed his hands into prayer position and lifted them toward the sky. "Thank you, God."

"Off-limits," A.J. reminded him as he watched Rory greet her brother down yonder at the firepit.

"My favorite two words. Or does the hyphen make it count as one word?" He shrugged and snatched a towel off the lounge chair.

"Trust me. The one guy you don't want to mess with is Jesse. Super protective of both Rory and Ella." A.J.'s brow scrunched when a thought struck him.

"What's that look you're wearing right now?" Chris waved a finger in front of A.J.'s face.

"Just wondering if Jesse doesn't think anyone is good enough for Ella because—"

"He's got the hots for your sis?" Chris nodded. "That much was obvious like five minutes into breakfast this morning. Good luck trying to get him to admit it, though."

Huh. A.J. stroked his closely trimmed beard, trying to wrap his head around the revelation as Rory laughed at something Shep said. "Well, back to Rory." He had too much on his plate right now to think about the fact one of his lifelong best friends might be into his sister. "Rory doesn't need her brother's protection, but—"

"That won't stop him from trying." Chris sounded a bit too nonchalant, as if he'd already given up on the idea of pursuing Rory. But when did Chris ever turn down any kind of challenge?

A.J.'s arms tightened over his chest with a pinch of irritation as he studied Brian climbing out of the pool, his focus back to the main subject at hand. "We might seriously need to access all the CCTV footage in Vegas from last weekend. Maybe use our facial recognition software to see what he was up to there."

"You don't think that's taking it too far?"

A.J.'s brows rose, the movement probably hidden by the brim of his hat.

"Yeah, yeah, okay." Chris caved before A.J. had a chance to school him on what it meant to have a sister since Chris was an only child.

A.J. removed his hat and dropped his eyes to his cowboy boots, his thoughts traveling back to the forest once again. To how real Marcus had seemed, as if he were still alive.

He'd met Marcus at college when they'd both worn crimson and white, the University of Alabama's colors, while playing ball. They joined the Navy together after that. Different classes at BUD/S, but they managed to wind up on the same squadron. After their stint in the military, they were brought back together when Luke Scott and his sister, Jessica, recruited them to join a different kind of team, one that completed off-the-books missions the military or government agencies couldn't or wouldn't handle for whatever reason.

Amigos por siempre, Marcus used to say to A.J. *Friends forever.*

And it did end. Way too early for Marcus Vasquez.

"When was the last time you talked to Savanna?" A.J. tried to pull his thoughts away from the day he had pounded his trident into Marcus's flag-draped casket.

"It's been too long," Chris answered, a look of regret in his eyes.

"I need to reach out. See how she's doing." Savanna was back in Birmingham. She'd remained single since becoming a widow. Surely struggling to move on from Marcus's death.

"Yeah. Time keeps slipping by." Chris's eyes thinned, and his forehead tightened as if the conversation was sobering him up.

"And we have no idea how much time we've got."

BRITTNEY SAHIN

When it's my time to go, it's my time. Don't you dare shed a tear, Marcus had said to A.J. a week before he died as if eerily knowing the future. *Ve al cielo y ve a mi padre otra vez.*

Your father doesn't want you up there with him. Not anytime soon, he'd replied to Marcus's words about joining his dad in heaven. *And what makes you think you'll go before me, brother?*

"What brought on the question about Savanna? Coming back home and seeing everyone?" Chris asked.

A.J. tore his head out of the past. "Something like that." He swallowed the lump the size of the Talladega National Forest down his throat. "Can you call Harper about Vegas after you dry off?"

Harper worked with the teams, in a similar capacity as Jessica, handling most of the intelligence and investigative components of their operations. The two women were the best of the best at what they did, and A.J. wouldn't spin up without their intel backing the missions.

"I'll go call her now. I'm not too worried about interrupting a Saturday-night date." Chris secured the towel that started to slip. "Harper is holding out for a certain someone. Same as you." He slapped A.J.'s chest and walked away.

A.J. focused on Roman in the pool. Maybe Roman would work up the nerve to ask Harper out someday. It'd taken Asher, Bravo Three, nearly losing Jessica to get his head out of his ass and share his feelings. But Jessica was the more stubborn one when it came to their relationship—and now they had twins.

A.J. supposed anything was possible.

Seeing ghosts, for example.

Calling Ana for a date . . .?

"I think I've had enough of this BUD/S drown-proofing

or whatever your buddies said they were having me do," Brian griped once out of the pool and did an about-face as if mocking those who served. Or maybe he really was just that stiff and uptight. "Not sure what family I'm marrying into. Does Ella have any idea the kind of hell you all planned on putting me through today?" Brian snatched a crimson red towel off the lounge chair. "Not sure if it's worth this."

A.J. puffed out his chest and stabbed a finger in the air, unable to hold back. "I reckon you better go unfuck yourself right now, then come back over here and decide if you want to take back those words."

"I didn't mean it's not worth marrying Ella. Damn, man." Brian scowled. "I think it's you who needs to—" Brian dropped his words as if sensing he was on the verge of getting decked by a man whose job it was to take down bad guys, and as far as A.J. was concerned, Brian was ranking high up on that list right now. "Nothing happened in Vegas," he shot out before retreating into Caleb's house, probably to change and cool off.

Maybe I need a moment to calm down, too?

A.J. pivoted to see Chris exiting the house, work phone in hand. Did he already have news about Brian from Harper? The woman was a goddess behind the keyboard, but that'd be pretty fast.

"Don't say it. Don't even say it," Wyatt called out as he hoisted himself out of the pool.

"Just talked to Harper," Chris announced, a nervous grin on his face.

"I'm guessing it wasn't about Vegas," A.J. said on a sigh.

"You bloody jinxed us, didn't you?" Wyatt scoffed as he joined them, water dripping off his body.

"Time to sober up, boys. We gotta get to the airport in Birmingham." Chris sounded like a kid who'd just been told summer vacation was canceled. Since when was he ever anything but ready, willing, and excited to spin up?

And then A.J. followed Chris's line of sight to Rory, who was standing in the glow of the fire talking animatedly to Caleb now. A.J. shook his head but kept his mouth shut. *Another one bites the dust.*

"Shit, if I don't make it to my wedding on time . . ." Wyatt growled out while grabbing a towel and drying off, Finn and Roman quickly doing the same.

"Our ops rarely take a month," Chris said with an upbeat tone that had A.J. cringing as he glanced at Wyatt. Echo Three grimaced as the significance of his words hit him. "Aww, fuuudge," he said as if Bravo Four's daughter was around, and he was trying to watch his sailor's mouth. "I shouldn't have said that."

"I think we need to throw your arse into the pool," Wyatt said, only half-kidding. "Hey, A.J., is there a swamp around here?"

"You got gators down here, don't ya?" Finn grinned.

"A few here and there have made their way to our neck of the woods." A.J. peered at Chris.

"So, anyway. D.C., at least we're heading toward your fiancée." Chris's smile broadened as he focused on Wyatt. "You know, bright side."

"Seriously, brother." Wyatt waved a finger in Chris's direction with one eye closed as if prepping to snipe him, but he was struggling to keep a straight face because, well, Echo Three had a habit of making all the guys laugh. And as far as A.J. was concerned, that was a good thing. He'd take humor any day over the wicked darkness that threatened to spring up on them from time to time.

"I guess my brothers and Jesse will need to wrap up Brian's interrogation," A.J. said, disappointed he'd have to leave home so soon after just getting there. Plus, part of him felt like he was leaving Marcus behind, too.

"Maybe Rory should give us a lift to Birmingham since we're all too drunk to drive," Chris suggested.

"We can Uber it." Wyatt rolled his eyes at Chris's lame attempt to spend more time with Rory.

"Hate to break it to y'all, but there ain't any Ubers out this way." They'd probably end up asking Rory, and Chris would get his way. Although, A.J. doubted they'd all cram into one SUV. "I'll have to call my dad to drive a few of us."

"And what will you tell him?" Finn asked, obviously curious as to how that conversation would go.

"He knows I work crazy hours. We'll be fine." A.J. turned back to Chris. "You happen to ask Harper about the Vegas thing?"

"She said, and I quote, 'You frat boys are on your own with that, and while you're at it, leave A.J.'s sister the hell alone,'" Chris repeated her words in a high-pitched voice, sounding nothing like Harper, but eliciting a laugh out of everyone nonetheless.

"There's someone I can ask," Wyatt commented. "If she can hack the CIA without getting caught, a few Vegas cams should be no big deal."

A.J. assumed Wyatt meant his cyber genius, twenty-one-year-old daughter, and he was on the verge of saying yes when Finn held both hands in the air, dropping his towel.

"She did what?" Finn's eyes widened in surprise as he grabbed the towel off the ground.

"You boys do remember we work for Uncle Sam, right?" Roman chuckled before heading inside Caleb's place without another word.

"Why does he always remind us of that?" A.J. smiled. "But yes, please ask Gwen," he said before starting for the firepit to say his goodbyes, promising himself he'd come back sooner rather than later this time.

Family was important.

The guys on Bravo and Echo were family, too.

But as he approached the firepit, his eyes moved to the flames licking the night sky, and his thoughts drifted to Marcus yet again.

Doesn't it feel like we're always chasing daylight? Marcus had asked the night before his final mission. *Just trying to make it to see one more sunrise? One more day? Sometimes I get tired of it.*

Yeah, and you'd be bored to tears doing something normal like finance or selling insurance, and you know it. We live for the chase, A.J. had said, a huge-ass grin on his face. He'd patted Marcus on the shoulder, both of them unaware that night was the last moonlit sky Marcus would ever see.

CHAPTER FOUR

WASHINGTON, D.C.

ANA SET A BOX DOWN AND REACHED A HAND AROUND TO brace her lower back. "I guess it's true, once you're over thirty, your body becomes more sensitive to everything." She continued to massage her back. "Or my cardio workouts aren't cutting it." Sleep deprivation from working nonstop didn't help either. Plus, her department clearly considered ergonomic office chairs a waste of money.

Adriana rested a tan forearm on top of a pile of boxes, not the least bit out of breath. "You can always join me for workouts."

"You work out with your husband whenever he's in town," Ana reminded her. And maybe what she needed right now wasn't rest or water but a bottle of wine. She allowed her hand to fall to her side, then circumvented the wall of boxes blocking her path to the kitchen.

When she turned with a bottle of pinot grigio in hand, Adriana was standing at the breakfast bar, which separated the kitchen from the living room in Ana's new rental. She set her palms on the counter and popped onto the barstool.

"Our reward." Ana uncorked the bottle with a regular corkscrew and not the complicated device her ex always insisted they use simply because it'd been a wedding gift from their old boss. He cursed the thing every time he opened a bottle, too. Inwardly, she'd always grinned because well, he was stubborn.

"I get satisfaction in just helping out. You don't need to bribe me with a glass of wine. But I won't turn it down." Adriana accepted the glass, her lips teasing into a smile.

She and Adriana were night and day in terms of looks, and, apparently, physical fitness.

Ana had red hair to Adriana's dark. Fair skin to her tan. Adriana was tall and well-endowed up top. Ana was petite and not even close to filling out a C, let alone a D. She was lucky to fit a modest B cup on a good day.

"I feel like a mistress, you know. A dirty little secret I don't want my husband to find out." A dark brow arched as Adriana sipped her wine.

Ana set her glass down and braced the counter. "I'm sorry. We'll tell Knox soon that we're friends and that I live in D.C. now. I promise."

"He won't be able to keep you a secret from A.J., so I get it." Adriana's expression had slowly changed to her thoughtful, *I want to say something but don't know how to* face. In the few months they'd been hanging out, Ana had learned to read her well.

Then again, between Ana's college degrees, training, and working for the FBI, it was basically her job to profile people. Couldn't turn the switch off, not even with friends.

Work. She didn't want to think about the nightmare at the office right now. She was being forced to take the day off, so she was doing her best to shut off her brain and forget who signed her paychecks.

"Any particular reason you don't want A.J. knowing you're living in D.C. and that we're hanging out?" Adriana asked, which wasn't her first time. But Ana was never forthcoming, and Adriana wasn't a quitter. Nor was she pushy. So, she inserted the question every so often to test the waters. See if Ana would finally swim.

"You saw A.J. with me back in Charlotte. You know how he is." Ana's eyes fell to her glass. She'd nearly drained the bottle with their two very full pours. "Flirty. Funny."

"Got your heart pitter-pattering, did he?"

Yes. "Kyle and I were only separated when A.J. and I met. Plus, we were on the hunt for the person who had tried to assassinate a presidential candidate. I shouldn't have, um, noticed him."

Before Ana's promotion to Headquarters, she'd worked at the Charlotte FBI field office. And because A.J.'s friend happened to be the son of then-presidential candidate Isaiah Bennett (now president), A.J. and his former SEAL buddies had provided security for Knox's dad. Well, in all honesty, they'd done more than that. They broke the case. Took down the real bad guys. Adriana had been assigned to Secret Service security detail for Knox's father as well.

"You don't need to rationalize whatever you should or shouldn't have been feeling for A.J. when you met him," Adriana came to her defense, like the strong kind of woman she was.

It'd been a nice surprise when Ana had bumped into Adriana outside the Hoover Building on her first day, and Adriana insisted they get a drink. The one caveat to hanging out was that Ana had sworn her to secrecy. At least for the time being. Adriana wasn't allowed to tell her husband or his buddies that she was spending time with Ana. It seemed ridiculous when Ana said those words out loud, but . . .

"We were busy. It was intense in general. I'm sure I'm remembering everything differently," Ana said in a near whisper.

But that spark. The insane connection I felt the moment he introduced himself to me. She was pretty sure she'd actually flirted with him, too. Engaged in witty banter. When had she learned how to do that? It wasn't her at all, and that part had been a touch exciting. Something different and new.

Thinking about A.J. was definitely a distraction from work. Probably not the distraction she needed, though.

"And if you didn't feel something then, you wouldn't be so afraid to see him now." Adriana was a master at pulling off an inquisitive look by using her brows and narrowing her eyes. She could have taught their UC division at the FBI how to get informants to better open up.

Adriana was right. Of course she was right. Or why else would Ana be avoiding A.J.? She was coming up on about eight months divorced.

With her glass in hand, Ana left the kitchen and made her way to the living room, dropping onto the gray-blue couch from IKEA with a sigh. It'd been her first official purchase following her divorce. "I'm not ready to test out my single shoes." *Especially not given my current assignment.*

"Does that mean he'd be the guy you'd like to date when you are ready?" Adriana came over to stand in front of the couch. She positioned her back to one of the columns that served as a divide between the room and the hallway off to their left.

"The fact I still haven't forgotten about him since we worked that case together last year . . . you really think that means something?" She frowned, embarrassed to be talking like this so openly. This kind of conversation wasn't in her wheelhouse, not when it came to discussing her own life. She could psychoanalyze and profile people better than anyone else, but she herself was off-limits.

Adriana sat next to her and slapped a hand to her knee. "I'm thinking so. But listen, Knox and I waited like twenty years to be together. So, I'm basically the last person on the planet to give dating advice. Probably the galaxy."

Ana smiled. It was easy to do with someone as nice as Adriana. So accepting. "I'm a shitty friend. Having you lie to Knox as to where you are tonight. I'm sorry."

"Hey, he kept me a secret from his friends for like forever," she replied, her tone casual. "I can handle Knox. I just think—"

"I should woman up and not hide from your friends?" *One friend in particular.* "And what if A.J.'s dating someone? If we ever see each other again, he might not be interested."

"Or maybe *you* won't be." Adriana was already on her feet again. Clearly, she'd gotten her eight hours of sleep last night, unlike Ana. She set her wineglass on the oak coffee table and faced Ana with her hands on her hips. "And A.J. hasn't so much as looked at a woman sideways since he met you. Now, I say that two people who still can't stop thinking about each other after so much time has passed, well, that definitely has to mean something."

"Has he mentioned me?" She swallowed the ball of nerves down her throat, nearly coughing like a cat choking on a hairball.

"What do you think?" Adriana asked while at the same time answering her question with a vigorous nod, then went over to a stack of boxes and cut one open. "You never want to talk about him, so I didn't bring it up. What can I say?"

"I'm not great at the talking-about-me thing," Ana admitted the obvious.

"Most of the guys on Knox's team are the same. Trauma can do that to a person." She closed her eyes as if regretting her words. "I'm sorry. I just assumed that maybe . . ."

Ana let go of a deep, uncomfortable breath and rose, her legs a bit wobbly. Her feet sank into the plush area rug beneath the coffee table. The air-conditioning was making a sputtering noise from the vents as if it were on its last leg. Another thing to fix. If it weren't for the rooftop patio and its view of the Capitol building dome in the distance, she probably wouldn't have lived there. The place was a fixer-upper that the owner clearly didn't feel the need to fix up before renting out. Her section chief, Porter, had mentioned it was available a few weeks ago when he realized she was still living out of a hotel. Since his place was only five blocks away, they took turns carpooling to the Bureau.

"It's okay," Ana finally spoke up. "Not many people can read me. You're talented."

"Occupational hazard," Adriana said with eyes now open, her focus back inside the box. "Plus, my husband is suspicious of everyone and everything, so I swear that man always has me on alert about who to trust these days."

God, she felt that in her bones more than she wished to admit. "Where is Knox, anyway?"

They usually only hung out when her husband was out of town, which was quite a lot lately.

"Overseas doing something with Luke." Her vague answer was typical.

They both had secrets, and maybe that was why their friendship worked so well. Neither would push or press. "And the rest of his friends?"

Ana had made a mental list of names when she worked

with A.J. and the guys from "Scott & Scott Securities" down in Charlotte, but she hadn't met everyone then, so Adriana had filled in the blanks. And yeah, she used air quotes in her head when thinking about A.J. and Knox's jobs because she had a gut feeling their security company was a front for something else. Most civilian security companies didn't manage to get themselves onto an active FBI, Homeland, and Secret Service investigation as "Scott & Scott" had last year, even if Knox's dad had been the one running for president.

"Well, you remember Liam and Emily had their baby, Jackson, this month, so Liam's here at home," Adriana began, and it was clear she was going to slowly work up to the one person she knew Ana was really curious about.

Emily worked for the Attorney General, and if she wasn't on maternity leave right now, Ana would probably have already bumped into her since the FBI worked with the AG's office a lot.

"Asher and Jessica are still at home with the twins?" Ana asked.

Jessica had been pregnant last fall when working the case with Ana, but she remembered Asher had stars in his eyes for that woman every time he so much as peered Jessica's way.

Ana had no idea what it was like to love someone that much since her first and maybe last marriage hadn't been all that passionate.

"They've been home for three months now, and from what I hear, they're going a bit stir-crazy. I'm betting they'll be working soon." Adriana set the box on the ground after removing a few candlesticks.

Ana reached for a box instead of simply watching her friend do all the work. "And the others?" she prompted.

"Samantha said their son is sick, so Owen hopped on an early flight home this evening," she said. "He was with A.J.

and the others at a bachelor party down in A.J.'s hometown in Alabama."

"Is this Wyatt's bachelor party?"

"No, Wyatt said he doesn't want a party." Adriana's long lashes lifted to catch Ana's eyes. "A.J.'s sister is marrying some banker who A.J. has decided he doesn't like for whatever reason. He asked the guys to have a so-called party, probably involving bullets, hopefully fake ones, to interrogate the future brother-in-law. See if he's good enough for his sister."

A smile flitted to her lips at the idea of A.J.'s protectiveness over his sister. And the surprising sensation of butterflies fluttering around in her stomach had her hand falling to her midsection.

"Is A.J. heading to D.C. after Alabama?" And why did her stomach do a little cartwheel at that idea?

"Yeah, but his sister's wedding is soon, so he'll be heading back South in two weeks." Adriana's brows rose with curiosity. "Are you thinking about finally seeing him when he's in town?"

"I can't." Her shoulders slumped. "The case I'm working . . . the timing would be bad."

"Trust me when I tell you the timing is never right. And then when it is, you realize you waited too long, and you don't have any time left on your side."

Ana forced a nervous smile.

"I have your back, though. Whatever you need." Adriana nodded. "This city can eat you alive, so just know I'm here for you. When you're ready."

When I'm ready to face the sexy Southern SEAL? Sure. But Adriana was right about the city. The harsh reality of what happened in D.C. when Ana was a teenager clung to her like a persistent ghost. The hovering dark shadow followed her everywhere, but for the first time, she was hopeful she'd finally be able to let go of the past and move on. Set the truth free.

Adriana lifted a framed photo out of the box. "This the ex?"

Ana tucked a hand in the back pocket of her jeans as she closed the space between them. Remorse was all she felt when eying the photo of her and Kyle standing on a beach in Bali for their honeymoon, which had been paid for by Kyle's parents. They'd paid for the wedding, too. He'd never let her forget that. Neither had his parents.

"Yeah, that's Kyle." She reached for the photo and tucked it back inside the box. "We don't need to unpack this one." She could have sworn she had a red X somewhere on the outside as a reminder it didn't need to be opened—just like she'd done with the boxes full of her childhood memories.

After folding the flaps back inside to close the box, she removed it from the stack and carried it to the storage area beneath the stairs.

"Was he FBI, too?" Adriana asked when Ana had returned.

Ana's ex was another topic Adriana had rarely broached. She danced and skirted around with finesse, but she never fully colored inside the lines.

"Yeah. He's currently stationed at an FBI attaché overseas in Hungary." Ana opened a new box, needing to make herself busy. Get rid of the knot in her stomach that was working its way to her throat. "He took a new role within the Bureau about a year ago. But yeah, we first met at the Charlotte field office."

"So, he moved before the divorce?"

Ana frowned. That tug of guilt yanking a bit harder at Adriana's innocent question. "Yeah. He was offered a job abroad. He said yes without talking to me first. And I said no to moving." It was a lot more complicated than that, but she didn't want to go down the rabbit hole that was her marriage, which might prompt more questions Ana wasn't prepared to discuss. Too much baggage to unpack after a day of actually unpacking boxes. "It wasn't meant to be."

Of course, Kyle didn't want the divorce. And for the first half of his time overseas, he kept calling. Trying to work things out. Eventually, he stopped calling as much.

Adriana gave a slight nod, accepting the conversation was over. She went back to unpacking, alternating between sips of wine and unwrapping decorations.

"You think that maybe you'd want to go to Wyatt and Natasha's wedding?"

"My coming-out party?" Ana joked. "Are you hoping if the truth about our friendship is spilled while everyone is drunk and happy at the wedding, you'll take less heat?"

"Look at that," Adriana said with a playful smile, "you already know me so well."

They clinked glasses, but the very idea of showing up at Wyatt's wedding had her palms sweating. Pulse fluttering a touch faster.

But because of her current case, the timing of the wedding was horrible, let alone to be friends with A.J. and the others. The feeling of defeat swiftly wormed its way in to destroy her hope for a chance at some sense of normalcy in her life. Or hell, a sense of romance. Real, unadulterated passion she'd never experienced before.

"I still can't believe Wyatt's getting married," Ana deflected instead of answering Adriana's original question about going to the wedding. "Based on what I remember when working with Wyatt, he didn't seem like he wanted to settle down." A British bad boy. A charmer like A.J.

"I guess you never know when you're going to meet the one." Adriana's comment was packed full of so much meaning, and nope, she wouldn't be unpacking that one tonight, either. Boxes were easier than feelings.

Adriana motioned toward the TV mounted on the wall across the room. "We've been at this for hours. Maybe we can take a break and watch a movie? You happen to like—" A knock interrupted her words and left her question hanging.

Ana set her wineglass down to go for her lockbox temporarily on the floor by her couch.

"Are you going for your gun?"

Ana retracted her hand from the lockbox, stopping herself from retrieving her FBI-issued Glock 19. "I'm not expecting anyone." And Adriana also had no clue how dangerous Ana's current assignment was, which meant yeah, she shouldn't answer the door without a weapon in hand. Always had to be prepared.

Adriana discarded her wine and went into the hall. "Your case must be inten—"

"What is it?" Ana asked when Adriana dropped her words and faced her.

"*Who* is it?" And now maybe she did need her gun.

Her friend's eyes widened. "I guess you weren't expecting Mr. FBI Attaché ex-husband, right?"

And shit. Really?

"It's me. You can put your gun away," her ex called out, loud enough to be heard through the door.

"Guess he knows you well," Adriana whispered as if unsure as to what to do next.

"One second!" Ana smoothed her palms down the sides of her jean shorts as she made her way to the front door.

"I'll head out. But if you need me, call." Adriana grabbed

her purse from where she'd set it on the small entrance table in the hall.

"Thank you." And was Kyle really standing outside her door right now?

When Adriana opened the door, Kyle took an immediate step back on the front porch stoop. His gaze clung to her like he was reading the ticker tape of a breaking news story.

Adriana, in her fitted jeans and red tee, with her glossy dark hair and stunning eyes, resembled Gal Gadot, the actress who'd played *Wonder Woman*. And Kyle took notice. He'd never been a man to go speechless by a woman's looks, but then again, maybe petite redheads like Ana just never did that to him.

Kyle forced his gaze past Adriana. "Ana." His attention on her lasted a fleeting moment before he locked back on Adriana as she attempted to maneuver around him.

"Adriana," she introduced herself. "I was just leaving. Excuse me." She peeked back at Ana, an offer in her eyes to reach out if she needed her, and Ana nodded her thanks before Adriana turned and started down the steps to get to her car parked at the curb.

"Hi," Ana said once she and Kyle were alone inside her townhouse.

"You look good." He wasn't even making eye contact, though. He was scoping the scene behind her. Assessing if Ana was alone now with Adriana gone.

"Thanks." She stood in the hall, not sure what to do next. When it was clear he was waiting for her to make the next move, she motioned for him to follow her into the living room.

Kyle stopped in front of her TV, barely inside her living room, acting as if he was leery of being there. *But* here he was.

"What are you doing here?" she finally managed to get the words out.

"I'm being transferred to D.C. for a special assignment, and I was surprised to learn you were at Headquarters now." When his hands went to the back pockets of his jeans, Ana took notice of the rest of his clothing. A navy button-down shirt left untucked. Brown loafers. Those were new. He'd never been the loafer type.

There were a few streaks of silver at the sides of his inky black hair. Same as before, but it was longer than when they were married. He was sporting a beard now, too. He looked different. On edge and somehow relaxed at the same time. It was all very strange.

Ana was so caught up in trying to get a read on him she'd barely heard his words. "Wait, what?" Two more steps had her close enough to smell his cologne now. Sharp. More distinct. Another difference. Who was this man?

Kyle's hands left his pockets. One patted the side of his leg. The familiar rattle of one too many keys on his chain in his left pocket. He had something he wanted to say but didn't know how to begin. "I'm worried about you." A lock of black hair swept over his forehead, and he pushed it away from his face.

"You're here in D.C., and now you're in my place. Who told you I was here and gave you my address?"

"I'm here. That's all that matters. We're back in the same zip code again. Not sure how long I'll be here, but I wanted to reach out. To see you." After another push of his fingers through his thick hair, his attention turned to her wineglass on the table.

Her arms went across her chest, covering the letters, FBI. It was her favorite T-shirt, given to her at Quantico when she attended the academy six years ago.

Kyle lifted a hand to his beard. Traces of silver and gray there as well. Each stroke drew his eyes over different parts of her body like an examination.

One of the downsides to being married to another FBI agent? They were constantly reading each other. Interpreting absolutely every move, every word, every change.

She snatched her drink, desperate for something to occupy her hands and smooth the tension she felt with her ex standing in her new place.

"I know I was mad when you wouldn't move with me, but you were right not to follow." He angled his head, his words taking her by surprise. "I should never have accepted the job without discussing it with you first."

She took a small step back, lowering the glass to her side. "It was about more than that, and you know it."

Your heart is cold. Dead. The words he'd spoken while they were still married would have hurt if she hadn't believed them to be, in part, true. She hadn't known her heart still worked until she'd encountered A.J., and it began to thump so loudly, desperately seeking to be heard. She was never one to blindly follow her emotions, though.

"The idea of you being here alone in this city, and in your new line of work, it's not—"

"You don't think I can handle it?" Kyle could talk all day long about her walls, her barriers, her inability to truly love . . . but question her ability at the job? No, she drew the line there.

"You hate this city, just as much as you hate Budapest, for reasons you never told me," he said, that same flare of frustration with her igniting. "I'm just surprised you took the job and moved here. And you're alone now."

Her tongue hit the roof of her mouth.

Memories she didn't want to deal with surged.

"I'm not alone. I have friends here." *A* friend. "And I'm an FBI agent. I can handle myself and you know that."

"I'm worried." He inched closer.

Ana turned, unable to look him in the eyes any longer. They'd been married for three years, but she'd never shared the dark secrets of her past. He'd tried many times to wrangle the truth out of her, using his tradecraft, but then he gave up. Took an assignment abroad. It was her secret to bear. But now . . . well, the story of her life that could've been a true crime series on Netflix might get a new ending. If she did her job right.

Ana set her glass back down, feeling a chill begin to settle in her bones.

She needed to clean. To do something. Get her apartment in order.

Everything would be okay if she only . . . "You should go. You shouldn't have shown up like this."

His jaw tightened beneath the beard. "I just wanted to be here for you. Help you." He paused. "Let me back in your life, even if it's just as a friend."

Even as a friend?

"We'll talk Monday, I guess," he said, knowing her well enough to assume she wasn't prepared to respond to his words. "You'll be at the office and not traveling with Porter?"

She did her best not to flinch at the mention of her section chief's name. Of course, Kyle would know his name. But how did he know Porter was going to be traveling? "Yeah, I'll be at Headquarters Monday," she said, still a bit confused.

He can't know about . . . no, it's not possible. Why would Kyle talk to Porter? Why wouldn't Porter tell her he'd spoken to her ex? And hell, what'd Porter tell Kyle as to why a man of his position was going out into the field?

Too many questions railroaded her mind, and she wasn't

sure if it was the wine, the lack of sleep from pulling an all-nighter last night at work, or her ex's presence, but she was growing dizzy.

She'd been working nonstop since last Wednesday. Porter had forced her to head home and try and relax that morning. He told her to remain calm. Not panic. He said it would all be okay. But she had needed to do something, to finally unpack and clean her rental, and Adriana had offered to help.

"You know Porter?" she couldn't help but ask.

"No, but I was at the office today, expecting you'd be there, and, well, you know as well as anyone, when a section chief decides to leave D.C. to go out into the field, news travels fast. People were talking." Kyle knew something. She could feel it, but he was waiting to see if she'd divulge. "Everyone in your unit is fairly tight-lipped about why he left, though."

Because we've been ordered to be close-mouthed about it.

"Lock up when I go," he said after a quiet moment passed between them.

She followed him to the door. "Kyle?"

His back was to her, a hand resting over the doorknob. "Yeah?" He glimpsed her from over his shoulder.

She lightly shook her head, unable to get the words out. His mouth tightened, and he returned his focus to the task of leaving.

He stepped outside and said, "Watch your back. D.C. isn't the safest of places." And then he left without looking back.

She locked up once he was gone and brought her forehead to the door, palms on each side as she grappled with the unexpected news her ex was in town, and from the sounds of it, they might have to work together.

The generic ringtone from her cell had her backing away from the door and tracking her personal cell to the kitchen.

Maybe it was Adriana checking up on her?

She snatched her phone from the counter, but the call had already gone to voicemail.

An unknown number. She wouldn't have answered anyway.

She waited to see if a message was left, then pressed the speaker to listen.

"Hi, it's me." A throat clear followed. "Sorry, I mean, it's A.J. Hawkins." The sexy, Southern accent had her throwing a palm to the counter. "I'm about to hop on a plane, but I had a few drinks. Maybe you can tell? I managed to scrounge up your number a month ago but haven't been drunk enough to work up the nerve to call you until now." He unleashed a string of semi-mumbled curses. "Shit, maybe I shouldn't have said that. Well, anyway, I wanted to tell you that I haven't stopped thinking about you since we met. Can't get you out of my head, and well, when you're ready . . . maybe we could go to dinner? I can head to Charlotte. I'm flexible."

Oh, God.

"I'd love to see you again. You know, sooner rather than later. If you're up for it and you even remember who I am, I thought it'd be nice to get together. So, well, I should probably go. Jet is about to take off." He swore again. "I better erase and *not* rerecord this message. I'll try calling again when I'm sober. Not that you'll even hear any of this. *But* since I'm deleting this, I guess it doesn't hurt to say that I've had you in my head so much I can't even ask another woman out. Months and months of no sex." He paused as if thinking, and her entire world was spinning off its axis at his words. "It's strange, right? It must mean something, the fact I can't even think about another woman. But I better go delete this drunk message and try you again another time. Take care, beautiful. Goodnight."

Ana stared at the phone, shocked. Stunned. All the synonyms on the planet that meant *holy shit*. She pressed play and listened to it two more times, still not sure what to think about it.

"You didn't erase it," she whispered to herself at the end of the next listen, and with that, she went in search of her wine.

She wet her lips at the memory of the first time he'd introduced himself.

"I'm Alexander James." He'd reached for her hand. *"But you can call me A.J."*

"His mom couldn't decide on a name. Don't mind him," Wyatt had chimed in.

"I haven't forgotten about you, either, A.J." *But I can't think about you,* she reminded herself. *Not now. Not with so much at stake.* Not when she was so close to unraveling the truth, the truth about the day her life changed forever.

CHAPTER FIVE

THE BOYS ON ECHO TEAM, PLUS OWEN FROM BRAVO, settled around an oval table with Harper, at what they were told would be their new meeting place. They were always moving to new black sites to prevent drawing suspicion, especially when meeting with those who ordered missions: the President, CIA director, and Secretary of Defense.

They were in a basement beneath an old closed-down jail on the outskirts of D.C. Better than being in that old psych ward like back in Boston, A.J. supposed.

The place had concrete floors, steel beams, and a few fluorescent lights overhead. Sparse and kind of eerie, and after A.J.'s strange hit-in-the-head-ghost-encounter yesterday, he wasn't in the mood for anything else that gave him the chills.

A.J. gripped the arms of the chair and forced it back, so the front legs were off the floor. The table they were sitting at must've belonged to the jail, based on the profanities and gang signs carved by probably a makeshift knife stolen from the kitchen by inmates. "You playing footsies with me?"

"You know you like it." Chris, who was sitting across

from him, playfully kissed the air. "You'd think in this huge-ass space they'd place a table that wouldn't cramp us so much." He elbowed Finn off to his side, and Finn nudged him right back.

Owen's son, Matthew, was feeling better, which was why Owen had shown up today when Harper had called him. At least that was some good news.

"Boys." The word teased out of Harper's mouth slowly, and A.J. noticed Roman's gaze immediately lift from the table and float her way as if on a breeze. An attempt to be discreet in his desire to check her out. God, that man needed to make a move. Man up and just do it.

Okay, so I'm a hypocrite.

"All this place needs is one of those impenetrable, glass-walled boxes in the center of the room to lock criminals in, and we'd be in an episode of *The Blacklist.*" Finn set his elbow on the table and rested his chin on his palm. "It's got the creep factor, for sure."

"I was thinking the same thing." A.J. nodded in agreement. "Well, the creepy feel. Not sure what in the hell else you just said."

"What show?" Harper secured her long hair into a high ponytail, the tips of her long black hair had been dyed crimson when she'd lost a bet. Harper should have known better than to make a wager on A.J.'s knowledge regarding every major football game played by the University of Alabama in the last forty years. Hell, his parents had created a trivia game based on the family's alma mater, and it'd been a weekly ritual growing up.

"A show about the FBI's Most Wanted criminal. And—" Finn began.

"How do you have time to watch the telly?" Wyatt asked. "You must not be working hard enough."

"Surprised you didn't say you watch *Jack Ryan* since you think you look like that guy from the series. You even grew your beard to match his, didn't you?" Chris swatted Finn's chest with the back of his hand.

"Har har." Finn rolled his eyes. "Anyway, this place gives me *The Blacklist* chills. The serial-killer-episode kind."

"That's a thing now, Mr. Krasinski?" Chris pushed away from the table and stood as if anxious to get a move on. To spin up to wherever the hell they'd be going.

"Who?" Finn asked, playing dumb.

"The actor who plays Jack . . . oh, forget it." A.J. directed his attention back on Chris. "And you weren't in such a hurry last night to leave," A.J. reminded him.

"That was, well, she was . . . different," Chris answered and waved A.J. off. "We need to operate, though. Get out there again. Been too long."

"We've barely had our boots on home soil since we were over in good ol' North Korea a week ago, and you call that a long time?" Okay, so maybe A.J. was usually ready to go as well, but something about being back in Alabama over the weekend had been a reminder that he not only missed home, but it was okay to slow down every once in a while. He only wished he had someone to slow down with.

A.J. shifted on his seat to grab his phone out of his pocket.

I didn't finalize the message, right?

Fuck.

I hope not.

Instead of sobering up before heading to the airport last night, Jesse had encouraged a quick "who can take the most shots and not fall down" competition, and he also placed a bet that A.J. would lose. A.J. had never been able to say no to a bet or to a competition, and in the end, he was victorious. But he'd been a drunken mess by the time they arrived at the airport. Probably not one of his best ideas, given the bump on the back of his head.

Wyatt and Chris had to practically carry A.J. onto the plane. And Chris had threatened to tape his mouth shut, worried he'd get them booted from flying commercial if he didn't stop talking about his firearm collection.

"You happen to know why we were called here?" Finn asked Harper.

"No idea why Secretary Chandler called us aside from the obvious." Harper's lips eased into a smile. "A mission."

It'd be their first official mission this year working for Admiral Chandler in his new role as Secretary of Defense. And now Wyatt's future father-in-law was officially one of the select few to know about Bravo and Echo Teams' off-the-books operations. To the world, the guys had retired, but hell, they were far from it. Of course, if they were to ever be captured during an op, they'd have to claim they were acting on their own accord under the guise of Scott & Scott Securities. They'd secured four more years of operating when Isaiah Bennett won the presidency, but if the media ever got wind of their ops, it'd be game over.

"How much did you drink last night, by the way?" Harper must have been asking A.J. since he was the only one with sunglasses on in the dark basement to hide his bloodshot eyes. All the ibuprofen in the world wouldn't get rid of his headache, either. It was worse than the one he'd had yesterday.

"His buddy made a bet." And that was all Roman needed to say for Harper to get the idea.

"Mmhm." Harper gave A.J. an accusatory but playful grin, her white teeth showing between her parted lips, coated in that nude gloss that Roman was clearly unable to take his eyes off. Captain Obvious was about as good at hiding his desire for Harper as Asher had once been with Jessica. Only, Asher and Jessica had done their best to make a show of hating each other while secretly wanting to rip each other's clothes off.

But Roman kept his cool because Roman was, well, Roman. Quiet. Always thinking. Probably calculating odds and measuring the risks if he were to make a move on Harper.

And then there's me. I drunk dialed an FBI agent. A.J. pulled at the brim of his ball cap in shame.

"You should've taken my phone away from me after all those shots." The cheap plastic government chair groaned beneath the weight of forcing it to move in ways it wasn't meant to. A.J. finally allowed the chair legs to meet the ground again.

"And miss out on the chance to watch you do something stupid?" Chris eyed A.J. with intense focus as if A.J. were coming around on the last lap at Nascar, and it was a make-or-break moment. Hell, A.J.'s life was all about those moments, wasn't it?

He removed his glasses at the sudden realization his drunken message last night had been Chris's doing. "You . . ."

Chris stopped pacing the length of the table and held both palms in the air. "I may or may not have been the one to encourage you to call her."

"What am I missing?" Harper asked, but then Roman tipped his chin in the direction of the metal door opening from the other side of the room.

"Harper, you didn't tell us the admiral was bringing Natasha to our, uh, supposedly clandestine meeting." Chris dropped back into his seat as if he'd get punished by the teacher for standing. "Um, Wyatt, what's your future wife doing here?"

Wyatt twisted to the side to peer at Admiral Chandler walking toward the table, his daughter at his right, a stack of folders pressed to her chest. He hurriedly stood, clearly surprised to see his fiancée in this so-called *Blacklist*-like setting.

Now that A.J. thought about it, the place did give off a bizarre feeling aside from being cold, dimly lit, and beneath a closed-down old county jail. Maybe there were ghosts of previous inmates causing that chill in the air?

Ghosts. Goose bumps exploded across his body as he remembered how clearly Marcus had appeared to him yesterday. *You here now?* Was Marcus in the room? It almost felt like . . .

A.J. heard a slight crack as he squeezed his palm around his sunglasses.

"What are you doing here?" he overheard Wyatt speak up.

A.J. snatched the bottle of water Harper had placed in front of him earlier, her nose scrunched as if she'd been able to smell the booze on him. Hell, his body was so infused it was probably like a fresh coat of paint on his skin.

"I thought you were working on last-minute wedding details," Wyatt said while Natasha kept the folders clutched to her chest with one hand and reached out and placed a palm on her future husband's chest with the other.

"I'll explain," Admiral Chandler spoke up, his deep tone deflating any of the residual humor that'd been left wafting in the cool air between the guys.

Wyatt hesitantly went back to his seat, but Natasha remained standing at the head of the table alongside her father, who was out of uniform and in a pair of jeans and a long-sleeved, gray button-down shirt. The casual look worked for the man, but it didn't make him any less intimidating.

It had to be weird for Wyatt to now report to his

fiancée's father, but no stranger than Knox working for his old man. AKA—the Commander in Chief of the United States.

Admiral Chandler gripped the back of the empty chair and looked at Harper, then on to the guys, before his eyes came to a halt on his future son-in-law. "We'd planned on making this announcement when everyone could be here, but the President and I will be phoning the others after this meeting." His voice was a bit raspy as if he'd smoked a cigar or engaged in a shouting match before showing up.

Wyatt shifted in his seat, clearly on edge with his fiancée, a CIA officer, in the room.

Natasha set the stack of folders on the table and tucked her blonde hair behind her ears, her gaze following the same pattern her father's had moments ago.

"When you men first began operating for the previous administration, you had a liaison between those in charge and yourselves." The admiral's words had A.J. releasing his viselike grip on the bottle of water, and he let go of the tight hold of his sunglasses, as well.

A.J. hadn't even remembered gripping them, too surprised by Natasha showing up to their meeting. Plus, that bump on the back of his head was still playing tricks on him, because for a moment, he could've sworn Marcus was in the room with them, in that empty seat, listening to mission instructions.

I don't believe in ghosts. Nope. He shook his head a little too hard, attracting the attention of Roman, who was now eying him with concern instead of focusing on the new Secretary of Defense.

"As I'm sure Luke will tell you when he speaks to you later, having that separation between our men and the President didn't work too well," Wyatt informed the admiral.

"We don't need someone else to report to. We don't *want* someone."

"And he speaks for all of us," Chris said in agreement.

"I thought you might say that." The admiral pulled out the empty chair and took a seat, but Natasha remained on her feet. "But this will be different. The President and I believe we need someone who can be the eyes and ears at the various agencies who can point out potential problems that need to be handled by alternative means."

"We're the alternative means, I assume?" Harper asked for clarification, and the admiral nodded.

"We've created a task force of agents. One highly qualified and heavily vetted agent or officer from the FBI, DHS, CIA, DIA, and lastly, the NSA," he explained, his voice low. A touch smoother than before. A ring of decisiveness coming from a man with decades of experience under his belt.

"You're on that team?" Wyatt's gulp was nearly as audible as A.J.'s own swallow at the news.

"Yes." Natasha's voice was pillow-soft as her eyes swept to her fiancé. "But I'll also be the liaison between that department and you all."

Wyatt immediately stood and turned his back to the room, his hands falling to his hips.

It was obvious it was taking Natasha every ounce of energy not to go to him. To remain professional, to prove she was up for the job.

But was she really ready to be not only a CIA officer on a new task force, but also an intermediary between the government and their team?

Bravo and Echo were a shadowy group of operatives that didn't follow the same rules as the CIA. Of course, Natasha had practically gone rogue from the CIA when hunting down the elusive hacker and criminal The Knight. What was he thinking? Natasha would fit right in.

"We can't risk anyone else on the task force knowing about you, and since Natasha is not only already aware of your operations but one of the best officers at the Agency, it was decided by the CIA director she was the right person for the position. And POTUS agrees. It wasn't easy for me to come to this decision, but I trust her." The admiral's voice dipped low like a challenge to Wyatt and Wyatt alone, as in, *Do you not trust her?*

Wyatt got the message and pivoted around, his eyes going straight to the woman wearing his grandmother's engagement ring.

"Are we okay with having these agents essentially spy on their own departments? I mean, that's what you're doing, right?" Chris asked before Wyatt had a chance to respond to the admiral's unspoken question.

"It's not so much about spying on our own people, but about having real-time access to all of the cases within each agency that may need an assist from you all," Natasha explained. "Agents on my team will only flag potential issues from within their own agency and share the details with our task force. Not all situations will require your help, but in the cases that do, I'll share that information with Secretary Chandler."

Secretary Chandler? Not Dad. "And the other four agents won't know you're coming to us?" A.J. asked, a bit alarmed at all of this. "Who do they think will be helping?"

"It's need-to-know, and well, they know they don't need to know," the admiral answered as if it were that simple.

Say that three times fast. A.J. resisted the urge to reach around for the knot at the back of his head. He was still off from that fall. He'd had a lot worse over the years, and for a rock to be the straw that broke the camel's back—well, damn.

"Most cases, this task force will be used as a way to communicate and better collaborate with our colleagues across agencies and won't involve you all," Natasha added.

"Can we have a word in private?" Wyatt moved toward her, and she quickly nodded, then followed him out of the room.

A.J. opened the water bottle and nearly drained every last drop as he allowed his mind to circle around the idea they'd be working with Natasha as a liaison for a covert task force.

"We're keeping this all a family affair, huh?" Owen directed his question to Secretary Chandler. "Jess and Luke co-run the teams. They're brother and sister. Jess and Bravo Three are almost married. Bravo Five's dad is POTUS. And now you, sir, well . . . you get the idea."

It also made it easier when the guys fell in love with someone who already had access to additional high-level security clearance, such as Owen's wife with ties to the Intelligence Committee before they married. And then there was Liam's wife, who worked for the U.S. Attorney General.

"I take it you have a mission for us already as a result of this newly formed group?" Harper brought the focus back to the immediate reason they were all there: an operation.

Admiral Chandler's attention turned to the stack of folders. "Yes, and unfortunately, this was not the way I wanted to kick things off, but for starters, we need to be certain we don't have a mole or a leak at the Bureau."

Yeah, and "for starters" means that's the tip of the iceberg. And damn, the FBI? They'd encountered an issue with the FBI in the past, and they weren't jonesing to do it again. The wounds were still fresh.

"I'll let my daughter explain the case when she returns,"

Admiral Chandler said as Finn reached for his phone. "You won't get a signal. This place blocks all devices. Safety precaution."

"Just gonna play some Candy Crush." Finn was withholding a smirk, and A.J. could see it in the quiver of his lips.

The admiral rose at the sight of Natasha entering the room with Echo One a few minutes later. Neither looked pissed. That was good news. It couldn't be easy for Wyatt to be in this position, but bright side? They'd get to spend more time together. Maybe fit in some last-minute wedding details.

"So," Natasha began once Wyatt was seated, "we brought you all here to do something that frankly you're probably not accustomed to doing, and I'm not comfortable asking."

Well, shit, way to start.

"We need you to follow a select handful of FBI agents from the Counterintelligence Division of the Bureau." Natasha passed out the gray file folders, ensuring everyone at the table received one. "Three, possibly more, confidential sources have gone off the grid. Any in the wrong hands would greatly threaten our national security."

Natasha circled back around the table once the folders had been handed out and stood off to her father's right. A.J. had to assume she was working harder than normal to remain business-like in the presence of her father, to prove she belonged in the room despite the fact she was marrying Echo One in July.

"So, are we assuming an FBI agent," Wyatt began while pointing at the folder he'd been given, "is behind the disappearance of the sources?" He set a hand on the folder instead of opening it, eyes on his fiancée. "Why isn't the FBI handling this internally? Or, I don't know, one of those fancy internal government agencies sent in to deal with leaks like this?"

A.J. was with Wyatt on this.

"The agent on the newly formed task force is only asking for an assist as a precautionary measure. He also doesn't want to tip off any agents to the fact that the FBI is onto the possible leak," Natasha answered.

"If there's a traitor in the Counterintelligence Division, we want to tie them to who they're working with," the admiral pointed out.

"And given our past experience with government corruption and betrayal, we didn't want to hand off this case to just anyone else." Natasha folded her arms. "So, as much as I hate requesting you to spy on agents, we need to find out what is going on. Clear the agents' names."

"Or find the traitor," A.J. muttered under his breath.

Natasha gave a tight nod. "The Bureau cross-checked every badge and ID code to see which agents or analysts accessed the case files connected to the missing sources in the last few months. But no one outside the particular unit within the Counterintelligence Division, or the connected field offices working with them, opened the files related to the missing sources."

"That doesn't mean someone didn't find a way around the system to get to the sources," Harper commented. "But I'm assuming the names you've provided for us to surveil are on the Counterintelligence Division's task force?"

"Unless something changes, yes, those are the names we have for now," Natasha said. "We'd like to rule them out first."

"What kind of sources are we talking about?" A.J. cocked his head. "What do they have in common?"

"You mentioned cases, plural. You saying these sources

were connected to different cases?" Roman spoke up for the first time since Admiral Chandler arrived with Natasha.

"Yes, the three sources are attached to different cases," Natasha clarified, "which is why we're ruling out the FBI field offices for now since it was only Headquarters that had access to all three names and their locational details. But the section chief in charge of the Counterintelligence Division has concerns about one of his sources down in Atlanta, so he's en route there now to check on him."

"Since when does a section chief go out into the field to check on a source?" Harper asked.

"The source is an Iranian the Feds managed to turn. He now spies on Iran for the FBI and CIA," the admiral explained.

Roman set his hands on the folder, eyes downcast as if working through the problem. "Three, maybe four, sources all go off-the-grid at the same time. Yeah, that raises some red flags."

"Spying on spies whose job is to spy on spies. Hmmm." Chris raised a brow.

"Sounds illegal-ish," A.J. shot back.

"I think the 'ish' makes it slightly less illegal," Chris said, no hint of a joke in his tone.

Harper cleared her throat and tipped her head in the direction of the admiral as a reminder he was in the room during their back-and-forth quips.

"It's okay," the admiral responded. "I remember my days in the service. Sometimes humor is the only way to make it through the tough times."

And A.J. liked the man even more. "So, do we have access to the case files related to the missing sources as well?"

Natasha pointed to the folders. "We figured you might

want to take a look at everything, so yes, that information has been provided."

"The assets we've confirmed to be MIA are connected to a Russian crime group, the Chinese government, and lastly, to Hamas." Something in the admiral's eyes when he'd spoken suggested to A.J. he was holding back, not telling them everything, but A.J. wasn't sure if he was prepared to press the issue.

"These sources are managed under the FBI's Confidential Human Source Program—HUMINT. You'll be monitoring a team of six agents, the ones operating those aforementioned sources in conjunction with the corresponding field offices under the leadership of their unit and section chief," Natasha said. "We were also alerted their unit is receiving an additional agent on Monday, but we're still firming up the details on that."

"The President agrees you all are best suited to handle this situation," the admiral began, drawing their eyes, and A.J. felt something big was coming, the "whatever he'd been holding back" was on the verge of heading their way. "Especially since there's a small chance that the Daylight Ledger may be mixed up in all of this."

"I thought that was an urban legend. A myth," Roman spoke up, since of course, Roman would know what in the hell the Daylight Ledger was when the rest of the guys, aside from Harper, looked puzzled.

Harper and Chris both opened their folders as if quickly ripping off the Band-Aid, intrigued to learn more.

A.J. wasn't ready yet to view the possible agents who were sworn to protect their country only to screw it over. There was a special place in hell for traitors. He also didn't know if he was ready to chase down an urban legend when he was already chasing ghosts from his past, ghosts that felt real since yesterday.

"Ohhhh shit." Chris grumbled before Roman had a chance to explain more about the ledger. A few more curses under Chris's breath stole A.J.'s focus.

Chris's eyes landed on A.J., and A.J. just knew what that "ohhhh shit" meant. It probably had nothing to do with the damn light-of-day, or whatever it was called, list, either.

A.J. flipped open the folder and stared at the photos of the six potential traitors before him, but it was only one that caught his eye.

The redhead he couldn't stop thinking about.

The woman he may or may not have accidentally drunk messaged last night.

CHAPTER SIX

ANA WAS AT THE OFFICE, SO SHE SHOULDN'T HAVE HAD HER personal phone glued to her ear, once again replaying A.J.'s voicemail from Saturday night. No, she should've been focused on the unit's major crisis, but she couldn't help herself from listening one more time.

She'd been right to fear A.J. would be a distraction, and a massively inconvenient one at that. Thoughts of him had bounced around her mind all day yesterday. And even now, his voicemail, his sweet words . . . while obviously drenched in booze, somehow brought a smile to her face on such a bleak day. A day when her world was quite possibly on the verge of flipping upside down.

She ended the voicemail before it finished and set her phone next to her keyboard.

Her desk was sparse. No picture frames. No knickknacks. Nothing personal. No way for others to glean any information about the type of person she was, and that was how she liked it.

Cold. Dead. Heart. But her cold heart had warmed a

touch when listening to A.J.'s message. It was all so strange. So unlike her.

Focus.

After her promotion, but prior to relocating to D.C., she'd returned to Quantico for a four-week course specific to her new line of work in counterintelligence, which was aptly nicknamed "Spy Hunting" by her colleagues at the Bureau. And catching spies was pretty much her job for the National Security Branch of the FBI.

Most of her work had to do with recruiting and creating sources. Turning criminals and spies to the side of Uncle Sam. For a price, of course. Some sources made six figures a year, substantially more than her salary, courtesy of the government.

Americans often believed the age of spies was a bygone era that belonged to the Cold War, but that was the furthest thing from the truth.

No, there was a race to steal secrets in every corner and crevice of American society. From universities to corporations—everyone was capable of becoming a target.

Absolutely everyone.

Even me.

"Hey, Red."

"Can't come up with anything more original?" Ana spun in her swivel desk chair to eye Dean, one of the six members on her task force. Most squads at the FBI field offices were made up of ten to even thirty agents and analysts. She'd quickly learned Headquarters was different, and also had a lot more layers of power and bureaucracy.

D.C. was where she needed to be, though, even if it wasn't easy for her to live there again.

Dean's forearm rested atop the cubicle partition

separating her from another workstation. He drummed his fingers. "Ginger?" Dean tested.

"How about Agent Quinn?" she offered with a smirk.

Dean smiled, showing the slight gap between his two front teeth. "You know I'm just teasing with you." He winked, the same wink she'd seen him give a source outside the courthouse last week before the commencement of a trial, in which he'd said, "Gonna take care of you at the end. No worries." That was code for, *Keep up your end of the bargain and testify, and you'll see a payout after.*

"Sure," Ana responded, but it came out more exasperated than she'd meant.

Dean wasn't an asshole. He didn't make passes at her, no sexual misconduct, either. He just liked to make jokes in a friendly way, which was one of his more likable qualities. But she was grumpy as hell, nervous, and a bit riled up by the fact her ex-husband was somewhere in the building, so much so she'd nearly spilled her coffee on herself in the break room when she'd walked right into someone who resembled Kyle.

And it didn't help that Dean had interrupted her while she'd been pining for a man she had no business pining over, all because of an adorably awkward drunk voicemail. But that voice. That Southern accent. Sweet and sinfully seductive. She wanted to take a bath in it and wrap it up around herself like a blanket when she slept, which was insane because since when did a voice get to her like that?

Since A.J., that's when. Great, now she was talking to herself. She needed to put her focus back to the here and now, which was Dean, still hanging over her cubicle wall.

"Sorry," she offered since she'd come off stronger than the dark, cream-free coffee she'd just poured for herself. She preferred sugary, unhealthy French vanilla, but the break room had been all out. "Just a bit on edge."

"The missing sources are on everyone's minds." He offered her a sympathetic look of understanding.

Ana's hand swept to the middle of her throat in an attempt to hide the hard swallow.

"Gray wants us all assembled."

Gray was their unit chief, but Porter, who left for the Atlanta field office yesterday, was one level above Gray as the section chief.

"I'm surprised Porter opted to go locate that source himself. I mean, I guess he has a lot riding on this, but the big dogs never go out." Dean lowered his arm from the partition and fixed the knot of his tie. "Not even for an Iranian spy."

"You know Porter," she replied with a smile, doing her best not to let him read her nerves. "He's hands-on unlike most." She took a breath, hoping Porter would call soon with good news. God, she really, really needed good news.

"We better not make Gray wait," Dean said. "He told us to meet in the SCIF. He's got his Monday-morning pissy look going for him already, and I'd prefer not to be the one to make him any angrier, not with the shit storm we're facing right now."

It was too early in her new HQ career to be dealing with a shit storm that might wind up getting pinned on her, but what choice did she have? Plus, she knew what she'd signed up for when moving to D.C., and in her mind, it was not only her duty, it was her destiny to be there.

"Right." Ana smiled. Another fake one. Perfectly crafted over the years. Most were incapable of knowing the difference in her expressions. Even the most skilled agents with the best tradecraft were unable to read her.

She locked up her personal and work cell phones in her desk since they weren't allowed in the SCIF, which was a sensitive compartmentalized information facility.

She followed Dean down the hall, and he swiped his badge to allow them access to the room. The rest of their unit was inside waiting for them at the conference table off to the side of the work area.

The office was at the backside of the building that faced Pennsylvania Avenue, and in the distance was the National Mall—well, that's what they would've seen had there been any windows.

Ana sat between Dean and Griff. Dean was in his late forties. A family man. Two kids at home. A nice and friendly smile. Always joking. He'd been in the Army before joining the FBI at the age of thirty. Griff, on the other hand, was what she called career-FBI. A rarity, like her. Joining straight out of grad school. Minimum age to join the Bureau was twenty-three, but most joined around thirty. The max age to become an agent was thirty-seven.

Griff was harder around the edges than Dean. Guarded. Not prepared to accept Ana as a new member on the team, given the loss of the man she replaced, as well as the manner in which he died—kidnapped, tortured, and brutally murdered. She wasn't looking to fill someone's shoes, or to get overly friendly with anyone in the unit, but she understood the hesitation by a few on her task force to welcome her with open arms.

Halle, who sat across from her, had been a bit cautious toward her when Ana first joined, but she'd started to open up within the last few weeks or so.

Halle was also the only other female on the team. The Bureau was doing its best to become more diverse, but the men-to-women ratio was still skewed toward men.

A smile played across Halle's lips, her way of saying good morning to Ana. Halle resembled the actress who, ironically, shared the same first name with her. Well, back when the movie star was in her thirties with shorter hair. Dean, of course, had nicknamed her Hollywood because of it.

Hollywood. Red. Yeah, Dean wasn't very original even though he worked for an elite task force to help bring down spies. But when it came to UC work or dealing with sources, Dean had proven himself highly capable.

The other three team members at the table were studying the chicken scratch notes they'd taken over the weekend during the brainstorming sessions to determine "what the fuck" went wrong, as Griff had so eloquently put it. It'd been his mantra since Friday, sounding like a broken record over the weekend.

Their unit chief, Gray, entered the room a moment later, and Ana was grateful she'd arrived before him. Tom Gray was basically every screenwriter's vision when creating his type of character for TV.

Gray wore a crisp black suit and navy tie. He switched back and forth between what Dean joked as democrat blue and republican red. From what Ana could tell, Gray did his best to act politically neutral, which was her preference as well, especially now that she was in the beating heart of the nation, the nerve center of the country where there was a political tug-of-war going on, even with the newly elected President Bennett.

Knox's dad.

Knox is A.J.'s teammate.

And here I am thinking about that man again when I shouldn't be. Repeatedly listening to his voicemail wasn't going to help get A.J. out of her head, either. Maybe if she deleted the message, the distraction would disappear?

Gray's lips twitched, barely noticeable beneath his thick,

black mustache. "Deputy Winters will be here shortly with an agent joining the unit on special assignment."

Special assignment? Kyle's words replayed in her mind from Saturday. *Double shit.*

"Let's recap before Deputy Winters gets here." Gray unbuttoned his jacket and worked his hands into the pockets of his slacks.

Ana much preferred Deputy Assistant Director Winters to Director Mendez. Mendez, who'd stayed on after Bennett won the election last November, wasn't Ana's biggest fan. The only reason the man even knew of her existence was because she worked with him on the attempted assassination case during the election last year. She'd also teamed up with Scott & Scott Securities, per Bennett's direction, and Mendez had blown a fuse at the idea of working with them.

"An accountant cooking books for an Albanian criminal organization in Boston has disappeared. Some of the money he was laundering went to acquire tech to help build dirty bombs for Hamas," Dean spoke up. "We haven't been able to reach him since Wednesday. Voicemail box full. We sent agents to the address where he lives, and no one was there."

The Albanians could've killed him for any number of reasons, right? Made an accounting mistake? she rationalized.

"A research scientist we'd turned, who'd been stealing proprietary secrets and selling them to the Chinese, is missing as well," Halle began. "We've been trying to contact him since Friday morning."

Maybe the scientist left? Abandoned his agreement with the FBI. It wouldn't be the first time it happened.

It was Ana's turn to share what Gray already knew but wanted to hear again like they were being quizzed before the big boss showed up.

"Katya, a ballerina for a small Russian theater company in New York City, is missing. The Volkov Russian crime family hired her to cozy up with American government workers, including congressmen, to obtain intelligence." *She was the only one who was supposed to go missing. The only freaking one, damn it. But not like this.* "Same story with her. She didn't show up for her last performance. No answer. No one at home."

"We've reached out to every source connected to all the active cases within our unit to ensure no one else is missing. We can't alert them to a potential problem, or that might have them running scared," Halle noted.

"All are accounted for except one, and as you know, Porter is personally following up on him in Atlanta," Dean pointed out.

"The Iranian spy," Gray said with a nod. "We can't lose him. Too much at stake." His cheeks filled with air for a moment before releasing it like a slow-leaking balloon.

"We're working nonstop with the field offices in Massachusetts, New York, and California in regard to the missing sources," Dean added. "And Porter will ensure the team in Atlanta is on high alert."

"I want to reiterate that neither Director Mendez nor the Deputy AD want the individual field offices made aware that sources, other than the one being investigated in their city, are missing," Gray noted what they all already knew. "Same goes for HQ. No one outside this unit is to know we have three missing sources. Am I clear?"

How in the hell was this happening? Everything had been planned so perfectly. It should've gone down flawlessly. *Katya should've—*

Ana ditched her thoughts when the door opened to reveal what she'd feared after Kyle left her townhouse on

Saturday—that her ex-husband would be working alongside her.

She straightened in her chair, her heartbeat going for a ride in her chest. Too hard. Too fast.

"Ladies. Gentlemen," Winters addressed them once he and Kyle were in the room, and the door clicked shut.

Kyle tucked his hands into the pockets of his black slacks, his eyes riveted to Ana as he stood alongside one of the most powerful men at Headquarters. No red or blue tie for Kyle. Purple. Bold. A statement that he was present and ready to go to work.

Kyle had clearly heard more about Porter traveling to Atlanta than the mere gossip he'd claimed during his surprise visit over the weekend. He was there to investigate the circumstances surrounding the missing sources.

Halle peered straight at Ana now, brows pulled tight. She must have noticed the distressed look on her face.

Ana had dropped her guard. She'd let the sight of Kyle rattle her, and as a result, someone was able to read her thoughts, her feelings, her emotions.

Ana gave Halle the slightest of nods, letting her know she was fine, and they'd talk later. Well, maybe.

She hadn't shared much about her personal life with anyone at Headquarters. Although, a Google search would throw the truth about her three-year marriage ending in divorce out for anyone to see if they were interested in looking. But she hadn't felt like sharing her backstory with any of her co-workers. Not yet, not until she knew her teammates better.

Deputy Winters, who was in his early fifties, gave off a Robert Redford vibe, from his expressive eyes to his blond hair and bone structure.

"This is Special Agent Kyle Jeter." Winters arched his shoulders back, adding an inch to his height of five-ten.

"No relation to Derek Jeter." Her ex-husband's joke that he wasn't related to the former pro baseball player was his standard opening, and even now, he couldn't help himself.

Kyle's gaze circled the table, taking in his audience, a group of non-trusting and skeptical agents. If most of them still viewed Ana as an outsider, then Kyle didn't stand a chance.

"Agent Jeter was on temporary assignment working with the Criminal Division in Hungary when he reached out to Headquarters about a possible assassination attempt on a Russian ballerina in New York," Winters explained, hints of his Texas upbringing in his tone.

"As you know, the Hungarian government asked the U.S. to help break up Russian mobs in Budapest," Kyle began. "We have a working squad there. Developing and operating informants. Gathering intelligence," he continued. "What we are doing there is unprecedented." His eyes swiftly moved to Ana. Did he know something? "I assume you all are well acquainted with the Volkovs since Katya was working for them."

"I'm more familiar with the Petrovs since they're the biggest Russian mob family in the world," Dean said. "The Volkovs are Ana's department."

Ana's mouth pinched tight, her focus falling to the table before her. No notepad there. She had every detail stitched into her mind from the moment the sources began going missing.

"The Petrovs were the FBI's greatest concern up until the leader's son died last year," Kyle responded to Dean.

"Don't tell me you're really buying this 'they've turned a new leaf' BS?" Dean asked, adding air quotes for emphasis.

"We'll have to give it time," Kyle said. "But right now, the group that concerns me the most is the Volkovs, because as of five months ago, they re-emerged after having been dark for about fifteen years."

Of all reasons for Kyle to be back in her life again . . . had he been looking into the Volkovs while in Hungary during his time there? *Fuckity fuck.* Why hadn't she considered the possibility. Of course, his assignment had been classified, and he hadn't told her why he'd been placed in Budapest when he left.

That awful gurgly feeling a person got when they were famished had Ana clutching her stomach.

"When Jeter reached out to Headquarters to warn us about the hit placed on a Russian ballerina in NYC, we realized the target was our unit's source," Winters said, interrupting Ana's downward spiral. "But we were too late. Katya was already gone. Given Jeter's close work with the Russians in Budapest, we requested his help."

"We didn't even believe the Volkovs were back and operating until we landed two new sources in the last few months, and they confirmed the Volkovs are discreetly operating again," Griff noted. "We did place our other Volkov source down in Miami under heavy protection the moment we learned Katya vanished, just in case he was a potential target."

"Remind me what happened fifteen years ago?" Dean asked. His expertise had more to do with Middle Eastern spies and terrorists, which was why he'd been assigned the accountant in connection to Hamas.

Kyle looked to Dean, but before he could speak up, Winters responded, "We believed the Volkovs were the right arm of the SVR following the days of the KGB and Cold War. But we've never been able to confirm that since the official line from the Russian government has always been that the two groups weren't connected."

"The Volkovs were a powerful Russian family that helped plant and manage Russian assets out in the field all over the world," Kyle added.

"But back in twenty oh five and six, the FBI began cracking down on Volkov spies. I doubt the Russians would have cared if they weren't worried the spies might expose the truth that their government bankrolled the Volkovs," Ana chimed in, choosing to finally join the conversation, though it pained her to do so.

"Why do you say that?" Dean asked, jotting notes as he spoke.

"Because planting Russian sleeper agents into the U.S. was the old way of doing things," Kyle answered for her, which he'd always done when they were married, and it had driven her crazy. "The SVR and the like found an easier way to gather intelligence." His hands dipped into his pockets as he scanned the room, eyes going to Ana last. "Bribe or blackmail *real* Americans already in positions of power. It saved them a lot of time and effort. No more training Russians to take on cover stories and blend into American society like the Volkovs had done."

Ana slipped her hands beneath the table, wrestling with the desire to speak up when she knew she had to conceal the truth behind tightly closed lips. "Shortly after the summer of oh six, the FBI could no longer find Volkov agents to arrest. Volkov spies had all but vanished, and the Volkov crime family seemingly ceased to exist overnight. Either killed or went underground."

"Until five months ago." Dean secured the chewed-up cap of his pen back in place and set it on top of his yellow legal pad. "I feel like there's more to this story I'm not remembering."

Halle looked up from her notes, gaze falling to Kyle as he circled the table to stand right behind Ana. "I would think as the Volkovs re-emerge, the new members would want revenge against the Russian administration for wiping the majority of them off the map fifteen years ago."

Ana shifted in her seat, uncomfortable with her ex looming behind her. "The Russians would have the most to lose with a Volkov comeback, especially if they were concerned they might wind up on the receiving end of a blackmail threat by them."

Dean snapped his fingers as though his memory had been jogged. "There was a list or something, right? One that would expose every spy the Volkovs had positioned around the world, including not-yet-activated sleeper agents, right? Proof the Volkovs worked for the Russian government, too." He paused for a second. "I would've assumed the Volkovs would have used that as leverage to prevent the Russian administration from turning on them. An insurance policy."

"We think it's possible Russian Foreign Intelligence got its hands on the book the summer of oh six, which may explain the domino effect of the fall of the remaining Volkov agents after that." Kyle moved back around the table to face her once again. "It was known as the Daylight Ledger." He repeated the words as they were actually known in Russian. "Not just a list of Volkov spies, but the name of every person murdered and by which spy. They may have begun collecting intel on the Russians' new American assets as well."

"Why was it called the Daylight Ledger?" Dean and his questions today. Normally she didn't mind, but she didn't want to be engaging in a conversation about the Volkovs right now.

"The rumor was that the list would shine the light of day on all those who wished to remain in the dark. It'd destroy lives. And powerful people," Kyle explained.

"The list doesn't exist. And if it ever did, the Russians probably managed to get a hold of it and torched the thing." Winters folded his arms. "No way did the Volkovs sit on that thing for fifteen years and suddenly decide to use it."

"Why wouldn't the Volkovs make a copy of the list if it was so important?" Dean went on anyway, curiosity in his eyes. The man loved a good mystery. "You know, a backup plan for if the book ever did fall into enemy hands, they'd have another one."

"The Volkovs were old school. Think Illuminati. They followed a code. Only one list, and only the leader Adrik Volkov had it. But the ledger was useless to anyone without the key to decrypt it." Kyle's intimate knowledge of the ledger was enough to put Ana over the edge. "Well, at least, that's what I learned while I was in Hungary this past year. Word is Adrik Volkov's nephew is now running the show and has the ledger."

"Which explains the Volkov comeback," Dean said with a nod.

"And what about the key?" Griff asked.

Winters shot an annoyed look at Kyle, one that said they were wasting time on what he believed to be a fairy tale.

"Grigory Volkov, Adrik's nephew, if he is in charge, has remained underground. The fact he hasn't fully emerged—"

"Suggests Grigory might have the ledger, but he's still in need of the key," Ana finished for her ex-husband, and her stomach was officially in the tightest of knots.

Kyle made eye contact with her, and his gratified expression said it all: *We still make a great team.* They had indeed been fantastic colleagues. "Right. If the ledger and key are real," he said while glimpsing Winters, offering the *if* for his benefit, "it'd make sense for Grigory Volkov to remain hidden until he has both."

Winters turned to Kyle, his stern no-nonsense face on display. "This is the Bureau, son. I appreciate all your insight into what you've learned about the Volkovs, but we're not going to focus on some fantastical ledger like we're in *The Da Vinci Code*. Our concern is the missing sources."

Ana's stomach dropped, but she resisted closing her eyes and gripping the arms of her chair. She didn't need anyone getting a read on her.

"I agree with Deputy Winters," Gray said, eyes moving around the table, the steely look on his face an indication he expected them to follow his lead.

Kyle offered a firm nod instead of words, but his eyes said it all to Ana, he didn't appreciate being dismissed by Winters or Gray.

"So, Agent Jeter," Halle said, seemingly trying to clear the sudden blitz of alpha male tension in the room, "do you believe the same assassin who may have been hired to take down Katya is also responsible for our other two missing sources?"

But no, that didn't make sense.

The assassin couldn't possibly have eliminated the other two targets. That "assassin" didn't really exist. Ana had made him up. Then again, she'd never anticipated for Katya to disappear *before* she was actually scheduled to vanish.

"Have we found ourselves caught back in the middle of a Russia-versus-the Volkovs duel two-point-oh?" Dean asked. "Maybe the SVR is hunting the Volkov crime family again in hopes they don't have the . . ." His voice trailed off in deference to Winters, but the word *ledger* was out there nonetheless.

"Intel would suggest Russian Foreign Intelligence was responsible for the hit placed on Katya, but we didn't get a name on who was hired to handle the matter." Kyle's gaze darted to Winters to see if he'd disagree with this theory as well.

"I'm not prepared to make that assumption, especially given the fact two other completely unrelated sources have also vanished," Winters challenged. "But I'm relying on you all to get to the bottom of everything."

"Is someone at the Bureau selling names of our sources to the highest bidder? Is this an internal issue?" Griff lifted his dark eyes toward Winters, and Ana saw the look of worry crossing Winters's face at the idea.

Did Winters not know how to answer? Did he think someone in the room was guilty?

"No one outside this unit accessed any case files related to all three sources. Not with their code, at least. We've already had the Bureau do an internal review. That doesn't rule out the possibility someone went around the normal means of obtaining information, though," Gray answered when Winters had refrained from doing so.

"Are you looking at us?" Halle asked what had to be on everyone's mind.

"You work for CI. You're already under one of the most closely monitored divisions in the Bureau." Was Winters's answer really an answer, though? "If someone in this room betrayed the FBI, we would've already known about it," he added, and Dean's shoulders slouched a touch with relief. "So, I'm counting on everyone here to come up with a how, why, and a way to stop any other sources from disappearing. I want answers." Winters turned to the side, his gaze moving back and forth between Ana and Kyle. "Will working together be a problem? A conflict of interest?"

"Not for me," Kyle answered immediately, smoothing a palm over his purple tie.

"Same, sir," Ana managed the response.

"We won't let you down." Kyle offered a reaffirming nod toward Winters, then to Gray. But his body had remained tense ever since the two men had rejected any talk of the Daylight Ledger.

Winters left a moment later, then at the sound of a knock, Gray stood and opened the door.

"Sorry to interrupt," one of the analysts who often worked for their unit announced, "but I have news."

Ana flicked her finger in Kyle's direction after Gray stepped outside to speak to the analyst. "Ex-husband."

"Ah." Dean slumped back down into his chair, but Ana kept her focus on the table, not sure what to make of this entire situation.

She startled when the door opened a minute later and Gray returned. "We have a possible hitman, and it's not good."

Ana's eyes widened as she waited. "Who?" Who in the hell had actually gotten to her source before Ana's plan had fallen into place as designed?

"Ivan Smirnoff," Gray announced.

What? She blinked in surprise at the name.

"Dubbed The Huntsman because of his ability to track anyone anywhere," Kyle added, clearly familiar with the name. "Famous for kidnapping and killing without leaving a trace behind. He's Russian, but . . ." He smoothed a hand over the few weeks' worth of beard he'd grown. In all their years of marriage, the man had never even tolerated a five o'clock shadow. "Well, shit."

"What is it?" Ana asked, recognizing Kyle's distressed look.

"The hit couldn't have been ordered by the SVR as chatter suggested," Kyle began, a look of confusion on his face that Ana felt down to her core, "because Ivan would never take the job. He hates the SVR."

"Because?" Dean asked.

"Before Ivan left Russia in his twenties, the government had his brother killed," Kyle explained. "The only way the Russian government is behind these hits is if Ivan's either not responsible or they went through a middleman—had someone else hire Ivan for them."

"Well, our people confirmed Ivan was in New York City last week. Got him on camera at the airport the day before Katya vanished." Gray paused. "He was flagged in Boston as well. So, it's looking like he's our guy."

"If someone is handing out source names and locations, what's the need for a hitman like The Huntsman?" Griff asked.

Ana's stomach lurched, and her hand dipped to her abdomen as she drew in a deep breath. Was the blame game amongst them about to start?

"Because no one gave up the names," Halle defended the team. "So, they needed the best of the best to track down these people for reasons unknown to us. *Yet*."

"If it's The Huntsman, he won't kill the sources right away. He'll keep them hidden somewhere for whoever hired him," Kyle said a moment later after some of the tension in the room had eased up.

"They have valuable information. Access to money, technology, and intelligence." Halle nodded in agreement. "Whoever is after our sources may first extract them for information, then offer them to whoever would be most interested. SVR, China, the Albanians, or Hamas. If they find out their spies turned on them and worked for the FBI, they'll want them back."

"For a price," Griff added, eyes moving around the table again, still suspecting that someone at the table may be a traitor.

This entire situation wasn't going to end well.

There was too much on the line.

Too much her ex-husband clearly already knew.

And she needed to get Porter on the phone ASAP.

"There's been a development. The team has a lead on who may have gotten to Katya and possibly the others. It's all one big mess over here. We need to talk. Please call me as soon as you get this." Ana's voicemail to Porter was brief, not wanting to leave too many details over his work phone.

The meeting with her team had lasted another hour before Ana could escape and make the urgent call. The task force had pored over case files, including digging up everything they knew about the Volkovs since Kyle firmly believed it was no coincidence a Volkov source had been targeted amongst the others. He'd even suggested the disappearances of their missing sources in California and Massachusetts were just to confuse the FBI and hide the fact that the true target was Katya, Ana's source.

"You okay?"

Ana flinched at the sound of Kyle's voice and slowly whirled around, lowering her phone to her side. "Trying to get a hold of our section chief."

"Porter hasn't checked in yet. Is that surprising?" He positioned a palm flat against the wall, effectively trapping her in the hallway. Her only other choice was to scurry into the bathroom.

"Last I heard from him, he was in the field with a special agent, but when he got in last night, Porter warned me the area doesn't have the best cell service," she lied, and how could she not? She had her orders.

"You and Porter sound close."

Was Kyle jealous? Of her boss? She couldn't deal with this right now. "Porter helped get me this new promotion. He's really taken me under his wing." *Porter changed my life, but how can I explain?*

"We should do dinner. Tonight."

"Huh?" she blurted, surprised by his question given what was going on. And he wasn't going to give up on regaining a footing back in her life, was he?

"We can make it a work meal. Discuss the missing sources. We used to be a great team," he added.

Maybe dinner wouldn't be so bad. She could peel back more layers about his work in Hungary with the Volkovs. It might help her shed some light on everything since he clearly knew a lot. Plus, she wanted to know exactly how he'd stumbled upon chatter about the hit against Katya.

"Dinner. Seven o'clock. My place, though," she agreed.

"I'll bring takeout." He smiled, lowering his hand from the wall, a look of victory in his eyes and in the crook of his lips. "Unless you learned to cook since we were married?"

"No, I'm still a lousy chef."

He placed a hand on her shoulder, and she'd almost swear he was going to lean in and lay one on her cheek.

"Can I ask you something?" She couldn't help herself. "Why didn't you tell me your move to Budapest was temporary?"

He inched back a step, releasing his hold of her. "Would it

have made a difference? Would you have come with me? Or tried long-distance while I was there?"

"I don't think so," she admitted. "Our marriage was over before the move." A bit of honesty could go a long way.

He didn't say anything, so she shifted the weight of her stance from right to left, left to right.

There'd never been any heat between them. No passion. Not on her side, at least. *A cold fish for a fiery redhead,* Kyle had said one night. His op had failed, and he'd returned home drunk, wanting sex, and she hadn't been in the mood.

But if she were truly a cold fish, dead on the inside, bland and boring, lacking sexuality, then why'd she slip her hand beneath the covers to get herself off after meeting A.J. back in Charlotte? Why'd she pretend that hand belonged to the sexy Southerner?

And why had she replayed his drunk voicemail over and over again since Saturday night? Why was she so afraid that if Adriana told A.J. Ana was in town, and they became friends, she'd—

"Ana?" Kyle sought her attention. She was trapped between a wish of what might be and the reality of what was.

"Yeah, sorry. What were you saying?" She dragged her focus up Kyle's lean torso and to his eyes.

An awkward throat clear from behind Kyle had her peeking around his large frame to spot Halle, who was probably attempting to get to the bathroom.

"Excuse me," Halle said, and Kyle brought his back flat to the wall to allow Halle access to the ladies' room.

"I have to go. Talk tonight." Ana followed Halle into the bathroom before Kyle was able to object.

"Wow." Halle folded her arms and leaned against the vanity in the restroom.

Ana unleashed a deep breath and looked in the mirror

alongside Halle and played with her bun, ensuring no strands managed to escape.

"You feel like talking about it?"

"No." Maybe that was rude? "Sorry, I just—"

Halle held a palm up. "No worries. I get it. I made the mistake of falling for someone at the Bureau, and I walk on eggshells every time we're in the same room together."

"Don't worry, I'm not the kind of person to ask who at the department you fell for." Of course, Ana already guessed with whom she'd been involved. She was trained to read people. Situations. And she'd felt the breakup between Griff and Halle vibrate through the building after it had happened.

"And that's what I like about you." Halle spun around to peer in the mirror as well. She fixed her short hair, teasing up the ends a bit.

"I'm thinking he may want to get back together." *Why did I just admit that?* She was normally a steel trap. Nothing in. Nothing out. And honestly, she was worried about a lot more than her ex right now, but she couldn't talk about it.

Maybe she was only doing her job, but keeping secrets from the team made her feel dirty. Like she was the one betraying them. And after what they found out in the SCIF today, Ana knew all fingers would soon point to her. Thank God she had Porter on her side.

"And I'm guessing you don't?" Halle set her palms to the counter.

She shook her head no.

"Is this gonna be weird working with him?"

"It'll be fine." As long as Kyle didn't try and stand in her way of completing her mission it would be. That'd been another obstacle in their marriage. He knew firsthand the dangers of their job, and he'd made her well-being and safety his business, taking every opportunity to keep her out of the line of fire—pushing her superiors to put her on a desk. His lack of trust in her competence, as well as his blatant disrespect for her wishes, had been infuriating.

Regardless, Ana was determined to unravel the truth and leave her past behind for good. And once she'd completed that mission, she could truly move on from the day her life changed forever. The day her parents died at the hands of the FBI.

CHAPTER SEVEN

"YOU REGRET VOLUNTEERING TO SURVEIL HER YET?" CHRIS asked, and A.J. shook his head in disbelief as Chris used chopsticks to shovel the contents of a container of lo mein into his mouth like he hadn't just scarfed down a burger a few hours ago.

They were sitting in A.J.'s Suburban rental on a stakeout of FBI Special Agent Anastasia Quinn.

Did A.J. want to see Ana again? Yes. For this reason? Hell, no.

A.J. draped an arm over the top of the steering wheel and leaned forward in the driver's seat where they sat parked outside the FBI Hoover Building. The exterior needed an update. Age had tarnished the structure. Ink stains were beneath the flag poles surrounding the entrance doors. The FBI police car out front didn't look up for the challenge of a high-speed pursuit and was in need of a good bath.

"I mean, I didn't actually think you'd opt out of the chance to stalk the woman you've been thinking about for basically forever, but still," Chris went on when A.J. had remained quiet, then placed the now-empty container into a bag by his feet and threw the chopsticks inside as well. And great, now the vehicle would smell like a Chinese restaurant for a week.

It was day two of watching Ana. She'd stayed at her office nearly all day Sunday. Then he and Chris had followed her to work today. Shadowing an FBI agent wasn't high on the list of things he enjoyed doing, especially when it was a woman he was interested in dating. Who, as it turned out, might be a traitor.

"I'm not stalking her," A.J. countered.

"Mmmhmm." Chris lowered his shades to shoot A.J. a *you're full of bullshit* look, one he pulled off well, then set his glasses back in place. "So . . . you really think POTUS believes in the existence of that Daybreak Ledger?"

"It's Daylight, dumbass," he corrected in his typical, sarcastically polite manner. "It amazes me you didn't get tossed from BUD/S by calling officers the wrong names."

"Funny." But hell, Chris and remembering names paired as well as ice cream and pickles (well, aside from what his mom said about pregnancy). "But annnnyway," Chris began dramatically, "I don't think we'd be sitting here right now, spying on a team of people who spy on spies," he said with a grin, "if the President didn't think we might get our hands on that ledger."

"Well, if there are a bunch of names in a record book from years ago, and some of those people are still living amongst us, they deserve to be outed as the traitors they are," A.J. quickly responded, the very idea infuriating him.

"That might be one reason POTUS wants that ledger. And well, also get ahold of the key that's supposed to decipher it." Chris smirked. "And can you imagine if there really is a list of murdering spies and their victims, not to mention Russian double agents in other countries? That'd be a powerful political tool."

Chris was probably right. And maybe the ledger would offer the U.S. some leverage over Russia for once.

Chris snatched Ana's case file from the back seat and opened it on his lap. "Man, your girl is smart." He thumbed through her records, reading them aloud to give A.J. a hard time. He'd done the same on Sunday. Chris didn't ever miss a chance to drive A.J. batshit crazy.

"She's not my anything."

"Born in New York City," Chris began, ignoring A.J. and faking a Southern accent for reasons unknown, but that was par for the course when it came to Echo Three. The guy should've been an actor. Of course, A.J. would sure miss him if he were to ever quit Echo Team. "Moved around a lot."

That had to be tough.

"Her parents were traveling salespeople. They died in a car accident when she was sixteen, and she lived in foster care until eighteen." A.J.'s gaze slid sideways to catch Chris shaking his head in sympathy. "Then she got accepted to Walden in Minneapolis. Psych degree." He tossed a quick look A.J.'s way as if the psychology degree would have been a deal-breaker had Chris been interested in her. The last thing Chris wanted was anyone trying to get a read on him. "John Jay College of Criminal Justice for her double master's degrees in criminal and forensic psychology."

"I remember all this from when you read it out loud this morning. And yesterday." *And when I studied the file until my eyes went blurry.*

"Did some consulting for the NYPD before joining the FBI at twenty-five." Yeah, Chris was relentless. "Wonder why she turned down the FBI recruiters two times before saying yes on a third. They must've wanted her pretty bad like someone else I know."

"Would you shut up?" A.J. teased. "I swear, sometimes you're more seal than Navy."

Chris made a barking seal noise, and the fact the man knew to do that, well, exactly.

A.J. smiled. "Polar bears. Seals." The time Chris had confronted a polar bear, Chris had worried more about saving the bear from getting shot than getting eaten by the thing or killed by the Russian agents nearby that would have happily put a round in his ass.

"Do not bring up that incident with the bear." Chris pointed at him. "Just because I like animals—"

"And so do I, but, brother, if it's me or a polar bear, well, all bets are off." A.J.'s hands went to the gear shift when he spotted Ana rounding the side of the building. He'd nearly missed her exit when a trolley tour vehicle blocked part of his view. "She's on the move," he said, resuming some sense of seriousness now, a reminder they were there for work.

Ana had her red hair in a tight bun at the back of her head. A gray pantsuit with white blouse beneath. Black heels. Sleek black sunglasses. He was too far away to see the color of her gorgeous eyes from where he sat, but he remembered them.

A darker green than his. Something akin to the color of the forest back home in Alabama. The same one where he smacked his head on that death trap of rocks.

"Can't believe she took a promotion and moved to D.C., and I had no idea." She'd made the move after the one time A.J. had Googled her. Wyatt and Asher had made fun of him for days about that, and he hadn't Googled her again.

"She deserves the promotion as far as I'm concerned," Chris commented. "She was pretty talented when we worked with her last year. And hell, she put up with you."

A.J.'s eye-roll was hidden behind his aviator sunglasses, but the grin on Chris's face meant he surely felt the scathing look shot his way.

A.J. fidgeted with the brim of his hat. Both he and Chris had ball caps and sunglasses on, but A.J. had the feeling if Ana looked back toward the SUV, she'd recognize them. Shitty Federal agent if she didn't, he supposed.

The woman seemed like such a straight arrow, but she'd surprised him by rolling out some humor when they worked that case together last year. She had a dry, sarcastic wit, and half the time, he wasn't sure if she was being serious or if it'd just been a slip, but the way her humor slid off her tongue was sexy as hell.

"She's not going to her Volvo." Chris threw a finger toward where Ana walked down the street. "Turning on Eleventh."

"I can see that," A.J. said while easing into traffic to keep up with her. He also had to stay far enough away so that a trained agent of her caliber wouldn't notice him.

"Why is she going that way?" Chris asked when Ana made another turn. Followed by another shortly after.

They were on 10th Street NW, heading back toward the Hoover Building, which made no sense. "Shit. You see that? Damn, she's got fast hands." Chris shifted his glasses down a touch as if rewinding the scene to re-watch in slow motion.

"A pass was made. She must have had to collect something from a source, and that's why the unusual walking loop," A.J. reasoned.

"Pull over. I better follow that guy." Chris pushed his glasses back in place as A.J. stopped near the sidewalk. "Hey, don't give me that look."

Had A.J. looked at him? Chris was feeling guilty, too, so it would seem.

"We're supposed to monitor all her interactions," Chris said as he opened the door. "This is to rule her out as a suspect. Okay?"

"You saying that to make yourself feel better?" But A.J. went ahead and waved him off. "Meet you after." He hated that they had to spy on her, but the team had been burned before, and he couldn't turn a blind eye just because he was ridiculously attracted to her.

A.J. waited for Chris to hop out of the SUV, then picked up his pace to catch up with Ana. She'd gone straight to her Volvo and climbed into the driver's seat.

After a few minutes, he was following her on Pennsylvania Avenue and heading past Capitol Hill, in the direction of her rental, which wasn't far away.

According to the profile, Ana had moved to D.C. about two and a half months ago after accepting an offer with the CI Division. She'd been living out of a hotel until recently.

"Did I delete my message?" he asked himself while turning up the volume on the radio when the singer Brett Young came on. "I think so." He expelled a breath through his nose. "Talking to myself again."

He rolled down his window once he was parallel parked on her street a few houses down from hers. He was close enough to put eyes on her as she exited her Volvo and hurriedly went up the steps to her front door, but far enough away not to draw notice.

Ana stole a look over her shoulder as she stuck the key in the lock as if she sensed someone was there. And damn, she was good.

He tugged at the brim of his hat and shifted back in his seat, moving fully out of view of her door.

A.J. texted Chris his location, then snatched Ana's case file once she was inside, and her front room light was on.

He flipped through the papers for the millionth time, but guilt slowly ate at him.

His phone began ringing, and he expected it to be Chris with an update, but it was his brother Caleb. Maybe he had news on how the rest of the bachelor party slash inquisition weekend went?

A.J. brought the phone to his ear, his eyes drifting from Ana's townhouse, its windows shielded by blinds, before his focus moved back to the photo paperclipped to the file folder.

Reddish-gold hair fell past her shoulders. Had the FBI asked her to put it down for the shot? There was the tiniest hint of a cleft in her chin. Straight red eyebrows and long dark lashes dramatically framed her green eyes. Her nose was straight. Not too upturned or wide. And her lips. Heaven help him. Thick, full, and luscious.

"You there?"

He blinked at the sound of Caleb's voice, nearly forgetting he'd answered the phone. "Yeah, what's up?"

"The wedding is still a go, I'm afraid to say. Two weeks and counting," Caleb announced apologetically. "Unless you happened to come across something that would convince Ella not to marry him."

God, he didn't want to be the one to break his sister's heart. To crush her hopes and dreams. But he also didn't want her making a mistake and marrying Perfect Brian, and he knew deep in his belly, the man was far from perfect for Ella.

"I should know soon about what really happened in Vegas," he announced.

Wyatt's daughter, Gwen, promised to look at the hotel surveillance to ensure Brian hadn't cheated on Ella or done anything else disgraceful.

"Okay, let me know when you hear something." Caleb paused. "Where are you at?"

"Working." And that was all he could say. He wasn't about to expose the fact he was sitting outside Ana's apartment like some creepy stalker.

I'm getting paid to watch her. His skin heated at the thought. Yeah, he hated this, but he also hadn't wanted anyone else to watch her.

This assignment also probably meant he'd never get a chance to ask her out. Once he cleared her name as a traitor, and that was the only acceptable outcome, how would he let her know about this? It wasn't a secret he was comfortable keeping from her if, by chance, he manned up and ever officially asked her out.

Date? What am I thinking?

"Okay, well, stay safe," Caleb said, taking on a bit of Beckett's dad-tone. "Don't die or anything." He cleared his throat. His brother was about as good at dealing with his emotions as the rest of the Hawkins brothers—and that was to say he was shitty at it. They'd been raised by caring and loving parents, but each brother had gone through the wringer in one way or another that had shaped them into the men they were today. "By the way, how's your head?"

A.J.'d had two hellish nightmares since bumping his noggin in the woods, and they all centered around painful memories. "I'm fine." It wasn't like he hadn't hit his head a dozen times before. "Talk when I have news on Brian." He ended the call before his brother had the chance to pry anymore, then almost dropped his phone at the sight of a man now standing on Ana's front step, a brown bag cradled in his arm. Was that takeout?

The man shifted to the side as he waited for Ana to open the door as if he had the same feeling as Ana that someone was out there watching.

A.J. flipped through Ana's file to another image, to the man standing outside her door.

Kyle Jeter. FBI for fifteen years. Thirty-nine years old. And Ana's ex-husband.

A.J. swallowed hard when Ana opened the door, then stepped aside to allow her ex entry. She'd changed into jeans and a black, cotton V-neck tee.

"Well, shit," A.J. muttered.

A tap at the passenger window had him losing sight of Ana's door for a moment as he looked over to see Chris standing there. "I make a horrible stakeout guy. Didn't see you there," he said after letting Chris into the SUV.

A lopsided smile played at Chris's lips. "I miss anything? Who's the guy she just let in?"

"Her ex-husband." Pings of jealousy, totally unwarranted, popped inside his chest like the Pop Rocks he ate as a kid. "What happened with the guy you were following? You got here fast."

"I lost him." Chris shook his head, disappointed. "Yeah, I know. I know. Not like me. I swear the guy basically vanished before my eyes." He held his phone out between them. "Got a photo. Not the best. Sent it to Harper to see if she can work her magic and get us a name." He tucked his phone back into his pocket and rifled through the bag on the floor. "I got an Uber here and didn't expect to see some guy at her door when I arrived."

"Yeah, I wasn't expecting that, either." Especially not her ex. Was he in town for work? Based on Ana's file, he was an FBI agent stationed in Hungary for a special assignment cracking down on Russian mobsters. *Annnnd shit.* He was the special agent the unit was bringing onto the team, wasn't he?

"Here. Check your fortune," Chris said in an attempt to distract him. He tossed one of the two fortune cookies that'd been included with the dinner Chris had grabbed during their stakeout of the Hoover Building. "Maybe all the answers are inside that cookie."

"Are you ever serious?" But A.J. removed the plastic wrapping from the cookie anyway, his nerves more shot than before he'd been assigned to stalk the woman he'd recently drunk dialed.

"Since when are you Mr. Doom and Gloom?" Chris popped the cookie in his mouth and squinted at the small white paper in his hand.

"Wouldn't you be a bit sour if—"

"The woman you want to have babies with was currently inside her townhouse with her ex-husband and was also a potential traitor to the United States?"

A.J. slapped Chris's bicep with the hand that clutched the cookie, and he nearly crumbled the thing in his palm.

"What?" Chris shrugged. "I've known you a long damn time, and I've never seen you like this."

"Which is why you had me call her in my drunken state Saturday, huh?" A.J. pressed.

"Someone needed to give you a push. I just didn't expect we'd be seeing her under these circumstances the next day."

That was a big fat ditto.

"You will chase fortune but win a heart," Chris read the note from his cookie. "Chasing fortune, huh?" He sat up and stuffed the note in his pocket as if he planned on keeping it. "Yours?"

A.J. cracked the cookie, and Chris swiped the broken parts and tossed the pieces into his mouth. "You're like a growing boy who never stops eating." He couldn't help but laugh at Chris. The man was good at a lot of things—one of them, making him smile even during the shittiest times. Case in point now.

"So, what's in your future?" Chris asked around a mouthful of cookie, crumbs dropping onto his plain black tee.

A.J. removed his sunglasses since it was after seven, and Ana wasn't around to spot him in the vehicle. "Trusting a traitor is dangerous, but falling for one is the deadliest sin of all."

"Noooo, really?" Chris's eyes stretched in surprise. He snatched the paper and peered at it, then flipped it over. "You got a blank one. You pulled that shit out of your ass? How very Confucius of you." He threw the paper back at him. "You know what a blank paper means, right?"

"No, but I'm sure you're going to tell me."

Chris pivoted his Red Sox ball cap backward and pressed his shoulder casually to the side door. "You get a fresh start. You get to determine your fate."

"Oh, and you don't?" A.J.'s brows rose as he waited for Chris to enlighten him.

Chris flashed his white teeth. "No, it sounds like I'm coming into money. And meeting a woman, too."

"Lucky you."

"Or, maybe I already met one." Chris had to be referring to Rory.

"And if you were to break her heart—"

"Jesse will break my legs? Or would you?" He grinned. Apparently, the threat of bodily harm didn't offend him in the least. "You know, you could vouch for me, since you're his friend and all." He held both palms open as if it were that easy. "And *I'm* your friend."

A.J. didn't want to talk about Chris's love life right now, not when he was sitting outside Ana's house, and his prospects with her were dwindling by the second. He set his blank fortune on the console between their seats and closed the file on his lap, unable to look down at Ana's gorgeous green eyes and not feel like some weird creeper. "You don't actually believe in fortune-telling nonsense of any kind, do you?" he asked, deciding to change the subject. "Or is this some new thing about you I don't know?"

"How can you not believe in something . . . magic or mysticism, whatever you want to call it, after meeting Elaina?" he asked, his tone dead serious.

Of course, Liam and Emily's adopted daughter was eerily prophetic. He had no intention of reading into her abilities because that was outside his wheelhouse.

But maybe after being in the woods near Shaw's cabin and feeling as though he'd seen Marcus's ghost, well, hell, he didn't know what to believe anymore about anything.

"You letting Harper go to voicemail or what?" Chris pointed to A.J.'s cell, causing him to blink at the realization his phone was ringing.

Chris pressed the speaker button before A.J. had a chance to do so. "What's up?" he answered. "Get a match on the picture I texted you?"

"Not yet," Harper said. "But I do have other news."

"You still in that basement?" A.J. asked her. "I thought there was no reception."

"The place got a few upgrades, so I can operate from here," she explained. "The section chief, Wilson Porter, is now MIA. Porter's rental was found ditched thirty minutes south of Atlanta. Tire marks suggest he was forced off the road."

"Shit." Chris shook his head. "The source he went to check on missing, too?"

"No, the Iranian is in an FBI safe house. Porter had him placed there earlier today."

"Some good news. But does that mean the hitman you told us about earlier had been in Atlanta and—"

"Ivan may have taken Porter so he could tell him where the Iranian is being held," Harper finished A.J.'s thought.

"Great," A.J. grumbled as Chris motioned toward Ana's townhouse.

"I guess this news explains why Kyle Jeter is being booted from Ana's place. She must have just learned about Porter's disappearance," Chris announced. "Want me to follow him?"

"Yeah." A.J. peered at Kyle hurrying down the steps. He took a right, going the opposite direction from where they were parked.

Chris exited the car and started down the street toward Ana's ex, and A.J. returned his focus to his cell phone.

"What else do we know?" he asked Harper. "Anything on Kyle Jeter, Anastasia's ex-husband?"

"Yeah." Harper was quiet for a moment. "Jeter's now working the investigation on the missing sources. He's the one who first intercepted news that a hit had been placed on Katya, the ballerina in New York. He has a lot of knowledge about Russian crime families, especially the Volkovs, given his work in Budapest, and he could be valuable *if* the Russian mob *or* Russian government is behind what's going on."

Kyle was Ana's ex for a reason, and A.J. couldn't help but assume that if the dude couldn't hang on to Ana, he was most likely a dick and never deserved her. "Where are we at on placing Ivan in California when that source went MIA? And hell, in Georgia, now?"

"Working on it, believe me. He's not known as one of the best out there for nothing," Harper rushed out as if worried he was challenging her abilities. "And a news outlet in Atlanta broke the story that a high-ranking FBI agent is possibly missing. Only a matter of time before more of the story breaks," Harper gave him the bad news. Whenever the media got involved, shit went sideways.

"Fingers will get pointed every which way."

"And if an agent on the CI unit is guilty, they might spook and take off, and we lose who they're working with," Harper finished for him. "Luckily, though, we're watching them all. But if it's Quinn . . ." She let her words hang, not wanting to finish them as much as A.J. didn't want to hear them.

Harper's switch to using Ana's last name bothered him more than it should have. She was trying to separate herself. Remain objective. Clearly, he was failing in that regard.

"It's not her. She's a solid agent. She helped us before. She's not a traitor." He knew it in his gut.

"Yeah, and I want to believe that, but we have to try and be—"

"Objective," he said grimly. "I know, I know."

"It's just not going to look good for her, you know. She's the newest on the task force. And after going through all the reports, I discovered the three missing sources were first developed by her when she joined Headquarters. Same with the other Volkov source in Miami, and the Iranian in Atlanta."

His heart nearly stopped at the news. "Wait, I thought two of the sources were assigned to other agents."

"Yeah, but Quinn was the one who put together the source identification packets before recruitment for the informants. *She* identified the subjects as targets. Gathered their vulnerabilities so the FBI wouldn't be blindsided down the road for any trials if needed. Put together psych evals and intel to be used against the informant to, you know, motivate them into cooperating. Only after the dossiers were compiled and targets approved to become FBI assets, did other agents and correlating field offices take over for the other two that are missing." Harper spoke so fast, which was typical, that A.J. had to take a second and digest her words.

"And?" More was coming, A.J. felt it.

"Quinn chose to remain the handler for the Volkov sources. And with Ana's ex-husband showing up to Headquarters, well, something isn't right. Everything is leading back to—"

"Her," A.J. finished, painful and foreboding dread leaching into him.

CHAPTER EIGHT

ANA BROUGHT HER HANDS TO HER KNEES, HER BODY SHAKING as she stood across the street from Wilson Porter's townhouse and out of view of any neighboring houses that may have had cameras positioned with a view of the street.

She snatched a breath of the hot, humid air and stood upright, preparing herself to go inside. Her hand dipped into the pocket of her black hoodie for her disposable phone, and she replayed the urgent voicemail from Porter she'd missed while Kyle had been removing the takeout from the bags.

"It's me. I'm sorry I couldn't reach out before, but I haven't been alone until now," Porter said, his voice breathless. From running? "I'm being hunted. Someone is following me. Ran me off the road. I've gotta go dark, but, Ana, I found him," he said, huffing around his words. "Initiate the backup plan and be at the set location in precisely ninety-six hours. I'll get him there, you have my word." He growled out in pain as if he'd tripped and fallen and was struggling to get up. "And watch your back. It's about to get ugly." The call ended abruptly.

She powered off the phone, knowing she'd need to

destroy it tonight. When both she and Kyle had received a call from the office alerting them to Porter's possible disappearance, she'd urged Kyle to go to the office, and she'd meet him there. After he left, she'd hurried to her safe to check to see if Porter had called her. The disposable phone in her safe was only to be used between her and her boss for an emergency such as this.

One message. The contingency plan she knew would, at least temporarily, have her looking guilty as sin.

I was trained and conditioned to handle anything, Ana reminded herself, shoving away the terror working to cling to her like wet clothes during a torrential downpour.

She had to remain unshakeable. She couldn't break now.

So, Ana kept her head low to avoid any neighborhood surveillance cameras while moving onto Porter's property and into his backyard.

Thank God Porter was single. No kids. No dogs. No one home so she could make an easy entry.

Ana opened the screen door and stuck her key into the lock of his back door. The key was reserved for shit-hitting-the-fan kind of moments like now.

She quietly shut the door behind her and pulled out her personal cell, using the flashlight to guide her to his office. It was down the hall and two doors on the left.

Ana circumvented his desk and set her phone down, positioning it so the light shone on the wall. She eyed the framed photo of George Washington before carefully lifting and setting it on the floor by her feet.

Ana punched in the code for the safe and waited for the small door to unlock and click open.

Her shoulders fell forward in panic when she saw the box was empty.

"No," she whispered and threw her hand inside to feel

around even though it was clearly freaking empty. The backup plan was failing before it even started.

She shut and locked the door and rehung the picture, not sure what else to do aside from getting the hell out of there.

But first, she had to access Porter's security system and erase the footage of her entry. Her being there would look suspicious, especially right after his disappearance, even if she was using a key he'd given her.

Ana started out of his office but paused in the hallway at the sound of a creaking floorboard above her. She wasn't alone. Whoever was there must've come for the contents of the safe, too. And beaten her to it.

She ducked into the office, unstrapped her sidearm, and retrieved her gun. Safety off. The individual would have to walk past her whether they went to the front or back door.

But hell, there'd been no signs of forced entry in the back when she'd arrived, and she highly doubted whoever was in the house had used the front door—unless they had a key? And what did that mean?

When the sounds of footsteps grew louder, she eased farther back to catch whoever was about to walk by the office.

Her heartbeat quickened when a dark figure appeared and halted right outside the door as if sensing her presence. Based on height and bulk, it was a man, his head and face covered with a full mask, gloves on his hands. Dressed in all black like her.

The second she sensed he was about to turn, she lifted her gun and aimed it his way. "Don't move," she demanded, but he came at her fast, forcing her arms up into the air. She gritted down on her back teeth as they struggled with her sidearm. His hands were everywhere. Pushing. Pulling.

Ana's back slammed against the wall, but she refused to

give up, even though something inside her told her she was on the brink of losing this battle.

A knee to his groin only made matters worse when a shot got off and pierced the ceiling.

He kept her body pinned to the wall as he stopped fighting for control of her gun, and in one fast movement, he reached around to his back. With his barreled chest so close to her, she couldn't even get her arms lowered to try and position her weapon on him.

Her eyelashes fluttered against particles of plaster falling from the ceiling.

Another knee to his dick had him hissing and growing angrier with her.

But as she stared at a pair of unnaturally colored eyes, it dawned on her he could have already shot her by now but hadn't.

"Stop," he growled in a too-deep-to-be-real voice. "Stop resisting."

"Who are you?"

The man stepped back, and they both pointed their weapons at each other, breathless.

He raised a forefinger to his lips with his free hand. "We're not alone." The man spun toward the open doorway, then gave her one last look before taking off.

She stumbled back in surprise, prepared to pursue but hesitated at the sounds of a skirmish right before the back door banged shut.

Ana carefully entered the hall, still confused as to what in the hell just happened, then halted in surprise as a shadowy figure started her way, one hand with a gun aimed toward the ceiling, the other holding the side of his head.

"You okay?" he asked.

She attempted to adjust her eyesight to see who was standing in the hall with her.

"It's me."

That voice.

"Anastasia." He teased out her full name, allowing it to slowly roll across his tongue. "The guy is gone. Are you hurt?"

"*A.J.?*" She edged closer to him, taking cautious steps. Once his face was in view, and she confirmed his identity, she lowered her weapon, and he did the same. "I'm fine, but what in the hell are you doing here?"

But damn it, there wasn't time to have a conversation, especially not there. Someone may have already reported hearing the gunshot.

"We need to get out of here," she urgently said before he'd answered her.

"I'm thinking that's a good idea."

"I discharged my weapon. And . . . the security cameras." The cameras she could fix, but the spent bullet was irrefutable evidence she'd been in Porter's house.

"There will be a secondary copy of the footage on the security company's mainframe. You'll need that one, too," he said as if it were the most natural conversation in the world.

She'd been so shocked by what happened tonight, she might have missed that detail had A.J. not shown up.

"My people will handle that." He motioned for the door. "I'll scrub the footage that's on-site and get the shell casing and bullet. You just get back home and wait for me there."

"Why are you helping me?" she blurted, worried he was a figment of her imagination. An illusion. Some big trick, one like her father used to pull.

"I, um."

He wasn't supposed to help her, was he? And what did that mean?

A.J. reached for her hand. A surprising and comforting feeling warmed her like a security blanket.

"Please, just go. Trust me, okay?" She stared at him, eyes wide. How could she trust him when she had so many questions? But for some insane reason, she did.

She pulled her hand free and walked right out that door without a second thought.

CHAPTER NINE

ANA BLINKED A FEW TIMES IN SURPRISE AT THE KNOCK ON her door and the accompanying voice. "It's me."

A.J. had said the same back in Porter's house as if they were already so familiar with each other that "it's me" held no question. But she had recognized his voice back there, same as now. Even through the door.

There was no hesitation when she moved to let him in. No question in her mind. Cast under some type of spell or something.

His mouth was set in a tight line. Worry in his green eyes. "I erased the footage from inside the home. And my people are working on wiping the recordings sent to the security company." He opened his palm to reveal the bullet and shell casing, the remaining evidence that put her inside Porter's house that night.

She mouthed thank you, a bit shocked she was letting him break the law for her, and that he was so willing to do so.

A.J. closed and locked up behind her, and she went down the hall into her kitchen, almost in a daze, assuming A.J. would follow.

The takeout Kyle had brought over for dinner was still on the kitchen counter, sitting there like a Japanese sushi roll-scented air freshener. The aroma was enhanced by the fact her A/C had stopped working that morning. Good thing she didn't have a cat, the smell would drive the poor thing crazy.

She began disposing of the food, not sure how to have a conversation with A.J. right now about what happened, and why he was even there.

Hell, she'd never asked A.J. how he'd known where she lived.

She wasn't listed, but if he'd been outside Porter's, well, he must have followed her from her rental to her section chief's home.

Her day, her night, her everything was spinning out of control, and she didn't deal well with out of control.

She quickly went through her mental SGW—Shit Gone Wrong—list for the evening: a panicked message from her boss, an empty safe, the discharge of her sidearm, and the gorgeous, unforgettable man who had shown up for the (sort of) save. Although, she probably shouldn't put A.J. on the SGW list.

But despite three of the things on that list closing in on DEFCON 1 status, disposing of the sushi as if it were a dead body was suddenly of paramount importance.

Ana grabbed her spray bottle and paper towels and began scrubbing down her counters where the brown bag had sat for hours.

"Cleaning, huh?" he asked. "Pretty vigorously, I might add."

She kept scrubbing, the paper towel tearing from her attempt at getting a stain off the counter that'd probably been there since the '80s. The once-white appliances were now a dingy yellow. And if A.J. stretched his arms open, he'd be able to touch both counters.

It was old. In desperate need of upgrades that she'd never see since it was a rental. But places in the city were expensive, and she was still paying off her ridiculously large student loan debt every month and couldn't be choosy about her new place to live. Plus, it'd been conveniently located near her boss.

She kept scrubbing, and given the heat, she was beginning to sweat between her boobs. At the feel of a hand on her shoulder, she flinched and faced him, letting go of the paper towel.

He raised both palms in the air in surrender when she pointed the spray bottle at him. "You, um, okay?" His eyes were soft. Thoughtful. The kind of warmth that flowed from a man you might be able to trust with all your heart.

"I panic-clean. One of my many flaws."

He leaned his hip against the counter and folded his arms, the black fabric taut over his biceps. His legs were encased in dark denim paired with black sneakers.

He was standing close. And he smelled of manly soap and fresh laundry. The scent wafted through the air and hit her nose, knocking out the odor of disinfectant.

Slightly drunk on the essence of all that was A.J., Ana ignored proper etiquette and gave him a thorough once-over. Discreetly, of course. He was broad-shouldered. Fit, but not overly muscular. She spied one tattoo on the inside of his forearm. A Navy SEAL Trident with the script, *Earn Your Trident Every Day*, beneath. His beard was trimmed. About three to four weeks of growth by her guess. A straight nose. Expressive eyes and brows that helped her read his emotions. She gauged his thoughts as she peered into those light green eyes, the color of the exotic water she'd only dreamed of swimming in.

The man was handsome. Cowboy-handsome. Okay, so maybe that wasn't a thing. But then again, guys in cowboy hats without a shirt on, showing off a six-pack, a lasso slung over a shoulder, sounded awfully sexy to her.

If she were a judge in a competition, she'd be waving a 10 up in the air, hiding a giddy smile.

And Ana didn't get giddy.

She read people. Found their flaws. Discovered reasons not to like or trust them.

So far, Adriana Bennett had yet to disappoint her. No deal-breaker traits. Ana also felt at ease with her co-worker Halle. She was classy, sophisticated, and brilliant. Even Dean, with his quirky nicknames, wasn't all that bad.

When moving to D.C., she'd had high expectations that she'd dislike most people she worked with. Ultimately, they always let you down. People, in general, had a way of doing that.

She'd let herself down, too. Marrying Kyle. Breaking his heart.

"Were you saying something?" She stole her focus from his body and looked up to see his gaze fixed on her, the slight wrinkles at the corners of his eyes enhanced by what she guessed was concern.

"You were saying you panic-clean," he reminded her, "and I got too distracted by *you* to respond." His hand went flat on the counter as she put aside the spray bottle. Strong hands. Strong forearms, too.

This was not a lip-biting moment, well, not for Ana, at least. She never bit her lip, but damn it, she had to pin her tongue to the roof of her mouth to prevent herself from doing it. She had to do something to rally, to focus, to get her head out of the A.J. zone. To concentrate on the plan. To think through the problem.

The safe was empty, the USB file with classified case evidence gone. But she'd have to keep moving forward. Focus on what she could do and not the SGW list.

She'd finish what she'd set out to do no matter what.

"My mother bakes and cleans when she's stressed," A.J. said, drawing her eyes to his once again. "When I was deployed, she single-handedly supplied every bake sale in the state of Alabama."

"She must still worry about you since you're clearly in a dangerous line of work."

"Nah, she thinks I just bodyguard famous people and such. She doesn't know the truth." He pulled that sexy, strong hand of his from the counter and stroked his jaw.

"And what kind of truth would that be?" She crossed her arms over her chest as she examined the man that had her disoriented when she should've been focusing on how she was going to get to Georgia without her colleagues discovering the plan.

When A.J. leaned in a touch closer, his hand going back to the counter as if bracing for impact, from trying not to fall straight into her, she peered up at him from her height of barely five-five and almost gasped.

What the hell?

She didn't bite her lip or gasp. Not over a man, at least.

The excitement of catching a criminal, knowing she was close to taking down someone, deserved a nibble on the lip. A deep inhalation of breath.

There'd never been a man who'd elicited that kind of response from her. And yet, A.J. had her flirting and teasing since the moment she'd met him last year. This man almost had her lip wedging between her teeth, too.

"I'm really an Avenger," he said close to her ear, her stomach tightening at his warm breath. "A bona fide caped crusader who saves people."

"Like tonight?" she murmured when he backed up to find her eyes again. "You heard the distress and you came flying in, huh?" She needed to be serious, but Mr. Cowboy Handsome was standing in her tiny kitchen, which hadn't been purposefully distressed like on an episode of HGTV, but was actually distressed, in a state of extreme sorrow. And there she was, ready to fan herself like some Southern belle on an episode of *Hart of Dixie*, the show fresh on her mind since she'd caught a rerun on Netflix a few months back, and of course, her first thought had been about A.J. because the show took place in Alabama. And now the man even had her inner thoughts a rambling mess.

Yeah, she'd done her research on A.J., too. Too many glasses of wine one lonely night when she still lived in Charlotte, and her fingers had hit the keys. She'd been tempted to bypass the rules and check from her work computer, but she'd told herself that'd be stalker-ish. Of course, that was before she'd been offered the position at Headquarters. Before she realized her life would change forever once she moved to D.C.

My assignment, damn it. "I have to work," she blurted, mostly as a reminder for herself.

A.J. was a distraction, but this specific distraction came to the rescue tonight, and he was in her kitchen, eying her as if he'd had a few fantasies of his own about her.

Ana doubted any of his revolved around him as a naked cowboy.

But what she needed to do was get answers from him about what the hell had gone down tonight. No panic-cleaning. No ogling his denim backside with the most perfect glutes she'd ever seen.

No naked cowboys.

Okay, every girl deserved a naked cowboy in her fantasies, right?

I've officially lost my mind.

"The nondescript clothes. Black hat, shirt, and sneakers. You were on a stakeout. In a psychopathic stalker kind of way or a work kind of way?" she asked after finally getting her head back on straight.

His eyes became thin slits. She could see his internal struggle about how much truth to share by the slight twinge of his lips.

A tentative step closer had her only inches away again. "You were at an FBI section chief's house tonight," she added when he'd stayed quiet. "So, even though part of me would prefer you were stalking me to find a way into my pants"—*did I just admit that?*—"I'm assuming you're here for work."

A.J.'s brows shot straight up. He made a whistling sound and tugged at the material of his black Under Armor tee. "Shooo. It just might be hotter than holding a firecracker at both ends in here," he drawled.

"AC repairman comes tomorrow." It was unusually hot for D.C. Maybe she could blame the heat wave for her brain fritzing out around A.J.?

"And are you trying to distract me to keep from answering my question?" The man was good, she'd give him that. "Your sexy smile and that swagger of yours won't disarm me." At least she hoped they wouldn't, not again.

"So, you think I got a sexy smile and, uh, swagger, huh?"

She hissed and turned toward the counter, unable to maintain a straight face when that was exactly what she should've been doing. "Why were you spying on me? I know you weren't watching Porter. We only just learned he was missing. And you were at that bachelor party and—"

"Come again?" At the touch of his hand on her arm, she slowly faced him. "How do you know where I was? Sounds to me like you may have been doing the spying."

Her eyes fell to his light grasp on her upper arm. Why didn't she want him to let go? Why did she want him to pull her against his chest, wrap his strong arms around her, and make everything okay?

She'd never relied on anyone in her life. Not for safety. Or for love.

"Adriana Bennett, the President's daughter-in-law. We hang out." She hoped she didn't get Adriana in trouble. It was the last thing she wanted for one of her only friends in the city.

He immediately released her and stepped back like she was literally too hot to handle. Eyes moved to the floor. Betrayal cutting across his face.

"She didn't tell Knox. I didn't want anyone knowing I was in town. Not yet." She wet her lips, drawing strength to continue, even though there were more pressing matters to deal with. "We bumped into each other when I moved here. I asked her not to tell anyone about me."

That had his attention. His light green eyes found her face, stopping on her lips before slowly skating over her features. "Why not?" He inched closer, his chest lifting with a deep breath.

"I-I don't know." *Yes, I do.*

"Yes, you do." So, he was an Avenger and a mind reader. Since when was she so easy to read? "Anastasia." There it was again. The swarm of butterflies taking flight in her stomach. The way he said her name, allowing each letter to somehow take form, to stand on its own, lust entangled in his tone.

Her hand went to the counter. Now she was the one bracing for impact.

"Why were you following me? Who hired you?" They had no time to talk about anything else.

"Why were you breaking into your section chief's house?" he countered, then reached for the side of his head and applied light pressure with the heel of his hand over part of his hat and hair. She hadn't noticed before, but did he get hurt?

She closed the space between them and lifted his hat. His hair was short in the back, a touch longer on the top, and closely cut at the sides. But there was a definite knot in the back of his head. A bump near his temple, too. "What happened to you? Was this from tonight?"

"Nah, the back of my head was much worse on Saturday. But the cocksucker tonight whacked me with the butt of his gun." He faced her and deftly but gently snatched her wrist. He removed his hat from her hand, set it back on his head, and let go of her. "I don't normally let a guy get the drop on me, but my balance has been a touch off since I hit my head this weekend."

"Thought you were at a bachelor party."

"My kind of party involves guns." He winked and secured his hat back on. "Even bachelor parties."

"Of course."

"I may have gotten a concussion on Saturday. Threw up

after hitting my head. That usually happens to me after a concussion, so I don't know. It's not important."

"And how many concussions have you had over the years?"

"Ones that were confirmed?" He smiled. A wicked grin that would've had her panties growing wet if she weren't already so damp from sweat to know the difference.

"Yeah, a tough Teamguy like you probably doesn't see a doctor unless forced, am I right?"

"You may be right, but I don't need some doctor blowing sunshine up my ass."

"You think a doctor would really do that . . . give you good news just so you could operate?"

Oh, sarcasm. Of course, he knew a doctor would yell at him.

She'd worked with veterans during grad school. The psychological effects and post-traumatic stress of war coupled with physical injuries—not a good combination. What if he didn't wake up one day? Or he began forgetting things? "You should see a doctor."

"Bottom line, you can't talk about why you were at that house," he said, ignoring her worries, "and I can't talk about it either. So, I'm not sure what we're even doing standing here right now, sugar."

Sugar? Why did that *not* irritate her like it would normally? "Good, so we're agreed. You'll be leaving." She pointed toward the hallway. "Thanks for the save. Maybe I'll see you around in another nine or so months? Or better yet, never." Maybe she was being sarcastic now, too. *Or* just plain mean.

"Considering you were undressing me with your eyes back in the kitchen, I assume you don't think that *I* actually believe you mean that, now do ya?"

She could feel the flustery blush racing over her body. Nerve endings on fire. This was new. "I was attacked tonight. My boss is MIA. My life might be in danger." She reminded herself the missing sources weren't public knowledge yet, so she kept her mouth closed. "I have a lot going on. I panic-clean. I don't have panic-sex."

"Well, maybe that should be a thing." A.J.'s dark lashes fluttered a few times. Men shouldn't be blessed with lashes like those, damn it. "Wait . . . your life may be in danger?" he asked, just realizing what else she'd said.

"I'm FBI. Clearly, you're familiar with my division since you were outside my boss's house, so you know my job can be dangerous," she said, attempting to dodge any more questions on the matter.

"Anastasia."

"Ana, remember?"

"*Ana.*" The sound of him saying her name, deep and gravelly, unveiled a strange feeling in her chest. It was probably due to the fear she'd been resisting giving in to, though.

Surely the agents at the FBI would turn on her once she left town, once she went off-the-grid. The backup plan was a hard pill to swallow. It would most likely make her appear guilty given what was going on, but there was no other way. The FBI could find the missing sources . . . she had another mission.

"Do you have any idea who the guy at the house was?" he asked, his voice softer this time.

"Colored contacts. Deepened his voice when talking. Mask and gloves. All black clothes." *Didn't feel like he wanted to hurt me.*

"And why'd you break in?" He'd folded his arms so only half of his tattoo on the inside of his arm was visible. He wore a military-looking watch with a thick, black band next to it, and she was unable to remove her eyes from it for some reason.

"I didn't break in. I had a key."

"Then why worry about the cameras?"

"I can't tell you anything, especially without knowing what you were doing there." Her eyes zipped back to his face. "It's complicated," she added, feeling a bit guilty since the man had helped her out of a major jam. "But maybe it's time we go separate ways since we're both closed books."

"How can I leave you after someone attacked you tonight?"

"It was a wrong-place, wrong-time situation. No one sought me out." *Only you, apparently.*

"You don't actually believe that, do you?" A.J. stepped closer, and she walked backward into the coffee table.

"Were you hired to spy on FBI agents? Are you being paid to follow me?" It was the only thing that made sense. Someone in the upper echelon of the FBI must have thought there was a leak and didn't want to spook anyone on Ana's team, so they outsourced for help. Winters hadn't believed in their innocence earlier as he'd claimed.

But the Bureau wouldn't outsource this to a civilian company. No, it had to be someone within the government with high-level security clearance. And that meant her theories about A.J. were correct. Scott & Scott Securities was a front for a covert team of operatives.

"Why would a man like me be hired to follow an FBI agent?"

She reached for his ball cap once again and removed it, hoping he didn't seize her wrist this time and feel the increase of her pulse, but she needed to see his entire face to read him better. "Because you and I both know what you really do."

He leaned in, the smell of mint on his breath—when did he pop a mint in his mouth?—and his eyes drilled straight into her. "And what is that?"

She lifted her chin and moved in closer, putting them almost nose to nose. "You're an Avenger, remember?"

CHAPTER TEN

AFTER THE PLAYFUL, SEDUCTIVE WAY ANA HAD MADE THE vigilante Avenger jab, A.J.'s heart exploded in his chest. His entire body was more alive than when in the middle of a gunfight with a bunch of Talibani terrorists.

The gorgeous redhead, with eyes capable of seducing him to the most dangerous of waters, had him wrapped tight around her finger without even trying.

No woman, including his only real relationship outside of high school, had ever had him tongue-tied before. And was it sad that he'd just turned thirty-eight and hadn't been in something real in over a decade?

Ana began straightening the pillows on her living room couch, then moved on to the stack of magazines on the coffee table, clearly anxious to hear news from A.J.'s team.

Panic-cleaning?

With his back to the column in the room, he eyed her as she bent over to retrieve the TV remote that had fallen on the floor, and he became mesmerized by the woman's ass in those black jeans. She had to do Pilates. Yoga, maybe. Something that tightened and lifted her butt to perfection.

Her top came untucked, and when she stood upright and faced him, she began fidgeting with the material. The woman was a bit high-strung, but . . . *damn.*

Headstrong, guarded, and stubborn one minute—playful, sexy, and witty the next. He couldn't always get a read on her, but he was pretty sure Ana was confused by her behavior when around him.

While sitting in his SUV an hour ago, watching Ana slip around to Porter's backyard, his hand had remained frozen and hovering over his cell phone to alert Harper to what Ana was doing, but he hadn't been able to rat her out. Not without knowing more. He wanted answers from the source herself as to why she'd go into her boss's house dressed like a burglar.

He hadn't expected the gunshot shortly after she'd gone inside.

And when A.J. had rushed through the unlocked back door, the masked man had caught him off guard and barreled straight for him, arm outstretched, a firearm in his hand.

He didn't want to shoot the man first and ask questions later since he was on U.S. soil and rules of engagement were a bit stricter. But damn, he'd swear ever since his fall Saturday, the random dizzy spells, the ones that felt like his head was filled with air, had him off-kilter.

A.J. hadn't shared this with Harper or the others yet. He couldn't bring himself to admit he may not be in tip-top shape to operate or that he may actually need to get his head examined. There was a real chance he'd been wrong to brush this off like he had so many times in the past. But usually, he felt better a few days after hitting his head. He'd been thrown quite a few times from IED blasts, so he had some experience dealing with losing consciousness. Never hallucinating ghosts, though. That was new. Or someone getting the drop on him to knock him in the side of the head.

And tonight, when that fucker had hit him in the head with the gun, he could've sworn Marcus was there. He could feel him looking over. He didn't have time to process the weird sensation since he'd had to let Ana know he was there moments later.

"It's Harper," he announced when his phone vibrated.

Ana crossed the living room to stand closer, her arms going over her chest like a shield.

"I have bad news," Harper announced the second he answered.

"Don't you know never to start a phone call like that?" he asked her.

"Someone beat us to it. The camera footage was already removed," Harper delivered the shitty news.

"Fuck." He held the phone away from his ear for a moment. "Security footage was wiped before we got to it," he told Ana.

"He got to the footage first?" Her gaze dipped to the floor before slowly sweeping back up and landing on his mouth for several heartbeats. A.J. could almost see her thoughts swirling in overdrive.

Was she torn between panic-cleaning and panic-sex? Okay, he had to focus and not allow himself to be "razzle-dazzled" as his niece, McKenna, called it when a boy became fixated on someone or something.

"I kept my hat on. Head low. Whoever got to the security footage first won't be able to ID me," he told Harper, knowing exactly what she was thinking. "What about you?" he asked Ana. But the look on her face and the fact she was as pale as a ghost said it all. She was concerned her face had made it on the screen.

"Are we really helping her, though? Doesn't this sort of prove she's the leak?" Harper kept her voice low as if worried

Ana might overhear her. "She's one of our suspects. I know how you feel, but—"

"It's not her," A.J. snapped out, then quickly muttered an apology. To both women, maybe. "I'll call you back." He ended the call and tucked his phone into his pocket as Ana surprised him by unleashing her auburn locks from her bun.

She tore her fingers through her hair, swiping it off her shoulders. "I have to go sooner than I thought." Her gaze darted to the stairs. Nervous as a rabbit about to bolt.

And he was right. Her shoulder bumped into him a beat later when she brushed past him.

He pivoted and reached for her arm in an attempt to stop her. "What are you talking about? Where are you going?"

"I can't wait three days to leave the city. If footage of me in Porter's house gets out . . . no, I need to leave now," she said, a resigned look on her face.

Three days?

She pulled free from his grasp and started for the stairs, leaving him unsure what to say or do next.

He took a few seconds to gather his wits and figure out what in the Sam Hill was going on with her. A.J. knew why he was there, but she'd need to open up and let him in on why she felt the need to leave.

"Don't you think running will only make you look guilty?" he asked once he found her inside her master bedroom closet grabbing a duffel bag. "Remember what happened with Aaron Todd last year?" Aaron was the Navy SEAL the FBI assumed was guilty of an assassination plot, especially because he ran. Running was never the best choice when trying to prove your innocence, and she should've known that.

"I don't have a choice. I need to go."

"Ana."

Before she had a chance to challenge him, to offer a response, her doorbell rang. Her eyes grew narrow when her brows slanted, a touch of fear coloring her green eyes darker.

She maneuvered around A.J. to get to the top of the stairs when they both heard someone yell, "It's me. Kyle. Open up."

"Shit," she said under her breath. "He can't know about this. About anything." She faced A.J. and whispered, "Please." Her eyes pleaded with him more than her words.

He nodded, not sure what else to do. He wanted to protect her. Something inside of him wanted to save her from every threat that came her way, even if she was capable of saving herself. She was in his life again, and this time, he didn't have it in him to walk away. Plus, right now it was his job. Okay, so maybe it was his job to chase down a mythical ledger while determining if there was an FBI leak, but . . .

"Thank you," she mouthed, then went downstairs.

Once the door was open, Kyle quickly stepped inside. "Are you okay?" he asked before his attention swung A.J.'s way, distrust filling his eyes.

With Kyle there, Chris would be nearby. That is if Chris hadn't lost him the way he'd lost Ana's source earlier that evening.

Ana moved backward and stood alongside A.J., her body language saying, *He's with me.* "This isn't the best time right now."

"Porter is missing, the neighbors overheard a gunshot at his place tonight, and you're here doing what?" One dark brow arched as he stared at A.J. as if he were looking to do some hand-to-hand combat. The man wasn't over Ana, and A.J. didn't blame him. A.J. had only worked one case with her. To marry her and have to walk away? Hell, no.

"A.J.'s my boyfriend. I'm sorry you had to find out this way."

"You're not serious. This Navy man?" His eyes were on A.J.'s trident tattoo. Kyle was FBI and as decent at reading people as Ana, so it would seem. Although, given Ana's psychology background, she could probably profile people down to the kind of breakfast they preferred to eat.

"Navy man?" A.J. tipped his head, acting confused just to screw with the guy, but he had to admit he loved the fact Ana had referred to him as her boyfriend, even though it was a lie to get her ex-husband off her back. Still, he'd planned a hundred different ways to ask her out over the last several months, so "boyfriend" might not have been out of the realm of possibility. But of course this would be how she wound up back in his life. On a list of potential suspects for being a traitor. *Of-fucking-course.*

"I don't believe you." Kyle ignored A.J. and moved closer to Ana. "You didn't mention him tonight, or the other night when we were together."

"You and I weren't together-together," she added as if worried A.J. might think she'd hooked up with her ex.

Kyle looked back and forth between her and A.J. but chose to drop the matter. "You should be worried that Porter is MIA, not worried about your love life. What's really going on?"

Love life? A.J. coughed into his fist. He sure as hell wished that was why he was in her townhouse right now and not because someone nearly shot her tonight. *Hell, everything happens for a reason.* If he hadn't been watching her, the guy at Porter's house may have killed her. Fate. Fortune. Whatever mystic shit Chris had been talking about earlier— was he right? And maybe the Daylight Ledger was legit instead of an urban legend. *And pigs can fly. Bigfoot is real.*

"I was chasing down some leads, and then I planned on heading in," she said, the snap in her voice a clear indication to A.J. that Kyle knew not to follow up with more questions, or he'd get his head bitten off.

"Unless this guy is a lead I need to know about, you should get to the office. Your being gone doesn't look good." Kyle was uptight and all-business.

And if her colleagues knew what went down tonight, they'd probably toss her in some box and question her forever.

"I'll be there soon." She sidestepped Kyle and held the door open. "Please leave."

Surprisingly, Kyle obliged, but he sent one last scolding look A.J.'s way before walking through the door. "Be careful."

Ana quickly slid the chain lock across the top once the door was closed. "Sorry about him. He probably thinks I haven't been with anyone since the divorce." Her cheeks tinted pink. "Not that I have."

A.J. took a second to process her impromptu confession and the fact the last person she'd slept with was her husband. Married to him for three years, so she hadn't been with anyone else in quite some time, then.

"I have to get ready." She turned back toward the stairway.

She was a woman with a single-minded focus, but he'd seen in her eyes tonight he was capable of making her a touch off-balance and distracted. She had the same impact on him, but he might need to use whatever this thing was to his advantage. If it meant keeping her safe, he'd do whatever he had to do. "This investigation just started, no one is looking at you in particular, so why not . . ."

Turning, her big green eyes swept his way, stealing his

focus. Locking his entire body still. "I'm sorry, but I have no choice but to go, and right now, the last thing on my mind is what people are going to think about me."

"Why not just explain to the Bureau why you were at your boss's house before it becomes a thing, then go to Atlanta wearing your sexy blue raider jacket with the flashy FBI letters on it?" He gave her a smile, hoping for a glimmer of something. Any reaction at all that said he could get through to her. Prevent her from running. "From where I'm standing," he went on when she offered no reaction to his words, "your boss is missing, and you have your hands full, and yeah, maybe you're new and all three missing sources were first identified by you, but that doesn't mean you're the leak."

Her brows lifted in surprise at his knowledge of highly classified details.

There was no point in keeping information from her. Cat was out of the bag as to why he'd been following Ana. She wasn't an idiot. Why bother pretending otherwise?

If he hadn't been in the presence of such a stunning woman after now having been hit in the head twice, he might not have been so forthcoming.

"I trust you. I believe you're not the leak," he declared in response to her continued silence accompanied by a tightening of her mouth. But he needed her to hear the truth. To know he was in her corner, so there was no reason to run.

Don't be wrong. Please God, don't let me be wrong about her. Because he was going to risk his neck, his reputation, and possibly his team to help this woman.

"Let me help you," he said, working the words loose while closing the small gap of space between them.

"No, I can't do that. And you were most likely sent to bring down the traitor. Not help me."

"But that ain't you, and we both know it," he quickly replied.

She shook her head. "Don't let your feelings for me cloud your judgment. Your sense of right and wrong." Her index finger poked his chest, right near his heart. "This is my fight."

He angled his head, lost in her gaze. "My feelings for you?"

Her lip went between her teeth. Why did he feel like that wasn't normal for her? He forced his eyes back to hers. "Your voicemail Saturday, I assume it was part alcohol and now part concussion—but you accidentally sent it instead of erasing it."

I knew it. A mumbled curse fell from his lips, and he dropped his eyes to the ground. *But what in the hell did I say?*

"You bumped your head. You were drunk. Don't worry." He waited for her to continue, sensing she had more to say on the matter. "But it's pretty obvious that there are some feelings on your side. Attraction, I guess."

He guided his eyes up like he was a teenager getting his first rejection from the opposite sex.

"I just didn't expect to hear a voicemail out of the blue from you, and then to actually face you forty-eight hours later. The timing is peculiar."

"I didn't know I'd be seeing you when I left that message, just so you know." He kept his voice as level and defenseless as possible. "I had no clue you were at Headquarters. Adriana obviously didn't say anything."

He took a mental note to talk to Adriana about that once the dust settled.

"I just can't have you helping me. I have to do this on my own. Plus, you're a distraction."

"If you're so worried about me helping me, maybe it's you who has the feelings." He stepped forward, and her grip on the railing seemed to tighten. "I wouldn't be such a distraction otherwise." His heart pumped harder the closer he got to her, inhaling her intoxicating scent. He didn't need Owen's super-smelling nose to distinguish a touch of honey and vanilla wafting his way when Ana leaned in close.

"Distraction problem. *Not* a feelings problem." Stubborn. Beautiful. Smart. And soon? Possibly a fugitive.

He stroked his short beard, their faces remaining close, so close he almost brushed his mouth over hers. "You can keep telling yourself that, girl, but that doesn't mean—"

"*Girl?*" Her brow arched, her attention dipping to his mouth for a split second. "Your Southern charm and terms of endearment won't work on me."

He cocked his head. "You're preparing to run away with the assumption you're going to look guilty for the missing sources, despite the fact your name has yet to be sullied. And we're having this conversation right now?"

"Exactly," she said, letting go of a flustered breath. She pulled her head back as if realizing they were close to kissing. "This is not me." Ana pointed a finger back and forth between them. "And if you try and help me, you'll only threaten my focus."

"Like you're losing your focus now?" He just couldn't help himself. He even laid on his accent a bit thicker, lifting his chin a touch when he spoke.

Her palms landed on his chest with a shove. He refused to budge. His balance was just fine right now. "I-I don't understand what it is you're doing to me, but—"

"I'm not doing anything to you, darlin'." *I'd like to be, but this is the definition of wrong time, wrong place.* There was something in the air, though. Magic, mysticism, whatever it may be . . . there was a pulsating electric current between them that drew him to her, preparing to forgo his mission and scoop her into his arms. To hell with the consequences.

"I'm sorry. I have to go, but please do yourself a favor and stay out of what's going on. Leave D.C."

He swallowed at her cryptic warning. What had she gotten herself involved in? "I can't watch you leave." He shrugged. "I'm persistent, and I don't forgo a challenge. So, if you remember working with me back in Charlotte, you should already know that this night ends in one of two ways."

Ana's eyes locked with his, a questioning eyebrow waiting for him to go on. Her hands remained on his chest, and surely, she felt his heart drumming harder beneath her touch.

His entire body was lit. Alive with her eyes and hands on him. "Either you let me help you, or I walk you into the Hoover Building myself, and we have a nice little chat about what happened tonight."

CHAPTER ELEVEN

"I can drive." It was his rental SUV, after all. "My head isn't that bad."

"You admitted someone got the drop on you tonight, and you lost your balance. You really think I want you behind the wheel in the dead of night?" She opened her safe inside her master bedroom walk-in closet and knelt to retrieve her pump-action Remington 870, 9mm, and K-bar knife. She handed him the weapons, then went for ammo.

His heart nearly exploded. "A woman after my own heart." *Wow.* "Every closet should come equipped with a Remington."

"And by the way, if I can handle firearms like these, I think I can handle driving your SUV."

"Really, I—"

"You want me going with you, then let me drive." She was also persistent, he'd give her that.

He zipped his lips. This was a woman not to be reckoned with. A Southern woman at heart, perhaps. "I'm gonna ask one more time, but are you sure you want to run?"

"It's not running. I need to be at a location outside of

Atlanta in"—she checked her Apple watch—"about ninety-four hours. And let me remind you that I'm perfectly capable of going by myself. I don't need a babysitter." Pivoting one knee to better face him, she threw a finger in the direction of the weapons bag. "I can probably shoot better than you."

"Ha!" He crouched, the weapons separating the two of them, because why wouldn't a shotgun be what was between him and the woman he wanted to kiss? And he did want to kiss her. Her eyes lowered to his mouth as if she were reading his inappropriate thoughts right now. That little twitch of her lips said it all. She was wondering how his mouth would feel on hers, too. "You do know what I do for a living, right?"

She rolled her tongue over her lower lip before drawing her eyes to his—*ohhhh,* she was screwing with him. It only turned him on more. "I thought you were retired. Since when do security contractors go around shooting on U.S. soil?" She braced herself with one hand on the floor next to the weapons bag, and they both leaned forward as if they were about to share a strand of spaghetti like the two dogs in that Disney movie his niece loved. "No, that's right, they don't. So, either you're full of bullshit thinking you can actually outshoot me, or you never retired."

He fell back onto his ass, losing his balance, and chuckled. "It's the bump on the head. No, sorry, two bumps!" He tossed two fingers in the air before she turned back to her safe and locked up.

Well, shit. The woman was damn good at reading people, and he'd have to remember that. She'd easily picked up on the fact he'd never really retired. "Retired or not, I'm betting I can take you."

"Yeah, well, I was at the top of my class at Quantico. And I shoot every weekend to let off steam." She stretched her arm beneath the rack of clothes next to the safe and retrieved a second bag.

"What's that one for? Your long gun?" he quipped.

"Clothes. I wasn't planning on going on the run naked."

"Aha, you just admitted you *are* running. All this naked talk has me wanting to go on the run with you now more than ever." He pushed to his feet and tugged at the material of his shirt. It was already too hot in there for her to be using the word naked in a sentence.

She turned around once she was on her feet and let go of the bag. Her skin was a bit flushed. The heat? Naked talk? *Him?*

"And before you try and take back what you said," he began while stepping over the guns to get to her, "I'd say it's running when you leave without informing your superiors."

Porter had gone missing outside of Atlanta, but beyond that, A.J. had no idea what to expect once they made it to Georgia since she wasn't being all that forthcoming. The fact she didn't want the government to know she was leaving was giving him a mild heart attack, but what could he do?

If for some reason his gut was wrong about her, it was better he was with her and tracking her movements. Let her lead him to whoever she was working with to betray the country.

God, even the infinitesimal possibility of that gave him a serious case of heartburn. And heaven help him when the team found out what he was doing.

Wyatt and Harper would lose their shit. But Wyatt would have walked through fire, separated the seas, done whatever he had to do for Natasha, so . . .

Shit, maybe my head is off?

"I have no choice but to go." She lifted her chin to look up at him since they were so close, and she was fairly petite.

He could easily scoop her into his arms, mold her body perfectly to his, and take her against the wall. On the bed. Every surface in her townhouse.

"Are you sure you want to come with me? Do you really understand what it is you're getting into?" She crossed her arms to add some kind of wedge between them, and her elbows bumped him in the process.

"Kind of hard to understand"—he lowered his face —"when you're being vague as shit, don't ya think?"

"Ugh, I just can't with you." A flustered breath later, she brought her hands to his chest as if planning on shoving him away, but they just stayed there. Two palms on his pecs. She'd surely feel his heart beating frantically beneath her palms. "We're like oil and vinegar, aren't we?"

"Nah, I'd say more like gin and tonic."

Ana closed her eyes, but the quiver of her lip suggested she was working damn hard not to smile. Shaking her head slightly, as if she were all kinds of confused, she took too big of a step back and bumped into the clothes hanging behind her, knocking a few shirts to the ground.

She quickly spun around and snatched up the shirts, her bottom bumping into him this time instead of her elbows, which he preferred much more. "Some space, please?" She cleared her throat.

"You've had a hell of an evening, and you're about to cut out of D.C. and raise some major question marks at the Bureau, but you're worried about those shirts on the floor?" He carefully stepped around the weapons bag, not looking to fall again, and eyed her as she hung her shirts. "Panic-clean," he said with a snap of the fingers. "Right."

She faced him a moment later, eyes dipping to her empty travel bag that she needed to fill so she wasn't "naked" on the trip. "Are you sure we have a safe place to go *if* I still agree to let you risk your life by going with me?"

"Why yes, my lady," he teased. "My buddy lives in Alabama just over ninety minutes give or take from Atlanta. He's on an assignment overseas, and his place is empty. Very secluded, too." *And ten minutes from my parents' house.* Ana didn't need to know that, though. "But we can only go there if you promise not to take advantage of me. You know, no panic-sex. And also, there is no *if* I am going."

"Fine," Ana responded. She may have been working awfully hard to sound businesslike, but her eyes sparkled with humor. She shooed him with her hand, nearly flicking him. "Let me hurry and pack. You're slowing me down."

"Whatever you say," he answered, catching a smile she'd been too slow to hide with the back of her hand.

A.J. turned to leave but then slapped a palm to the interior frame of the closet door. "By the way, my buddy has an arsenal at our disposal and a helo if we need one while we're there. He's in the Air Force." He wasn't quite sure what kind of trip this would turn out to be, but just in case . . .

"And you can't fly, so trying to woo me over with a helo is a waste of your efforts unless you've taken up flying lessons I don't know about."

He was loving every verbal jab from this woman, and he'd happily take them all day long. "Now you got me curious just how much you know about me."

She opened her mouth, probably to protest something, but her eyes fell to the black silk robe now suspended from the hanger in her hand.

He couldn't unsee it. Couldn't unimagine what it'd be like to have her wearing it for him. Pull at the sash and reveal her pale, creamy skin. Naked body. Perky breasts.

"You won't be seeing me in this," she quickly informed him. "Don't get any ideas."

He lifted his palms in surrender. "I wouldn't dream of it, sugar." He worked his eyes back up to her green ones, full of fire right now.

"I guess 'girl' and 'sugar' aren't any worse than Ginger or Red." Her response was almost disappointing because he enjoyed a good back-and-forth with her.

She turned on her heel and went back to the business of packing, most likely checking off a to-do list of Things To Wear On The Run in her head.

A.J. finally left the closet, not before grabbing her weapons bag first, because it really was too damn hot in there, and he was from Alabama, so that was saying a lot.

He set the bag down by the door, then turned to look at her bedroom, which had yet to be decorated. A simplistic plain brown headboard with a gray-ish-hued bedspread. Clean lines. She wasn't a frills or fuss kind of woman from what he could tell. The lockbox peeked out from under her bed—her secondary weapon she probably had on hand nearby for nighttime. *Good.*

"My people will figure this whole mess out, by the way," he said when she exited the closet a quick sixty seconds later, her bag packed. Clearly, he had been slowing her down.

"I don't need their help," she answered with her typical stubborn sass. "But could you ask someone on your team to reach out to Adriana for me? I don't want her to worry, but I can't make contact with anyone once I leave."

God, there was so much more he needed to know before he drove off into the proverbial sunset with Ana, but this woman was going to take some time to unravel.

"Sure." He nodded. Doing his best to get mission-focused

once again and stop fantasizing about her wearing the silk robe. "You all set?"

"Just about."

"I'll check in with my team while I wait for you." He dialed up Wyatt when she disappeared into the bathroom.

"Hey," Wyatt answered on the fourth ring, his voice ragged, or maybe out of breath.

"I bet you and Natasha are in that basement safe house having a quickie." And if it were true, he wouldn't blame him. Wyatt had finally found love, and the man was in deep. "You need to finish first and call me back?"

"Shut the bloody hell up." Standard answer from Echo One. "Where are you?"

"Still with Ana," he replied. "There's a change in plans." A.J. provided Wyatt with a location outside D.C. "Can you meet me there in forty minutes or so? And can you bring my stuff with ya?"

"Don't tell me you're planning something stupid," Wyatt replied.

"Nah, Boss Man. What would give you that idea?" Without thinking, A.J. set a hand to the back of his head, carefully probing the lump there. A little hit on the head shouldn't have jarred him so much. *Two bumps*, he reminded himself.

"Anything else you need me to pack for you? Like condoms?" Wyatt asked, and A.J. heard the smirk in his tone.

"Hey," Natasha snapped over the line at Wyatt's question.

"I knew it," A.J. said with a smile. "Finish up. See you in forty." A.J. ended the call before he had to deal with any protests.

"I'm not sure how I feel about meeting up with your friends on the way out of town," Ana said, exiting the bathroom with a small blue bag.

"I need my stuff, and they need to know the plan if they're going to help us." And this was as non-negotiable as her leaving D.C. alone.

"I said I didn't need their help. And I meant what I said before. I don't need yours." *Such a firecracker.*

"But you want it." He tucked his phone in his pocket and crossed the room to be near her, his favorite place to be tonight. "We both know The Huntsman is probably out there collecting sources like it's his day job, and hell, that sort of is his job, so it'd be better if we stick together. Maybe track down who is after your sources. Find your boss. And then, we'll clear your name because once you *run,* there'll be plenty of people dragging it through the mud."

"I can't believe I'm involving you." Ana huffed out a breath and tossed the blue bag onto the bed, then flicked her gorgeous red-gold strands to her back as if having her hair down was an inconvenience. "I only trust you because of Adriana and because of how you performed on the case we worked together last year."

He brought a palm toward her face, and she flinched, but she didn't shove his hand away when he thumbed the last few lonely strands of hair behind her ear. "Nah, it's more than that, and you know it." He'd tried to pull off a teasing tone, but his voice had come out as raspy as a country music legend singing a love song. "I believe you're a good person. A good agent. And I'm a betting man, and right now, I'm betting on you."

She caught his wrist in the air between them when he'd started to pull his hand back, and held on to him for a long moment, her expression contemplative. "I'll try not to disappoint you." Ana's manner was more FBI special agent than the woman who'd finally let her hair down. In one fast movement, her hand slid from his wrist to settle in his palm, and she stepped back.

A handshake? Or a truce? Whatever it was, he liked having her hand in his.

She was chewing on her bottom lip, and the fingers of her free hand feathered over her mouth. For one adorable moment, it appeared she was pleasantly startled by his touch when her eyes blinked rapidly, her dark lashes fluttering. But the moment was quickly over, and she pulled her hand free, then stepped away.

"It's okay, you know. You can have feelings for me that make no sense," A.J. said candidly, not kidding around at the moment.

"I don't have feelings for you," she stated, her green eyes intently focused on him.

He nodded, eyes thinning. "Mmhm."

Ana turned and set her attention on the open doorway of her bedroom, then reached up and slid her fingers through the auburn locks that fell in soft waves just past her shoulders. "I should probably dye my hair."

"No," he quickly sputtered, unable to stop himself. He loved her red hair. It reminded him of home, when the sunrise threw streaks of color into the sky as daylight unfurled itself.

Daylight. Ugh, the ledger. The real numero uno objective. He'd never think of daylight the same.

Ana turned to face him and fingered the collar of her black shirt, a slight touch of sweat on her chest from the heat wave D.C. was experiencing. She must've tossed her hoodie when she returned home.

Her eyes moved over his body, taking him in, and he grinned like he'd won his first rodeo.

"You have a lust problem, not a distraction problem," he teased before she had a chance to defend her gawking.

"Same thing," Ana murmured. A.J. couldn't help smiling when her eyes widened a fraction, obviously realizing what she'd just unwittingly confirmed.

He leaned in closer and playfully waggled his brows. "So, you admit it, then?"

A flick of the back of her hand toward the door was all he got. But he'd take it.

"Let's get you out of here and to someplace safe."

"I'm still not so sure the words 'you' and 'safe' are synonymous." Ana's voice was soft. Nervous now. She needed to panic-clean, didn't she? She was worried he was going to wear her down—make her fall for him.

And would that be such a bad thing?

"THIS IS GOING TO END BADLY." HARPER STOOD NEXT TO Roman and Wyatt in front of her Chevy Suburban rental. "We were brought to D.C. to find the leak and maybe that ledger, and now you're running off with a suspect?" Harper folded her arms, eyes pinned in the direction of A.J.'s SUV, where Ana sat behind the steering wheel, windows closed.

A.J. glanced back her way, confirming she was still in the car as he'd requested, then focused on his teammates. "I know this is crazy, but she's on the brink of becoming the fall guy the way Aaron was last year. At least, she thinks so."

Aaron Todd had gone through BUD/S with A.J., and A.J. couldn't help but go to bat for him when he'd been maliciously set up as the man who attempted to assassinate Isaiah Bennett. A.J. had never been great at standing by when a friend was in trouble.

"I don't think she trusts her team, which is why she's

intent on going to Atlanta without their knowledge," A.J. added.

"And aside from Porter going missing in Atlanta, she won't tell you her reasoning as to why she needs to be there on Friday?" Too many unknown variables made Roman uptight.

"No, but I think she knows something about where Porter may be. She doesn't act like a woman whose boss just died. Maybe she thinks he's alive," A.J. pointed out, and Wyatt's brows dipped inward.

"And you don't think it's because she—"

"Don't say it," A.J. cut off Wyatt. He didn't need Echo One suggesting Ana was behind Porter's disappearance because she was some cold-hearted killer or traitor. "Someone on Ana's task force must be behind the missing sources. Or the Volkovs. Or the supposed owner of the mysterious ledger. But *not* her." A.J. tucked his hands into his pockets, uncomfortable with his lack of information and having to rely on his gut to justify to his friends his decisions.

Wyatt stepped forward and set a hand to A.J.'s shoulder. "I know you've been thinking about this woman for quite some time, but we have to look at the facts. We were brought in by POTUS to protect national security."

"Not to run away with one of the suspects," Harper chimed in, and Roman nodded in agreement.

It was one against three. And he knew they didn't bring Chris or Finn with them to this face-off because Echo Three and Five would probably side with their hearts, like A.J.

"Luke and Knox will be in D.C. tomorrow. They wrapped up their assignment, and they'll be providing an assist," Harper announced the news. "Jessica is back behind her keyboard in New York to help, too. She's going to try and confirm it's The Huntsman who kidnapped the sources."

"Sounds like you're good, then. Won't need me here." A.J. pulled his hands from his pockets and fidgeted with the brim of his ball cap.

"A.J." He knew that tone from Harper. She was going to try and talk him off a cliff of crazy.

And maybe it was crazy he was blindly trusting Ana, but he knew she wasn't a traitor. And if he had to prove it to his best friends, that was exactly what he'd do.

"Listen." A.J. stepped closer to them, hating what he was about to say, but he needed to convince his team to let him go. "You want me to find out the truth, this is the best way. Let me get her safe and near wherever it is she wants to be. I'll gain her trust. We're working in the dark now. Once we get real insight into what's going on from her, and believe me, she knows a lot more than us, it'll expedite our assignment. But her in an FBI holding cell won't do us any damn good, and you know it."

Wyatt removed his hand from A.J.'s shoulder and exchanged a quick look with Harper.

"We need to know what the Feds neglected to include in the files we were provided," A.J. added. "And find out what Ana was after in Porter's house."

"Then we'll go, too," Roman firmly stated. "You can't be twelve hours away from us without any backup if needed. We can stay in Birmingham instead of Atlanta to prevent being noticed, which will also put us closer to your immediate location. Just don't tell her we'll be nearby."

"No more solo ops, remember?" Wyatt's words had A.J.'s eyes shutting, a memory tugging at his mind.

"Never again. Understood?" Luke had once eyed the guys on the teams, stabbing a finger in the air, emotion choking his words. *"No more solo ops. No more falling in*

love. No weddings. No babies. No more fucking heartbreak. Got it?"

"Marcus should never have gone in alone. We shouldn't have followed orders," A.J. had responded and lowered his hat to his chest, his eyes on the ground beneath his boots.

"A.J.?"

A.J.'s eyes flicked open at the sound of Harper's voice. "Yeah, well, this isn't an op. It's just me keeping an eye on someone while we all work to piece this case together." *To see where the hell she needs to be in three days.*

"I don't know if we can get approval for any of this." Harper faced the SUV and set her palms to it.

"Natasha can," Wyatt said after the longest few seconds of A.J.'s life. "I'll talk to her."

"Thank you." A.J. stepped forward, grabbed Wyatt's hand, and leaned in to slap his back twice. "I should get on the road now." They were going to drive to Roanoke and finish the drive in the morning.

"We'll head back to the city, put together a plan, then some of us will go to Birmingham," Wyatt said, his tone low.

"Look at it this way, the sooner we wrap this up, the sooner you can get back to focusing on your wedding." A.J. smiled, but Wyatt's lips didn't budge. He was worried. About a lot, probably.

"Speaking of weddings," Wyatt said, his tone grim. "Brian didn't cheat. Gwen pulled the surveillance footage from Vegas."

A.J.'s stomach tightened at the news. Why did he feel so disappointed? He should've been happy Brian hadn't done anything to break his sister's heart, but he still didn't like Perfect Brian, and he truly believed Ella was going to get hurt down the road. "Okay." He wasn't sure what else to say. "Thanks."

"We'll check in once we get back to the safe house in D.C. Probably wait until tomorrow to head to Alabama," Harper said. "Well, if some of us get the green light to go, that is."

"Thank you." A.J. looked at the bag on the ground by Wyatt's boots. "Everything in there?"

"Can't go back to Alabama without your cowboy hat and boots." A smile crossed Wyatt's lips. "Gotta blend in and all."

"To think you just left home and now you're going back." Roman lifted the bag and handed it off to him.

"Keep your head down. Stay out of trouble," Wyatt commanded, and A.J. saluted them with his free hand and started for the SUV.

"You're not driving?" Wyatt called out in surprise.

"She doesn't trust me," he shot back.

"No idea why," Wyatt replied.

"Hey," Roman called out.

A.J. stopped just shy of the vehicle to find Roman coming up behind him. "Yeah?"

Roman's dark eyes studied him. "Watch your back, okay?" He kept his voice low so as not to be heard by Ana inside the SUV. "Every once in a while, you make a bad bet."

A.J. nodded. "This won't be one of those times, brother."

"And you don't make promises you can't keep," Roman reminded him.

"So, then you know everything is good," A.J. answered, doing his best to ignore the sense of foreboding gnawing in his chest.

CHAPTER TWELVE

"They don't like that you're doing this, do they?" *And why would they?* If A.J.'s teammates were sent to spy on her and her colleagues, surely they would object to A.J. not only helping her leave town but also riding along in the getaway vehicle. So to speak. Although, Ana still refused to call it running away.

"Your phones are off, right?" he deflected.

"Of course." She knew the second she failed to show up at the office as she'd promised Kyle, he'd be blowing up her phone. And by the fourth time his calls were sent straight to voicemail, he'd go over to check her place. Probably have a team of investigators there soon to search her townhouse. And then the allegations would start flying out of the chute, and the rodeo would begin. She just needed to stay on the horse until she met up with Porter. *And when did I start thinking in cowboy analogies?* Since the sexy cowboy sitting in the passenger seat had walked back into her life and jump-started feelings she never knew existed.

Allowing A.J. to go with her wasn't the best idea. But he hadn't given her much of a choice, and there was a dangerous hitman out there somewhere, so maybe she could use the help until her meeting Friday.

A.J. would demand answers at some point, but she'd need to carefully consider how much to divulge. Her promised silence about this classified assignment had practically been signed in blood on those non-disclosure agreements.

"Hey, you okay?" A.J. asked softly. He placed a hand on her arm as she clutched the wheel tightly with both hands. "You're shaking. I never thought I'd see that reaction from you."

Goose bumps pebbled her skin beneath his palm.

She relaxed her jaw at the realization she was biting down on her back teeth and forced a nod.

He gave her arm a light squeeze before letting go.

"Blindly trusting someone like this is a new thing for me." *And oh my God, I looked at him with stars in my eyes and bit my lip earlier. What was up with that?*

Distraction, sure. But feelings? It made no sense.

"I get that. Trusting people ain't exactly easy for me, either. Not outside my circle. But here I am doing it for you."

She stole a brief look at him. "You run in a pretty tight circle, I assume?"

"Not much choice in my line of work," he said with a light tone, "you know, Avenger and all."

She graced him with a small smile. It was a nice reprieve from the jittery sensation that had filled her with dread moments ago. "Right."

"But, um, on a scale of one to ten, how much of a fool did I make of myself on that drunken slash bump-on-the-head phone call?"

"Oh, an eleven, for sure." She didn't have to look at him to know there was a grin on his face. Probably a wickedly sexy one, too. "I would've loved to play it for you, but I had to delete it tonight. Can't risk anyone knowing about our connection."

He cursed, then grabbed his phone from the center console and jabbed a finger at the lit screen. It took her a second to grasp what he was doing, but then it registered. She wanted to kick herself for not thinking of mentioning it earlier. It wasn't like her to overlook details like that. "Hey, Harper, can you delete the record of my call to Quinn on Saturday?" He said a few more words, then hung up. "They may pull your records."

"May?" She smiled. "Oh, they'll pull my records as soon as they realize I'm gone." Standard operating procedure.

"But let's get back to the 'Anastasia Quinn saved A.J. Hawkins' voicemail message' thing." Oh jeez, he actually sounded proud.

"I didn't save it." She shrugged. "Just didn't delete it. Well, until our road trip."

Road trip. What an odd choice of words. Porter was out there somewhere, and hopefully he was safe, but he needed her. And she was sitting here talking about a voicemail. A rambling, drunken voicemail from a guy telling her he had a crush on her. Could this be any more like high school? Well, like high school in the shows she'd seen on TV since she'd been homeschooled.

What else would they talk about, though? She wasn't sure if or when she'd share the truth, so maybe small talk was all they had. *No talk. How about that?*

"Mmhm." A touch of cocky floated through the sound he made.

"You sure we should stop in Roanoke and not drive straight through?" If she were more focused on driving, then maybe she wouldn't be distracted by the zing of chills that'd been wrapped around her body from the moment they were on the road. She was well aware of the source of that zing, too. They were trapped in this SUV together, so there was no escaping his powerful male presence.

"It's near midnight. I think you've had a jam-packed night already, considering only three hours ago you discharged your weapon in your boss's house, so I'm thinking driving straight to Alabama isn't the best idea, even if we take turns. We'll be fine at a hotel."

"Not a motel? Shouldn't we be more discreet?"

"Think about this. In a hotel, we know where all the cameras are located. They're visible. We know where not to go. In some small, off-the-road Bates Motel, they could have cameras hidden God knows where to catch shady shit happening."

"Alfred Hitchcock, huh?"

"I mean, I'm not itching to be in what might feel like the set for a horror movie. Been there, done that. No desire to do that again. I hate creepy shit."

A light laugh left her lips. "I'm sensing there's a good story there."

"The last one involved a Russian ghost town. It was no *bueno*."

Russian? She tucked her chin down a little and cleared her throat, hoping he hadn't noticed her slight gasp. How much did he already know about the Volkovs? About the ledger? Maybe talking wasn't such a bad idea after all . . . get him talking and pry out more details from the Southern Teamguy who didn't seem to have a problem opening up around her.

A.J. fidgeted with the controls of the radio. "Anyway, I have a credit card in a different name and lots of experience evading cameras and authority of all types. You're in good hands."

She had no doubt about that. Her instincts told her that even if this was all a bit insane. One minute she was at Headquarters with the Deputy AD of the FBI, then about to have dinner with her ex to try and get intel out of him . . . and the next thing she knew, A.J. was charging into Porter's house prepared to throw down his life for her.

"Oh, love Blake Shelton and Gwen Stefani," she said when A.J. settled on a song, deciding to table the heavy work conversation.

When A.J. began softly singing the lyrics to the song, *Nobody But You*, Ana experienced what felt like a cataclysmic event inside her body. *Of course, you can sing.* Her nipples pebbled, probably poking through her lacy bra and tee. Thank God it was dark.

He stopped singing a few seconds later, and she felt his eyes on her. "I'm digging the fact you recognize the song . . ."

She glanced at him, catching his smile. He had straight white teeth, and one side of his mouth charmingly hiked up a bit more than the other. Yeah, A.J. had a great smile. One that could easily seduce her, even at a time when she was risking everything to get answers, to get to the truth. "I'm eclectic in my music tastes. Plus, I was a big Gwen Stefani fan growing up when she was in No Doubt."

"Believe it or not, I am, too." He leaned his seat back a touch and then set those strong, masculine hands of his on his jeaned legs.

"A Gwen fan or eclectic in your music taste?" she teased.

His brows pulled together, and his smile deepened before she tore her gaze back to the road, so they didn't crash. "Definitely both."

Why hadn't she felt even an iota of whatever was happening to her now when she was with Kyle? A.J.'s mere presence had her body reacting, tightening with a need she hadn't known was inside of her.

She'd been around good-looking men before. And a lot of them had hit on her. None had made such an impact.

Cold, dead heart. Why wasn't it cold and dead around A.J.?

She'd enacted Porter's backup plan, and it'd begun with a bust. But yeah, she was lusting after this man next to her. And the last thing she wanted was for a good man like A.J. to be collateral damage in her pursuit of truth and justice.

"Something about being on the highway late at night soothes my soul," he said. "It's calming."

"Like, so calming if I'd let you drive, you would have fallen asleep behind the wheel?" She captured a quick look at him again, and his eyes were out the side window.

"Nah, I've got sleep discipline. I can stay awake when needed but fall asleep at the drop of a hat when allowed. We had no choice back in the Navy." His tone was a touch heavier when he spoke this time, as if remembering someone or something from his past. "You get rack time whenever you can."

"What makes the road calming, though?" Being on the road only reminded her of the past, of all her time traveling as a kid. Her few good memories had all been destroyed by the bad ones when she'd turned sixteen. Totally decimated.

"My folks had an RV. Used to pack all five of us kids up and go on road trips to the middle of nowhere. No plans or reservations. Sort of like throwing a dart at a map to see where life would take us. Of course, my brothers and I would sleep in a tent outside while my parents and sister, Ella, stayed in the RV."

A big family. Must have been nice.

Daddy, can I have a brother? A sister? She remembered

begging her parents for a sibling and wishing for one every year when she blew out the candles of her birthday cake.

We got lucky with such a perfect daughter. We don't want to jinx it and try for more. You're all we need, my red angel, her dad would respond.

"I bet you loved sleeping outside." She drew her hand into a fist and set it to her chest, pushing away the happy memory from her past as she'd trained herself to do because the pain of remembering was too much to bear.

"Tents are great, but nothing beats lying out in the back of your pickup beneath a canopy of stars. You don't get night skies in the city like you do back home. You'll see when we're there." His voice was warm and soft and nearly wrapped her like a blanket.

As nice as staring at a bunch of stars on a dark night sounded, she had to do her best not to let this man get under her skin, or under her clothes. "We're going there to make a plan, not to—"

"I know," he interrupted. "Don't worry, I may be a country boy, but one thing you can count on is the fact that I always get a job done. Close a case. Complete an op."

"And I'm your op?" She gulped and slid her gaze to the side to catch his eyes.

He tilted his head to the side. "I reckon you're going to be a lot more than that."

CHAPTER THIRTEEN

Aɴᴀ ꜰᴏʟʟᴏᴡᴇᴅ ᴛʜᴇ ᴀʀᴏᴍᴀ ᴏꜰ ᴄᴏꜰꜰᴇᴇ ɪɴᴛᴏ ᴛʜᴇ ʟɪᴠɪɴɢ room of the two-bedroom suite A.J. had booked upon their arrival in Roanoke in the early hours of the morning. They hadn't slept too long, but it was enough for her to feel refreshed.

Bonus points to the hotel for having decent water pressure. The scalding hot shower she'd taken once they'd ensured the suite was secure, had loosened her sore and knotted-up muscles enough that as soon as her head hit the pillow, she was lights-out. Which was definitely not her norm.

Sensing her presence, A.J. turned from the coffee station situated in the corner of the room and smiled. God, that man had the best smile. His brownish-blond hair was slightly damp from his shower, the color a little darker when wet. A few strands stuck up every which way as if he'd used his hand to swipe the water free without a brush. The style suited him. He had on dark jeans, a plain white tee that showcased his muscular arms, and instead of the sneakers he'd worn yesterday, he had on brown leather boots, a round toe unlike typical cowboy boots she'd seen him wear before.

"Morning," he said as he approached her carrying two paper cups, swirls of steam escaping into the air. The few hours of sleep had done him good. Not that A.J. didn't always look great.

"Don't tell me whatever file you have on me also includes how I take my coffee." She was only half-kidding. And surely, he'd seen or was in possession of a file on her. Whether the details included her real backstory, or as Porter had called it, Anastasia 1.0, she had no idea.

Porter had always warned her that her true story had the potential to be dangerous in the wrong hands. The truth would paint a target on her head, and now look at her, at what she was doing . . .

"Ana?"

"Sorry, I, um, what?" She blinked and peered up at A.J., now standing so close she had to tilt her head back. *Shit, what was he just talking about?* She knew it was more than "Ana?", but she'd slipped inside her head, lost in her thoughts and worries.

He extended a cup, and she eyed the light brown liquid. "I said that I remembered how you drank your coffee back in Charlotte when we worked together. I saw you pour two creamers into your cup. No sugar." He smirked. Proud of himself for paying attention to such details.

She took a sip and scrunched her nose.

"Yeah, I couldn't do much about the ash-like taste of hotel coffee, though. Sorry."

"It'll work." She looked toward the door, nervous about the trip today. Well, more so about being alone in the car with A.J. for so long. The console between them in the SUV didn't provide enough space to prevent her from breathing him in last night. It didn't prevent their arms from bumping. The slight touches sent jolts through her body causing inappropriate thoughts. "We better get going since we have a lot of driving to do."

He made no move to follow her suggestion. Instead, he flashed a grin, that playful tease of his lips lighting yet another fire in her chest, the one that had a tendency to throw off sparks and light fires elsewhere in her body. "You're still surprised I got us a two-bedroom suite, aren't you?"

"Oh come on, tell me you didn't consider discreetly bribing the woman at the front desk to say they were all out of suites so we'd have to stay in the same bedroom? Or try to persuade me that we had to pretend to be a Mr. and Mrs.?"

"It is the twenty-first century." A.J. took a swallow of his coffee and winced. "Men and women can travel together without people assuming they're sleeping together. But I draw the line at pretending you're my sister."

Ana had no desire to pretend he was the brother she never had, considering there'd been at least fifty naughty scenarios starring A.J. streaming through her head during the drive to Roanoke last night. Fifty more than acceptable.

"I'll be driving today," he informed her when she'd remained quiet.

One more quick sip of her bitter coffee had her deciding to chuck it into the trash. "And how's your head?"

It was certainly possible he'd hit his head one too many times over the years. And getting whacked in the head with a gun last night could very well have been, to loosely interpret the idiom, the straw to break the camel's back.

"I'm normal again, don't you worry." Was he trying to convince her or himself?

She narrowed her eyes. "Yeah, not sure if normal on you is much different."

He tossed his coffee cup in the trash before opening the door. "Shall we?" He positioned his ball cap backward—that looked far too sexy—then he secured their bags that were sitting by the door in his one hand while keeping the door open with his back. "I'm fine. Really," he added as if sensing her hesitation about letting him drive. "Are you sure you're okay? Feel like panic-cleaning? Panic-sex? How about we kill two birds with one stone . . . go back inside, have wild sex in my room, and then you can make the bed."

"You did not just say that." But really, the man had her smiling so much since they'd left D.C. that her cheeks physically hurt.

"Humor not your thing?" A.J. asked once they were in the SUV a few minutes later. "My buddies in the military—we have a tendency to say shit that others might not find funny or appropriate under certain circumstances, but it helps. For some reason, the humor helps us get through it all." The deep timbre of his voice caused goose bumps to form on her bare arms.

She'd gone with a yellow tank top paired with white pants today, hoping to pull off a relaxed vacation vibe and not an FBI agent. Of all the places she'd lived growing up, the South had never been one of them. "I think I get it," she spoke up once he pulled onto the highway that'd be almost a straight shot to Alabama. "People cope in different ways."

"And how do you cope?"

She pivoted her focus his way. "What makes you think I need to cope with anything?" Okay, so she did already admit she panic-cleaned when stressed, so maybe he had her there.

He lowered the aviator shades he'd put on when they'd gotten into the car, stealing a quick glimpse of her that said *I already have you figured out* before setting his attention to the road.

Sunglasses. She'd forgotten hers and would definitely be needing a pair around this man. She wasn't used to people getting a read on her so easily.

"So, um, did you speak to your colleagues before we left the hotel?"

"You mean before you walked out of your room looking like a ray of sunshine?" And there was that goofy but still sexy grin again.

"Trying to look a little more Southern than uptight FBI."

"You admit you're uptight, then?"

Of course, I'm uptight. She sighed instead of confessing what they both already knew was one of her main qualities (or was that a flaw?). "I'm not gonna survive this drive with you. I can feel it. Maybe we ought to go back to being quiet like the ride last night." And yet, a smile pulled at the edges of her lips.

"That was pure torture." He tossed an overly dramatic palm to his chest. "I'm a talker."

"I can see that." She fidgeted with the strap of her seatbelt. A touch of nerves at having to endure being in the car with him for seven or so hours and in the daylight . . . this was going to be hard. She was not an open book, and she had no intention of getting sucked into talking about her life. But for some insane reason, around him, she had the urge to at least turn a few pages and see what might happen.

"You still haven't answered my question, by the way. Perhaps all this talking is your way of avoiding questions you don't want to answer." She leaned back in her seat and tightened the knot of her ponytail, waiting for a rebuttal that never came. "See, I'm right."

"To answer your question, I did talk to my people. They

checked every house that had a front door surveillance camera around Porter's place to try and get a look at who may have entered his house before you. The guy was good. You too, so it would seem. Neither of you were on any other cameras." He paused. "Also, there's no mention of you being on the run with a handsome cowboy." She assumed he chased away whatever concerns had entered his mind when his lips went from drawn tight to curving into a smile. "And lastly, my buddy is fine with me staying at his place. He just said no sex in the master bedroom."

"Does he know I'm with you?" And wait, she probably should have led with another response, one that shot down any ideas that they'd be sleeping together.

"No, I said I'd be traveling alone." His voice lowered, almost like he was once again a Tier One operator in the middle of a serious mission. Did he suddenly remember why they were on the road? "Not that he believed me," he tossed out a moment later.

"So, he assumes you'll hook up with someone in town. Is that your reputation?" she asked, her voice pitching softer than normal. A strange feeling of—was that jealousy?—had her stomach tightening.

He shifted on his seat, looking back and forth between the highway and her, which was making her more uncomfortable. Too many eighteen-wheelers on the road. "Do I look like a player?" His signature playboy grin with a side of cocky touched his face. "And I thought you didn't want to chitchat?" *Annnnd operator mode gone.* The A.J. she'd grown accustomed to in their short time together had returned.

Well, if he'd been telling the truth on her voicemail—he hadn't been with anyone since he met her. She had a hard time believing that, though. It was probably a drunken attempt to woo her.

She hadn't been with anyone since Kyle, and even when they were together, their sex life hadn't been great. She was never in the mood. She'd destroyed the redheaded stereotypes Kyle had had in his head before dating her.

Cold, dead heart. Her eyes fell to her ring finger.

"What happened with you and Kyle?" A gentleness ebbed through his words this time. "You, um, over him?"

"Is this your way of feeling me out?" she asked. "Seeing if you have a chance?"

"Just trying to get to know you a little better." His answer almost sounded sincere. Not like he was working a case. Working her for information.

Maybe now was the time for them to discuss what A.J. already knew about her background. Better yet, there was probably a file on her somewhere in his car. She'd love a peek, and she casually stretched her arms up and turned her head toward the back.

"It's not there."

"How do you know what I'm looking for?" she challenged.

"I've been wondering when you were going to ask me about whatever file I have on you, but since you don't like to talk, we can just—"

"No," she cut him off. "Let's talk about what you know."

"I know a lot, sugar. About horses, weather patterns, guns, conspiracies. You name it, I probably know a thing or two about it. Better be more specific with what you'd like to know."

"Me. What do you know about me?" She shifted to face forward, and the movement pulled the strap of her tank down, exposing the top of her bra. *Shit.* She quickly adjusted the seatbelt and righted her top. The last thing she wanted was to flash her boobs when he needed to keep his eyes on the road.

She'd order him to pull over so she could drive, but her hands and fingers were still cramped up from strangling the steering wheel last night.

I'm basically a fugitive. If not yet, I will be soon. But she'd known the risks when she'd agreed to her assignment the day Porter offered her the promotion. She never expected it all to go down like this, though. Or for A.J. to walk into her life and offer a hand when she needed it the most.

"Born in New York. Moved around a lot. Parents traveled for work before they died." He paused. "I'm, um, sorry for your loss." When it was clear she wasn't going to respond, he added, "You excelled in all your studies. Recruited by the FBI. Their third time courting you was the charm. You were assigned to Charlotte after Quantico. Bounced around a few different squads over there. Married Kyle Jeter. No relation to the baseball player. I checked." He cleared his throat. "And then you got divorced shortly after we worked that case together. Took a position in D.C. with the Counterintelligence Division. Six people in your unit, plus your unit and section chiefs," he added, speaking very matter-of-factly. "Lots and lots of blank spaces, though. I'd much rather hear your story from you since you lived it."

She slumped back into her seat after A.J. had summed up her life in just over thirty seconds. He had the Anastasia 1.0 version.

Part of her was relieved he didn't know the tragic circumstances of her life. The other part almost wished he did know, thereby sparing her the need to reveal everything face-to-face when or if she chose to do so. She'd never mustered the courage to tell her husband of three years the truth. How could she confide in this man who *should* have felt like a stranger but didn't?

"Who hired you?"

"Classified," he abruptly answered, then his shoulders sagged apologetically. "Sorry, I, uh, well, you know how it is."

And she supposed she did get it. Her world was one classified bubble. Even with the Hatch Act, she wasn't supposed to share political opinions given her job, let alone classified intel.

Ana's gaze veered out the side window, her thoughts flitting about as she tried to piece everything together. "Well, someone suspected a leak since all of the sources that went missing were attached to my unit. I'm guessing they didn't want to tip off the mole by sending someone from the FBI to watch us, so they went outside the lines on this one, which is how you're involved."

Porter would have warned her if he'd had any idea about the external investigation being conducted on her team. Well, he would've warned her before shit hit the fan last night. God, she hoped he was okay.

But aside from her and Porter, who else knew about the files in his safe? Who the hell was that guy in Porter's house last night?

"Does it really matter who hired me?" A.J. asked a few deep breaths later. "All you need to know is that you're in good hands. If someone at the Bureau is a traitor, we'll take him or her down. And my team has excellent facial recognition software. If anyone can find your missing sources and The Huntsman, it's Jessica and Harper."

"I thought Jessica was on maternity leave."

A.J. side-eyed her. "How much did Adriana tell you about my team?"

She was quiet for a moment, trying to figure out how to handle the direction of the conversation. "Not much. Does Adriana know about us?" She regretted the use of "us" almost immediately, knowing A.J. would most likely spin her words.

"Adriana knows you're with me, yes." Wow, a straightforward, non-flirtatious answer. What was up with that? Operator mode again? Of course, she heard that Navy SEALs had the ability to be a warrior one moment and help a woman with her groceries the next. Warrior to gentleman to warrior within the blink of an eye. A.J. was most likely the same. "And Knox will soon know she kept you a secret."

"It's not her fault," Ana said, worried about a marital fight because of her.

"And yet, according to Wyatt, Adriana is not throwing you under the bus and blaming you for withholding your friendship from us."

"Well, she should." Guilt pushed through her at ever asking Adriana to keep a secret from her husband.

"And real friends go to bat for each other. It sounds to me like you're not too familiar with what it's like to have people in your corner like that." His tone was sad, as if he truly felt pity for her.

"I, um." Shit, was she getting emotional right now? No, it had to be bad mascara. The stinging in her eyes was because she forgot to buy a new tube, too preoccupied with her assignment to remember to shop. "Kyle was never in my corner," she continued, slightly surprised she was making such a confession. "Well, more like he tried to box me into one. Too protective. I didn't need that. I don't need—"

"You don't need help? Someone to care about you?" he asked, and how was this conversation taking such a sharp and personal turn?

"I don't need protecting. I can handle myself." *Cold and dead. Heartless.*

"You ever consider that keeping someone safe isn't because they don't believe you're capable, but because they just care?"

"Are you really defending Kyle?" she asked in surprise, twisting to the side to gain a better view of him.

A.J. shifted lanes and pulled off the side of the highway so fast she'd barely had time to steel herself for the action. She jerked forward, the seatbelt catching her, when he firmly applied the brakes.

When A.J. unbuckled, whipped his sunglasses off and faced her, his eyes were the color of the ocean during a storm. His forearm rested over the top of the wheel as he studied her. Words on the tip of his tongue, and this time, she didn't have a clue as to what he might say.

She gulped and studied him while the vehicle shook as cars and trucks flew past them.

"No, I'm not defending your ex," he growled out in a low, raspy voice. "But I am defending the kind of man *I* am."

Her fingers feathered across her chest as he kept his eyes pinned on her in an intense gaze. "And what kind of man are you?" she whispered, her body tensing up.

"I'm a man who will do absolutely everything in his power to protect the people I care about, and right now, that person is you. I can't imagine you being out here alone, FBI agent or not, and if my wanting to help keep you safe bothers you, well, tough shit," he hissed between his teeth, edging his face even closer.

Chills coated her body as she waited for him to continue, knowing he had more to say.

"And no, hiding out with you was never the original plan. You look guilty as sin when you stack all the cards up, but I believe you. I just fucking do. So, maybe you don't like getting help, or having a man protect you, but I'm here now, and you ain't gettin rid of me, sugar." He jerked his focus back to the road and reached for his seatbelt, but she extended an arm, unable to stop herself.

He tensed and let go of a deep breath but kept his eyes set on the road. Jaw tight. Angry. This was a man hurting. A man who'd experienced pain, and it was pouring right out of him so hot and heavy she physically felt it.

"Look at me," she requested, her tone soft. "Please."

"I'm looking at you," he announced when facing her. "Right now. Right here. I see you." He pointed a finger, and it nearly touched her chest. "I see a woman afraid to let her guard down, especially to someone like me. But you need to, or you'll get us both killed. And I reckon you don't want that, now, do you?"

She leaned in closer, unaware she was even doing it. "I don't know how to do that, how to let my guard down," she murmured, surprised he'd managed that confession from her.

And yet, here he was, shattering her world alongside a highway.

"I can teach you." He added a genuine nod that had her nearly believing it was possible.

Cold and dead on the inside didn't feel like the truth with his eyes and his trust pointed her way. More like warmth and sunshine. "I'm not an easy student. I'm stubborn," she admitted, those annoying tears creeping back into her eyes as she spoke, and when he cupped her face with his warm hand, one tear slipped free like a drop of truth had snuck through the cracks. "And I can be hard to deal with. A total pain in the ass."

He wet his lips, his tongue peeking out for the briefest of

moments, drawing her attention to his very kissable mouth. "Then it's a good thing I love a challenge."

His warm hand on her flushed skin felt decadent and delicious. And she wanted nothing more than for that hand to travel all over her body. To awaken every fiber of her being.

She had a mission to complete, so did he. But she was beginning to wonder if A.J.'s mission now involved having Ana fall for him. And if so, did she want him to succeed?

CHAPTER FOURTEEN

A.J. ROLLED UP TO GRANT WALKER'S PLACE LATER THAT afternoon. Ana had been a champ the entire trip and didn't request a pee break but once, nor did she complain that they survived off gas station snacks for food on the way down.

When they were forty-five minutes away from his friend's house, A.J. stopped at a Piggly Wiggly to grab groceries. He didn't want to risk being seen out in public in his small town. Even though the townsfolk kept secrets from outsiders better than most, he wanted to avoid questions as to why he was staying at Grant Walker's house instead of with his family.

Grocery shopping with Ana had felt normal somehow. Easy. Like they were a married couple, quibbling over which brand of milk or flavor of chips to buy.

They'd loaded up their cart with all the essentials, including wine and beer. He didn't normally drink on the job, but if he was going to be alone with Ana, they needed something stronger to drink than sweet tea or Coke.

After their impromptu roadside chat that morning, they'd mostly spent their time in the car fighting over the radio controls while avoiding serious conversation. Ana had shored up her walls shortly after giving him a glimmer of hope she might be ready to open up. Still, he was satisfied he'd made some progress with her. Sooner rather than later, though, he'd need her to reveal more and trust he was there and with her for the right reasons.

"Not bad for a hideout." Ana opened the SUV door, stepped outside, and stretched. "And you said this place belongs to an Air Force buddy?"

"Yup." He came around the vehicle on the circular driveway to stand alongside her and eyed the house. "Six bedrooms. Nine bathrooms. Infinity pool, pond, and hot tub out back. Plus, a hangar for his bird. Not too shabby." Maybe he'd even have a place like this someday. Probably half the size and without a helo out back.

"I never understood the idea of having more bathrooms than bedrooms." She smiled and pointed to the bed of pink flowers in front of the gray-bricked home with a wraparound porch. "Pretty flowers."

"They better be. Camellias. Alabama state flower." He motioned toward the side of the house where a three-car garage was located. "I should park and get the groceries inside."

"Don't want the ice cream that's surrounded by the two bags of ice you bought to melt." Her lips teased into a fuller smile.

"Nothing comes between a man and his ice cream."

"Sure you don't mean a kid and his ice cream?" She winked, and he resisted the urge to slap a hand to his heart.

By some miracle, Alabama was already doing her thing and loosening Ana up.

"But, um, did the Air Force get a pay increase I'm unaware of? I'm thinking the Bureau should do the same."

He set a hand on top of the warm hood of the SUV. "One

of our friends started a bourbon business a few years back, and Grant used some of his inheritance to invest in the company. Let's just say I'm regretting my choice not to buy in."

She tugged at the bottom of her yellow tank top as if trying to coax a breeze. "Looks like the heat wave followed us here."

"Nah, the heat wave was born in Alabama." He pointed to the trunk. "And that ice cream—"

"Is about to die a quick death." She kicked the tip of her shoe at the driveway. "Who from your team is coming to Alabama?"

He hadn't planned on revealing the fact some of his teammates would be arriving soon for backup should they need it, but the woman was worse than a bloodhound.

"It's fine. I'm not too keen on the idea of involving more people, but I take it you all are a packaged deal?" She crossed her arms while waiting for a response she clearly already knew the answer to.

He cocked his head and smirked. "It's almost as if you got a thing against ice cream, distracting me with conversation, so I don't go rescue it from melting."

"I'll admit I've never been a fan of anything sticky. I hate when it gets all over my hands as it drips down the side of the cone." She scrunched her nose.

"Now I'm thinking you've been eating your ice cream wrong." He opened the driver's side door as she came over to stand beside him, shielding her eyes from the sun to view him.

"You haven't answered my question," she reminded him.

Yeah, well, she went and distracted him with thoughts of licking a little chocolate off her hand. Putting her finger in his mouth. Sucking it clean.

Damn, his dick was gonna get as hard and stiff as a pole if he didn't get his head on straight.

He sat behind the wheel and restarted the engine. "Not sure who you met last year or if you remember them," he began, "but Wyatt decided to stay in D.C. since his wedding is coming up soon." His smile broadened. "So, it'll be Chris, Finn, Roman, and Harper heading here. Harper was planning to stay in D.C., but she decided it'd be better to have someone watch over us down here in case we need a quick digital assist with anything."

"The women are the brains behind your work, huh?"

"We're not so bad ourselves, but thank God for them, that's all I can say." When his phone rang from where it was positioned on his dashboard, he sighed. "The bags of ice and ice cream are gonna be as good as gone if they bake out in this heat much longer, even with the A/C running."

"How about I bring the SUV into the garage and unload the groceries, and you handle the call?"

He snatched his phone and hopped out. "The key to the door is under the third rock to the right in that flower patch over yonder. You can open the garage door once inside." He pointed to the flowerbed and brought his phone to his ear.

When Ana was out of earshot, he answered Wyatt's call. "We're here. Good timing." *Minus the ice cream issue.* "Any news?"

"Ana's still not on the FBI's Most Wanted list. Not yet, at least. Feds have searched her home and are going through her phone records, though," Wyatt replied, knowing full well that was what A.J. was asking. "Her unit is definitely tossing her name around as the potential mole, especially since she's the newbie on the team. Plus, I guess something about her background is not what it seems, and we're not quite sure what that means yet. But all of this isn't exactly going to do wonders proving her innocence." Wyatt paused as if regretful at the news he'd delivered. "Running doesn't help, either."

"Not really running," A.J. defended, trying to shirk the concern about Ana's background now creeping into his mind. "And for all the Feds know, she could be missing, same as her sources and Porter."

"It is shaping up to look like the Volkovs, not the SVR, hired The Huntsman to kidnap Katya in New York, which means they may be behind the disappearance of the other sources," Wyatt said. "Well, that's what our contact at the Bureau told Natasha, but we need to do our own digging."

"Shit, okay. I'll let Ana know."

"The guys and Harper should be setting up in Birmingham by nightfall," Wyatt added.

They didn't have a safe house there, so they'd need to rent a place. "You sure they don't want to stay here?"

"And if I say yes, you'll kill me. You know you want a chance to spend time with Ana. Hell, you wouldn't shut up about her on the way to the airport Saturday night."

Hence the drunken call. "I hit my head. Plus, I was intoxicated. Bad combination."

"Sure, sure. So, you're not risking our necks because you got feelings for the woman?" Natasha chimed in.

"Am I on speakerphone?" A.J. lifted his sunglasses a touch and cocked his head, his eyes glued to the scene before him. Ana, in those tight white pants, sashaying toward the flower patch. Fuck if she didn't have a gorgeous body. He let his glasses go, brought a fist to his mouth, and bit down on his knuckles as she bent over to grab the key from beneath the rock, the snug fabric stretching across her perfect ass.

She must have felt his eyes on her because at the moment, instead of getting back up and going to the front door, she held her position and slowly turned her head to peer at him from over her shoulder.

"Yes, you are," Natasha answered as A.J. stepped back and turned to the side. He needed to be stealthier.

"Hey, I'm not risking your necks. This was my choice. If something goes wrong, it's on me. Not y'all."

"That's not how we roll, and you know it," Wyatt said as Ana finally climbed the steps to the wraparound front porch. "And Luke and Knox will be arriving in D.C. soon. They've been apprised of the situation."

"Is Luke pissed?" A.J. asked, closing one eye as if he might get punched in the face and part of him wanted to see it coming.

"I'd say Luke took it better than Knox did when he learned the news that Adriana is friends with Ana and kept the truth from him."

His expression relaxed at Natasha's words. "Well, considering Knox kept a few secrets from her, I'd call it even." Ana going to the trouble of keeping A.J. from discovering she was in D.C. meant one of two things in his mind: she hated his guts, or she was so attracted to him that it scared the hell out of her. He hoped for door number two since fate, as fate tended to do, intervened and brought them together.

"And what does Admiral Chandler have to say about all of this?" That was the dicey part. Now that Natasha was working with them and reported directly to her dad, it was all a bit . . . yeah, dicey.

"He wants you to find out what Quinn may know about the Daylight Ledger and key. But the admiral said if we're wrong about her, and she's a traitor and a threat to national security, he'll arrest me himself for aiding and abetting a fugitive." A.J. wasn't sure if Natasha was kidding or not. Her dad wouldn't really arrest her, right?

He shook his head. "Well, if you get arrested, that would ruin your wedding, now wouldn't it?" A.J. joked. He had no doubt if they were all in the same room, Wyatt would be shooting daggers at him, probably worried he'd just been jinxed for the second time in less than a week. "But seriously, thank you for trusting me on this. I know it can't be easy, especially in your new position, Natasha."

"Just watch your back. I don't want her getting you killed. Let us handle the investigation," Natasha spoke up, sounding all mother-like. "We've got this, and with Jessica looking into The Huntsman, you know—"

"I hope the angry papa bear isn't upset we pulled him and his better half back into work," A.J. said.

"I'm pretty sure they both begged to help," Natasha responded, a smile in her voice. "Jessica's parents are helping out, and I think she's eager for a chance to do some work."

"Okay." That was a relief. He'd rather piss off POTUS than Jessica. "What's the status on Jeter, her ex?"

Had Ana really taken an issue with Kyle being overly protective, or had there been more to it?

"Owen is keeping tabs on him right now. Kyle seems to be taking Ana's disappearance the hardest. He mentioned Ana had been with some military-type at her townhouse before she went MIA," Natasha added before tossing out, "Don't worry, I covered for the both of you."

"Thank you." That was all A.J. needed—a pissed-off ex on top of things.

"And we're hoping to have an ID today or in the morning on the target Chris snapped a photo of last night, the person who Ana passed something off to," Natasha stated.

A.J. still needed to press Ana about why she'd been in

Porter's house last night, but he was hoping she came forward about it herself.

"Okay, good. What about the FBI agent on your special task force? He doesn't know we're helping, right?" A.J. clarified as Ana sauntered back his way to get to the SUV after she'd unlocked the house and presumably opened the garage. "Or that Ana is with me?" He turned his back to the car once the driver's side door was closed, and she pulled away.

"No," Natasha quickly answered.

"Who is it, by the way? Can we know that?" A.J. was curious who'd provided Ana's case file. Was he a friend of Ana's, or was he going to be an enemy when it came time to clear Ana's name after all was said and done?

"I'm sorry," Natasha answered. "That information is need-to-know."

"Even from us?" A.J. challenged, irked by her response.

"You know how things go," was all she said, and he knew he'd have to suck it up and take it. For now.

"I, uh, should go get settled in." A.J. cleared his throat. "Call me if you hear anything."

"Stay out of trouble," Wyatt reminded him.

"You know me, Chief," A.J. responded.

"Yeah, brother, I do. And that's what scares me." Wyatt ended the call, and A.J. made his way past the side of the large home and into the garage.

"Everything okay?" Ana asked, both arms full of grocery bags.

"Yeah. You're not on the wanted list yet," he said as nonchalantly as possible, "and the Feds are leaning toward believing the Volkovs are behind the missing sources."

The bags started to slip from her hands, so he quickly

stepped in and grabbed them. She wet her lips and swallowed. "Did they say how they knew that?"

"Nah, that was just Bureau news, and we prefer to formulate our own opinion on matters." He smiled, then side-eyed the back of the SUV. "Well look at that, the ice is still intact. Maybe the ice cream will live to see the inside of my stomach." Humor. Only way to survive.

"Thank God for the small wins," she nearly whispered while reaching for another bag.

He followed her up the short wooden steps to get inside the house. The place still had that new-home scent. The paint only a few weeks old.

"And your friend won't show up unexpectedly?" she asked while he set the bags down on the massive marble island at the center of the kitchen. There was a panoramic wall of glass windows on the opposite side of the room that opened to the back.

"No. He was here a few weeks ago. Wrapped up the interior design with the designer on his weekend off, but he's overseas right now."

"And will the designer be coming by?" she questioned, opening the stainless-steel fridge to stock it with the food, her tone still a touch distracted or distant. Talk of her case and the Volkovs must've gotten to her.

"Well, my mom is the designer. Does it for fun, but no, last I heard, my mom won't be coming around anytime soon." He hoped not, at least. He'd have a hell of a lot of explaining to do. "And all this cabinetry," he added while pointing to the wall of white cabinets, "is courtesy of my boy Jesse. He has a business, and he's meticulous with details."

"Well, your mom has great style, and Jesse's very talented, too." She raced a hand over the stove. "Nice six-burner gas range." She glimpsed him and smiled. "Not that I cook."

"Well, you're in luck. I happen to be an excellent chef."

"Why did I somehow expect you to say that?" She lifted her eyes to the vaulted ceiling, taking it all in.

"I promise to dazzle you with my skills." He just could not control himself around this woman. He'd meant to sound casual about his cooking skills, but his voice had come out deep and husky, giving the words unintentional meaning.

Ana cleared her throat, and based on the red flush on her face, A.J. guessed she'd been thinking the same thing.

"Er, you should check out the roof deck off the master upstairs," he said quickly. "Nice three-sixty view of the property." He'd taken a quick tour before borrowing the chopper last Saturday.

"But no sex in the master, right?" Ana's eyes grew wide and her face redder as if she hadn't meant to vocalize those words.

But hot damn, if she was thinking about sex . . .

"Yeah, that was his only rule." A.J. walked past the butler's pantry and back into the garage, wanting to give her a second to let the heat in her cheeks dissipate, *and* so he had a chance to adjust his pants and his thoughts.

She's about to be labeled a fugitive. Probably accused of treason. Stop picturing her naked.

"Hey," she said softly a minute later, standing off to his side in the garage.

A.J. set their travel bags down by his feet, grabbed the last bag of groceries, then closed the back hatch. He glimpsed Ana standing in front of Grant's black BMX bike, looking at him intently. "Yeah?" He left the bags on the ground and approached her.

"I was just wondering if I've actually said thank you?"

179

Her lashes fluttered as if she were pausing to find the right words. "Not many people would do what you're doing." Her green-eyed gaze swept over his length, starting at his shoes and working up to his face. "So, thank you." She extended her palm for a formal handshake.

"Doing the right thing doesn't deserve a thank you. But, since we're in Bama, and we do hugs instead of handshakes, I wouldn't mind one of those." At this moment, he'd give anything to pull her into his arms. Comfort her, promise everything was going to work out just fine. But he couldn't make that promise yet, could he?

She took a hesitant step to close the space between them, and honestly, he hadn't expected a hug, only a rejection wrapped in humor.

But when she moved in and reached around his back, bringing her chest against his, he stilled in surprise. And then he wrapped her tight in his arms, resting his chin on the top of her head since she was a good six inches shorter than he was.

"Thanks." She stepped out of his reach after a moment and smiled.

He'd witnessed a few different kinds of smiles from her, some he saw from afar while watching her, others had happened since their collision course inside Porter's house. This smile was the kind that broke his heart. It was one of mourning and pain and it had him wanting to scoop her back into his arms and shield her. Make everything right. But she wasn't a fan of being protected, so he didn't want to push her into being someone she wasn't.

"I, um, could use a shower," she said, appearing a bit awkward after their hug.

"Sure." He grabbed the luggage, and she lifted the last of the grocery bags. Once inside, with his hands full, he kicked the door closed behind him and followed her into the kitchen. "Thought you took one at the hotel this morning?"

"Were you spying on me?" She looked back at him. "*Again*?"

And did they need to talk about her wet, glistening body in the shower? How he imagined her mass of red hair flowing over her skin. Chin tipped up, eyes closed, her mouth parted as a drop of water fell on her lip that he'd suck off.

"I heard the water running," he said with a smile, one he sure as hell hoped she wouldn't be able to read. "I can give you a tour of our new hideout, then drop your things off in one of the guest rooms."

Ana reached for the gray duffel she'd packed last night. Had she brought that black silk robe? Maybe she'd put it on after her shower without anything underneath?

"You okay?" she asked as they walked down the hall and toward the stairs near the front door.

"Maybe it's the fresh paint getting to my head."

She stopped, one foot positioned on the bottom step, and turned. "Are you dizzy? Is your head bothering you again?"

Which head? He closed his eyes at his vulgar thought.

I'm here to stop a traitor. Take down a threat to the nation. Possibly more than one threat. Or find some unicorn ledger. I do not need to get excited about spending alone time with this redheaded goddess. "I'm good." He wasn't seeing ghosts at the moment. Hadn't had any nightmares last night. So yeah, he'd (hopefully) survive living under the same roof with her while they worked to discover the truth that appeared to center around Ana.

"Okay." He knew she didn't believe him, but she let it go and went upstairs, her ass looking way too good in those white pants. She had to be wearing a thong given the lack of panty line showing beneath the material. "This is a man cave if I've ever seen one," she called out before he joined her in the media room.

"This room was all Grant. My mom didn't decorate it." He set the bags down once inside the large room and smirked.

Ana's back was to him, her eyes set to the wall of framed photos that covered decades and decades of memories for Grant, many including A.J.'s family.

"Now why didn't you tell me you were friends with Michael Jordan?"

"Because I'm not." He smiled.

"Not the basketball player, the actor. The sexy guy from the movie *Creed*. You know, he played Apollo's son from *Rocky*."

"Please don't tell my boy Grant he looks like that guy. He's got a big enough head as it is." He chuckled. "But I have to say, I'm impressed with your *Rocky* and *Creed* knowledge."

A.J. walked past the two massive side-by-side LCD TVs mounted on the wall to get to her.

"Oh my God, wait. Noooo." She faced him, her eyes bright. "Grant's dad is Booker Walker? *The* Booker Walker? Well-known blues and country singer?" She turned back to the wall.

"Yeah, that's him." A.J. leaned in and pointed to the guy playing guitar next to Grant's father. "That's my old man next to Booker."

"I had no idea." The deep green of her eyes appeared to darken in surprise.

"And why would you?" he asked. "We, you know, haven't done too much talking."

She frowned. "I'm thinking I had a different upbringing than you, so I just don't like to—"

"That's fine." They didn't need to get into her backstory.

Not this second. "But yeah, my dad met Booker while they served in Nam together. They said music helped get them through it." He tucked his hands in his jeans pockets, smiling at the memories his dad used to share around the campfire when A.J. was growing up. "My dad taught Booker country music, and he taught my dad blues and jazz."

"Booker has the voice of an angel." Ana went quiet and faced the wall.

"When they got out of the Navy, my dad talked Booker into going to the University of Alabama with him. Now, you have to remember, this wasn't long after the Civil Rights Movement, the March of Birmingham . . . but, I tell you what," he said while pointing to the photo of his dad and Booker, their hands clasped in the air, "they served as a symbol of unity instead of divisiveness, and I swear, through their music, they brought our little town into the light."

"Walkins," Ana said with a smile as she turned to face him. "The name of your town . . . it was also the name of their group when they went on tour after they graduated college, right?" She wet her lips. "My dad was a fan of them. Had their records."

She was surprising him at every turn. "Yup." A.J. swallowed hard, emotion literally choking him up. "Walker and Hawkins combined. The town was renamed Walkins Glen about a decade ago when Grant's dad died."

"Is there even a glen around here?"

He leaned in and whispered, "No, but don't tell anyone. Kind of a local secret. It just sounded fancy, so."

She playfully zipped her lips before parting them to ask, "But um, why'd your dad leave the tour so soon?"

He lifted his hands from his pockets and removed his hat. "My granddaddy got sick. My uncle died in Nam, and my other uncle didn't get along so much with my dad or granddaddy, so my dad needed to come back home. Help out with the family ranch."

"Oh, I'm so sorry."

A.J. shrugged. "My dad and Booker remained the best of friends, though. He kept a house near my parents', and his wife lived there. Grant and I grew up together."

Ana moved to the side and spotted a photo of Grant and A.J. from decades ago. "That's you two in school? You played football?"

He grimaced. "Not very well, but we tried. Grant and I eventually gave it up and started our own band instead. We played at the local dives after a big football win. My music talent was better than my ball skills. But don't tell anyone I admitted that."

Her lips slightly tipped up at the edges. "Did you sing or play an instrument?" She faced him, one brow cocked. Eyes sparkling.

"Both." He settled his hat back on his head, emotion stretching through him as he shared his life with this woman. No woman outside his forever-ago girlfriend had known this much about him. He'd never wanted to share his life with anyone. And here he was working a case, and it was as if he were sharing his soul.

"I guess you all are hardcore Alabama fans, huh?" Ana directed her focus to the rows of brown leather couches set up in front of the two big screens. The throw pillows and blankets were all from the University of Alabama. The walls were white with a thick stripe of crimson cutting through one wall opposite the pictures.

"Let's just say we have two rules for the men in our house." He held up two fingers for emphasis. "No dating anyone who went to the University of Tennessee or Auburn—our rivals."

She smiled. The honest and warm one that had his heart pounding harder. "And the other?"

"Know how to cook so no Tennessee or Auburn alum could try and win us over through our stomachs."

"You're kidding?" She folded her arms and did her best to keep from smiling.

"Am I?" He leaned closer to her, catching a whiff of the lavender shampoo from the hotel he'd smelled during that brief hug in the garage. Their first hug in a garage of all places. "We take football and food very seriously down here in Bama."

"I can see that." Her fingers splayed across her collarbone as her gaze moved from his chest to his face. "I really should get cleaned up before dinner, which I assume you'll be making?"

"And if I win you over through your stomach?" he asked, the question tumbling from his lips.

"I don't think anyone is that good of a cook."

He tipped his hat. "That another challenge?"

"I figured you'd say that. Know you so well already."

He dipped his head, their faces much closer. "Why do I get the feeling you're not betting against me to lose?"

CHAPTER FIFTEEN

ANA SLIPPED INTO THE EN SUITE WITH HER TRAVEL BAG AND set it on the counter. She flipped on the shower and fished through the bag for one of the disposable phones she'd packed.

Door shut and locked. Water running. Check. Check. Check.

She closed her eyes, pulling to mind the number she'd committed to memory and then released a shaky breath. A breath on which floated a boatload of guilt, that is if guilt were able to manifest itself in a tangible form. She opened her eyes when the call connected and announced, "Hi, it's me."

"It's about time." He was quiet and restrained, which Ana had come to know meant he was reining himself in to keep from yelling. She assumed he'd tried to get to the second Volkov source in Miami and had discovered the man was under Federal protection. "We cannot get our man out of Florida. He is too heavily guarded. This is the second target you have failed to deliver as proof of your loyalty."

"I shouldn't have to prove my loyalty given who I am,

and don't forget, I reached out to your organization first," she reminded him, doing her best to keep her tone confident and sharp. "I'm trying to help."

"I still don't trust you. You may be working with any number of my enemies. Or setting me up with the FBI." The man had lived outside of Russia for so long his accent was more Jersey than anything else.

"I can assure you I am not. I want vengeance for what happened to my parents. Why do you think I joined the FBI? I needed access to their resources. Their case files."

"And they hired you despite knowing the identity of your parents?" He'd asked this the first time she'd spoken to him. Was he trying to catch her in a lie?

"I was sixteen when my parents died. As far as management is concerned, my history toughened me up and gives me an edge over my colleagues," she answered, shifting away from the door, hoping the walls were well-made and thick enough to prevent A.J. from overhearing. "You have to understand, I had no idea there were any living Volkovs until the FBI acquired two of your people and turned them as sources."

"Where were you earlier?" he asked, seemingly satisfied with her answer. "My cousin says you were not at the meet today."

"I had to leave D.C. to follow a lead," she rushed out. "But we learned who got to Katya. Ivan Smirnoff, The Huntsman, is in the U.S. The FBI believes your people hired him."

"This is not true," he said coolly. "And there is no way Ivan would take a job for the SVR either."

"Unless the SVR contracted someone else to hire him?" she proposed. "To put distance between themselves and the hit, especially because they are still not certain whether or not you have the key. They may be testing you. Or setting you up to draw the attention of the FBI." Anything was possible at this point. "But I did find who we've been looking for." Those words would buy her the time she needed and so much more. "I need you to trust me. Give me until Friday night, and I promise you'll be one step closer to having what you need."

"If you're wrong . . ." He left the unfinished threat hanging in the air. Ana was well aware his fierce tone was designed to scare her, but he couldn't contain the hint of excitement in his voice at the hope her claim might prove to be true.

It was the threat, however, that had her clutching on to the vanity counter to steel her nerves. "I won't let you down." She ended the call before he could say more, then powered off the phone.

Her heart hammered wildly and with fierce intensity. "What am I doing?" she wondered, eyes on the mirror where steam gradually worked to hide her reflection.

After a few calming breaths, she hid the phone in her bag and peeled off her clothes to go through the motions of showering before changing into clean clothes.

She put on a sheer white bra and panty set beneath her white, loose-fitting V-neck tee paired with pale green shorts. Her hair was still wet, but she hadn't thought to bring a hair dryer, so she tied it into a side braid, added a little mascara, then went to find A.J.

From the smell of it, A.J. was cooking. Well, maybe burning something.

The man had proven through his words and his actions he was in this until the end, and he was there to protect her. Maybe a part of her did want him in her corner, though she'd be reluctant to admit that to him.

A.J.'s protectiveness didn't seem to bother her the way

Kyle's had. Then again, Kyle's protective nature always felt like it stemmed from a place of control. Or maybe she'd just always kept walls between them. Walls he continually worked to demolish—without success. He finally gave up and left her. And honestly, she'd been relieved he'd stopped trying.

A.J. was offering to teach her how to open up instead of demanding that she do it like Kyle had done. And she found herself wanting to accept A.J.'s invitation.

What was different now? Was it him or the fact her world changed four months ago when Porter came to her in Charlotte with a special assignment?

"That doesn't sound good," Ana shouted over the shrill blare of a smoke alarm upon entering the kitchen. She waved smoke from her face as A.J. cursed and tossed a sizzling hot pan into the sink and quickly turned on the faucet to douse the . . . blackened chicken? "I thought you knew how to cook."

Ana couldn't help but giggle as she watched A.J. plant his hands on his hips and stare at what was supposed to be their dinner. The smoke detector stopped beeping, and he arched his shoulders back before turning to face her. "I do, but it's been a while. I took a phone call and forgot the stove was on."

"Ah. That happens." She smiled and maneuvered around the kitchen island to be nearer to him. "And now aren't you glad I insisted on buying the frozen pizza?"

"You were right, madam," he said while preheating the oven.

"Who was on the phone?" *Work?*

"Jessica. She has an update, but I told her I'd like her to share the news with you as well, so we'll have a video call with her soon. You know, since I'm trying to be open and honest with ya." He took off the white apron that read **SEALs ARE BETTER** in bold crimson letters and tossed it onto the counter.

Ana stifled a laugh. "Let me guess, you got that for your buddy as a housewarming gift?"

"Damn straight." He'd changed clothes and was now wearing navy blue cargo shorts, a gray V-neck, and black flip-flops. She did a quick and hopefully discreet scan of his lower half since it was the first time she'd seen the man in shorts. He had the perfect amount of drool-worthy muscles on his tan legs. His feet were tan too, strong looking like those of a surfer. *And when did I start finding that sexy?* "We like to rag on each other."

"I can see that." Ana rested a hip against the counter and watched him slowly close the space between them, coming to a stop mere inches from her.

Taken off guard, her breath hitched when he leaned in, braced a hand on the marble countertop off to her side, and sniffed her neck like she was the Alabama state flower. "Mmm, coconut. You tried Patty's soap, didn't ya?" he murmured in her ear.

His warm breath caressed her neck, and when she drew in a shaky gasp, their chests lightly touched. *Oh geez.* She reached her arms back and grabbed the edge of the counter, holding on for dear life. The warm, tingling sensation flowing through her body just might cause her to melt into a puddle right there on the floor. This man was making her all kinds of hot and bothered. And based on the devilish smirk on his handsome face when he leaned back, he knew it.

"I, um." Her eyes dipped to his parted lips, still so close to hers, and she wondered if he would move in to see if she tasted like coconut as well. She was curious how his mouth would feel on other parts of her body, too. Her face was so hot she was almost afraid she'd spoken her lustful thoughts aloud, but she forced her eyes to his. "I guess I did." *Oh God.* Was that her voice? It sounded raspy, sexy . . . like desire had wrapped itself around her vocal cords.

The edge of his lip shifted between his teeth as he continued to study her.

So. Much. Lust. It swirled in his light green eyes and had her squeezing her thighs together. Passion radiated from his body and hit her like a storm. Bolts of lightning and cracks of thunder struck her fast and hard.

Naked cowboy. A new fantasy formed in her mind, and in it, A.J. wasn't quite naked. He had on well-worn jeans, chaps, and a cowboy hat.

"Patty makes the best homemade soap this side of Alabama," A.J. said as if either of them gave a damn about soap or Patty right now. He tilted his head, his eyes twinkling.

"Oh? And who makes the best on the other side?" She arched her back a touch, drawn to him like a magnet, desperate with need.

"Damn, woman, I really like you." This was not a declaration of his undying devotion. His tone was teasing, playful, and yet he was still occupying her space and staring at her like he wanted to eat her for dinner.

She took a few shallow breaths and willed herself not to collapse into his strong arms and beg him to have his way with her, like he probably expected to happen.

"I think Alabama might actually be doing her thing and turning you into a Southerner." His gaze dropped to her braid hanging in front of her shoulder, and he reached out to take the end between his fingers. "You're wet."

"I am," she murmured, and then blinked in shock at her admission.

The side of his mouth did some cute curl, and she followed his gaze to her shirt.

"Ohhh." Her face heated with the force of a thousand suns when she saw the now-sheer white fabric where her wet braid had lain, directly over her right breast. The sight of her nipple poking clear as day through her sheer bra had her slinging both arms across her chest, resulting in the loss of her balance. If she weren't so mortified, she'd have laughed at her clumsiness.

A.J. released her braid, quickly gripped a hand around her hip, and pulled her close to steady her.

Their playful teasing suddenly took a back seat to unmistakable desire the second her body was up against his strong frame.

Her arms were wedged between them, but he brought his free hand beneath her chin, and with a finger, tilted her face, silently demanding she look at him.

Once Ana was face-to-face with A.J., fear grabbed hold of her. Just looking into his trusting, caring eyes made her feel like a fraud and a liar. She squeezed her eyes shut as thoughts of what was currently her life sailed to mind—the truth about her parents, the mission Porter had given her . . . Porter. *Please let Porter be okay.*

"Look at me," A.J. commanded, a sexy rasp in his tone that had her wanting to let go. To forget every sentence that began with "No" or "I can't."

She relaxed her arms, allowing them to fall, and without that barrier, there was nothing else between them. Nothing but her worries.

"Look at me." His tone was rougher this time, and it was as if his palm had stroked her center and parted her legs when he'd spoken.

"I'm scared," she confessed, her voice wobbly. "You may not want to kiss me once you know the truth about me."

He was quiet for a moment, but he didn't step away at her words. He didn't release her. "What makes you think I want to kiss you?" he challenged, ignoring her admission because A.J. was A.J., she'd quickly learned, and he couldn't help himself whenever he had a chance to playfully give her a hard time.

But his teasing question did the trick, and she opened her eyes. He got his way. She was looking at him. And what she witnessed had her knees buckling. His green eyes held a gentle warmth and conveyed an intense longing she hadn't believed existed.

"I got you," he said with a firm but tender voice, instinctively knowing to hold her tighter to keep her from sinking with the weight of all the emotions she was experiencing. "And I do want to kiss you."

"You do?" Dumb question. But she wanted to hear him say it again.

His lips crooked into a semi-smile as he brought his hand from beneath her chin to cup her cheek. "I really, really do." He lowered his head, prepared to do exactly what he said he wanted to do, but the sound of chirping, or a ring of sorts, had him stopping just shy of kissing her.

"Is that your team?" she whispered, his warm palm still on her cheek, his mouth hovering an inch from hers.

"Yes, but—"

"We shouldn't make them wait." With a sigh, he set his forehead to hers.

She wanted his kiss. His touch. But he needed to hear the truth first. Their kiss had to be pure and innocent. No guilt clawing at her. She would do things differently this time.

He leaned back, his hand falling from her face, a flood of disappointment in his eyes. It was a painful sight to see.

Ana set a hand over his palm on her hip the moment he'd started to turn, stopping him. "A.J.?"

"Yeah?" he mouthed as if it was too difficult to use his voice.

"Just so you know, I really wanted to kiss you, too."

CHAPTER SIXTEEN

ANA EASED INTO THE BIG LEATHER CHAIR IN FRONT OF THE oak desk in Grant's first-floor office, which was one room down from the kitchen.

Her head was still in the clouds from the intense near-kiss moment they'd shared a few minutes ago. She wasn't prepared for a video-call with A.J.'s teammates, but she'd need to put her game face on and transition back to FBI-mode.

A.J. wasn't making it easy, though. They'd missed Jessica's call, so A.J. was presently standing as close to her as a tick on a dog—and, Alabama *was* indeed doing "its thing" to her, as A.J. suggested. He leaned forward to access the keyboard, his tee stretching taut and putting his back muscles on display. That, combined with the fabric straining around his powerful bicep as one hand braced on the desk for support, was making Ana lose focus.

He tossed a quick look at her from over his shoulder, thoughts of what he wished had happened in that kitchen clear in his thoughtful expression.

The hum of their intense chemistry vibrated between

them, and she fidgeted with her braid to prevent herself from doing something crazy. Like snatching his shirt and tugging him around to face her. Instructing him to drop to his knees and go down on her right there at the desk.

What happened to me? She blinked and noticed A.J.'s eyes locked on her shirt. His gaze was heated as if he were imagining taking her nipple between his teeth and lightly biting.

The cotton fabric of her shirt was still wet, and A.J. lifted his chin, sending a silent warning that her nipple was still quite visible.

Right. Asher and Jessica would be on the video call.

She adjusted her shirt to ensure there was no nipple action but crossed her arms just in case. Better to be safe than sorry.

Her thoughts whirled back to their moment in the kitchen, and— "You turned off the oven, right?" she blurted.

"Yeah, guess dinner will have to wait," he said softly and pushed upright to a standing position once Asher filled the screen.

"Hey, guys," Asher said around a yawn. The loose-fitting black tank he was wearing showcased his muscular arms, each one currently cradling a daughter. His hair was longer than the last time she'd seen him as it was now up in a messy man bun.

"Hey, man," A.J. commented, arms folding as he stood alongside her chair.

"Congratulations," Ana said with a smile. "Beautiful."

Asher lowered his attention to his daughters. "Juliana and Arabella, this is Special Agent Anastasia Quinn, can you say hi?" He gently rocked back and forth in the desk chair, a view of Manhattan outside the window behind him.

"They might have Jessica's brains and good looks, thank

God," A.J. teased, "but I doubt they can wave or talk at three months old."

Asher rolled his eyes before looking at Ana. "I imagine you're ready to knock the cowboy in the back of the head by now?"

Ana peered at A.J., catching his profile as he kept his eyes steady on the screen. "There have been moments."

"I bet," Asher said with a grin. "Jessica should be here in a second."

"So, how's it being a father to two girls?" Ana asked while they waited, trying to fill the sudden uncomfortable silence, nervous Asher might pick up on the sexual tension between her and A.J. through the screen.

"They're more work than infiltrating a Pakistani compound in the dead of night without any ISR to back you up and no QRF on standby," Asher answered, continuing to rock ever so slightly, and he positioned a pacifier into his one daughter's mouth without losing hold of either little bundle. That took skills.

"You have your in-laws, and your mom, oh, and your sister, Sarah, as your QRF. Luckier than most," A.J. said, his tone light and joking. "But, man, we miss you out here with us."

"I'm itching to spin back up, but I, um." Asher cleared his throat and dropped the rest of what he was about to say. Had he caught himself on the verge of exposing the truth about his team? "I mean, I miss all that highly fulfilling private security work," he corrected himself.

Before anyone could speak, Jessica sat in the swivel chair next to him and gently took one baby girl. "Hey, how are you holding up?"

"Hanging in there." *And nearly making out with A.J. in the kitchen.*

Jessica's eyes made a scrutinizing sweep over Ana. *Shit, did she know something?* "My contact confirmed Ivan Smirnoff, The Huntsman, was in fact in Miami this weekend before going to Atlanta."

"Our working theory is that Ivan went to Miami for the second Volkov source," Asher added. "I assume even the great Ivan was unable to get to him because the FBI had already placed him in protective custody."

"So, we think Ivan led the Bureau to Atlanta, under the impression his next target was going to be the Iranian, when in fact it was for the purpose of drawing out and abducting a Fed to press for intel about the Volkov's location in Miami," Jessica went on.

"Which, frankly, is why the big guns shouldn't be going out into the field to begin with," Asher pointed out. They made a great team the way they bounced back and forth off each other.

"If you're suggesting Ivan got to Porter, well, Porter's tough," Ana said quickly, because Asher had no idea what was really going on, and how could he? She hadn't revealed anything to A.J. or his team. But no, Porter wasn't really in Atlanta for the Iranian.

Ana felt A.J. twisting to the side to peer her way, and when she checked—yup, his eyes were set on her. A question mark hanging between them that said *What do you know that we don't?*

"Our contact at the FBI also said Porter no longer has access to the FBI servers in case he is being tortured for information." Jessica tickled her baby's stomach and made a *coo* noise as though the subject of torture was akin to talking about the weather. But her comment gave Ana a reprieve from A.J.'s unspoken question, at least. "Your access has been revoked as well. Half your teammates believe you were taken, and the other half think you're the mole." She'd spoken more casually than Ana expected, or maybe Jessica was exhausted from sleep deprivation. *Or* Jessica was attempting to use spy tradecraft on Ana to continue getting a read on Ana's true intentions. Based on the way Jessica was looking at her, it didn't seem like she was as eager to trust Ana the way A.J. had.

"I assumed they would change our passcodes." Griff was probably leading the charge against her. Halle and Dean were most likely on her side. The others were a coin toss. And she wasn't sure where Gray would fall.

All of the passion that had sizzled through her body began to fade with their conversation, and she flinched at the feel of A.J.'s hand on her shoulder. When had he come to stand behind her?

"But still not on the wanted list yet, right?" A.J. asked for confirmation.

Yet. He must've assumed she would be at some point. The cards weren't going to stack up great for her, but she'd known that. The risk was worth it.

"No, I think the Bureau is hesitant to do so because then they'd have to explain why you're on the wanted list," Asher pointed out. "Also, they don't want to scare the hell out of people about The Huntsman running around America. So, we have some time."

"But probably not very much," Jessica noted, her voice lower, the baby in her arms falling asleep. "Also, it appears The Huntsman, or whoever is pulling the strings, had the Albanian wire money out of an account that belonged to Hamas."

"Yeah, I'm guessing this story doesn't end well for the Albanians, especially since Hamas's money was supposedly going toward making a dirty bomb." A.J.'s hand left her shoulder, but he remained behind her.

Ana's arms slipped at Jessica's announcement, but then she remembered why they were crossed, so she returned her forearms to cover her chest.

"Yeah, it's not good," Asher said with a grimace. "Hamas has twenty-seven million reasons to be angry."

"Let's just say the Feds in Boston are trying to prevent a total bloodbath from happening between the Albanians and Hamas," Jessica added.

"Well, bright side, looks like Ivan Smirnoff may have inadvertently helped the Feds catch a few baddies by kidnapping that Albanian source." A.J.'s hand brushed against her head, and she stole a look over her shoulder to see his hands gripping the back of her chair.

His focus swept to her face for a brief moment, and that intense look in his eyes was a reminder that no, maybe not even work talk could totally crush the feelings inside of her. One look and she was blazing hot again. How was it possible? "We have any idea where the twenty-seven million went?" A.J. reset his attention on the computer screen.

"Twenty-*two* million went to an account in the Maldives, and if it weren't for the help of Harper and Natasha, I may not have found that one so fast. But the five million that went to a bank account in the Cayman Islands was an easy find," Jessica said. "I still haven't cracked who the accounts belong to, but I'm working on it. The assumption is the five million is payment to The Huntsman."

"If someone shows up to collect from the bank in the Maldives, the FBI won't be able to make a move," Ana said with irritation. "No extradition there."

"Well, the good news for us is that the bank in the Maldives requires on-site access for removal or transfer of the funds. Someone will have to come and sign for it to access the twenty-two million," Jessica commented. "We'll have a team watching the bank and waiting. Once we identify the account holder, they'll already be there to move in."

She made it sound so easy. Bypassing red tape. No forms to fill out. No judge approval.

"The Feds only sent a team to the bank down in the Caymans since they haven't actually tracked the other transfer yet, and we're not in a hurry to tell them. We won't be going to the Caymans. The Feds can handle that. Not interested in any run-ins with them." Jessica's explanation meant that whoever hired A.J.'s team to follow Ana's unit wasn't the FBI.

"So, who is heading to the Maldives?" A.J. asked. "Don't tell me Luke and Knox have to hop back on a plane already." He released the chair, which had it moving ever so slightly at the loss of his grip.

"Yeah, but hopefully it's a quick trip," Jessica answered.

"Twenty-two million is a pretty good motivator for kidnapping the Albanian accountant," Asher commented. "But why take the scientist? The ballerina? Why go after the Volkov source in Miami now?"

"The mole at the FBI, assuming there is one, cherry-picked those sources for a reason. Maybe each one has the potential to provide a big payday, I don't know. But until we figure out the motive, or possible connection between the missing sources, we'll be chasing our tails," A.J. said, eyes back on the screen. "But my money is on the Russians."

"Which Russians?" Asher grinned. "Team SVR or Volkov?"

These guys and their humor. "Do you mind telling me who directed your team to identify the leak? What if they want you looking at my unit as a distraction from the real problem?"

Based on the way Jessica's mouth tightened before peering at the father of her babies, it was clear she wasn't going to offer a name. Classified. "We're under good authority to believe the man *or* woman who hired us is clean," Jessica announced after an uncomfortable few moments passed. "But the FBI did learn *you* may not be exactly who your file claims you to be. We're waiting on an updated dossier now." Jessica's next pause spelled more bad news. "In fact, we learned the man you made a pass with yesterday near your office was Dominick Volkov. And well, Dominick hasn't been seen in fifteen years, just like his older cousin *Grigory* Volkov."

Ana's eyes dropped to the shiny, new wood floors, taking a moment to breathe. To figure a way out of this mess. But there was only one way, wasn't there?

Ana pushed back in her seat, slowly stood, and faced A.J. to look directly into his eyes. "My real last name isn't Quinn," she whispered, her voice shaky. "And my parents were Volkov spies."

CHAPTER SEVENTEEN

Aɴᴀ ᴄʟᴜᴛᴄʜᴇᴅ ʜᴇʀ ᴀʀᴍs ᴛɪɢʜᴛʟʏ ᴀᴄʀᴏss ʜᴇʀ ᴀʙᴅᴏᴍᴇɴ, concern about her see-through shirt forgotten at the sight of A.J.'s mouth dropping open in surprise. The hurt and shock in his green eyes struck her with fierce intensity and had her drawing in quick, panicky breaths. "I'm sorry." She turned and brushed past him, bolting for the door.

"Ana, wait!" he called out, but his words only had her moving faster.

She paused in the hallway to determine a direction. The right would lead her outside.

"Ana," A.J. called softly this time, his voice heavy with disbelief. When she glimpsed back into the room, finding his hands on his hips, his gaze set on her, there was more than shock in the lines of his face. Disappointment. Disgust. Her worst fears.

"I'm sorry," she mouthed, then chose her target, the back of the house.

Once outside on the porch, she hurried to the railing that overlooked a landscape that appeared to go on for miles. She clutched the wide-plank strip of wood and sealed her eyes closed, gasping in fresh, although hot, air.

The sight of A.J.'s expression was enough to crush her, to stamp out her hope that something would develop between them. This was why she'd vowed to reveal her true identity before she let her guard down, let his lips touch hers.

The pained look on his face had enveloped his features like thick fog over San Francisco Bay. What if he still viewed her with apprehension even after she explained herself? What if a seed of doubt now grew in the back of his mind and he'd always worry she'd betray the country as her parents had?

Her body went rigid. Strung tight, like always. The relaxed sensation from their playful and flirtatious banter in the kitchen was gone, and she desperately wanted it back.

She wanted A.J. to look at her with affection and longing as he'd done when she was pinned against his strong, muscular frame. Like a woman deserving of love and passion. Not the daughter of Russian spies who made a career of betraying the U.S.

Tears leaked from her closed eyes. Unexpected and unwanted.

She clenched one hand into a fist and slammed it down onto the wood, so angry at herself for believing anything would ever change. Even if her mission was successful, she'd always be Anastasia Chernyshevsky, the daughter of Volkov spies. Daughter of traitors.

Years and years of punishing herself for her parents' sins had a painful sob ripping free from her chest. All the signs she'd missed from her parents while growing up. Signs she'd probably, in part, ignored because she loved them.

My red angel, my sweet Russian doll, her dad had once said upon entering her bedroom while her mom brushed the tangles from her hair, the view of the Golden Gate Bridge out her window.

You're silly, Daddy. I'm not a Russian doll. I'm an American one.

Her dad had revealed a surprise behind his back, and her mom had to stop combing her auburn hair when Ana turned to face her father, excitement in her eyes, knowing he was about to perform a little magic. The blank scrolled paper in his hand was much more than it appeared.

Abracadabra, her father had said with a broad smile and sprinkled his "magic potion" across the page. A drawing of a beautiful doll that resembled Ana appeared before her eyes.

Wow, Daddy. That's your best sketch yet! She'd clutched the paper and lifted it to show her mom before the image would fade away like normal. Like "magic" as her dad had always said.

At the feel of strong hands clasping her upper arms, Ana pulled herself out of the memory and went still as A.J. pressed his chest tight to her back, his chin settling on top of her head. "Shhh, it's okay. It'll be okay, I promise."

Her shoulders slumped, and her entire body became racked with chills at A.J.'s soft, surprising words. And she broke down and cried even more, turning toward him and burying her face into his chest.

He wrapped his arms firmly around her body as she let her emotions free. She didn't understand why he was hugging her. Or why he was trying to make her feel better before demanding answers to questions that were surely on his mind, but she didn't have the energy to challenge his kindness.

"I was shocked. I'm sorry." *He* was apologizing? "I didn't mean to look at you like that," he said near her ear when her tears began to slow. "I'm so sorry."

His continued apologies and attempts to make her feel

better put her over the edge again. Fifteen years' worth of tears she'd held in since her parents died were pouring out of her.

His hands soothed her, moving up and down her back. Her face was turned to the side so she could breathe, but she wasn't prepared to detach herself from his comforting and forgiving embrace.

"I'm the one who is sorry," she said around a hiccup.

"No, you were being brave sharing what must've been hard to say." A.J. placed his hands on either side of her head, urging her to look at him, then stepped back and slid his palms down to cup her wet cheeks as he viewed her with such a sweetness her legs nearly gave out. "I can't imagine what your life must have been like, but I'm here for you. I'm right here," he said with a nod, his brows pulled together.

Her shoulders trembled, and she wanted nothing more than to give in and cry again, but he needed to hear the rest. He deserved the uncomfortable truth she'd never shared with her ex-husband.

"And if you don't want to kiss me anymore after you learn what I have to say?" she whispered. He brought one palm to her mouth and pulled down her lip with his thumb.

"I reckon when the time is right, there ain't a thing in the world you could tell me that will ever stop me from kissing you, not if that's what you want me to do," he said, his voice rough, emotion bleeding through.

"I'm the daughter of spies. I'm slightly OCD. I hate being sticky. And I make way too many lists. I'm stubborn and controlling. I panic-clean," she rattled off her list of reasons why he should stay away from her.

A.J. brought his face within inches of hers. "I don't care."

"But—"

"I. Don't. Care," he said in a low, growly voice. "You're

the woman I haven't been able to stop thinking about for nearly a year. The woman who makes my heart race." He seized one of her palms and set it to his chest. That tender act had her lip quivering with the threat of tears again. "I don't need you to give me a list of reasons to stay away, none of them will compete with my very own list that I got going on myself."

"You have a list?" she asked softly, then shook her head. "Don't tell me, not yet. I, um." She wanted to hear every last word he had to say. To have him kiss every inch of her. But . . . she wouldn't be able to breathe easy and accept what he said as the gospel truth until he heard her story. He had to know what he was getting into before she'd truly let her guard down. "I have so much to tell you."

"I figured that." A small smile touched his lips.

"I should start from the beginning."

"Usually the best place to start." A touch of his typical playful tone had returned, and hearing it loosened her up a little bit. He took her gently by the elbow and motioned to the two white rocking chairs that sat at the center of the grand porch.

Apparently worried she'd lose her balance, A.J. kept hold of her until she was seated, but chose not to sit in the rocker next to her. Instead, he tucked his hands into his pockets and brought his back to one of the posts that held up the porch roof.

She sniffled and swiped whatever smudges of mascara were beneath her eyes, trying to pull herself together.

Had Kyle ever witnessed her cry? Had anyone aside from the Feds outside the movie theater where her parents were shot and killed seen her tears?

No one had seen her cry until A.J., and he was willing and ready to support her. How'd this night ever come to be?

"There is at least one spy within my unit, and it's me."

A.J. swallowed, and his hands shifted out of his pockets at her news, but he was doing his best not to react too quickly. To trust her. And it had her heart doubling in size.

"I'm undercover," she added quickly since she'd failed to mention that crucial fact straight away, too wrapped up with concerns about how A.J. might react. She was so accustomed to carrying around such an enormous amount of guilt about her parents that she'd almost convinced herself she was as guilty as they were, therefore deserving of A.J.'s anger. "I was brought to D.C. with the sole purpose of infiltrating the Volkov organization."

His brows relaxed. "Okay," he said with a nod, followed by one more hard swallow.

"My parents were shot and killed by the FBI when I was sixteen." She held back her tears this time. "It was then that I discovered not only had they been professional con artists my entire life, but they were also Russian spies." Her eyes fell to the wood plank boards. "I never knew my real last name was Chernyshevsky, or that my parents had moved to the U.S. in their twenties from Moscow."

When she peered up, A.J.'s focus was riveted to her. There was no pity in his eyes. Nor was there disgust. It was . . . well, it reminded her of how her parents had often looked at her, whenever she allowed herself to think of the good memories, that is. It was a look of unconditional love. Compassion.

"The Feds' explanation made sense about my parents once I took the time to reexamine my life after they died. The constant moving and name changes they had said were part of new adventures . . ."

A.J. shifted on his feet and put his hands back into his pockets, looking uncomfortable and unsure what to do or how to stand given her news. It wasn't exactly Southern porch-swing conversation. "Why'd they get shot?" he asked, his voice low. "How'd it happen?"

"We were living in D.C. at the time," she began, drawing her hand back over her stomach in hopes to quell the nervous, gnawing pain there. "We'd been out of the country for my sixteenth birthday, and as silly as this sounds, all I had wanted was to go see a movie as my present. To go out and do something normal teenagers did. *The Da Vinci Code* had recently been released, and I begged to go when we got home. My parents agreed to a late showing." Her mouth tightened as she tried to work through the memory without her tone wavering too much from emotion. "I had dropped my new cell phone in the theater, and they waited for me out front while I went to get it." She pressed her forearm even tighter against her abdomen. "I was just passing the concession stand, the smell of fresh popcorn in the air, and at first, I didn't notice the gunshots outside because the popcorn machines were working at full force."

Her eyes fell closed as she relived the moment as if she were sixteen again and not thirty-one.

"When I opened the door to go outside, people were screaming, and a sea of blue—cops and FBI agents—flooded the sidewalk out front. It was disorienting, and I just wanted to find my parents. They'd keep me safe." Her breath hitched. "They always kept me so safe."

Her parents had been criminals. Spies and imposters. And worst of all, traitors. But they'd loved her. And it killed her that she still loved them, even knowing the truth. She wasn't supposed to, but . . .

"But they were the ones who'd been shot. Weapons were on the ground near my parents' outstretched hands. The agents blocked off where they lay. Had to keep the crime scene intact, they said." She slowly opened her eyes to find A.J. crouched before her. He set a hand on her knee and began sweeping small circles over her skin. "I pushed through the officers guarding their bodies to try and get to them. The officers had to practically tackle me to the ground because I refused to give up."

"Jesus, Ana. I'm so sorry." His free hand cupped his mouth.

"They said my parents resisted arrest. That they were armed and opened fire on the agents first. I-I just couldn't believe it. They had their quirks, but criminals? Spies?" Ana shook her head in disbelief exactly as she'd done while sitting at the metal table inside an FBI interview room later that night. "They threw too much at me at once. Volkov spies. The ledger. Counterfeit artwork. Stolen artifacts. They wanted to know why we were in Hungary at the Buda Castle the week before. Did I see anything there? Know anything. They said my parents were sleeper agents and had only been activated the year before. I was so overwhelmed. Spies. Activation. I was clueless. For God's sake, I was only sixteen." She took a moment to catch her breath and steady her nerves.

"You don't have to keep going if this is too much." A.J. removed his hand from her leg and stood, then offered his palm and helped her out of the rocking chair.

"No, it's okay. I need to get through this." She went over to the railing and peered out at the pool that had yet to be filled.

She placed a hand to her neck, knowing it was bare, but her thoughts drifted to the ruby pendant her father had given her the night of her birthday in that castle in Budapest. Her dad's palms had been empty, but in the blink of an eye, he was holding the necklace, offering it to her. Just like magic.

She had to remind herself he wasn't a magician. He was a con artist. A Thief. A Spy. Maybe he even stole the pendant?

"When they died, and I learned my entire life had been a lie, I was so angry. So mad at myself for being manipulated. And upset that I missed them. Frustrated I couldn't stop loving them in the face of the truth." She side-eyed him, finding his elbows resting on the railing, his gaze set on the backyard that stretched for acres.

"That's why you studied criminal and forensic psychology, to ensure you could read people and know their motivations from then on?" He was a quick study.

"Yes," she whispered, her voice hoarse.

"And it's why you have such high walls?" He turned to the side, standing tall again.

She nodded.

"What happened next?"

"Once the FBI decided I'd had no knowledge or involvement in my parents' activities, and I wasn't useful in taking down any other spies, they put me in protective custody. They were worried about the Volkovs looking for me, or the Russians killing me."

"That was when you changed your name?"

"Quinn is the second name change the Feds ordered." So many names over the years she could barely keep them all straight. "I became Quinn when I was eighteen, when I decided to leave protective custody. By then, the Volkovs were yesterday's news, and the FBI agreed I could start a new life. They wiped my history clean to protect me. My records were sealed."

"But then your work profiling for the NYPD gained the FBI's attention?"

"Yes, and after turning the Bureau down twice, it was Porter who changed my mind."

"What?" he asked in surprise. "Why him?"

"He was one of the agents on scene the day my parents died. He'd taken me under his wing. Helped me start over with my life," she admitted, and the news had him pushing back upright. "But when he came to me at twenty-five, requesting I join the Bureau, he helped me understand that becoming an FBI agent would be my chance to make up for all the bad my parents had done."

"He guilt tripped you," A.J. hissed low and under his breath, but Porter saved her, and he was the last person she wanted A.J. angry at. Porter had been the only person she'd been able to count on since her parents died. Having no one else with whom to talk about the truth, he'd been who she had turned to. A father figure. He'd been the one to encourage her to get married and set some roots like she'd never had growing up. The one to give her away at her wedding with Kyle.

"It wasn't like that," she defended. "But I didn't think I had a shot at being hired because of my past."

"And I'm guessing Porter took care of that?" He arched a brow, concern still clinging to his expression.

"He said it wouldn't be a problem, and that my past would be need-to-know outside of those hiring me. He guaranteed no agents I worked with on a day-to-day basis would know the truth."

"How does the 'you're a Russian spy' thing come into play?" he asked after taking a few seconds to process.

"That's kind of where things get complicated."

His lips twitched into a surprising smile. "And what you said before wasn't already complicated?"

"I—" An embarrassingly loud growl escaped her stomach, interrupting her line of thought. *Perfect timing, hunger pains.* Maybe part of that pain in her stomach had been from her lack of any real food aside from gas station snacks earlier and not just the incredibly difficult conversation.

"Hungry?" His smile broadened.

"I think it was a good idea you bought the wine and ice cream. You feel like having that for dinner while I reveal classified intel to a man who has yet to come clean with me?"

He leaned in, and his mouth hovered near hers as if he were going to kiss her.

"You're not planning on going with Avenger again, are you?" she softly asked.

His gaze moved from her mouth to her eyes. "Do you really need to know the truth about me to share your truth?"

She rolled her tongue over her lips. "No." She knew in her heart this man was brought to her for a reason, now more than ever. "I trust you."

CHAPTER EIGHTEEN

A.J. SECURED A BOTTLE OF RED WINE FROM GRANT'S WINE cellar—this occasion now called for something better than what he'd picked up from Piggly Wiggly—and left to find Ana. *I fell for the daughter of Russian spies,* he thought in surprise while trekking up the steps. He'd never had much luck with the Russians in the past, but Ana wasn't her parents, and he refused to believe anything different. No blinders on his eyes.

A.J.'s thoughts kept spinning like he was on a Tilt-A-Whirl as he grabbed a corkscrew and two glasses, then searched for where Ana had disappeared.

He opened the back door and glimpsed Ana off in the distance down by the pond. *Wine in Solo cups it is, then.* He paused mid-turn, his attention falling to the white rocking chair that had him squeezing his eyes shut for a moment. He'd swear it'd been moving. *Losing my mind.* Letting the door shut behind him, he went back to the kitchen to exchange the fancy wineglasses for the red cups he saw stacked in the pantry when he'd been preparing for the chicken dinner.

He grabbed his cowboy hat and went back outside. One quick check of the chair to ensure it wasn't moving—it wasn't—and then he started down the steps and toward the path to get to Ana.

The man-made pond was fifty or so yards away from the house. About twenty-five by thirty in size. Probably stocked with some decent fish, knowing Grant.

Ana had her legs tucked beneath her bottom, looking every bit the gorgeous vision from his dreams. "You're wearing your cowboy hat. Looks good on you." She shielded her eyes with her hand and smiled while looking up at him.

His hands were full, so he couldn't tip his hat like he normally would have. "We should get you one."

"Oh, I don't know about that," she said, her voice softer. She was most likely worn out from crying.

He sat in front of her on the blanket and stretched his legs out before him, while setting the items on the blanket between them.

"*Ménage à Trois*." Her French accent had his skin heating. "Love that brand of wine."

"*Moi aussi*." He responded, *Me, too,* in French, unable to stop himself even though he literally knew nothing of the wine other than it was red.

And no, he did not need to think about the other meaning of the brand's name. Two women in bed with him. Ana would be way more than enough woman for him. God, did she have any idea how she made him feel with those green eyes on him? What her luscious lips did to him?

"*Parles-tu Français?*"

And hot damn, that accent. He could listen to her speak French all day.

"Plus Portuguese, Spanish, and a little bit of everything

when needed." He smiled. "Russian, at times." That merited a throat clear from him.

The mention of Russian was a reminder why they were about to binge on wine and ice cream. He sure as hell wished they were there for another reason. He was pretty sure he was still in shock from her revelation, too.

Seeing her crying on that porch, before she'd shared her story, had shattered any doubts in his mind about her that may have crept in when she announced her parents had been Volkov spies in Grant's office.

Ana's gaze fell to the red and white checkered blanket, her hand smoothing over it. The crickets were beginning to chirp even though it wasn't yet dark. "I found this in the laundry room."

"You sure you want to sit so close to the water. Not worried about gators?"

She immediately started to spring up, but he leaned forward and hooked an arm around her side to keep her in place. "I'm kidding." He unhanded her, reminding himself this wasn't the time to finish the moment they'd shared in the kitchen earlier. He eased back to a seated position, hands going to each side of his body. "It's rare to see a gator around here. We're good."

Her eyes darted suspiciously in the direction of the dark water. "You're sure?"

"Now would I do anything to put you in harm's way?" he asked, laying on his accent a little thicker.

She hesitantly relaxed. "I brought some crackers to help soak up the ice cream and wine."

He followed her eyes to the roll of Ritz. "Certainly an interesting meal to discuss Russian espionage over," he said in a joking tone to try and keep the dark weight of the world from crushing them. "In what order should we ruin our stomachs?"

"I'd say crackers first, but we don't want the ice cream to melt." Her fingers went to her cleavage, a slight sheen of sweat there. "Like I already am."

He bit down on his back teeth, doing his best to return his focus to her eyes instead of wondering how her breasts would feel in his palms. When her wet braid had soaked the spot right over her nipple earlier, it had taken all of his restraint to keep his hands to himself. To not reach out and roll the peaked point between his thumb and forefinger.

"Ice cream," he finally agreed. "Just don't get yourself sticky since you hate that."

"Right." She offered him a spoon and removed the lid, then set the tub down within reach for the both of them.

He watched her take her first lick, then casually lowered his forearm to cover the bulge he anticipated might appear if she kept eating her ice cream like that. "So, Porter."

Ana had been mid-dip into the tub of ice cream for another spoonful and froze at his words.

Mood killer, for sure.

She rested her spoon on top of the lid and shifted her legs, stretching them out in front of her. They were long for such a petite woman.

Ana nervously fidgeted with her braid. It was a "tell" about her mood he doubted she would've ever allowed before arriving in Alabama. "My parents and I were in Budapest a week before they died, then after their death, the Volkovs were all but slaughtered or forced into hiding. It looked as though my parents—"

"Were at the center of everything?" he asked, and she nodded. "How'd the death of your parents trigger the collapse of the Volkovs? I mean, I thought the Volkov leader had created the ledger and key specifically to keep him protected from the SVR."

"How much do you know about the ledger?" she asked, sounding a little surprised at his knowledge of the book.

"Enough." More than he wanted to at this point. And the fact POTUS wanted his hands on it spoke volumes. "How about you tell me what you know?"

She worried her lip between her teeth, eyes on the blanket. "When I was first questioned by the FBI after my parents died, they asked me if I'd ever seen a book. And a code-breaker. I had no clue about it at the time." Ana's green eyes focused once again on A.J. "Not too long after that, the Feds who'd been working the Volkov case for years decided there was never a ledger. I suppose since they couldn't find any evidence of it. Meanwhile, the Russians began killing off Volkov spies. Not only to prevent the U.S. government from turning the Volkovs but because they were also worried Volkov spies would pin their work on the SVR. The Russian administration wanted to prevent going down with the ship, so to speak. And since the SVR had begun converting Americans into spies for money, they didn't need the Volkovs anymore. Well, this is what I learned after joining the FBI, at least."

"But that's not your theory, I take it?" He tipped the brim of his hat a touch lower, shielding his eyes to better see her.

"No, I believe the ledger and its key are real."

"What makes you think that?"

"When Porter approached me four months ago about taking this UC job, he laid out more of the story behind my parents' death." Ana took a moment, most likely composing her thoughts. Cataloging them in the proper order that made the most sense to share. "Shortly *before* my parents died,

Porter said he arrested a Volkov agent. The man was offered a cushy deal in exchange for intel, and the man claimed both the ledger and key had been stolen from Adrik three months before, which Adrik adamantly denied."

"Because if the ledger and its key were real and the only thing keeping the SVR in check, Adrik wouldn't be fool enough to let anyone know they were no longer in his hands." That made sense, and as much as he hadn't really believed in the book before, well, he believed in Ana, so . . .

"Then rumors began floating around that a redheaded female Volkov agent and her husband were the ones who somehow stole the ledger and key from Adrik. Porter's source offered multiple stories as to how the couple actually stole the items, but all that mattered was the items were out of Adrik's hands." She grimaced, and he knew where her mind was going.

Visions of what Ana's mother may have looked like came to mind. The golden-red hair. Same green eyes, too, he imagined.

He couldn't stomach the idea of anything or anyone ever coming between him and his family. He hated Ana had to handle all of this, and without ever feeling as though she could share with the man she'd married . . .

He forced his focus back to her. "You think your parents are the ones who stole the ledger and key from Adrik?"

"It fits with the timeline. Our trip to Hungary over my birthday wasn't my first time there. We'd also attended another party at the labyrinth around the time the ledger and key went missing," Ana responded. "And my mother had distinctively red hair."

"Okay, let's say they did. The more important question is, why?"

"Best guess? Greed." She let the admission hang in the air, clearly frustrated for not being able to solve the puzzle.

"So, how'd they do it?" A.J. mused.

"Think about what the Feds told me my parents did before they were activated to spy for the Volkovs."

"Con artists. Thieves." He wished they could go back to her licking ice cream from the spoon and his dick stirring— no, saluting her—in his pants.

She nodded, her brows scrunched tight. "My dad was practically an illusionist. Made things appear and disappear literally before my eyes all the time. His magic tricks were my favorite memories of him." She closed her eyes for a second as if scolding herself for allowing any happy thoughts to remain in her mind.

"Both the Volkovs and the SVR would have reason to kill your parents if they discovered they stole them."

She sat taller, her spine going straight, outwardly relieved to be sharing everything even if it was a painful subject matter. "While my parents and I were at the theater, our house was ransacked. Porter told me when the team showed up to my home, the place was already destroyed."

And damn did he admire her strength. She was opening up to him in a way that, only yesterday, he hadn't been sure was possible. "Would your parents have kept the ledger and key at their house?" That didn't seem all that smart to do with such valuable items. Not even in a safe, well, unless someone wanted them found.

"Maybe not the *originals,* but I think whoever tore apart our home believed they'd found them. Or at least one of them," she answered, a mirror to his thoughts.

She tucked her lips inward for a moment, and for the briefest of guilty seconds, he wanted to suck that lip. Tease it between his teeth. If only he could make all her pain and suffering go away with a kiss. If only life were so easy.

"My parents had no qualms about stealing, so they certainly wouldn't hesitate about making copies of the ledger and key. The Feds said my parents used to counterfeit everything. Obviously, I didn't know the paintings I saw come and go from our house over the years were fakes, but thinking back, they couldn't have been real. Van Goghs. Picassos." Her tight, nervous expression loosened a touch. "What if my parents stole the ledger and key while we were in Hungary, three months before their death, just like Porter's source had claimed? They could have hired the forger they always worked with to create copies of both. And before you ask, at the time, I didn't know he was a forger, but it makes sense that they would have one given their line of work."

"You know, you reading my mind is kind of unnerving," he said, going for a sip of wine because this really was like the plot of a Tom Cruise *Mission Impossible* movie.

"Occupational hazard," she smirked. "Knowing my dad, he planted the forgeries in our home, but hid the real ones. Probably in two separate locations. An insurance policy perhaps? So, while the FBI were busy killing my parents, Russian agents probably stole one or both of the forged copies. And since no one came forward with another copy of either after that night, the SVR felt it safe to target the Volkovs."

His eyes fell to the ice cream as the chocolate liquified. "And if the real ones were hidden by your parents, they became lost forever with their deaths."

"Well, lost for fifteen years, at least. Grigory claimed to have found the ledger and key to keep the SVR at bay, but I know he doesn't have both. And as to whether he has the original ledger or another forged copy, I have no idea."

A.J.'s gaze whipped back to her face, first to her full lips before meeting her hunter green eyes. "Yeah, no way does Grigory Volkov also have the key, or he wouldn't be so willing to cooperate with you. He needs the key to protect himself from the SVR." A.J. paused for a moment because something wasn't adding up. "How can you be sure Grigory found the ledger? It could be another rumor."

"Because I've spoken to Grigory Volkov." Her admission sounded more like a plea of "guilty" in a courtroom. What did she mean she spoke to Grigory Freaking Volkov? Was she already in that deep?

"What?" He retracted his hand from her leg on reflex, but he didn't want to be that guy again. That guy back in the office whose shocked reaction had her fleeing the room in shame.

A lifetime of betrayal flashed in her green eyes, but he refused to hurt her. He set his hand back on her thigh and looked into her eyes. He offered her a tight nod he hoped conveyed, *I won't let you down.* Her lashes were wet, but there weren't any more tears. She was a stunningly beautiful woman who'd been put through the Russian wringer of life.

"After Porter came to me with my new assignment—to infiltrate the Volkovs—he presented a few possible Volkov sources to look into to help me gain access to the organization."

"Katya was one of them?"

"Yeah, I tracked her every move for about a month. She was dating Dominick Volkov, and I caught him having an affair." A soft blush crawled over her cheeks as if embarrassed she caught Dominick having sex. "I used that as my chance to turn her to work with the Bureau. She admitted she never really wanted to be a spy for the Volkovs, but Dominick had pressured her into it."

"Katya helped you make contact with Dominick, then?" *But what about Grigory?* He'd do his best to let her unravel the "complicated" story, now understanding why she'd opted for part two of their talk down by the pond.

"No, not officially. It'd be too risky for her since she was going to work with the FBI. But from my surveillance of her, I was able to track Dominick to an apartment in Newark, New Jersey. I made first contact, but he was hesitant to trust me."

A.J. removed his hat, swiping the slight sheen of sweat from his brow before setting it back on. "You had to offer him Katya?"

"Yes, but in exchange, Katya was going to receive a cushy payout, new identity, and a chance to be free of the Volkovs. She was okay with the arrangement," Ana explained, her tone confident.

"What exactly was the plan? How were you going to do that?" He'd swear he was smart, but every so often while they spoke, he found himself wondering if he'd be able to find his ass with both hands in his pockets. Maybe he'd blame the two bumps on his head.

Ice cream—no, milkshake break, anyone?

"Since the Russian government was the most notable enemy of the Volkovs, why not ensure the Volkovs in Hungary intercepted word that a Russian hitman had been hired to take out a Volkov asset in the U.S.?" She paused for a breath as though her thoughts moved faster than her mouth could. "Once I gave Dominick Katya's identity as an FBI asset, the plan was to have her moved into witness protection and make it look like she'd been killed by a Russian hitman before the Volkovs got a chance to get to her themselves."

"With her believed to be dead, she really could have started over. No one would be looking for her," he said with a nod, trying to keep up with her. "Plus, you would've given Dominick what he wanted, proving your loyalty. But it wasn't your fault that the SVR got to Katya first considering the beef between the two organizations." *Damn brilliant.*

"Only something obviously went wrong. There was never supposed to be a real kidnapping, but Ivan Smirnoff must've somehow got to Katya hours before the plan was set into motion to move her to WITSEC for what was supposed to be the fake hit."

"So, where does this forger who supposedly worked for your parents come into play?" In this heat, and with his shirt beginning to cling like something fierce, she might need to spell it out for him. He was growing a bit light-headed.

"When I told Porter about my dad's only lifelong friend, who also happened to show up with artwork every time he visited, Porter suggested he may be a forger, and he began looking for him."

"Did Porter confirm he was a counterfeiter of sorts?"

"Yes, his name is Anthony Vincenzi, an Italian artist by day, and a forger by night. And if Anthony can verify he made copies of the originals, maybe he made more? Or knows where my parents would have hidden the real ones?"

"So, now you're offering the Volkovs the forger, am I right? You told Grigory copies were made?" Heat exhaustion or not, it was clear why everything hinged on her leaving D.C. regardless of what the Bureau would think about her actions. A woman on a mission, but even if Porter kept the UC assignment on the down low, there had to be evidence of her work in the FBI server, right? Someone over Porter's head had to have signed off on the UC operation.

"Yes, and that's how my contact with Grigory comes into play. A few weeks ago, I told Dominick that the Bureau believed *someone* forged the original ledger and key fifteen years ago. I told him I would track down the forger. And the next day, I heard from Grigory Volkov himself. He was interested in the key, not the ledger, which I assume means he is already in possession of either the original or a copy. But if I can find the key, I can use it to draw out Grigory and take him down, as well as identify any remaining spies in the U.S. listed in that book."

"What I don't get is why your parents would hide a real or a fake ledger in Budapest, the location where it was originally stolen. I assume they did it that week before they died. But that doesn't make much sense to me."

Her hand went to the column of her throat before sliding beneath the fabric of her tee telling him the heat was now getting to her, too. "There are so many ideas spinning in my head, and it's mostly speculation for now. But that's why I am down here. To get answers. Porter left me a message yesterday to go dark. He said he finally found the forger, and he's planning to bring him to our safe house on Friday. Anthony's my best shot."

"Best shot at what?" A.J.'s stomach dropped. He had a good idea what she was going to say and really didn't want to hear it.

When Ana looked away and toward the pond, he knew he was fucked. How would he protect a woman who'd resent his protection as she'd done with her ex? "Trying to understand what my parents were up to. Find the real key."

"And you agreed to do this because . . .?" His back, shoulders, neck—everything tensed up, including his hands as they rested on the blanket on each side of his body.

"Because my parents are the reason why so many people died. Because they were criminals. Spies. Because I'm the

Bureau's best hope to get on the inside, and Porter didn't know who to trust. He's worried there are still spies working for Russia at Headquarters." She held her palms open. "You pick a reason." Her tone switched to defense-mode, anxious he'd try and stop her mission.

He scooted closer and brought a hand to her knee.

"I knew what I was signing up for when Porter laid the truth out four months ago. I was well aware of the risks. I had to prove to the Volkovs I wasn't entrapping them. But now, with the missing sources, it's clear someone at Headquarters is dirty. Possibly sabotaging me. The timing can't be a coincidence, not when I'd planned to have Katya go missing last week. Everything was falling into place until—"

"The missing sources," he finished on a frustrated sigh. He was terrified for her, but he also admired her determination. Now more than ever, he knew why Ana was so tense and wound tight. Saying she had a lot on her plate would be an understatement.

"Yesterday, I tried to buy myself some time and offered up the identity of the FBI's second Volkov source, knowing full well they wouldn't be able to get to him in Miami."

He thought back to the car with Chris just yesterday outside the Hoover Building. It felt like a week ago, though. "That was the pass you made with Dominick yesterday?"

"Yeah, and earlier today, I told Grigory I found the forger, but I had no choice. I didn't want him to question my loyalty and lose the chance to get to him."

A.J. closed his eyes at her admission. His heart squeezed uncomfortably. "You talked to him today?" he asked again to ensure he'd heard her correctly, doing his best not to feel betrayed at the news she'd been on the phone with a dangerous criminal without his knowledge.

"Yes, and as poorly as everything turned out with having

to look guilty to my colleagues, this plan might actually work. I think Grigory will arrange a meeting in Budapest. He wants the key himself. He won't trust anyone else to get it first."

"You're seriously considering meeting with the new leader of the Volkovs, a man the SVR wants dead, without the FBI backing you up?" He did his best not to sound sarcastic, but damn, was she insane?

"Of course not. Porter was going to arrange a team to follow me, but then he had to go dark, and now I am too, so . . ."

"I'm thinking I won't be able to stop you from going through with this, but can I at least back you up?" If she said no, though, he'd have to piss her off and protect her anyway.

"Are you sure you're okay with that? I don't want to endanger your team."

His eyes stretched. "I'm here with you through this. My team is in Bama, too. We'll figure this out together. You don't have to keep all this bottled up inside anymore. It's not good for you."

She swiped a fallen tear and looked away from him as if suddenly worried that one tear was more painful or revealing than the ones on the porch earlier.

His palm slid up her leg, stopping shy of her shorts. "But, Ana, what if Grigory Volkov knows your parents were the ones who stole the ledger and key in the first place? They're the reason forged copies exist. What if the revenge he might be looking for includes hurting you?"

"Porter mentioned that risk, too."

"And you ignored it?" His free hand knotted at his side with his need to protect her from the likes of the Volkovs of the world. And from men in suits at the Bureau who were willing to do whatever it took, including risk Ana's life, to close a case.

"It's worth the risk." She reminded A.J. of Natasha and her conviction to chase down The Knight. But that case had brought Wyatt and Natasha together, and now they were getting married in a month.

"Not in my eyes." He stood and removed his hat, on edge thinking about the million things that could have gone wrong had A.J. and his team not been assigned to surveil Ana.

Everything happens for a reason.

"A.J., please." She rose and stepped around the blanket to get closer to him.

"Who else, aside from Porter, knew about your undercover work?" Something was still bothering him about all of this, well, aside from all the other things bothering him.

"I don't know, but Porter didn't want a record of my assignment in the system at the Bureau, too worried about sensitive information being hacked, or falling into corrupt hands."

"And you don't find that suspicious?" He wasn't too keen on Porter at the moment.

"He had to get someone to sign off on the assignment. Someone he trusted, but they won't be able to vouch for me when shit hits the fan, and the blame gets pointed my way. They won't be able to risk clearing my name, especially since someone else is clearly leaking sources. And I'd rather the world think I'm loyal to the Volkovs for now. This might be my only shot to take them down once and for all."

He closed the space between them and seized her shoulders, unable to stop himself, worry and frustration tearing him apart. "Ana, you can't throw your life away for one mission."

"My reputation can be repaired," she said, lifting her chin to find his eyes. "You don't need to worry about me."

"It's kind of hard not to worry." He bent closer, still holding her shoulders. His heart and mind were too heavy. "But everything will be okay," he promised because he needed to hear it himself. To believe he wouldn't lose Ana like he'd lost his best friend.

CHAPTER NINETEEN

"YOU SHOULD EAT." A.J. QUICKLY FOLLOWED ANA ONTO THE porch. "You don't need to go clean the mess by the pond. I'll get that." But like the adorably stubborn woman she was, she kept on moving.

"You know I panic-clean. I can't relax knowing we left a mess out there." She tossed him a smile over her shoulder, which was damn near shocking since they'd just spent the last half hour on a video-call with Asher and Jessica retelling the story Ana had shared with A.J. He was fairly certain it'd been much more difficult for her this time around. He'd helped her fill in the blanks whenever she stopped speaking mid-sentence as though lost in her own thoughts.

"I'm surprised you can relax at all after tonight." He hurried to catch up with her and they nearly collided when she abruptly stopped and whirled around to face him.

"So, help me."

"I said I'd . . ." He raised a brow. Ah, she was playing with him. A.J. put his hands on his hips, deciding to play along. "Help you do what exactly, darlin'?"

Ana flattened her palm against his chest, and it was a reminder his attraction to her was still very much on the forefront of his mind even after the news she'd dropped on him.

"Help me relax in a way that doesn't involve cleaning." Her words were laced with seduction, bringing a cocky grin to his face and dirty thoughts to his mind. "I don't want to be high-strung and tense."

He brushed the back of his hand over her cheek before reaching for her braid. "Your beautiful red hair," he announced, giving it a small tug. "The first step is to let it down."

"My hair?" Her forehead tightened. The opposite of what he wanted to happen.

"You know that saying about letting your hair down and living a little?" He pulled the black hair tie free and tossed it in the grass. She stared up at him, her green eyes wide, as he loosened the braid with his fingers, his pulse quickening at the feel of the silky strands. The memory of their near kiss in the kitchen coming back to mind. She had wanted to wait until he knew the truth. Well, he knew now, and he sure as hell wasn't going anywhere.

She shook her head once her hair was hanging free. "Now what?"

He peeked around where she stood and put eyes on the pond. "When I was a boy, and I had a bad day, I used to swim. Go jump in a lake, pond, river—you name it. It helped cool me off. Literally and figuratively."

She slowly turned to face the pond. "Cool off in there?"

"Mmmhmm." He marched past her, deciding not to take no for an answer.

"No way. Too many unknown variables."

"So what?" He removed his hat and placed it on the

blanket, away from any melted ice cream, then peeled off his gray shirt. "This is about relaxing."

"Not sure how relaxed I'll be if I'm worried something will swim up my shorts." Her tone softened as she spoke, her eyes roaming over his abs. She drew a finger down the line of her chest to her navel as if picturing her touch was on him instead.

It took all of his strength to stifle the low growl that'd nearly escaped at the image of her hand caressing his bare skin.

Ana fidgeted with the material of her shirt, and he had the feeling she was itching to remove it but was scared. "You sure?"

He stepped in front of her and offered her his palm. "I've never been surer about anything in my life." He banded a hand around her waist and tipped his chin to the sky. "Sunset is at eight, and by my estimates, that was twenty-two minutes ago. You won't get a better sky to swim beneath than a Southern one like this." Streaks of gold, pink, and blue lazily rolled overhead.

Ana reached for his left wrist and pulled it closer to eye his waterproof watch. "You peeked at the time first, right? No way are you that accurate."

"I was probably off by one or two minutes." He winked, and she playfully swatted his chest before allowing her palm to rest on his pec.

As her gaze glided down to her hand, he brought their bodies so close he was sure she'd be able to feel the hum of electricity, of want, pulsating off him.

"You got a bra and panties on under there?"

"You want me to take my clothes off?" Her focus flew to his face. "Is my relaxed state contingent upon that?" A challenging eyebrow had his smile stretching. It had him forgetting about Russian espionage. American traitors. The danger Ana was in.

"It'll be a hell of a lot more freeing to swim without your clothes on. And what's a bra and underwear but a bikini, anyway?"

She made an adorable hissing sound. "You know damn well my bra is see-through, especially when wet."

"I barely remember that." But his grasp on her hip tightened at the memory. "Maybe you ought to remind me."

"Oh, sure." Her chin lifted in challenge to his words. "I guarantee you remember—"

"Exactly how much you were turned on back in that kitchen?" Keeping his tone playful was proving harder than normal with her hand on his chest, his palm on her waist. He was itching to do a lot more with her than stand by the water and listen to the chorus of crickets chirping off in the woods behind the edge of the pond.

"I, um." It sure was fun rendering her speechless.

A.J. forced himself to unhand her and backed up. "So, I'm taking off my shorts and jumping in. I hope you'll 'relax,'" he said with air quotes, "and join me with or without your clothes on."

He unbuckled his brown belt and unbuttoned his shorts before kicking them off to the side. He glanced over to see her eyes glued to his boxers so intently that if she looked much harder, she might see right through them.

"Of course you'd have patriotic underwear." And there her hand went, trailing down from her breastbone to the waistband of her shorts again.

"You counting the stars?" He winked once she'd ripped her focus back to his face. "You can believe me when I say there are fifty. One for each state." And with that, he reached forward, grabbed her upper arms and spun her around quickly before she realized what he was doing. He gently pinned her back to his chest and held her still, their bodies facing the motionless water. "Look." A.J. nudged her cheek with his chin. Little fireflies blinked in the air before them, their light barely a twinkle since it wasn't too dark out yet. Her skin was warm, and her body relaxed against him. "I can hold your hand. We can go in together."

"No." She shook her head. "And what are those sounds?" She tipped her head to the side as if searching to define the "sounds" of Alabama surrounding them like a symphony of nature.

"You ain't ever heard an owl before?" He chuckled, his mouth dangerously close to her ear. Based on how her body had responded to him in the kitchen, he knew if he whispered his words against her skin, she'd go weak in the knees. He wanted to see her tremble like that again. "No bullfrogs in those big cities you lived in, either, I'm betting," he teased at the sounds of the crying frogs.

"No, none." He felt her body tense in his embrace, and he was worried Alabama's normally seductive voice wasn't quite Ana's song. A few more days, and he was sure that'd change.

"Well, I'm going in. It's your loss if you don't join me, sugar." He smoothed his thumbs down the sides of her arms, then sidestepped her to jump into the pond, remembering Grant had said it was shallow. Less than five feet deep, so no diving.

A.J. dropped to the bottom of the pond, fully submerging himself, and held his breath for a bit. He always found himself at peace when underwater.

He popped up and swiped the beads of water from his face and hair. Ana's rounded mouth, followed by her crossing her arms with dramatic emphasis, meant she'd been worried about his length of time beneath the surface. "You do remember I'm a Teamguy, right? We have to hold our breath for a long damn time." When he grinned, she shot him daggers. The soft, pillow kind that soothed his soul because it meant the woman cared, even if she didn't want to admit it. "Awfully refreshing in here."

Her nerves were still all tangled up, but he was fairly certain it was more about letting go and jumping in and not because of the truth she'd laid on him about her family.

"I just don't know if I can do it." Indecision warred across her face, but the cute way she wrinkled her nose told him she had an aching need to join him and relax—he could feel the imprint of that need as surely as he heard Mother Nature cocooning them with her lyrics and ambiance.

"No snappers in here." He lowered himself in the water up to his chin and tipped his head back. "And probably no snakes."

"Probably?" she shrieked.

Holding in a small laugh, A.J. stood up straight in the water. "Kidding." *Mostly.* He cupped his hands together on the surface of the pond and then squirted water in her direction. "It's clearly not that deep. You're good. Promise." He motioned to his tossed shorts. "And I have a knife in my pocket if we find ourselves on the other side of an angry turtle."

"You're hilarious," she responded, *but* she strode closer, now mere inches from the edge of the pond.

"Come on, it feels great, and you need a refreshing swim. Nothing like pond water to clear your head."

An inquisitive brow shot up. "Oh, is that a thing?"

"If it needs to be a thing, why then, yes." He waded another few feet in Ana's direction, pinning her with a determined look meant to let her know he'd not hesitate to spring up, grab her, and pull her in with him. Of course, he'd prefer her to discard her clothes first, but baby steps. "You're coming in one way or another," he warned. His words were playful, but the deep, rough tone of his voice did nothing to hide the lust coursing through him.

"You're going to be my undoing, Mr. Hawkins." She backed up about ten feet and mouthed *one, two, three,* then ran forward and leaped into the pond, tucking her legs to her chest.

The sight of her letting loose had his heart tightening with emotion.

When she sprang up out of the water, only inches away from him, he couldn't help himself—he reached under the water and tickled her leg.

She yelped and leapt into his arms, right where he wanted her. "You!" she exclaimed, her nose brushing against his as his hands settled around her bottom. He held her against him and secured her legs around his hips.

"And looky there," he began, eyes moving to her wet shirt now molded to her skin. "Shirt or not, I can see you as plain as day."

Her chin dipped to assess her body. Her nipples practically strained through the bra and fabric, begging for his mouth to take a taste.

"I get the distinct feeling I'm the cause of that lip constantly slipping between your teeth," he said at the sight of her bottom lip tucked inward.

With her arms slung over his shoulders, hands resting at the nape of his neck, she whispered in a sensual tone, "You may be right."

Ana's breathing quickened, and her soaking wet shirt only made her breasts more enticing. The sight of her almost nude like that was fucking erotic. A.J. had to fight to slow his own breathing and restrain himself from sucking her lip between *his* teeth instead. "I know it doesn't make a lick of sense," he began, his accent thickening, "with all these obstacles in our way, but I've never wanted anyone more than I want you." He'd been torn on whether or not to reveal his feelings, but after everything she'd shared with him—she deserved to know what he was thinking. And he wanted her to hear it.

"Even after you learned the truth?" Broad strokes of surprise had the depth of her tone lowering to a feminine huskiness.

He kept his hands positioned beneath her ass so as not to lose hold of her, then tilted his head. "Yes, but I'm pretty sure all you gotta do is look in my eyes, and you'll be able to read me. See exactly how I feel." They bobbed in the water a little as he moved them side to side, never wanting to lose this moment. "Isn't there some saying that a woman can tell how a man feels by looking in his eyes?"

"And how can a man tell how a woman feels?" Her lips tipped into a beautiful smile.

"There." He nodded. "It's all in your smile."

"And what does my smile tell you?" she murmured as he continued to slowly move them in a circle, mesmerized by this enchanting woman.

"That you want me to kiss you."

The crook of her lips and her playful, "Oh, do I?" had his pulse speeding up.

"You do," he whispered, never having felt so nervous about a kiss in all his life.

She slid her hands up the back of his neck and into his hair as she sucked on her bottom lip like he'd wanted to do. "Then what are you—"

His mouth captured hers. Stole her words. Her breath. His breath, too.

Slowly and sensually. Close-mouthed. Soft kisses. A trace of her lip with his tongue. A war within his mind as he battled not to bruise her mouth with a crushing kiss given the fierce intensity with which he wanted to make love to her. To kiss every inch of her pale skin.

Her lips relaxed against his, but she let her eagerness for more passion show when her hands went to his shoulders, her nails gently biting into his skin. He accepted her invitation for "more" by releasing a growl from his throat and parting her mouth with his tongue.

A blazing trail of heat scorched through him when her tongue met his. His eyes were closed, but he'd swear the fireflies were lighting up all around him. The crickets chirped louder. The sounds of night embraced them in that moment.

With his knees slightly bent, he continued to hold on to her, keeping their shoulders above the water as they kissed.

Her walls were down for him. The undulating of her hips grinding against him beneath the water drew a soft mewl sound from her mouth.

"Mmmm," she said on a sigh when their lips detached a minute later. "Please tell me whatever I feel pressing against me is your cock and not something that will bite me."

Cock? That word made him wonder if she might talk dirtier in bed, and damn was he anxious to find out.

He nipped at her lip, teasing it between his teeth for a moment. "Not sure if bite is the right word for what's going on down there."

She lightly chuckled, and the sound had his heart exploding. "That's it," he said, mouth next to her ear. "Let go. Relax. I've got you." When he found her eyes again, he didn't expect to see them glossy.

"Why do I feel so safe in your arms? So protected even though I normally hate that?" Her voice was shaky this time.

"I don't know." He braced her even tighter, never wanting to let go. "But maybe we ought to find out?"

"And how do we do that?" Her hand went up his back and slid through his wet hair, her hunter green eyes riveted to his light green ones.

"Stick together for longer. Get to know each other more." He angled his head. "Maybe kiss me again?"

Ana darted her pink tongue between her lusciously full lips, which had his cock jumping. The woman knew exactly what she was doing. A temptress. A smile played on her lips, and he leaned in to take possession of her sweet mouth again but grunted when his phone began ringing.

He growled out his frustration. "Impeccable timing."

"It is becoming a habit for your team to interrupt us, but um, did you really set your colleague's ringtone to Beyoncé's *Run the World*?" She smiled.

"*Harper* set my ringtone to Beyoncé," he corrected.

"Well, you better answer. Can't keep them waiting."

He waded through the water in the direction of the grass and perched her up onto the bank. She untangled her limbs from him, allowing her legs to rest on each side of his body, and if the barrier of her shorts were gone, he'd probably lose himself between her thighs.

"What are we doing?" Her back arched, her breasts lifting with the movement, as if she was as desperate for him to run his mouth on her flesh as he was.

"I'm taking one more minute with you is what I'm doing." He grasped hold of her hips, then moved his hands up and pushed her wet shirt out of his way before leaning in to press a kiss to her abdomen. And then another. She hooked her ankles around his back, drawing him closer.

A.J.'s mouth drew closer to her breasts on display through the sheer bra, and he dipped in to nip at her peaked nipple. He swirled the tip of his tongue in lazy circles around her areola.

Ana bucked her hips and nearly slipped back into the water with him. "You're going to make me wetter than I already am," she confessed after a long sigh of pleasure fluttered free from her mouth. He firmly set his hand on her toned upper thigh and skirted the line of her shorts with a gentle finger. "I've never wanted to be touched so badly in all my life."

He quickly released the hem of her shorts as if she'd issued a command, set his palms to the ground off to her side, and hoisted himself up.

She kept her eyes locked on to him, following his movements with desire in her gaze.

After helping her onto the blanket, A.J. positioned her onto her back, then climbed over her. Her fingers went to the buttons of her shorts, and his throat moved with a swallow at the sight. He sure as hell hoped this was real.

When she shimmied her shorts to her thighs, exposing her matching sheer white panties, well, hell—if this was a dream —it'd be a wet one.

Ana's hand went beneath her shirt, pushing the fabric and bra up to expose her nipples, and he growled out a low, animal-like sound when she palmed her breast, her deep green eyes never leaving his.

He lowered himself closer and positioned his face at the soft V between her legs. When Ana eagerly lifted her hips, silently begging for more, A.J. dropped his mouth to her right thigh and scraped his beard against her sensitive skin. He took his time, breathing in her sweet feminine scent, his mouth tracing the panty lines between her thighs.

"A.J., I, um. I don't normally do this so . . . but I want you to. Please," she cried, seemingly pleading him not to let her retreat inside her own head and stop the moment. "This is crazy, I know, but I . . ."

He lifted his chin in search of her eyes. "I told you, I got you. Don't worry." He framed his words as a gentle but firm order for her to stop feeling guilty about finding pleasure at a time like this.

She responded with a sweet smile before lying back down and surprised him when she dove her fingers into his hair and held on. God, he couldn't get enough of this woman.

He ran the flat of his tongue over one breast. Then the other. Set small kisses over her abdomen.

And with one hand, he shoved down her panties and inched down her body with his mouth to position himself over the creamy, smooth skin between her thighs.

When he circled her clit, and parted her folds with his tongue, she screamed out his name, adding to the symphony of the sounds of nature all around them. "A.J.," she hissed as he kissed and sucked her sweet flesh.

He moved his mouth over her skin, feeling the tremble in her body, noting the tightening of her thighs when his lips hummed over her sex. He positioned a finger inside her pussy to reach her G-spot while he licked and licked.

"Oh God," she said on a moan, and damn did this woman taste better than he could've imagined. Nothing sweeter than her. And she was finally letting go and relaxing. It only took the coaxing of his mouth, the flicks of his tongue. "Oh, oh, oh . . . don't stop. This is, oh my."

Her arousal on his tongue, and her pleasureful cries, had him harder than he thought possible. He was on the verge of exploding his load listening to the beautiful woman come undone.

When she orgasmed, her hands fell to his shoulders and

she slightly shoved at him as if she wasn't able to handle riding the wave of ecstasy any longer.

He shifted fully on top of her, supporting himself on his forearms. His body sated with satisfaction that he'd made her come. Made her release some of that tension she was holding. "You're a lot sweeter than sugar. I'm gonna need a new name for you."

She eased up onto her forearms and found his eyes. "I don't know," she said with a small smile, "those names are beginning to grow on me."

CHAPTER TWENTY

ANA TIGHTENED THE KNOT OF THE BLACK SILK ROBE SHE'D thrown in her bag at the last minute. A lightning-quick shower after her dip in the pond while A.J. phoned Harper had done nothing to cool off the desire her sexy cowboy had awakened.

I let him go down on me. What was I thinking? She cursed the guilt trying to rope her in. *Stop thinking. You were giving yourself permission to finally live after refusing to feel anything real for a long, long time.*

She clamped her legs together and set a hand to the wall outside her bathroom door when little pulses of need began clamoring for her attention yet again at the memory of A.J.'s hands and mouth on her body.

When she told him the truth about her parents, it felt as though the weight of her past had been lifted. A.J. accepted her, flaws and all, and she wondered, as crazy as it seemed, if she was starting to—

"It's me. You decent?" A knock followed A.J.'s words.

It was unlocked, but she slowly strode toward the door. Nervous and excited at the same time to see him again. Was it ridiculous that she felt like a teenager about to open the door for her prom date, hoping that he'd like her dress?

Prom. Something she'd only wished she'd experienced. A.J. would've made an amazing date. He probably had every girl in school hoping he'd asked her to the dance.

"One second." She took a deep breath and placed her palms on her warm cheeks, praying they weren't as red as her hair at the memory of his mouth between her legs.

She swung open the door and stepped back. One hand braced against the wall outside the door, the other positioned at his side. He looked clean and smelled delicious.

His fingers began to drum against the leg of his khaki cargo shorts, and she followed the length of his body up to see him staring at the plunging neckline of her silk robe. Was he nervous, too? "You promised I wouldn't see you in that."

"Yeah, well, things change. This robe seems downright modest after the pond and, you know . . ." And there went her cheeks, probably firecracker red now.

His brows pulled together, making a show of pretending to be confused, and then he brought his arms across his chest. And oh, those arms. Defined, but naturally sculpted, like A.J. had tossed bales of hay over and over again, not like he'd pumped iron at the gym.

And that six-pack with the V that disappeared beneath his boxers . . .

His strong back muscles. The trim waist that went up to broad shoulders. Per-freaking-fection.

"No, I don't actually know." His lips curved into a knowing smile. "You should tell me."

She set a hand to the fresh white tee he wore, her palm settling on his chest above his crossed arms. His heart was beating fast. Was it because he had news from Harper or because they were no longer denying their scorching chemistry?

"Now that I think about it, I seem to remember you taking your shorts off and pretty much begging me to lick that sweet pussy of yours. So, I guess you're right, that robe doesn't do much considering I've seen what's underneath." Humor infiltrated his tone.

"And you're such a bad liar. This little thing still turns you on." She surprised herself with a jab right back. "Undressing me with your eyes right now."

His cocky grin had her playfully rolling her eyes and using her hand on his chest to push herself away. She turned and walked back into the room, expecting he'd follow, but when she stole a look back, he remained in the doorway. "You're right, which is why I shouldn't come inside." His forehead was tight, lips barely parted as he spoke. An attempt at restraint?

"Phone call that bad?" She sat on the bed and fidgeted with the belt of her robe, adjusting it to ensure there was no boob action. She peered up, finding him still standing rigid in the doorway.

And . . . maybe stiff below the belt? His pants were a bulky material, but there'd been a twitch of something down there just now.

She never had a chance to get a look at him beneath those starred and striped boxers down by the pond, but she'd certainly felt his hard length press against her.

"No, because if I come into your room, that robe will be on the floor faster than you can say 'Yes, please.'"

And does it need to stay on? *Probably. Maybe. Well, for now.* She had zero regrets about what happened at the pond. But on the other hand, what sane and rational person got down and dirty and had oral sex when her very life and reputation were on the line? *I was living. Feeling,* she reminded herself again, hating the buttoned-up, straight-edged FBI agent who kept taking over inside her head.

Maybe instead of a checklist of everything that'd gone wrong, she ought to make one for everything that had been going right? A.J. showing up in her life when she needed him, for starters.

Memories licked her mind with furious intensity once again about what happened at the pond. The soft strokes of his tongue coupled with the scratchiness of his beard along each thigh.

"My team is settling into their current location. They ended up finding a place about twenty minutes away," A.J. said, sounding regretful that he had to force himself back into operator mode. "I gave them the Cliff's Notes version of what we already told Jessica and Asher." He pushed away from the frame of the door to stand straight and scratched the back of his neck. "My team knew some of your story already. And your unit is now aware of your real name and the new identity given to you by the FBI when you turned eighteen. They also know what happened to your parents."

This was to be expected, and yet, it had her shaking on the inside a little. "They think I'm the spy, right? The leak?"

"Which 'they'? My teammates or yours?"

She'd seen a touch of doubt in Jessica's eyes earlier when Ana had shared her story. Not so much Asher because she'd swear that man was rooting for her and A.J. to be more than "on the run" together. "You pick which one to tell me about first."

A deep inhalation through his nose probably wasn't the best of signs. "I've convinced my people you're who you say you are, and they've promised to trust my judgment."

"Because you trust me, they'll trust me?" She leaned

forward slightly and brought her hands to her bare knees, the silk sliding higher up on her thighs.

"Right," he answered, slowly nodding. Ana was becoming quite fond of A.J.'s Southern accent, especially when he said this word in particular. *Riiiight.* She kind of loved that drawl. And she was now stalling as to how to respond.

"And my team?" Halle and Dean might give Ana a chance to explain, but her disappearing act wasn't going to do wonders for her innocence. "Aside from Porter, we still don't know who else is aware of my UC assignment."

"You may not believe this, but Director Mendez admitted he was the one to sign off on your hire six years ago. As well as your promotion to HQ. He hasn't mentioned your UC assignment, but that might mean he was the one who gave Porter approval in the first place for you to infil the Volkovs."

"Mendez hated me back in Charlotte." Her tone was weak as she recalled working with the FBI director.

"Don't take it personally. He sure as hell hated my guys then, too. And I may not like Mendez, but if you're going to have someone on your side at the Bureau, he's the guy to have." A.J. added a nod meant to make her feel better, but she was still swimming in a sea of doubt about who to trust at the Bureau. The memory of the pond was quickly slipping from her mind when all she wanted to do was wrangle it in and think only about her feelings for A.J.

And maybe now wasn't the time to tell A.J. the USB file from Porter's safe contained the evidence of her UC assignment, which meant someone out there knew where her loyalties truly lay.

"Your, um"—A.J. cleared his throat—"ex-husband is leading the not-guilty charge. He insists I hijacked you or hurt you." A smile curved at his lips. "Not that he knows who I am, but his description of me to your unit was colorfully inaccurate."

She could imagine what Kyle had said. "Are you going to be okay? I don't want your work with me coming back on you."

"Natasha has me covered. Plus, I'm pretty good with POTUS." He winked, and it was exactly what she needed. A touch of sweetness in a moment of brutal truth.

"Other than Kyle, does anyone believe I'm innocent?" she asked again since he hadn't answered her the first time. "What about Deputy Winters or my unit chief? They didn't seem to have a clue about my UC assignment based on our last meeting yesterday."

And wow, yesterday was lightyears ago. Today had been one long but surprising day that'd started on the road at sunrise and ended with an orgasm at sunset.

"Winters didn't even want to entertain the idea of the existence of the ledger yesterday, so I don't know what that might mean," she added. "And Gray was in agreement with him."

"Well, you can rule out Gray. He definitely wasn't aware of your history before tonight, but he's solid." Ana had a feeling A.J. knew something he couldn't share, and as honest as she'd been with him and his team, it stung a touch, but she understood the nature of classified work. Just because she'd broken her oath to speak the truth to A.J. didn't mean he'd be able to do the same with her. "But several in your unit have turned on you. With the Volkovs returning five months ago, you starting work at HQ shortly after, and then you insisting on personally dealing with both Volkov sources . . . it paints a shitty picture."

"Whoever leads the charge against me the most vehemently—"

"Is probably the real leak," A.J. finished for her.

Her attention wandered to the three framed photos stacked on the hallway floor just outside the door, a hammer resting on top. She kept her focus fixed on that red-handled hammer, a pounding sensation driving into the side of her head as if the hammer were hitting her.

"Anastasia." And there it was, his concern from earlier coming back into play. She heard it in his voice, in the way he'd dragged out her full name. He was about to lay something on her he knew she wouldn't want to hear. "The idea of you going anywhere near the Volkovs still makes me a bit crazy. I don't trust they won't kill you the second they have what they want." His husky tone had her drawing in a deep breath and standing. She took a step closer to where he remained in the doorway. "The FBI gave you a new identity for a reason, to keep you safe."

"I completely understand that this entire situation makes you uncomfortable. You're taking a lot of risks, and I know you hate this." She tensed when he finally stepped into the room, his gaze focused intently on her.

"I can't help but hate anything that involves putting you in danger," he answered honestly.

The throbbing in her temples kicked up as a concerning thought came to mind. "But you won't try and stop me from meeting with them, right?"

A.J. crossed the room to get to her and cradled her face between strong hands, no hesitation whatsoever. His thumb moved in small circles on her right cheek. His light green eyes thinned. "Whatever you need from me, I'm here for you. No matter what," he said softly.

"Even if it means crossing lines?"

A small smile graced his lips while his fingers threaded

her hair. "My job is all about crossing those lines, don't you worry."

Was he for real? "And for some reason"—she leaned in closer, her hand going to his hip—"I'm not worried."

"We do have a rule on my team. No solo ops. People die when they're on their own, and I know you have Porter, but you've got me, too. Okay?" He continued to swirl the pad of his thumb over her skin, his touch and words lighting up everything inside of her.

"I never set out to be a Lone Ranger."

"Wrong state," he teased and brought his mouth closer to hers. "I really want to kiss you right now, but if I do—"

"You won't be able to stop." Her eyes fell shut as reason and responsibility nearly faded from her thoughts. But then a question whirred to mind. "Have you really not been with a woman since you saw me in Charlotte?" she murmured curiously.

His mouth closed in on the side of her neck, and he worked his lips to her ear. Her hands slid up the sides of his torso, over his tee as she braced him for support.

"Did I confess that on my voicemail?" he asked, the depth of his Southern voice hitting her like a soft-cushioned arrow right to the heart.

"Yes," she croaked out when he nibbled on her earlobe. "Is it true?"

"It's true," he admitted.

Her fingertips bit harder into his sides when his breath touched her ear. He kept one hand on the back of her head, the other went to her hip, and she wanted more than anything for him to take off her robe. Kiss her all over. Work his way down her body. *But, but, but*—damn her brain.

He released her suddenly, taking her by surprise, and when she peeled her eyes open, he was standing a foot away, dragging both palms down his face. "Yeah, I can't do much thinking about Russian espionage when you look and smell so good." He took another giant step backward like maybe there was a line he had to get back behind, even though he'd just admitted he was all about crossing lines. "I know it's late, but how about we get some food in our stomachs and talk?" His fingertips raced down his tanned throat and then he set his hands to his hips. "Unless you have something else on your mind you'd like to do right now?" He was letting her set the pace, but he sounded hopeful.

"Dinner and work talk." Getting those words out was harder than she'd anticipated, especially because desire swelled to epic proportions inside of her.

A brief touch of disappointment flashed across his face, or maybe she'd read him wrong. Hell, maybe her skills were on the fritz while on the run and in this Alabama heat? But then he surprised her with a big smile.

"What?" she asked.

"I've been waiting nearly a year for you," he said, his tone a touch hoarse, "and the reasons are shit, but I'm just happy you're in my life again, and I don't want to screw anything up. I don't—*we* don't need to rush, just so you know. We are in the South after all. We can take things slow."

"Are you real?" she softly blurted.

He patted his chest, sides, then chest again. "I think so, but I have been seeing ghosts, so . . ."

"Wait, what?" She smiled, but well, she was also worried maybe he wasn't kidding given his recent bumps on the head.

"That's a story for another day. I think we've probably hit some sort of record when it comes to what a human can handle in one day, right?"

"You might be right." She drawled out the word "right" to

imitate him, and he grinned. That cocky one he liked to shoot her way, and she'd never dare admit how much she loved it.

"So, dinner and strategy, then?" She pointed to the door, but he shook his head. "What?"

"Clothes first." He lifted his hands as if praying for strength. "Otherwise, the only strategy we will be discussing is the many different ways I can make you come."

Her thighs tightened.

It was only Tuesday night.

Two more full days and three nights with this man . . .

He may have proposed they take their time and not rush, but Ana had the feeling that this time she'd be the one standing before him begging. Begging him to show her all the different ways he could make her come, regardless of the fact she had to focus.

Begging. Yeah, one more item on her "Things She Never Did Before A.J." list.

Multiple orgasms would be something new, too, and heaven help her, the way A.J. was peering at her with those gorgeous green eyes of his and that sinful smile . . . multiple orgasms was going to make it to the top of her freaking list. And that one, she wouldn't even mind.

* * *

"You were right about needing food. I don't do hungry well." Ana sat back in her white chair at the square, four-person table in the breakfast nook where they'd shared the pizza and held a hand over her abdomen.

"I honestly don't know anyone that does hungry well, and I'd be worried if they did." A.J. reached across the table and refilled both their glasses with the red wine they'd had by the pond earlier.

They'd yet to talk about work. Instead, A.J. had peppered her with questions about herself for the past hour, and if she weren't worried about his motives, she'd think he was crafting a source identification package on her.

And the crazy thing? She'd freely given every detail, her walls basically nonexistent around him.

"He really wasn't the right one since I was never able to confide in him," the admission whooshed free from out of nowhere after sipping more truth serum, aka, wine.

A.J. set his palms on either side of his gray placemat. "Your ex?"

Kyle was one topic A.J. hadn't pressed her on in the last hour, and she had a feeling he didn't want to cross that particular line without an invitation first. "Yeah. I just think it's wild that you literally showed up at Porter's house"—she glanced at the big white clock on the wall off to her right —"twenty-five hours ago, and you already know the truth about me. I've known Kyle for five years, and he's clueless."

"Guess you didn't have much of a choice in telling me considering our situation." He reached for his glass, and she fixated on his strong hand, catching sight of his tattoo as he drank his wine. There had to be a story there with the ink.

"I could've kept my secrets. Ditched you before Friday like I'd contemplated doing on our drive here."

"Oh really?" A brow lifted as his glass returned to the table.

"Can you blame me? I'm working a top secret case to out Russian spies by tracking down a ledger that requires a key to decode it. To paraphrase Winters, it sounds like something from *The Da Vinci Code.* Most don't believe the book exists. Who would *want* to believe me? Looks like my unit certainly doesn't."

"And they haven't heard your side of things, but they will in time," he said, conviction ringing through his tone.

"I guess this means we should probably talk about work now," she said on a sigh, preferring relaxed-Ana, who jumped into ponds fully clothed with an almost naked cowboy, to uptight-Ana, who panic-cleaned spoiled sushi rolls.

"Probably, but can I ask you something? You don't have to answer, but—"

"Why'd I marry Kyle?"

"Damn, you really are a mind reader." A.J. shifted farther back in his seat and toyed with the stem of his wineglass between his fingers. His green eyes took a slow journey over her as if she was still in the robe and hadn't changed into black cotton shorts and a red tank top.

"I married Kyle," she began when remembering his question, not wondering whether he was able to see the outline of her nipples since she was braless, "because I thought I had to fit some perfect mold. Check off certain boxes. College, career, husband, and baby. I never got to the fourth one." She took a moment to gulp back a large swallow of wine. "And he's by the book like me. Likes lists and being organized. Well, I *was* by the book. I don't feel that way right now."

He was quiet for a moment, possibly mulling over her words. "Did you love him?"

Did I? "I think I did in the only way I knew how to at the time. Friendship. Companionship. A caring relationship."

"That's a lot of ships."

She cracked a smile. Of course, he'd be able to provoke such a reaction during this kind of conversation. "But every time I tried to remove the wall I'd placed between us, to show him the real me, I'd shut down. I couldn't do it. I didn't think he'd be able to look at me the same way again after he learned the truth. He'd see me as the daughter of traitors forever. Like I was worried you'd look at me." She paused for a breath. "But you were worth the risk," she softly admitted.

A.J. sat taller, hands going flat on the purposefully distressed tabletop. His gaze connected with hers, and the look of lust in his eyes had her skin blushing instantly. "Well, I can tell you that from the moment I met you, I knew you were a woman I wanted to get to know."

"And here you are getting to know me." Her hand began to tremble ever so slightly as her past cut through their moment. She didn't want to remember her parents in the way they died, or the reasons why they died. Not everything had been rainbows and sunshine, or gloom and doom.

"What are you thinking about?"

"My parents." She really was an open book with this man, and he seemed fairly eager to keep reading.

"You're allowed to still love them, you know." He was on his feet and moving around the table before she had a chance to process his quick movements.

Oh. There were tears. That's why he was before her, one knee on the floor as if proposing, the other leg bent back, his hand on her cheek. "I'm sorry."

"It's been what feels like a forty-hour day. We can talk about work tomorrow. You should sleep." He scooped her into his arms before she had a chance to protest.

Ana wasn't used to surrendering to her tears, and yet with A.J., she allowed them to freely fall. And they kept coming as her arms circled his neck.

"Thank you," she whispered when he carried her up the stairs, his powerful body holding her like she weighed nothing. She brought her face closer to his chest, nuzzling against him once he'd sat on her bed, holding her on his lap. "I, um."

"Shhh," he said when she lifted her head. "You don't need to say anything. Relax."

She didn't normally relax. No, she panic-cleaned. And now? Could panic-orgasm be a thing? She really was thinking like A.J. now.

"I'll wait to go until you're asleep."

But this was a place she never wanted to leave.

In his arms.

And maybe being protected wasn't such a bad thing if it was A.J. doing the protecting?

CHAPTER TWENTY-ONE

A.J. WAITED UNTIL ANA HAD FALLEN ASLEEP TO LEAVE HER room. He'd have preferred to stay and hold her, but he begrudgingly had to call the team and check for updates.

He'd failed to mention to his team that, in a roundabout way, he'd dropped the news on Ana that her unit chief Gray was on his team's side. Of course, A.J. had only discovered that tidbit when he'd spoken to Harper and Natasha by way of split-screen while Ana had taken her post-pond-orgasm shower. Natasha had been resistant to tell his team Gray's identity as the colleague on her new task force, but with Chris and A.J. both trying to throw Gray's name into the guilty hat, she'd been forced to speak up.

When Harper had informed him she'd had enough of his yawning and insisted he get some sleep, he hadn't objected.

He felt bad taking rack time when his team was working, but within a minute of lying down on the bed in a guest room after removing his shorts and shirt, he'd passed out cold.

"She's a hot one." The familiar voice came out of nowhere, shocking him awake. "Smart. Funny."

"Huh?" A.J. turned his head to the side trying to

257

determine where the voice was coming from, not to mention why the hell he was lying on a hard surface. Hadn't he just gone to sleep? In a bed?

He pushed up on his forearms after finding himself flat on his belly on the porch out back, shifted to a sitting position, and came face-to-face with Marcus, who was sitting in one of Grant's rocking chairs.

A.J. blinked and slapped his cheeks twice. *Am I dreaming, or is this real?* He stood and peered down at his body, finding himself in only his boxer briefs.

"Oh, and the back-and-forth between you two is the thing of romance novels," Marcus went on, ignoring A.J.'s confused stare.

"Whaaaaat? Did you read one of Savanna's novels?" He smiled, deciding to stay in this dream if his buddy was going to pay him a visit. "You did, didn't you?"

"No, I read a couple before I met her." Marcus flicked a hand in the air. "How do you think I won over a woman like Savanna? Learned from the pages of a novel how to woo a woman."

"Am I dreaming?"

"You tell me." Marcus shot him his signature smile and braced the chair arms, closing his eyes as he continued to rock. "That bump you got on your head Saturday wasn't that bad, but how many times have I told you over the years, you gotta stop being an idiot and see a doc every once in a while. You get banged up too often."

A.J. scrubbed his hands up and down his face and tried to get a grip, to determine if he was sleep walking, or still back in the guest room sound asleep and dreaming. "My head is fine."

"You always say that. Stubborn." Marcus shook his head, eyes remaining shut. "At least you don't sleep commando."

A.J. rolled his eyes, forgetting for a moment this wasn't real. Marcus was buried in Birmingham thirty minutes away from there. He wasn't on Grant's back porch right now. And A.J. probably wasn't either.

"So, let's talk about this FBI hottie. Why'd it take you so long to reach out to her? You scared she might bite?"

"I wasn't scared," A.J. protested, folding his arms across his chest and pouting like a kid in trouble.

He had so much he wanted to say to Marcus. So much to apologize for. A.J. should have been at his side the day he died. If he had, Marcus might still be alive. Fuck orders from the top. The top didn't always know the best course of action for an op.

"You haven't had a serious girlfriend in years. Actually, no girlfriends since I died." Marcus opened his eyes and slowed his rocking, his brown gaze meeting A.J.'s. "I've been worried about you. But based on that kiss I saw you lay on your FBI hottie, maybe you're finally coming to your senses."

"Have you been watching us? Spying?"

"I'm not so sure you have room to talk. Weren't you spying on her?"

A.J. pinched the bridge of his nose. "We should be talking about you, not her right now. You're here, and I have stuff to say."

"If you even think about dropping a *lo siento,* I'll get up out of this chair and knock the shit out of you. Understood? Terrorist motherfuckers killed me. They're now toast. Justice served. What happened to me ain't on you. Or Luke or anyone else. You would've died, too, if you'd been with me, and that would've killed me." He grinned. Dark humor even in death. "*But* I'm here because I'm worried about you, brother."

259

"Because of my lack of a love life?" he questioned. A spiral of guilt that Marcus was gone still clung to him like the humidity after an Alabama afternoon rainstorm.

"Trusting a traitor is dangerous, but not letting yourself fall for the woman of your dreams is the deadliest sin of all."

A.J. jerked his head back in surprise. "Did you just paraphrase my made-up fortune cookie message?"

Marcus cracked a smile, showing his white teeth, then brushed back a lock of dark hair from his tan skin, pushing it away from his forehead. "Seriously, bro, I just want to make sure you're good. It's time to move on. Be happy. Stop being so guilty and stubborn." His tone grew more serious. "No more letting your dick take the lead to avoid feeling anything in your heart or head."

"My dick is just fine." A.J. muttered an amused curse under his breath. "And so is my head." Another curse. "This head," he said while tapping at his skull.

"So, once you fall for this woman, you're not going to freak out and take off? Feel guilty when you start to experience some happiness?" he challenged. Typical Marcus. "Because this woman is different, I can tell. I think she's the one for you. And I don't want you giving her up because of some bullshit notion that you shouldn't have happiness because I'm dead." He was quiet for a moment. "You have to stop blaming yourself for my death. It wasn't your fault."

"But I—" A.J. dropped his words at the sound of a woman's voice.

"I better go, brother. Someone is here for you." Marcus tossed a hand in the air, waving goodbye. "And, A.J., be careful. I don't want to see you on the other side anytime soon."

"A.J.?" Someone was patting his cheeks. Saying his name.

A.J. jerked his eyes open in surprise.

So, he was on the porch. Marcus wasn't in the chair anymore. But what did it mean that it was still rocking?

"Hey, what are you doing outside?" Ana asked.

A.J. blinked slowly, letting his eyes adjust to the floodlight she'd turned on.

"You were talking in your sleep." She was on her knees next to where he sat.

His eyes darted back to the rocking chair that was no longer moving.

Was it ever moving, or am I really losing it?

"I haven't sleepwalked since I was seven," he confessed. "I don't remember coming out here."

"I came downstairs to get water, then realized the back door was open. I looked outside and saw you out here."

"Shit, I'm sorry if I startled you." He was too tired, too confused, too embarrassed. "What was I saying out here?"

"Something about a fortune cookie." She stood and offered her hand for an assist. "No American flag boxers this time?"

He followed her gaze down his nearly naked body to his black boxer briefs. "Nah, I save those for special occasions," he managed a joke somehow, still trying to shake off the weird dream where he'd had a conversation with his dead best friend. "Like a first kiss." And he hoped it was the first of many.

A.J. stole another look back at the chair, the memory of Marcus still so fresh in his mind he was struggling to believe what was real right now. When he faced Ana again, he set a hand to her shoulder. To make sure she was really there.

"You okay?" she asked, a worried look in her eyes.

"Of course." Although after his weird sleepwalking dream, the answer was more of a coin toss. "You should get back to bed. Sun isn't up quite yet." He retracted his hand and walked across the porch. Taking a deep breath, he leaned his forearms on the railing and raked a hand through his hair.

He twitched when she placed her hand to his back, but she didn't back away. "What's going on? You can tell me." Her tone softened. "I did bare my soul on this very porch a few hours ago. You could do the same if you'd like."

His eyes went to the tattoo on the inside of his forearm, and he straightened, tracing the letters of the inscription inked on his skin with his forefinger. "A lot of the guys got tattoos after Marcus died," he said softly. "Liam got the lion. Everyone always said Marcus had the heart of one."

"Marcus was the guy Asher replaced, right?" Adriana must have filled Ana in.

The day A.J. was recruited in 2013 by Jessica and Luke Scott to leave his SEAL platoon and work off-the-books missions popped to mind at her question. *Not my fault you died, huh? But wasn't it?* "Yeah, but Marcus joined Scott and Scott because of me. I didn't want to join without him, so Luke and Jessica made the offer to him as well. Marcus was one of the best trackers anyway. We needed him." His stomach wrenched at the memory. "We were best friends. Went to college together. I was the best man at his wedding. So, you see, how could I start a new adventure without him?"

Her hands smoothed up and down his back in reassuring, comforting strokes.

"It'll be six years in November since he's been gone. We were on an op, and we needed recon near an alleged terrorist cell. To prevent drawing attention, and with no drones at our disposal, only one man was deployed. Marcus volunteered. Somehow, he was spotted, and he didn't make it back. Captured and killed." He was somewhat vague since the operation was top secret and not with Scott & Scott, but he owed her honesty after she'd opened up to him. "Marcus was one of the best of us. Said we had to earn the privilege of being a SEAL every day, not just on the day we got our trident." He pointed to his tattoo. "This ink is a reminder to do that in his honor. Be the best man I can be every day, especially on the hardest days."

She brushed a hand over his tattoo, eyes remaining frozen on his arm as if working through the weight of his words.

"And this black band was Marcus's. We rotate wearing it in his memory," he explained while Ana smoothed her thumb over the black band, which resembled rubber, though it was made from leather. "Weird thing is, ever since I bumped my head Saturday, I keep seeing Marcus. Feeling him everywhere." A.J. blinked and squinted as his eyes burned with the threat of shedding his emotions. He'd witnessed her tears. Brushed them from her cheeks. But he rarely allowed his own tears to fall in the presence of others. And when possible, he used humor to fight off any painful memories that might provoke tears. "He was out here in that rocking chair talking to me. I swear it was real."

She clutched A.J.'s forearms and turned her head to study the rocking chair for a moment. "For years, I saw and talked to my parents. I may have been furious with them, but they remained with me for the longest time." She slid both hands up his arms to brace his biceps, eyes set on his green ones. "Everyone heals differently. You're not crazy."

"Marcus died six years ago. I feel like I might be a bit crazy." He swallowed the knot in his throat.

She tightened her grip on his arms and held on to his eyes. "Maybe that knock on the head isn't making you see things," she began, "it's just helping you finally process. Go through the stages of grief."

"I grieved when he died." He thought he did, at least. But hell . . .

"But for how long? Did you truly move on? Forgive yourself for your friend dying instead of you?"

And shit, the woman had multiple psychology degrees, so yeah, she knew a thing or two about this, but she treated him less like a patient and more like someone who understood loss.

She gingerly touched his cheek with the back of her hand before her thumb caught his bottom lip, tugging it down ever so slightly. "You took me in your arms and let me grieve my parents' death. I've never let myself do that. I was always too angry at them, too angry at myself for being so sad that I never truly just cried for my loss. Fifteen years later, it took a cowboy SEAL with a heart of gold to get me to open up."

He half smiled, still working to fully accept her words and what she was trying to convey.

Had he spent the last six years being angry? Had he been mad at himself and the world for the death of his best friend?

Justice was served to the terrorists who murdered Marcus, and while it had appeased the SEAL in him, it had barely put a dent in the pain he felt at the loss of his best friend.

I think she's the one for you. The words of Marcus's ghost strummed through his mind, plucking at his heartstrings. *It's time to move on. Be happy.*

Marcus was gone, and he'd left behind a wife. A widow now. How was that fair? But was Marcus right? Had A.J. been avoiding love and happiness out of guilt? Was it time to move on?

He gently swept Ana's hand from his face to seize hold of her cheeks. She was real, right?

"How'd I get so lucky to have you walk into my life?" he whispered, trying his best to take Marcus's words to heart.

Ana was the first woman in six years who'd made A.J. want to keep his feet firmly planted on the ground. No taking off out of fear of deserving happiness.

"I guess it's all those lines you've been crossing that brought you to me." She lifted an auburn brow, her eyes still a bit red from crying before she'd gone to bed.

It's time to move on. Be happy. He'd swear he heard Marcus's voice again, and it had him releasing a shaky breath.

But then he followed Marcus's advice. He gently held Ana's face between his palms and slowly captured her lips with his. She clasped her hands atop his as he placed quick, urgent kisses on her mouth, neck, then back to her lips again.

With Marcus's words surrounding him, the heated kiss he was sharing with Ana felt like a release from the prison of guilt he never realized he'd been trapped in until now. The power of this one kiss brought him to his knees, and she dropped with him so as to not break their connection.

He lowered his hands from her face, tracing the lines of her silhouette from her waist down to the curve of her ass. She arched into his touch as they continued to kiss, moving with frenzied need, touching every part of each other without releasing their lips.

They were both reeling.

Spiraling.

Right into each other's arms.

CHAPTER TWENTY-TWO

"Someone is either setting up the Volkovs, or Grigory Volkov is a freaking idiot, and since he's survived this long, the latter is doubtful," Harper announced, sitting next to Roman during the web call Wednesday morning, five hours after A.J. had bared his soul to Ana out on the porch.

A.J. folded his arms and glimpsed Ana out of the corner of his eye. She was in the leather chair in Grant's office, hands knotted together on her lap, most likely bracing herself for whatever news Harper planned on sharing.

She was tense again. In desperate need of relaxing. On the other hand, after his strange ghost-dream encounter with Marcus in the middle of the night, he felt the opposite of rigid. The burden of guilt he'd shouldered for years after Marcus died had started to lift. Dream or not, something had clicked. Made him feel a little better about allowing himself to be truly happy.

As much as A.J. had wanted to take Ana back to his bed after the hot, emotionally charged kiss on the porch, he was doing his best to behave and wait for her to let him know when she was ready.

So, he'd been a good boy and jerked off in a cold shower after tucking Ana back into bed, same as he'd done after going down on her by the pond.

But based on her posture now, he'd need to help her loosen up again. For her sake, of course.

"The proprietary research the missing California source had been working on was sold on the Dark Net by a Volkov agent out of Budapest, but I think it's a pseudonym," Harper explained, "and the funds were traced to—"

"Let me guess, the same account in the Maldives?" A.J. finished for her.

"Yeah, we still haven't been able to lock down a name. And although the Feds are aware of the sale by the alleged Volkov agent, they haven't tied the transaction to the bank in the Maldives yet." Harper pushed back from her desk a few inches, revealing one of her signature T-shirts, this one black with gold letters that read "You Matter" with a gold atom beneath the words. "So, I think it's safe to say someone wants the Feds to believe the Volkovs are behind the disappearance of the sources."

"But they'd prefer the Feds not locate the funds in the Maldives," A.J. concluded.

"And the backup plan . . . no extradition if the FBI does track the money there," Harper reminded him.

"I have to assume," Ana began, "that if the Bureau easily tracked the one account to the Caymans, it was because whoever is pulling the strings wanted that account found?"

"I'd say yes." Harper flicked her dark hair to her back. Her glossy locks pin-straight today instead of casual and wavy.

Roman's dark eyes narrowed as he peered in their direction. "We believe the SVR is setting up the Volkovs, but I don't think they'll make a move against the Volkovs until they can verify Grigory Volkov isn't in possession of another copy of both the ledger and key. So, they're using The Huntsman to set up the Volkovs and draw the focus of the FBI to them," Harper explained. "They must have a middleman, though, to create a layer of separation between them and what's going on. And that's who hired Ivan. It's quite possibly the mole at the FBI."

"Yeah, because Ivan accepting a job from the SVR makes about as much sense as a screen door on a submarine." *No damn way.* "The SVR murdered his brother. So, if this is the work of The Huntsman, he sure as hell doesn't have a clue the SVR is pulling his strings."

Ana swiveled the chair to face A.J. "Yeah, I think the middleman—the *real* mole at the Bureau—would have hired him on behalf of the SVR."

"Also"—Harper drew their focus back her way—"we did get a hold of the case file from the day Ana's parents died. The names of all the acting agents have been redacted. I'm working on getting the non-sanitized version, but Director Mendez isn't prepared to hand it over to our contact there."

"Orders will need to come from above." A.J. stole a quick look at Ana. She was wearing the same pajama shorts and red tank she had on at dinner last night, but he'd changed into a pair of black running shorts and white tee after his jerk-off session in the shower.

"Above as in *who* above?" Ana peered at A.J., waiting for an answer, and he'd nearly forgotten she didn't know his team was on good terms with the President not only because Knox was his son, but because they directly reported to the Commander in Chief.

"Just above-above." Harper shot daggers A.J.'s way when he returned his focus to the screen, warning him not to expose their secret.

"Damn, woman, I felt that." A.J. set a hand to his side and playfully winced as though she'd actually jabbed him with a knife, and Harper rolled her eyes.

"We'll try and get the files," Roman said with a confident nod. "The movie theater had security cams positioned on the parking lot, but there was damage to the footage. Jessica is doing her best to fix the film and piece together what she can."

"Kind of suspect to me," A.J. commented. "Sounds like someone doesn't want that footage to be seen."

"What exactly does the report say?" Ana asked, curiosity in her tone. Was she having doubts about the story Porter told her four months ago regarding the events of that night?

"The Bureau received a tip five minutes before the movie ended, notifying them that an armed couple, Volkov spies, were at the theater. No names provided, but your parents' descriptions were given. An agent happened to be doing surveillance for another matter nearby, so he was the first on scene."

"Annnd like I said . . . suspect." A.J. snickered. "A hundred bucks says that agent was also the one to shoot your parents." He gave Ana an apologetic look. He hadn't meant to come across as cavalier or casual about her parents' death.

She offered him a light shake of the head that said *It's okay,* but he still felt like a jerk.

"The report claims two agents were face-to-face with your parents when they resisted arrest. The agent who arrived first to the scene was, in fact, also the agent who fired the fatal shots. We'll call him Agent One until we have his real name." Harper's brow scrunched. "Well, wait, did Porter give you a name?" Harper positioned her eyes on Ana but continued before Ana could respond. "Surely the man who took the shots wouldn't escape his memory. Did he memorize all the agents on scene that night?"

"Unfortunately, Porter said the man who killed my parents died of a heart attack not too long after my parents died," Ana responded.

"How convenient," A.J. said with more than a touch of sarcasm.

After Ana provided the name of the shooter, along with a list of every agent's name Porter had given her, A.J. asked, "Is it possible the shooter was a Russian spy for the SVR, and he was never really nearby doing surveillance? Maybe he was even the tipster."

"And while the Feds were at the theater, the Russians tossed my house in search of the key and ledger," Ana finished A.J.'s line of thinking since they'd had a similar discussion by the pond last night, but with the new details about the case, it was looking to be more fact than theory.

"If we assume the ledger and key are real, and the Russians did get their hands on at least one of them, which then led to the end of the Volkovs . . . then yeah, I think it'd make the most sense that the FBI shooter was also a spy for the Russians," Roman answered. "You and Porter find anything out on the other agents who'd been on scene that night?"

"Aside from a few using their badge to get out of some local parking tickets, they came up clean from what we could tell. No patterns in their cases or arrests that would suggest they were or still are Russian spies." Ana sat back and gripped the arms of her chair.

"We'll take another look at the names you gave us, but I still want the original report to ensure we aren't missing a crucial piece of information," Harper said. "And once Jessica gets that footage pieced together, I think we'll know more."

"But?" Ana had quickly read Harper.

"Since Porter was one of the agents who'd been working the Volkov case prior to the shooting, and he was there that night—plus, he took an interest in helping you . . . we have to look into him, too. And I know that makes you uncomfortable, which is why we'll be the ones handling it." Harper's tone was apologetic. "Porter was aware of your plan to place Katya into WITSEC, and at this point, we don't know who else knew."

"I'm pretty sure Porter was being chased by The Huntsman on Monday," Ana quickly countered while standing, pushing the chair back, ready to defend her boss.

"Or he lied about his car going off the road when he called to tell you to enact the backup plan and run, knowing the truth would come out about your past, and you'd look guilty. Then he had someone remove files from his house before you got there to keep the truth about your assignment from being revealed, and you'd be none the wiser." Roman's dark words and ominous tone had Ana turning from the screen.

Damn Roman and his way of cutting straight to the facts without sugarcoating them.

And wait, what files?

"How'd you know about the files?" Ana asked, purposefully avoiding eye contact with A.J.

"I didn't, but you just confirmed there were indeed files." Roman leaned back in his chair and crossed his arms. "There had to be a damn good reason you went into your boss's house that night, and getting your Volkov case files, the evidence to prove your innocence, sounded like a good one to me."

Ana finally faced A.J. and mouthed, "I'm sorry," but all he could focus on was the fact someone out there knew the truth about her undercover work and what that meant for her safety.

How could he have been so stupid? She'd avoided talking about why she'd been in Porter's house, and now it made perfect sense why she was keeping the truth from him.

He'd freak the fuck out that she was in far more danger than he realized.

"I'm not an idiot," Ana went on, "I was not conned again." A.J. saw the tears from past betrayals on the brink of spilling over, but she was fighting to stay strong. And he hoped like hell the bomb Roman had just dropped in her lap wouldn't prove to be true. "Porter is not setting me up. There has to be another explanation that makes more sense."

"Sometimes it takes someone on the outside to help with objectivity," Roman added, and A.J. was well aware the statement was also meant for him. He was obviously still worried about A.J.'s unwavering support of Ana.

Ana held a hand in the air like a shield, fending off further disappointment. "Porter wasn't one of the first agents on scene that day."

"According to *Porter* he wasn't the first on scene. What if he conveniently gave you the name of someone who died to protect you from finding out the truth," Roman insisted, playing devil's advocate. "Maybe Porter even fired the fatal shots?"

"Get the footage fixed from that night. It'll prove his innocence, I'm sure." Ana's voice trembled. "Please," she croaked out. "And if you really want to help, we need to make sure the forger shows up at the safe house Friday. It's my way in with Grigory Volkov."

"But, Ana, what if the man in Porter's house that night was a Volkov agent, and he knows you're undercover?" A.J. asked.

Ana dragged her hands down her face. "Shit, I don't know what to think."

"Let's handle one issue at a time. Based on your last conversation with Grigory, it didn't seem like he suspected you're undercover, correct?" Harper came to Ana's rescue as the voice of reason.

"Not from what I could tell," Ana replied.

"Let's get to the safe house and scope the place out. Get a lay of the land." Roman grabbed a pen, preparing to write down the address. "What's the location?" Ana offered the address of a cabin in Carrollton. "I'll send Chris and Finn over to do some recon. It's not that far from the Alabama-Georgia border."

"Thank you." Ana's hands went to her bare arms, and she smoothed her palms up and down in a comforting motion. "What about The Huntsman's location? The missing sources? Or you know, pick a problem and answer." A hint of a smile brushed across her lips.

"Still working on The Huntsman's location, but I think we can draw him out to the safe house in Carrollton. Kill two birds with one stone. Find out where he stashed the sources, if they're still alive, and who hired him," Harper suggested, and the blood drained from A.J.'s face.

"And put Ana in even more danger?" A.J. spoke through gritted teeth. He couldn't handle much more conversation that resulted in further jeopardizing her safety.

"You promised to help no matter what," Ana reminded him, her eyes thinning.

Shit. This was not going to be easy.

"The longer we drag this out, the worse it will get," Harper said. "And I know what you're thinking, A.J., but she'll have us outside that cabin. We won't let Ivan, or anyone for that matter, hurt her. And keep in mind, she's a trained Federal agent."

A.J. forced his gaze away from Ana to let Harper in on exactly "what he was thinking"—well, he'd planned to, but then he took a breath and pulled his shit together. "And Ivan is the freaking boogeyman of hitmen, so . . ."

"So, it'll be nice to take him down, right?" Harper flashed an innocent smile. The one she used when she wanted to wrap the guys around her little finger—her dark brows lifted, a casual curve to her lips. It worked every time, especially on Roman.

A.J. quickly shifted his attention to Ana when he felt her soft touch on his arm. The plea in her eyes just about did him in. Both strong-minded women were weaponizing their skills on him at the same time.

And he was screwed.

CHAPTER TWENTY-THREE

A.J. SET ANA ON THE KITCHEN COUNTER AND WRAPPED HER legs tight around his waist, then slung her arms over his shoulders. He nuzzled his nose into the crook of her neck and breathed in her delectable scent mixed with a hint of Patty's coconut soap. "You just might be the death of me, woman."

Ana traced her finger down the center of his chest as he leaned back to catch her eyes. "Now, whatever are you talking about?" she asked, teasing her words into a thick Southern belle accent that had him chuckling.

"Let's see." A.J. gave her what he hoped was a stern look, but it only served to make her giggle. "For starters, when you bent over to pick up your fork off the floor this morning, you popped that ass of yours up like you were practicing for a pole dancing competition. Doing your best to turn me on, no doubt."

"Yeah, I can see it now. Anastasia, the erotic dancer, coming soon to a gentleman's club near you," she said, and he slipped his hands to her hips, gently squeezing his fingers into her sides. "If you're lucky, I might even show you some moves." He let out a soft groan and closed his eyes, holding her tighter as her words played out like a movie in his head, and it sure as hell wasn't PG-13.

And if he didn't know any better, he'd think she'd gotten into Grant's bourbon or homemade moonshine at some point between their call and now.

"How else have I been teasing you?" she prompted, her eyes lit up like a woman without a care in the world. Or a past that she'd spent fifteen years working to keep buried.

"Well, there was that little stunt you pulled inside the helicopter. I mean, you straddled me in the cockpit and swiveled your hips, making me hard as a rock before hopping off and leaving me high and dry."

"Is that what happened?" Oh, the woman was good. Toying with him like there was no tomorrow, and hell, in his world, when tomorrow wasn't guaranteed, he was all for living life to the fullest.

"Yes, ma'am, you did. And then you grabbed my cowboy hat right off my head, which was downright mean. I had to chase after you until you tripped me, you little sneak. Although, it was fun taking you down with me, rolling around in the grass. I got stains all over my T-shirt, and I didn't even get a kiss—"

Ana sealed her mouth to his, cutting him off. A tender touch at first before her tongue slid along the seam of his lips and pushed into his mouth.

About damn time. At the end of their sweet and sensual kiss, it suddenly dawned on him—this brilliant woman was a master in tradecraft, and she'd . . . "You've been distracting me all morning, haven't you?" he finished his thoughts aloud as she unhooked her legs from his waist.

She placed her palms on the counter at her sides and parted her legs ever so slightly, drawing his eyes to the only

Southern place he was in the mood to be right now. Back between her smooth, toned thighs.

When his focus returned to her face, she shot him a huge grin that said she was proud of herself. Maybe she'd been purposefully distracting him to keep him from worrying or changing his mind about their next move. He was definitely not on board with offering her up as bait at the safe house in the woods. Between everything she'd shared over the last few days and the theories they'd been discussing, the woman deserved a break.

With Luke and Knox on their way to the Maldives, Chris and Finn scoping out the cabin in Georgia, and Jessica and Harper working their intel magic—there wasn't much else Ana and A.J. could do aside from spin more theories that'd make the both of them dizzier than sitting in one of those cheap county fair amusement rides.

"More like being a tease. And I'm adding that to my list," she announced with a confident nod.

"Which of your lists?" His hands went to the counter on either side of hers, but he eased back to look into her forest green eyes.

"The mental list I keep of all the things I've never done until I met you."

His eyes dropped to her mouth. "That's one list I like." He captured her bottom lip between his teeth and gently pulled, preparing to ravish her in the name of letting her "distract" them both. "Tease all right."

She secured a fistful of his shirt and feathered her mouth over his, her tongue skirting his lips before disappearing back inside her mouth.

Tease or not, kissing like they were horny teenagers was more than enough for him. That erotic sweep of her tongue in his mouth helped him focus on all that mattered right now. Her.

"I have to admit, I'm surprised you own this little jean skirt. Seems a bit rebellious for you." His hand skated up her thigh, and she parted her legs and lifted her chin a fraction. The sultry look in her eyes daring him to slide his palm higher.

"UC assignment eight months ago. I had to blend in," she admitted. "I thought it might come in handy down in the hot South with you. I was right."

"It's certainly handy." He coaxed her thighs farther apart as his fingers drifted up under her skirt.

He positioned his free hand at the hem of her white ribbed tank and pushed it up, shoving her bra up along with it, then cupped her breast. "Perfect."

She moaned when he gently twisted her nipple, while his other hand teased her inner thigh using small, sweeping circles with his thumb.

"I know we're taking things slowly, but you have needs, too," she whispered seductively. "We can stop the teasing and advance to the action."

"You don't need to worry about my needs," he drawled, even though "action" with her sounded significantly better than his hand on his own dick like the last two times. "I might be patient, but I also hate the color blue when it comes to my balls."

"Ah, I see. When life gives you lemons . . ." She was a quick learner, giving him the same cocky-as-hell smile he'd no doubt tossed her way over the last few days in spite of everything going on.

He brought his mouth to hers while sliding his palm up to her panties beneath the skirt.

"*Who the* . . . Alexander James, is that you?"

A.J.'s shoulders jerked, and he instantly retracted his hand from beneath Ana's skirt. The booming voice with a Southern accent belonged to his mom.

Shiiit. He and his brothers must have taught stealth and tactical skills to their mom a bit too well if she got the drop on A.J. and a Federal agent.

A.J. swiped his thumb over his lips, still swollen from all the hot kissing, and faced his mom, not expecting to see her with a shotgun in hand. "Can you lower the gun, Mama?"

"'Mama'?" Ana shrieked.

"What are you doing here?" He blocked Ana with his body, giving her a chance to discreetly adjust her clothes.

His mom placed the Winchester down on the counter, barrel pointing away from him and Ana. After fixing the strap of her tank top, she folded her lean arms across her chest and gave A.J. the once-over with her sharp green gaze. A rainbow of dried paint splatters adorned the denim overalls she wore when doing her projects, claiming they gave her "good mojo." His mom may have been sixty-nine years old, but even after raising a bunch of hellions, she hardly looked a day over fifty—her hair, currently in a messy ponytail, was still more blonde than gray, and the lines on her face were laugh lines. "I came over because I forgot my favorite hammer, and when I walked in, I heard a noise. I went out to my truck to grab my gun. I'm not about to have some fool running amuck in Grant's house and stealing his stuff."

A.J. bowed his head toward the ground for a brief second. "Mama," he dragged out. "You should've called your sheriff son to come over if you thought there danger. You could've gotten yourself killed if I had been a bad guy." Hands secured to his hips, he stared at his mom from across the kitchen island, not sure how he was going to explain what *he* was doing at Grant's place.

"But it was you," his mom protested.

"But what if it wasn't?"

"But it was." Her gaze lingered on Ana, and A.J. quickly peered across his shoulder, catching Ana's eyes to assess how she was holding up given the awkward situation. "And what are you doing here, Son? Rory and your father drove you drunken boys to the airport Saturday night, so why are you back, and why didn't you let us know?"

"I, um." What lie would his mom believe?

His mom circled the kitchen island to stand closer to him and Ana. "Are you my son's girlfriend?" she directed Ana's way. "I reckon you are since he was groping you."

A.J.'s worst nightmare might've been this moment right here and now. Forget Iraq. "Mama," he tossed out, a plea in his tone to back down.

"I'm Ana." She stepped forward and offered her hand, and his mom accepted her palm.

"Deborah Hawkins, but you can call me Deb, everyone does."

"We're working together," Ana explained before pulling her hand back.

"Oh?" His mom brought a fist beneath her chin and scrutinized them both. "You always make out with people you work with?"

"That, um, no," Ana sputtered. "We weren't, you know, doing anything." It appeared that Ana's tradecraft was failing her in the presence of his mom.

Welcome to Alabama and Southern moms. "I'm her bodyguard, and I can't tell you more than that." That was the story his family and friends believed. Bodyguard, sure. "Grant knows we're staying here for a few days."

"Is Ana in danger?" Her arms fell to her sides at the idea A.J. had brought "danger" to their little town.

"I'm sorry we startled you," Ana apologized, hopefully relieving him of having to answer his mom's question. "Your hammer is in the guest room upstairs. Red handle?" Ana's cheeks were about five seconds away from matching the color of her hair.

"You have, like, fifty hammers, and you came over because you left *one* here?" This hadn't been in his "What Could Go Wrong" plans. *And now I'm making lists?* Ana was rubbing off on him, and hell, he didn't mind.

"It's my favorite. McKenna got it for me for my birthday in March, not that you made it home to know that." And there it was, he was going to get an earful from his mom. She'd held back last weekend, too focused on Ella and Brian's upcoming wedding, but she was going to take the time to jab now.

"I sent you a gift." He stepped forward, eyes sweeping to the gun on the counter his mom had pointed at them. In fact, the Winchester, with the mossy oak finish he'd chosen to appeal to his mom's decorator sensibilities, had been his gift, and this was not how he envisioned she'd be using it.

His mom tucked a few loose strands of hair behind her ears. "One of my favorite movies is *The Bodyguard.* Such a shame what happened to Whitney Houston. Absolutely loved that woman." She waved an accusatory finger in front of him and Ana. "Is that what's going on here? You falling for your bodyguard?" she yammered on. Typical. Embarrassing. "I mean, I don't blame you. My boy is the best of the best, but isn't there a rule about sleeping with the woman you're protecting, Son?"

"Mama, you should go. And don't tell anyone I'm here, okay?"

His mom's green eyes shot to Ana. "I'm fixin' to make

lunch. You'll join us." A.J. didn't fail to notice it wasn't a question.

"Oh, thank you, but I don't think that'd be a good idea," Ana rushed out, but she didn't know his mom. When Deb Hawkins set her mind to something, there would be no arguing.

They couldn't possibly go there, but, shit.

"Lunch"—she pointed her finger at A.J.—"and I'll forgive you for missing my birthday." *And now you're just playing dirty.* "I'll go grab my hammer and be right back. Be ready." She marched out of the kitchen without another word. A.J. faced the kitchen island, placing his palms down in front of the gun.

"I don't even know what to say," he grumbled, and Ana set her hand on the center of his back. "She's not going to back down. You just don't know my mom."

"You're lucky you have a mom, especially one like her," she answered softly, her wistful tone a reminder her parents were not only gone, but they'd betrayed the country that Ana put herself in harm's way for every day to defend and protect.

"That mean you want to go to my house for lunch?" he asked in surprise and turned around. But could they? Would they be putting his family in danger? *No one followed us to Alabama. We're safe*, he reasoned with himself as he debated the possibility of lunch.

Ana's hands went to his arms, and her eyes journeyed from his chest up to his face. "You said she won't back down, and since I'm not yet marked as a fugitive," she responded in a whisper, "I think we'd be okay to have lunch at your parents' house. Well, as long as they don't tell anyone we're in town."

"Are you sure you want to go to my parents' place?" he asked, finding his voice unusually timid.

Her lips twitched into a smile. "You said we can't be of any help to your team, right?" One shoulder lifted. "And if we stay here alone, there's a pretty good chance we might do more than kiss."

They'd been on the brink of doing a lot more before his mom showed up.

He leaned in and brought his chest closer to hers while she maintained her grip of his forearms. "Oh yeah, and would that be a bad thing?" he rasped, visions of their naked bodies entangled as they made love coming to mind.

"Not bad at all," she murmured when he took hold of her hips, locking her in front of him, forgetting his mom was upstairs.

He angled his head. "But?"

"But I wouldn't mind getting a glimpse into your life, what it's like to be surrounded by a warm and loving family." Her brows scrunched and her gaze pinned to his. "Is that crazy?"

"Maybe, maybe not," he responded, eyes narrowing on the incredible woman before him. "But taking you home feels right somehow. Having you here in my hometown. It feels really, really right." He leaned in and gently pressed his lips to hers.

"You two can't keep your hands off each other, huh?"

Holy hell. A.J. set his forehead to Ana's, and he felt the soft rumble of a chuckle escape her body when they both should've ducked for cover. But he gave in to the laughter, too, because why not?

"This ain't a dream, is it?" he whispered into her ear. "I'm not still unconscious in the woods by Old Man Shaw's cabin?"

"Now you know better than to go near his place. That

man will shoot you," his mom warned, somehow overhearing his hushed words.

A.J. stopped himself from bellowing out another "mama" and pulled away from Ana, part of him wishing they were going to stay at Grant's and make love instead of having lunch with his parents. "Just lunch," he gave in, facing his mom with a hand in the air, hoping she wouldn't protest because heaven help him, she always won.

His mom winked and tucked her shotgun under her arm. "We'll see."

"Maybe dessert, too?" Ana smiled. "I heard you have some of the best pies in Alabama."

And now Ana was in trouble. His mom would never let her go.

But that wasn't such a bad thing since he had no intention of running this time.

CHAPTER TWENTY-FOUR

A.J. HAD OPTED TO TAKE HIS OWN VEHICLE AND FOLLOWED his mom to the Hawkins Ranch. The last thing he wanted was to be trapped into staying there all day. He wasn't sure if Ana had deliberately distracted him during the short drive with all of her flirtatious shenanigans, but there'd be payback later regardless.

He'd nearly sent them careening into a ditch when she'd spread her legs and snuck a hand beneath the hem of her skirt as though she might dare get herself off. Who knew there was a little vixen beneath all those layers she began shedding since her arrival in Alabama?

"Nice view." Ana's hands were set on the granite counter in his mom's kitchen as she observed a good portion of the Hawkins Ranch from the large picture window. She stood on her tiptoes and angled her head, trying to take it all in.

His mom had stepped out of the kitchen to fetch Ana an apron from the laundry room. She'd hosted a girls' baking party the previous evening and her collection of University of Alabama aprons were all in the dryer.

A.J. hooked an arm around Ana's waist from behind and

set his chin on her shoulder, joining her to take in the view. He pointed out the pasture lands, then the stable off in the distance. "I'll take you on a tour after lunch."

"That sounds nice," she murmured, then surprised him by wriggling her ass against his crotch.

He bit down on his back teeth and ordered his hands to stay on her waist . . . no roaming. He'd already been caught in the act of groping her once by his mom. "Be careful, sugar, you keep on provoking me, and we'll be skipping that dessert you're looking forward to," he growled against her ear.

She gave him a saucy look over her shoulder. "What will you do?"

"I grew up on a ranch, and I'm a sailor, which makes me damn good with knots. I might just have to bind your wrists and torture you with my tongue if you keep at it." He could play the tease game, too.

"And there you two go again," his mom said, crushing the moment. *No wonder I never got away with any bullshit as a kid. She has ninja skills.* A.J. sighed in frustration but stepped back and unhanded Ana as his mom continued to talk. "I remember those days with your father."

"We were discussing Ana's lack of cooking skills."

"Oh, you can't cook, my dear?" Deb handed Ana a red apron, which had a giant white A at the center, then put on a matching one. "I can teach you a few things. But don't worry, A.J. can cook for you, too. I raised my boys not to expect women to wait on them." Her expression suddenly changed to one of mild shock, and she clutched her imaginary pearls. "You're not an Auburn or Tennessee alum, are you?" This was part jest, part serious on his mom's part. He just never knew which way she was leaning at any given time.

"Mama," he said, delivering a warning flavored with a little love.

"No, ma'am. I assure you I'm a newly proud Bama fan." Ana's lips tipped into a broad smile. Her cheeks were a soft pink, still flushed from having been caught in the act with A.J. again.

"Glad to hear you have good sense," his mom replied as A.J. helped Ana tie on the apron.

She pulled her hair up into a high ponytail, which was a shame since he was loving the relaxed version of Ana, her auburn hair tumbling over her shoulders in soft waves. She'd let it air dry today, which enhanced her naturally wavy hair, making it look like she belonged on a beach, not on the run from the FBI while chasing down Russian spies.

"Where is everyone?" he asked while his mom busied herself with washing her hands in the farmhouse sink.

She dried her hands on her apron. "It is Wednesday. We don't all have wild hours like you. But Caleb will be in soon for lunch. Dad had to run some errands. And Ella and McKenna are around here somewhere."

"Why aren't they in school?" he asked before turning to Ana. "McKenna is my niece, and Ella's my sister. She's a teacher."

"It's summer, or have you forgotten? And you know Ella helps Beckett by entertaining McKenna while he's at work." His mom tipped her chin at A.J., and he got the message. Go find Ella and apologize about the "bachelor" party.

The fact his sister had yet to call A.J. and yell at him meant she was still too angry to talk to him.

"I need to go find my sister." He looked at Ana for permission to leave. "You'll be okay?"

"She's in good hands," his mom answered for Ana, and Ana shooed A.J. away. Her body more relaxed. Already fitting in. She'd make a great Alabama woman, wouldn't she?

And did he want to move back home someday? He sure did miss his small town and family.

A.J. raked a hand through his hair as he wandered out of the kitchen in search of his sister. This was all a bit strange. He really was beginning to wonder if he was fast asleep in the forest, and Mrs. Shaw was playing some mind tricks on him.

He shook off his doubt, or nerves, whatever it was, while checking the rest of the house. After finding it empty, he made his way outside. He snatched his shades from where they hung on his shirt to protect his eyes from the glaring June sun.

Ella stood outside the white and green horse stable with McKenna off in the distance. As he strode their way, McKenna spotted him and trotted her colorful, spotted Appaloosa closer to Ella and dismounted.

He cupped his hands around his mouth and called out, "Yo!"

Ella spun around in surprise, her cowboy boots kicking up dust, and shielded her eyes with her hand beneath the brim of her straw cowboy hat. "What in blazes are you doing back here?"

"Uncle A.J.!" McKenna tore the thirty or so yards to get to him while Ella handed off the horse to one of the guys who worked on the ranch.

"Hey, sweet pea." He scooped her into his arms, forgetting she was eleven, not five, and spun her in a circle. Her long black hair, which she'd inherited from her mother's side, fanned out behind her. McKenna's birth mom was part Cherokee, and McKenna had been blessed with her grandmother's rich, silky black hair.

"You're back already!" McKenna exclaimed once he set her down, her face beaming. "Why are you here?"

He didn't want to lie to a kid, so . . .

He shot an uncomfortable look Ella's way as she took her sweet time to get to them. "I'm here with a friend for work, but can you do me a favor?" He leaned down to eye level with her. "Can you not tell anyone I'm back home? It's kind of top secret."

McKenna brought a finger to her lips and nodded before he pushed back upright. "Who is your friend? Mr. Chris? Mr. Finn?"

"No, you haven't met her. Name is Anastasia, but she goes by Ana." He jerked a thumb back toward the house. "She's with Nana in the kitchen."

McKenna glimpsed Ella and faced him again. "I'm going to go see her!"

"Right." He set a palm to his thigh in anticipation as Ella made her way over while McKenna took off in a sprint toward the house up the hill.

Can I go back to making out with Ana back at Grant's?

"What are you doing here?" Ella's blonde hair was plaited in two braids, one on each side of her face. Her blue eyes—she took after their dad—were sharp on him. She was giving him her signature teacher stare she whipped out for her students to let them know they'd done something wrong. "Dad and the others know you're back so soon?"

He mimicked her stance, arms across his chest, attempting to hold his ground against a Hawkins woman. Ella was as strong, if not stronger, than their mom. "I'm here for work, and if you wouldn't mind, don't let anyone outside the family know I'm home."

Her brows stitched together with mild curiosity before she said, "Brian's not here if you were wondering. Back in Mobile until the wedding. And thanks to your shenanigans, he won't be taking a local banking job. He insists we move to his place once we're married."

"What?" His arms plummeted to his sides. "Your job is here. Your family."

"And his job is in Mobile, and he's not looking to sacrifice everything for our crazy family."

"Sounds like Mr. Perfect ain't so perfect to me, then." He huffed out an angry breath, momentarily forgetting the real reason he was in Alabama after hearing the news that his sister was hurting, and it'd been, in part, his fault. "Mom know you're going to move to Mobile?"

"No, and don't you dare say anything. Not until I find a way to tell everyone, especially McKenna." Disappointment from her harsh stare cut him hard.

"I swear, woman, you just—"

"What?" Ella stepped closer and lifted her chin to bring her face closer to his from her height of five-six. "*You* need to apologize to Brian is what you need to do." A finger stabbed his chest. "Since you're down here, take a trip to Mobile and tell him you're sorry."

"I can't do that, and you know it. I'm here for work, and even if I wasn't, I don't want to see him," he admitted, an angry bite to his words. He hadn't meant to come across that way, but he didn't like the fucker for whatever reason. "Brian's not good enough for you."

"You don't know him." She spun away to face the stable off in the distance as Jesse exited the building alongside Caleb.

"Jesse's here, too?" Too many people would know he was home.

Jesse and Caleb spotted A.J., and Jesse made a "yeehaw" noise and kicked up his pace to approach them. His gaze hung on Ella for a few seconds before he threw his attention to A.J. "Whatcha doing back here, man?" He reached around and slapped a hand to A.J.'s back as his version of a hug.

"Work," A.J. said, still a bit taken aback at Ella's news about moving to Mobile.

Ella placed a hand at the side of her mouth as if she were about to divulge a secret. "Don't tell anyone he's here or *Alexander* will get his skivvies in a twist." Great, Ella was pulling out his first name. She really was pissed, and given Brian's reaction to the bachelor party, he couldn't say as he blamed her.

Did he have time to make things right? Did he *want* to make things right?

Brian. Brian. Brian. Screw that guy.

"What kind of mischief are you up to?" Caleb asked once he reached them, having taken his time to get to A.J. "We just got your ass out of here, and here you are again. You real?" He waved both hands in the air as if there was some mystical force field between them.

You and me, brother. You and me. He was right there with him questioning just about everything, including his sanity, given his dream slash ghost encounter last night.

"Work," Ella quickly answered for him with enough sass to make a grown man quake in his boots. "And a woman is here. Anastasia."

A.J. slapped a palm to his face when he remembered Ana's name had been revealed at the bar Saturday night.

"The FBI agent?" Caleb asked, putting two and two together, unfortunately.

Damn it.

"Wait, what?" Ella sputtered in surprise.

A.J. lowered his palm from his face. "Different Ana," he attempted to bullshit a bullshitter. Caleb wouldn't buy it.

"Well, I gotta go see the woman who has you all tickled pink in the face like this." Caleb swirled a finger in A.J.'s direction and then scurried off to the house.

"Don't mention the FBI thing, please," A.J. called out in a low voice. Caleb whipped around and zipped his lips shut like he used to do when they were kids. "Shit," he cursed under his breath and looked to Jesse for—help? He wasn't so sure.

"You protecting a Fed?" Jesse asked once Ella took off toward the house as well.

A.J. gripped his temples with his thumb and middle finger and applied pressure. "Something like that. And coming here wasn't the plan, but Mom showed up at Grant's rather unexpectedly while I was making out with Ana."

"Whoa, rewind." Jesse slapped a hand to A.J.'s chest. "You did what with the pretty Fed? And she's a looker, right?"

A.J.'s chest puffed out with a deep breath as he lowered his hand to his side. "More than pretty," he said on a sigh. "And you can't tell a soul we're here." He removed his glasses so Jesse could see his eyes and understand he meant every word.

Jesse held both palms in the air and smiled. "You've kept all my dirty secrets. I suppose I could return the favor and finally keep a few of yours."

A.J. trusted him. McKenna, too, despite her youth. No one would rat out his location. Small towns were great at gossiping, but they'd protect a secret from outsiders down to their dying breath. "Let's not talk about why I'm here, though. I'm worried about Ella and Brian."

"She told you about moving to Mobile?" he asked with a wince. "She didn't tell me, but I overheard her talking to Brian Sunday night before he hightailed it out of town."

"And you didn't knock the shit out of him?"

"I wanted to, but then Ella would hate me," Jesse said. "She's pissed at all of us."

"Well, we gotta fix this. I just need some time to handle a work matter first. But before their wedding—"

"She's gonna marry him," Jesse said, his tone defeated. "The more we try and stop her, the more stubborn that woman becomes."

"Hawkins women," they both said at the same time.

"Uncle A.J.! Mr. Jesse! Lunch!" McKenna called from the back porch, hands on each side of her mouth.

"I guess it's time I go meet the girl that's got you all googly eyed." Jesse grinned, and A.J. quickly placed his shades back on.

"Shut up," he mumbled as they started up the hill to get to the house.

"I absolutely insist you stay for dinner!" Ella said the second he opened the sliding glass door to go inside. "I just won't take no for an answer. I'm cooking tonight, and it'd be inhospitable of you to turn down a Southern meal." Ella was laying it on thick. Revenge for Brian.

"Please, please, please, Ms. Ana," he heard McKenna beg next as he and Jesse entered the kitchen.

Ana's gaze cut straight to A.J. for a clue as to how to handle the situation. The woman could take down Russian spies, but throw some sassy and stubborn Southerners her way, and she was waving a white flag of surrender.

"Ohhh, you must be the one I've heard so much about." Jesse left A.J.'s side to introduce himself to Ana, offering her a momentary reprieve from answering the dinner question.

"So, it's agreed." A.J.'s mom slapped her hands together while Jesse pulled out a chair for Ana to sit at their big white kitchen table. "After lunch, we'll give you a tour of the ranch —not too many of them in Alabama, so our place is all the more special—then after, you'll clean up and have dinner."

What just happened? And he saw the same look in Ana's eyes once she sat at the table.

"You just *have* to stay," Ella insisted as she helped set out the barbecue sandwiches and sides.

"I'm, um, sorry, but we probably won't be able to stay for too long." An A for effort from Ana, but the woman was toast with *three* Hawkins women in her presence. She really had no idea what she'd gotten herself into. Russian espionage would be a cake walk after a day with his family.

Maybe he could fake a call from his team, and they'd be able to escape that way?

He sat opposite Ana at the table between Caleb and Jesse and placed a sandwich on his plate alongside some homemade pasta salad.

When McKenna reached for Ana's hand to say grace, A.J.'s throat thickened at the sight.

Ana took Ella's hand on the other side, and she caught A.J.'s eyes before bowing her head.

Ana wasn't an FBI agent on the run right now.

And he wasn't a clandestine operator crossing a whole bunch of lines to help her.

He didn't know exactly how to define the two of them, or the moment, but he wasn't so sure he needed to. Instead, he took Jesse's and Caleb's hands and said grace, then sent a silent thank-you up to Marcus for helping to get him there.

CHAPTER TWENTY-FIVE

THERE WAS FULL, AND THEN ACCORDING TO A.J., THERE WAS "Alabama home-cooked meal" full. Ana set a hand to her abdomen, wondering if the buttons on the dress Ella had insisted she wear were in danger of popping off. She did a discreet check. Nope, she was good.

After their tour of the ranch, Ella had promptly led Ana to her old bedroom to wash up for dinner and refused to take no for an answer when she gifted Ana with a cute dress she'd designed. In the small en suite, Ana had tried to wrangle her windblown hair after taking a quick shower but gave up, deciding it looked pretty good with her sun-kissed skin and her new outfit. The sleeveless V-neck dress fell to mid-thigh and was made of soft denim with turquoise buttons down the front and a butterfly on the back fashioned out of turquoise stones. It was actually quite impressive.

Wait until after dinner to wear the hat. A.J. will lose his mind, Ella had said, while she held a tan women's cowboy hat in hand and took in the sight of Ana in the ensemble. Ella had also insisted Ana wear her hair down. Apparently, every

Hawkins felt Ana was in need of relaxing, and "hair down" was pivotal to that happening.

And after the hours spent touring the ranch, during which A.J. stole private moments to tease *her* as payback for earlier —stealing kisses, nuzzling his face in her neck, whispering sexy words in her ear—Ana felt as though she'd had a two-hour massage. So, she was, in fact, relaxed.

She and A.J. hadn't talked to his team since that morning, but A.J. continually reassured her that his people had everything covered whenever signs of worry crossed her face.

We're used to missions like these, he'd said. *Walk in the park*, he'd added before sweeping his tongue between her lips and cupping her ass with that strong, rough hand of his—*just* as his niece, McKenna, caught them and clapped with excitement, which drew a blush from Ana and a "skedaddle" from A.J.

"The meal and dessert were incredible." Ana smiled at A.J.'s mom, who was sitting next to A.J. across from Ana at the outdoor dining table on the deck overlooking the stunning property. Varied shades of gold, pink, and blue spread across the sky and were a reminder of her sunset kiss with A.J. in the pond yesterday. It'd been a picture-perfect moment last night, and spending time with his family today had also been amazing. "Thank you," she said to both his mom and Ella for cooking.

A.J.'s other two brothers, Beckett and Shep, hadn't been able to make it for dinner. Beckett, the sheriff of their small town, was dealing with an urgent matter, and Shep was on call at the firehouse. Basically, if Ana were stuck inside a Hallmark movie about a small town, this would be it. And she was loving Alabama more and more with every passing moment.

"You're very welcome, dear," A.J.'s mom answered, and

Ella responded with a smile and a nod, but her gaze was focused on their friend Jesse at the table.

"We're more than happy to have you here," A.J.'s dad, Rick, commented.

"Thank you." Ana watched with wide eyes as A.J.'s mom slid another huge slice of pecan pie onto her son's plate. When he let out a mournful groan, she simply said, "You need to eat up, Son."

He grumbled and cursed, then snatched his fork and dug in, his eyes lifting to meet Ana's.

She hid a laugh at the comical expression on his face, then panicked at the sight of another piece of pie heading her way. "Oh, I honestly think I may not be able to walk if I eat more." Between the Bushwacker, which was basically a creamy chocolate piña colada, the pie, and the three servings of homemade cornbread served with the duck, she didn't have room. "But thank you." A.J.'s mom tilted her head and squinted, obviously suspicious of anyone who turned down her pie, so Ana reluctantly gave in. "Um, okay. Maybe a sliver."

Now it was A.J. chuckling as he patted crumbs from his mouth with his red-and-white linen napkin. She jumped in her chair when the tip of A.J.'s cowboy boot tapped hers. *Footsy?*

Buuut, she was wearing the cutest short boots with side fringe Ella claimed needed to be paired with the dress. Lucky they were both a size 8. They were another design of Ella's. On her tour, A.J.'s father had said he'd created a studio on the ranch for Ella's sewing and leatherworking hobby.

A.J. also looked sexier than ever in a black tee that highlighted his amazing arms, broad shoulders, and chest. His shirt was matched with a pair of classic stonewashed jeans that showed off another amazing "asset" of his. Brown leather boots and a hat to finish off the sexy cowboy look. The beige hat had a hand distressed finish with a cattleman crease. Well, that's what Ella explained while Ana stood in a daze, mentally undressing A.J. as he'd strolled onto the patio just before dinner was served.

She'd never known cowboys were her weakness until meeting him. And Ella was trying to turn her into a cowgirl.

"I hope you two are planning on staying a bit longer," A.J.'s dad said. "I do know your secret, so—"

"And what is that?" A.J. used his playful tone, the one Ana knew well and loved, and positioned his attention on his father, but Ana's heartbeat suddenly took a wild ride.

His dad waved a hand in the air like he was swatting a fly. Heck, maybe there'd been one. After all, they were in the South where the flies were big enough to ride like a horse, according to McKenna. Plus, the smell of the roasted glazed duck wafting through the air, coupled with the pecan pie, had to be an insect attractor. "That Ana let you win during that little shooting competition down at the range before y'all showered and got cleaned up for dinner."

A.J.'s focus whirled to Ana, who let out a breath of relief upon hearing *that* was the secret he knew. A.J. flashed her a sneaky grin. "Or maybe I let her think that she let me win, but really—"

"Sure, Son," his dad interrupted. "You keep telling yourself that." Oh, and his dad was a jokester, too.

But also, his dad was right. "I may have taken it easy on him." Since the cat was out of the bag about her being FBI, she hadn't felt it necessary to hide her shooting skills, but she was in A.J.'s home, and it would have been impolite to let A.J. lose, right?

"You should come to the wedding," Ella blurted out before A.J. had a chance to offer a comeback to Ana's teasing words. "What do you say?" The question had Ana dropping her fork when she realized Ella was speaking to her. "I mean, we have plenty of room." Ella's gaze tore across the table to A.J., and the stiff way she held her shoulders back left no doubt she was angry about something. "In fact, A.J., you ought to invite all your friends for the nuptials." Her accent was thicker than A.J.'s, same with the rest of his family members. "You know, bring back those Teamguys that were here this past weekend. The ones who worked so hard to try and scare my fiancé out of marrying me."

Ohhhh. Yeah, she was pissed at A.J. Ana could practically see the steam rising from Ella's ears like a kettle about to blow. And everyone at the table must have felt it.

A.J. set his fork alongside his plate and lowered his gaze to the remaining bites of pie. He'd taken off his hat before dinner, which Ana assumed was a sign of respect down South. "And where is Brian right now? With the wedding so close, why ain't he here?"

Jesse abruptly stood from the table as if he'd rather be anywhere but there at the moment. "I think I hear an alarm or something beeping inside. I best go check that out." He positioned his eyes on Ella from where he stood on the other side of A.J. for several heartbeats, and it was then that Ana knew why he wanted out of there.

Jesse had a thing for Ella.

Once he was gone, Ella set her napkin on her plate, and her eyes remained cast down. "Brian will be back the Friday before the wedding."

"Oh, Ana, it's gonna be beautiful." A.J.'s mom waved a dramatic hand toward the backyard. "Church wedding, then the reception will be right here. Fireworks at night while everyone dances. Magical." She was clearly doing her best to keep the peace between her kids.

"Yeah, maybe it'll rain." Caleb reached for the neck of his beer, eyes on his sister, but Ella didn't look his way. And from the looks of it, Caleb wasn't a fan of this Brian guy, either.

"Rain on the wedding day is supposed to be good luck for marriage," McKenna said with a big, innocent smile.

"Then I highly doubt—"

"It'll be the Fourth of July weekend," A.J.'s dad spoke up, cutting off whatever A.J. was about to say, which probably a good thing. "I bet your teammates could use another weekend off."

"Wow, the Fourth is coming up soon," Ana chimed in, hoping to help dispel some of the tension. Though it seemed like an issue between siblings, and therefore none of her business, Ana felt compelled to do what little she could to protect A.J. from Ella's silent fury. But knowing A.J., if he'd done something to try and scare off Ella's fiancé, he had a good reason. Ana trusted his judgment.

"The Fourth of July down here in Alabama is like Christmas," A.J.'s mom commented with pride. "You were planning on staying with Grant for the wedding weekend, right?" She fidgeted with her silverware, straightening them beside her plate.

"I'll offer the invite to the team," A.J. answered, his tone turning glib. "Wyatt and Natasha are getting married toward the end of July, so I'm not sure they can fit two *joyful* occasions in one month." The way he'd said "joyful" had the hairs on Ana's arms standing.

"Alexander," Ella hissed in warning.

"What?" A.J. pushed back from the table. Footsies were officially done. "You're marrying the wrong man, and you know it." He stood. "Now, if you'll excuse me, I better help Jesse with that beeping."

"Me, too." Caleb followed A.J. into the house, leaving Ana at the table with a few awkward throat clears from A.J.'s parents.

"Sorry about the boys," A.J.'s dad began, eyes moving to Ana from where he sat at the head of the table, "but they get a bit protective of those they love."

"That's all it is, Ella." A.J.'s mom reached across the table and set a hand over Ella's. "Ignore them."

"Yeah, sure," Ella said softly. "Anyway, Ana is our guest, so let's talk about something happier."

Happier than your wedding? Hmm. Did she really want to marry Brian?

"A.J. hasn't brought a woman home in, hell, more than a decade." A.J.'s dad was similar in height to A.J., about six feet, and had a full head of silver hair, thick beard, and kind blue eyes. His skin was tanner than A.J.'s, probably from all his outside work on the ranch over the years. "So, we're happy you were able to join us."

"You know, I reckon A.J. hasn't had a girlfriend since Brooke, and that was in his twenties," his mom said. "Brooke is one of Ella's closest friends. Bridesmaid. Of course, if Rory doesn't make it home for the wedding, she'll be the maid of honor."

"Rory will make it," Ella quickly defended, then peered at Ana. "Rory is Jesse's sister, and she sure took a liking to one of A.J.'s friends last weekend. Well, she didn't use those words, but—"

"Chris?" Jesse asked as he returned to the table with A.J. and Caleb.

"Beeping gone?" Ella asked with a sarcastic tone.

"Taken care of," A.J. answered before sitting. "And what were you all talking about?"

BRITTNEY SAHIN

"How Rory has the hots for that friend of yours, Chris," Jesse explained. "From what Ella is saying, at least."

"Oh." A.J. scratched his beard. "Yeah, feelings might be mutual." He tossed out the words as casually as possible. "Anyway."

"So, A.J. told me all about your professional singing career, Mr. Hawkins," Ana quickly said, and A.J. looked up and sent a silent thank-you for the reprieve with his eyes. "I'd love to hear you sing."

"A.J.'s the better singer," his father admitted. "I think it'd be nice if you sing a song or two after dinner, don't you?"

"Oh, I don't know about that." A.J. shook his head.

Ana had heard him sing in the car the other night, and her ovaries would probably burst if he were to serenade her in front of his family. But, how could she pass up hearing him sing again? "I'd love that."

"Yes, please, Uncle A.J.!" McKenna pleaded. "Maybe we can dance, too. Good practice for the wedding."

"How can I say no to that?" A.J. stood from the table. "My guitar in the usual place?" he asked his mom.

"Of course, dear." Mrs. Hawkins stood and set her hands on her hips. "These dishes can wait. Let's go out onto the patio down below."

"Now is the time for that hat," Ella said with an easy smile, the recent tension in regard to her wedding seemingly forgotten. "I'll go get it."

As Ella disappeared into the house, McKenna came skipping across the deck toward Ana with an outstretched hand. "Come on! You can dance with Jesse first." She motioned toward A.J.'s good-looking friend. "Oh, wait." McKenna made a huge show of shrugging her shoulders before pulling her hand away from Ana. "You probably

302

shouldn't since Uncle A.J. was making out with you earlier, right?"

Ana felt the heat rise up her neck and take over her face at McKenna's comment.

"That's okay, sweetheart, we all know how that boy feels about you. A.J.'s eyes say it all." Mrs. Hawkins pointed to the backyard indicating they needed to get a move on.

Jesse saluted her and started for the steps off the back deck.

"I miss anything?" A.J. asked when he returned outside and found them on the patio area. He was now wearing his hat, the guitar strap positioned over his shoulder.

Holy shit. Now I have a thing for singing cowboys. Her body tensed, overcome with need. Memories of his kisses on her bare skin circled around in her mind as he stood close to her. "Just my near death by embarrassment. No biggy, though."

He crooked her chin with his index finger and tilted her face up to find her eyes. "You okay?" he asked with a gentle sincerity.

"More than okay." Despite everything, she was swimming in a crystal-clear ocean of "more than okay" right now. "And I can't wait to hear you sing."

"I ain't that good. Don't get your hopes up." He withdrew his hand, and she wished instead he'd set his lips over hers.

"Here you go," Ella announced. "This will look great on you."

"Oh, hell yes," A.J. drawled when Ella set the cowgirl hat on Ana's head.

"Now you look like a Bama gal." Ella winked. She started to walk away but glanced back when A.J. captured her upper arm.

"I'm sorry," he said to Ella, remorse in his tone and in his eyes. "If Brian is who you want to marry, I'll make things right. I just want you to be happy."

Ana slipped away and left them alone, worried about intruding on a moment A.J. needed to have with his sister.

Ana glimpsed Jesse positioning a stool in front of the patio chairs, making her think a night like this was the norm for this family. Jesse's eyes were on Ella, his clean-shaven jaw tight as he regarded her. Oh, he had it bad for that woman. *The eyes say it all.* "Your cabinets at Grant's house are spectacular." Jesse ripped his focus from Ella and released the stool.

"Thanks. The master bed was handmade as well." A knowing smirk traveled across his lips. "But I assume you haven't seen that one."

"No, I haven't." *And now I'm about to fan myself like a Southern belle.* Thoughts of A.J. pinning her to a bed, the ground—hell, anywhere—had her body heating up.

"Mmmhmm." Jesse's smile stretched before he took a seat next to Caleb. A.J.'s parents and McKenna were already seated.

"Come on, A.J.," Mrs. Hawkins called out. "I promised Beckett I'd get McKenna to sleep by nine."

"Yes, ma'am." A.J. strode toward the stool, and Ella chose the seat next to Ana. Despite A.J.'s apology, a tense energy emanated from his sister, more so, Ana noticed, when Ella's gaze lingered Jesse's way.

But when Ana moved her focus to A.J., one booted foot on the ground, the other on the rung of the stool, and the pick between his teeth while he tuned the guitar—her attention was solely on him. Where else could it possibly be?

A.J.'s eyes sparkled, a mischievous look she already knew all too well. She couldn't help but picture his strong hands strumming her body instead of plucking the guitar strings.

"Any requests?" A.J. called out.

"Blake Shelton!" McKenna exclaimed. "The 'Hell Right' song, and no, Nana, I'm not swearing. That don't count."

"I think I remember that one." A.J. closed one eye and took the pick from his mouth as if trying to call up the lyrics in his mind. "Okay, got it."

Ana did her best not to clutch her chest when he began singing, his deep, husky voice delivering the uplifting song. Jesse and Caleb began dancing with McKenna, taking turns twirling her around, and then before Ana knew it, even A.J.'s parents were on their feet, clapping and swaying.

Was this what Southern life was like?

I could stay here forever.

"Dance with me!" McKenna offered her hand while dancing in place. Ana took it and let McKenna pull her up off the chair.

Let loose, she reminded herself. Dancing wasn't her specialty. It required letting go, allowing your limbs to be loose and free. That wasn't quite natural for her yet.

When Jesse requested Luke Bryan's "What She Wants Tonight"—well, Ana's insides melted while listening to A.J. croon the lyrics.

Yeah, A.J. knew exactly what Ana wanted.

Forget slow. Forget why they were in Alabama to begin with. She wanted A.J. tonight.

Caleb surprised Ana by pulling her in for a dance, only for the briefest of moments, and it was clear he was doing his best to try and rile A.J. up. But Caleb's actions did have A.J. on his feet, eyes pinned on Ana.

"How about a little Lee Brice, 'I Don't Dance'?" The unmistakable husky tone of A.J.'s voice was heard by everyone. He left out the *This one is for you*, but Ana felt it in her bones as he sang. The lyrics had her swaying from side to side, unable to remove her gaze from him the entire time he sang. Her heart was going to explode. Each verse of the song had her feeling the intent of the words.

When A.J. finished, he handed off his guitar to Caleb, who then picked up playing, and made a straight line for Ana.

He wrapped her in his arms, not giving a damn who saw, and lifted her off the ground. He held her hat on and tipped it back to better see her eyes.

"I don't want to take it slow," she whispered softly, but the gleam of her desire was loud and clear.

CHAPTER TWENTY-SIX

"Damn, woman, I'm gonna get us in an accident," A.J. growled as Ana did something she'd never in her life done before: tossed her inhibitions out the window.

His hand was on the back of her head, his fingers threaded through her hair while she took all of him in her mouth as they drove back to Grant's house. "You want me to stop?" she panted out, coming up for air.

"Hell no, don't stop," he groaned and gave her a quick smile before returning his focus to the road. Ana grinned and returned her own focus to his lap, where his shaft poked through the opening of his jeans.

Her panties were soaked, slick with desire, and they'd been that way from the moment A.J. belted out the first song in his rich, husky voice. A short while later, he artfully negotiated their departure from his parents' ranch as if de-escalating a hostage situation. And the moment they were alone in the SUV, his tongue was in her mouth, the top half of her denim dress undone and a hand inside her bra to cup her breast.

And now she was sucking his . . .

I'm allowed to think the word. Damn her inner prude for scolding her inner bad girl, who had apparently never been let out to play before A.J.

Coooock, she allowed the word to glide through her mind with certainty. It'd flown so easily from her mouth in front of A.J. last night, so no reason to let it hang her up now.

She licked slowly, circling the head with her tongue before sliding down his long, thick length. With one hand holding the base of his shaft, she bobbed her mouth up and down, feeling like Anastasia the pole dancer and loving every flipping second of this incredibly sensual act of going down on her sexy cowboy.

"Letting her hair down" had officially been bumped out of first place on her "How To Relax" list, replaced by "pleasuring her man." Ana was wild about A.J.'s grunts and groans of desire.

His quad flexed beneath her palm as she continued to suck eagerly. "Mmm," she moaned, aroused by the taste of him and his reactions to her touch.

"Fuck, girl, I'm gonna bust my load in that sweet mouth of yours if you don't pull off soon," he roared as the truck made a sharp turn, probably into Grant's long driveway. The home sat far back on the property, acres of woods making up his front yard. "And the first time I get off with you, it's going to be in your pussy." He gently fisted her hair and urged her off him.

"But you taste so good," she moaned, "and I don't want to stop."

Even when the SUV slowed to a brief stop, the mechanical sounds of the garage door signaling they'd arrived at the house, Ana continued to work him with her mouth.

She needed this, maybe more than he did.

"Darlin' . . . I-I changed my mind." The words cut through his clenched teeth as he cupped the back of her neck. "Puhhhlease don't stop now."

She swallowed every last bit of cum that exploded into her mouth a moment later.

His breathing was ragged and his hands a bit shaky as he let go of her. Ana slowly sat up, brushing the back of her hand over her mouth, relishing the satisfied expression on his face, especially since she was the one to put it there.

Not so cold and dead now.

"You're naughty."

After untangling herself from the seatbelt, she confessed with a touch of shyness, "I've never been like this with anyone but you."

A.J. secured his length back inside his pants and zipped his jeans, leaving the top button undone. He unbuckled his seatbelt, gently lifted Ana's hand, and placed a soft kiss on the inside of her slender wrist before using his hold to guide her over the center console. Her denim dress slid up to her hips as she straddled his lap with a little shimmy, wishing he was still exposed so she could grind against him.

"Good. I'd prefer it stay that way from now on, too."

She wet her lips. "You don't like to share, I take it?" Ana had no idea her voice could sound so breathy and provocative, but she embraced it, giving herself permission to be the naughty girl, Anastasia the dancer, without fear of judgment, knowing this man would love her for whatever she gave him.

"Absolutely no to sharing." The words were infused with a sexy kind of possessiveness that turned her on. He banded a hand around her hip and tightened his hold of her as if to emphasize his words. "And when you're ready for more . . ."

More orgasms? Or more . . .? Hope clutched her heart

and had her inhaling a deep breath. She never wanted *this* to end between them. Not after tonight. Not after the meeting with Porter, and especially not after the Volkovs were gone once and for all.

Did that make her crazy?

Do I care?

Maybe she would have before yesterday. Before this man had flipped her world upside down.

A.J. killed the engine so they wouldn't die of carbon monoxide poisoning. That would totally ruin "more."

As she sat atop his lap, a sense of pride and power surged through her.

He removed his hat and set it on her head as he held her gaze. "When we make love, this hat is the only thing I want to see you wearing." He pressed his mouth to hers in a sweet kiss, parted her lips with his tongue, and held nothing back as he gave her the most intoxicating kiss she'd ever experienced. Ana pressed her ass down onto his lap and rotated her hips to let him know she wanted it all.

"Oh, really?" she asked, pulling back slightly while clutching two handfuls of his cotton tee. "And what will you be wearing?"

"Just rubber." He wedged a hand between their bodies and shifted her bra to palm her breast. "One of these days, hopefully nothing at all."

A thrill raced down her spine. "If you play your cards right, that just might happen."

"Shall we go inside, then?"

She nodded, temporarily robbed of speech as desire took over, and her body trembled like the aftershocks of an earthquake.

He nipped her lip before kissing her again, then quickly moved her back to the passenger seat.

Once out of the vehicle, A.J. scooped her up and carried her in his arms all the way to the large living room at the back of the house.

The moment he set her down, she immediately began unbuttoning her dress, anxious to get free of the thing.

"Hell, there are too many." He yanked at the material, sending the turquoise buttons flying. "Sorry." But there was no hint of remorse in his tone.

A fever was racing through them, their need for each other fierce and beyond question.

"This is what I want. Right here." Ana gasped when he squeezed her ass cheek.

Sliding her hands from the top of his jeans up to his chest, Ana whispered, "Take off your clothes." At her command, he released her, stepped back, and retrieved a condom from his billfold. "Always the prepared sailor."

With the foil wrapper gripped between his teeth, A.J. tossed his wallet, then shucked his shirt. Boots. Jeans and boxers. The man undressed with tactical precision.

Naked in all his glorious, muscular splendor, she gasped, "Wow." *My naked cowboy.*

His cock was hard again. Thick and roped with veins. Two confident strides brought her cowboy closer. "Your turn." His hooded green eyes blazed with desire as she removed what little clothing remained.

And wow, we're finally doing this. They'd only known each other for a short time, but being with him felt incredibly, undeniably right. The connection she had with A.J. was so strong, it felt as though they'd been together for years instead of a mere handful of days.

He ripped open the condom wrapper with his teeth and gripped his shaft, sliding his palm from root to tip as he watched her undress. "I think I'm in heaven." She stood naked before him with absolutely nothing to hide. She'd bared her soul, shared her secrets, and he hadn't turned away.

He rolled the condom over his length and lifted her with ease, guiding her legs around his waist and bringing her pussy against his hard length. She shifted and moved, desperate for more.

A.J. walked them backward, the bounce from each step creating a delicious friction at her core. His back hit the window and he spun around, reversing their positions. "Drop your legs down, sweetheart," he murmured.

The hat had fallen, but he seemed too preoccupied to notice.

Threading their fingers together, A.J. pinned their linked hands against the glass just above her shoulders and nuzzled her neck. The heat of his mouth was an exciting contrast to the coolness of the window on her bare bottom.

His hips moved in tight circles, adding more friction that had her yelping between the hot kisses he peppered all over her mouth.

"You're so beautiful," he said between kisses. "So damn sexy." He tightened his clasp of her one hand while letting go of the other.

His free hand explored and lovingly tortured her body. A slight twist of her nipple. A sharp nip of his teeth on her other breast. A slow graze of his nails down the side of her torso. Ana's breaths came fast and shallow.

But A.J. wasn't finished. He ran a finger along the side of her breast and on down to her hip before his hand cupped her wet center. Muttering incoherently against her mouth, A.J. slid a finger along the seam of her pussy, separating her folds. "Fuck, you're ready for me," he said on a groan before plunging a finger inside and curling it in a come-hither motion, hitting her right where he knew would make her—

"A.J.," she cried out before lowering her mouth to his shoulder and biting down. She pulled her other hand loose of his grasp and clutched his back for dear life as he worked his hand over her pussy. "I need you."

"Do you now?" he rasped, a slight twang in his tone when he brought his mouth to her ear. "How badly do you want me?"

"More than I can possibly explain," she answered honestly. Quickly. The searing heat of her desire sidestepped reason and responsibility. Having him inside of her was all that mattered right now.

There was no Anastasia Chernyshevsky tonight.

No Ana Quinn, the FBI agent.

Just the redheaded, sexual goddess that A.J. brought out of her. A woman who wasn't above begging him to make her body writhe with his touch and stars explode in her vision while luxuriating in the best orgasms of her life.

"Look at me." She lifted her eyes, unable to deny him anything at the moment. "Tell me, one more time. Tell me what you really want." His tone was gentle but commanding. He was talking about more than sex, wasn't he?

She cradled his cheeks between her palms. "I want you," she admitted. "All of you."

He slanted his mouth over hers with a crushing kiss that she was certain was also a freeing one for the both of them. It was a kiss that allowed him to move on from whatever else may have been holding him back, same as her.

She sank to the plush carpet moments later, not needing a bed or anything other than him.

"On top of me," he rasped. "With the hat."

She sat up, grabbed the hat, and secured it on her head, then waited for him to get on his back. *Sex with me on top.*

Yes, oh yes, yes, yes. What's that saying? Save a horse, ride a cowboy? She understood it now more than ever.

But this wasn't just sex, and they both knew it.

Once she'd straddled him, her knees sinking into the soft carpet, he leaned up on his forearms and eyed her pussy as she positioned the tip of his cock to her opening. The sight of him watching as their bodies connected was as erotic as it got for her.

She lowered her gaze and clenched her teeth, worried his thickness would hurt, at least initially. It had been a long time since she'd had sex. But she guided him inch by inch. Taking her time. And A.J. looked as though he might die. Ana knew it was taking every ounce of his willpower to resist the urge to grab her hips and take control. To penetrate her hard and fast. But he was letting her set the pace. Letting her choose how and when to lose the control she'd spent years trying to maintain.

Let go. Now. And with those words echoing in her mind, Ana sank down and took all of him. A.J. cursed under his breath as her palms landed on his chest and she adjusted her position, then began rocking. Moving up and down. Experimenting. Any and every which way felt phenomenal.

She leaned forward, sliding her hands alongside his muscular arms to bring her lips over his. He groaned against her mouth as she raised her bottom up and down in small motions.

"Ana," he said through gritted teeth.

He gripped her sides, digging his fingers into her flesh as he thrust with her, their bodies in a rhythmic dance. She eased to an upright position again to admire his carved muscles, to trace her finger over the lines of his V, the sex lines.

He palmed her small tits as they bounced. Perfect

handfuls for him. She gyrated and moved, and her body tensed as the impending orgasm mounted and built.

It was too soon. She didn't want to come yet.

But there was more time.

There would be more time for them, right?

As desire consumed her, Ana began moving faster, grinding against him, losing control. "Oh, oh, oh." While her little sounds grew louder and louder, A.J. brought his hands to her hips to steady her.

"Let go, sugar. Let go."

Ana tipped her head back and cried out a guttural moan, which was quickly followed by the feel of A.J.'s cock pulsating inside of her.

She collapsed onto his chest, her energy totally spent. The muscles in her thighs deliciously sore already from holding the position. "That was incredible."

He brushed the pad of his thumb over her lip, a taste of saltiness there when her tongue peeked out of her mouth. "More than incredible. And I think we need to do it again."

"No," she said with a firm shake of the head. "There is no 'I think'—we must do it again. And with you behind me. On top. Every which way."

A light rumble of laughter broke from his chest. "You're my kind of woman."

I am, aren't I? she thought with pride before folding her arms on his chest, resting her chin on her hands.

"A.J., what the fuck!" A deep, roaring voice had A.J. flipping Ana to her side and off of him.

Twice in one day, but this time, it wasn't his mom.

Tremors of embarrassment rocked through her body as she stole a glimpse of a man in uniform, his eyes closed, head turned to the side.

"Beckett, what are you doing here? Don't you knock?"

A.J. grabbed her pile of discarded clothes and handed it to her, then picked up his cowboy hat and stood, using it like a fig leaf to cover himself.

Ana quickly put on her dress, sans underwear, and backed against the window out of sheer horror that A.J.'s older brother—the freaking sheriff, and McKenna's father—had caught her butt naked on top of A.J.

"You can open your eyes," A.J. said once Ana was covered, but he hadn't taken the time to do anything other than protect his condom-wrapped dick with his hat.

Now that hat would never look the same.

Beckett slowly opened his eyes and scoffed. "I can see your naked ass in the window's reflection." He shook his head, grabbed A.J.'s jeans from the floor, and tossed them his way. "I'm betting your phone must be on silent—for obvious reasons—but it's probably been ringing nonstop." He turned his back so A.J. could pull on his jeans.

Not so easy. Condom had to be dealt with first. "One sec." He removed and tied off the condom, then hid the thing before pulling on his jeans.

Oh, jeez. She was going to die of humiliation.

"I don't know what happened." A.J. snatched his phone from his pocket. "Jesse must've put my phone on silent," he mumbled, probably assuming his friend had snuck the ringer off to give A.J. "alone time" with Ana. "Ten missed calls. Fuck."

"What's going on?" Ana worked her hands down the dress, attempting to find a few buttons that'd survived A.J.'s urgent hands earlier.

Beckett faced him, drawing a hand over his beard. "Ms. Anastasia Quinn, aka Anastasia Chernyshevsky, can you tell me why I shouldn't arrest you since you're now on the FBI's Most Wanted list?"

CHAPTER TWENTY-SEVEN

THE FBI'S MOST WANTED LIST. DESPITE ANA'S CLAIM THAT her affinity for lists soothed her soul, A.J. was damn certain Beckett's news she was now on *that* list would prove to have the polar opposite effect. Anastasia Chernyshevsky was officially in deep shit. And so was A.J.

A.J. held his palms up, phone clutched in one hand, while he eyed his brother. "I can explain," he blurted.

"How about you explain why a wanted fugitive spent the day at our house in the company of my daughter?" The vein at Beckett's temple visibly throbbed.

"It's my fault." Ana rushed to stand as a buffer, her arms outstretched between him and his brother. "I'm so sorry."

"She's not a fugitive," A.J. gritted out and sidestepped Ana. She didn't deserve Beckett's wrath.

"Her name and face are all over the national news." Beckett angrily tossed a hand in the direction of the TV.

Ana whirled toward the television, a horrified expression on her face, then frantically grabbed the remote and was clicking through channels before A.J. had a chance to muster a response to his brother.

"I need to call my people." He looked down at his phone like it might bite him. Which angry woman should he call first? There was an equal number of missed calls from both Harper and Jessica. "Can I explain after? Please, Beck, you know I'd never do anything to hurt the family."

"And maybe you weren't thinking with the right head." Beckett removed his sheriff's hat and tapped it alongside his thigh, eyes set on Ana as if she were an enemy of the nation, a traitor.

"Just one minute." A.J.'s phone vibrated in his palm before he had a chance to make a call.

Beckett waved him off with his free hand and then rested it on the holster of his gun, appearing ready to break leather and pull out his Glock at a moment's notice.

A.J. brought his phone to his ear, his gaze locked on Ana standing a few feet in front of the TV, her body one hard line. Arms crossed tight against her chest.

The same FBI photo of Ana from his case file was on screen, and he assumed the photo of a woman, with hair the exact color of Ana's, standing beside a dark-haired man were her parents.

"Hello?" A.J. turned away from the room, eyes on the window, hoping his brother wouldn't cuff Ana.

"What the hell, A.J.?" Harper hissed straight away. "Was your ringer off? We've been calling."

"I know, I know. Ana's made the news. And the wanted list," he said, his heart breaking for Ana too much to turn and look at her again.

She'd known this was a risk when she took the assignment, but seeing her face on national news as an alleged Russian spy, her name dragged through the mud along with her parents' . . . unimaginable.

"It's more than that," Harper said after a moment, her

tone remaining businesslike despite the shit situation. "We tracked the identity of the Caymans account holder."

"It's Ana, right?" He suddenly had a horrible, aching pain in the pit of his stomach.

"We've been operating under the assumption the account was for Ivan, but this must be another setup," Harper explained. "And it surely can't be a coincidence that within minutes of the FBI connecting Ana's name to the account, the surveillance footage of her entering Porter's house was leaked to the media, along with her real last name."

"Damn it." He cursed again. And then again. "Whoever was in Porter's house knows she's undercover, but—"

"But they chose to be selective in the intel they leaked to the national news," Harper added. "Which means they're using her as a fall guy, and they forced Mendez's hand to declare Ana a fugitive."

"The timing of the release of both the video footage and Ana's real last name only solidifies that someone at the Bureau has been moving pieces in place, maybe to put Ana right where they want her." *Porter?* His gut said not to trust the man. And if Porter had anything to do with setting up Ana, the last thing he wanted was to use her as bait to draw out Ivan Smirnoff. Well, assuming that's who kidnapped the sources. But based on intel, they were fairly certain The Huntsman was their guy. "Anyone know about me? That Ana and I are together?"

"Aside from Kyle's poor description of you to Ana's unit, no," Harper answered. "And speaking of Kyle, right after news broke about Ana, he was called back to Budapest."

"Wait, what?" At the moment, A.J. was too out of sorts to process the significance of Kyle's sudden return to Hungary. "Are we sending Owen to follow?"

"Admiral Chandler wants to wait and see what happens Friday at the safe house," Harper replied.

At least the admiral was still on their side. "Maybe we should cancel the meet on Friday? Too many unknown variables."

"No!" Ana exclaimed. "If I don't show up, I'll lose my chance with Anthony and to see if Porter is okay."

"Can I, uh, call you back?" His shoulders slumped when his eyes connected with Beckett, now standing off to his side in a watchful stance, hat back on, hand still on his holster.

"Of course, but you need to pack up and leave ASAP. I'd rather you leave the rental vehicle there. Grant have something you can drive?" Harper asked.

"Yeah," he said quickly, needing to de-escalate the tension in the room. "Call you soon." He ended the call and stuck the phone back into his jeans pocket. "We'll talk about Friday," he said to Ana. "But first—"

"You need to tell me why I'm not handing the Russian spy over to the FBI." Beckett and his straight-edge, no-bending-the-rules attitude, damn it. It had always been a source of contention between them over the years.

Ana faced the TV screen again, grabbed the remote, and turned it off. Probably a good idea. She didn't need any reporters getting into her head, not after she was finally freeing herself of some of the guilt she'd held on to about her parents' lives.

"She's undercover, but things went sideways," A.J. rushed out.

Beckett shook his head. "Trouble follows you everywhere you go, Alexander James."

He didn't need a lecture from his forty-year-old brother. Beckett may have been older, by a mere two years, but he wasn't A.J.'s dad, though he often acted like it. "And you haven't made any mistakes?" he challenged, which was a low blow because he didn't want to throw Beckett's past in his face right now. The man had his own demons. A.J. hung his head and took a few deep breaths to calm himself down. His brother wasn't the enemy. "Can we start over? Ana's not a threat to anyone in the family, and you must know I'd die before letting anything happen to my niece." How could Beckett ever think otherwise?

Beckett's hand slipped from the holster and relaxed at his side, but just because he didn't want to shoot him anymore, didn't mean he didn't want to throttle A.J. for bringing a "fugitive" to the ranch, innocent or not.

Ana snatched her bra and panties from the floor, apparently just noticing they were there, then held them behind her back and stood next to A.J.

"You two were here having sex at Grant's house, meanwhile her face is on every major news outlet in the country." Beckett curled his hands into fists at his sides. Tension gathering like an impending afternoon storm.

"Since when do you watch the news? You hate the media." *Not the point. Focus.* "We have to go. I'll explain everything once it's safe to do so. Please, just don't report we were here, not unless you want us getting killed." He hoped his brother would set aside his high-and-mighty moral compass if it meant keeping A.J. alive.

Beckett's mouth opened, prepared to speak, but then he tightened his lips.

"I really am so sorry." Ana stepped forward, keeping her undergarments hidden behind her back, and reached out with a tentative hand in Beckett's direction, but Beckett walked back a step.

Beckett stared at her with such contempt it had A.J. wanting to knock his brother in the jaw for daring to hurt

Ana's feelings. "You never come near my family again. You got it? If I see you back here, I'll be the first to bring you in," Beckett warned, eyes pinned on Ana.

She blinked, then bowed her head and returned to stand beside A.J. in defeat.

"You're out of line." A.J. stepped in front of his brother, hating Beckett had two inches on him, and he had to look up to meet his eyes. "You have no right to talk to her like that. You don't know a damn thing about her aside from what bullshit the media has cooked up." Anger at Beckett radiated off A.J. in hot waves, and he nearly forgot the gravity of the situation.

But they needed to get out of Grant's house ASAP.

"And maybe you shouldn't come back, either. Skip Ella's wedding." Beckett angled his head, eyes thinning. "If you don't have the good sense to know not to bring trouble to our town, to our home—regardless of your reasons—then you don't belong here."

A.J. was ready to lash out, but at the feel of Ana's hand on his arm, he faced her, witnessing a plea in her eyes to back down.

"Get out of here. You have five minutes. If you ain't gone by then, I'm calling the Bureau myself." Beckett turned and started for the hallway but then paused and threw a look back at him over his shoulder. "Don't fucking die," he said in a softer voice. "Mom wouldn't like that."

Once Beckett was gone, A.J. dropped his face into his palm. "I'm sorry about him. He's a good guy, but he doesn't do gray areas. Very black and white."

Her hand was on his bare chest when he opened his eyes. "It's all my fault. I never wanted to come between you and your family. And I shouldn't have involved you in my mess."

He gently seized her wrist when she began to pull away. "You can't mean that."

"I don't belong in this place. It was a fairy tale being here with you, but I don't deserve a storybook ending."

"Ana." He let go of a ragged breath. "Your story ends however you want it to, and if you think for one minute I'm going to let Beckett change my mind about you, you're mistaken."

GRANT WOULD FORGIVE HIM FOR BORROWING HIS TRUCK AS long as he didn't return it riddled with bullet holes. The BMX that A.J. decided to load into the truck bed at the last minute —yeah, Grant would kill him for taking that. But it might come in handy if he and his team did go to the safe house in Carrollton as planned Friday night.

A.J. settled his wrist over the steering wheel as he drove on back roads. Harper had been concerned that if he and Ana went to the team's location on the outskirts of Birmingham, they'd have trouble crossing into Georgia later. It was best they got a head start even though it was doubtful anyone knew Ana was currently in the South. And since the FBI manhunt had officially begun, A.J. didn't want to chance being stopped at a state line checkpoint.

They crossed into Georgia after a ninety-minute drive that should have taken an hour. The back roads slowed them down.

"Mendez had no choice," Ana spoke for the first time since they'd rushed from Grant's house. "The Cayman account, the surveillance video outside Porter's house, and the media getting wind of my identity," she listed. "I knew this could happen, but I didn't expect it to hurt so much. Or for the national news to learn my real last name and bring up my parents' sordid story. I might as well kiss my job at the Bureau goodbye."

"Don't say that." He slowed his speed, worried about deer in the backwoods. "You're an incredible agent."

"How can I be an agent again now that my face and story have been broadcasted all over the world? The words 'Russia' and 'spy' will forever be attached to my name even after the case is closed. You know how people are." Her tone was somber. The stubborn intensity he loved gone. Defeat in its place. Hopefully that was temporary.

"You don't need to give up. That's not like you."

"And if I want to?" she whispered. "If I only became an FBI agent to fix the wrongs of my parents' past—well, what's the point after this is over?"

"If you don't want to be an agent, that's one thing, but don't let my brother or the media influence your choice." His parents, Ella, Jesse—they'd all been blowing up his phone since he left Grant's house. A.J. had no idea what Beckett had told them, but surely his family would be pissed, too.

"I don't know." She went quiet for a moment. "I should never have gone to your ranch. Let myself get caught up in what it'd be like to be part of your family."

The impact of her words had him lifting his foot from the gas pedal for a second. *Part of my family. It has a nice ring to it.* And it may have been crazy, but that was what he wanted . . . her in his life for much longer than one case.

When he'd been singing to her earlier that evening, his heart exploded in his chest watching her with his loved ones. She did belong there, and there was nothing she, or anyone else for that matter, could say to change his mind about that.

"Your parents, your town, they'll hate me. You saw how your brother looked at me."

"They'll get over it," A.J. protested, not wanting her to have any reason to turn her back on what they had—and they did have something. And for once in his life, he had no intention of running, so like hell would he allow *her* to run.

"Where are we heading anyway?" Ana asked after a few more minutes of heavy silence. They'd turned off the radio, purposely avoiding the news for the time being. So now, nothing but deep thoughts filled the air.

"I was wondering when you were going to ask." A small smile touched his lips. "We have a place outside Atlanta so we can be near the safe house in Carrollton. My team will rendezvous with us there tomorrow." *If we go to Carrollton.* He wasn't so sure Porter could be trusted, and he didn't want to walk her into a possible trap.

Ana's body visibly relaxed at his words, seemingly comforted by the fact they were still going to the safe house given what he'd said back at Grant's. He just wasn't looking to argue with her after what she'd had to deal with between the news and his overprotective brother. "Why didn't we, or your teammates, stay there in the first place?"

"You didn't tell us the location of the safe house until we arrived at Grant's," he reminded her. "And my team preferred to be close by in case—"

"In case I was a threat. No more solo ops, right?" Her voice dipped lower. "Oh, God, what if we had been followed from D.C. by Volkov agents, and they'd shown up at your parents' ranch while we'd been there? I could have put your family in danger. I'm putting you in danger now." She covered her mouth with a shaky hand and looked away from him out her side window.

He slowed down and came to a stop. There'd been no cars in sight for miles, so he parked on the side of the road.

"In hindsight, I probably should have declined my mom's

invitation to lunch at the ranch, if that's what you could call being bulldozed by Deb Hawkins. Should have left Grant's right then, too." He reached for her hand on her thigh and squeezed it. "But I got caught up in the moment. Wrapped up in the idea of what it'd be like to have you in my life under normal circumstances. I made the decision. I can't blame the bump on my head or seeing ghosts for the choices I've been making. And I can't sit here and tell you that today wasn't one of the best days of my life when it was. Having the woman I . . ." A.J. swallowed when her eyes swung his way. "Having you with my family was a slice of heaven I never knew I needed until today."

"You're a good man, Alexander James," she said with a shaky voice, her lip quivering. "I don't know if I deserve—"

"You deserve everything I have to give and more," he cut her off and leaned over the console, maintaining a grip of her hand. "And you and I are only just getting started, you hear me? After this case is closed, I'm taking you to my sister's wedding."

Shame cut across her face. Worry clouded her eyes. Fear of judgment from his family.

"My family is fiercely protective of their own. My town, too." He brought his mouth close to hers. "And once they know what you mean to me—they'll have your back, too. I promise." He set a gentle kiss to her lips. "And, Ana, I don't make promises I can't keep."

CHAPTER TWENTY-EIGHT

A.J. REACHED HIS ARM OUT TO THE SIDE AS HE LAY ON HIS back in bed, only to find Ana's place next to him empty. He'd slept like a log all night and had no idea what time it was, but as far as he was concerned, there was still too much sunlight in the bedroom of the two-story cabin they were using as a safe house.

He sat up in bed slowly, kicked the covers off him since they'd slept with the A/C blasting, and lifted his watch from the bedside table. "Ten?" *Holy hell.* When was the last time he'd slept until ten?

Memories of making love with Ana at Grant's house flew back to mind as he dropped his bare feet to the wood floors. He'd planned on a round two and three, but then his brother had shown up and everything changed.

When they arrived at the new safe house last night, he and Ana were emotionally and physically spent, so they'd crawled into bed. He'd wrapped her in his arms, waited for her to sleep, then allowed himself to pass out.

But where was she now?

He grabbed the sidearm he'd stowed just beneath the bed

for emergencies and left the bedroom. The aroma of coffee hit his nose as he neared the stairs. The smell of eggs and burnt toast, too. When did Ana get food?

He went down the steps two at a time and halted in the entryway to the kitchen at the sight of Ana, Chris, and Finn sitting at the small round table in the breakfast nook that overlooked the forest behind the house.

"So nice of you to join us," Finn said, catching A.J.'s eyes first. Finn's greeting had Ana turning in her seat to peer at him.

She had on a pair of jeans and a loose-fitting black top. Her hair was down and wavy, still damp from a shower, and her cheeks had a healthy glow now that she'd had some sleep. "I didn't want to wake you."

Chris stood and stretched his back, coffee mug in hand. Then reached into his pocket, pulled out a twenty-dollar bill, and slapped it into Finn's extended palm.

"Told you he'd join us in his skivvies and holding a gun," Finn said with a laugh, accepting the payout.

A.J. dropped his eyes to his red cotton boxers as he strode farther in, then set his gun on the kitchen counter off to the side. "When did y'all get in? I didn't hear you."

Finn winked and stood, going for a refill of coffee. "Stealthy like that, bro."

A.J. opened his mouth to crack a wise-ass comment, but he lost his train of thought when Ana padded his way.

"Good morning." He wanted to pull her against him, but he had Echo Three and Five watching his every move. There was probably another bet about whether he'd already hooked up with Ana.

Just wait until you fall in . . . He cleared his throat and blinked a few times. "Where's Roman and Harper?"

"On the phone with Jessica in one of the rooms down the

hall. That or making out." Chris walked by Ana, then shoulder-checked A.J. as he made his way to the coffee pot as well.

"Yeah, right," Finn said. "That man will never get his head out of his head for that to happen."

"His 'head out of his head'?" Chris glared at him with an amused expression. "I swear, brother, you're way more John Krasinski *The Office* than you are John Krasinski *Jack Ryan*."

"You left the pot empty," Chris said, his tone light. "Rule number, like, fifteen or something, no leaving the coffee pot empty."

When both the guys had their backs turned to A.J., he took a quick second to step in and sneak a kiss on Ana's cheek. Yeah, he could be stealthy, too. As long as his mom wasn't around. Or Beckett, apparently.

"Smart picking up groceries before you got here." A.J. leaned his back against the counter in the wide-open kitchen and folded his arms, in no rush to go put on clothes.

"Better than MREs," Finn commented casually, facing him again. Though his words said otherwise, A.J. knew Finn was in recon-mode, gathering as much intel as he could by observing Ana and A.J. while Chris brewed a new pot of coffee, and it was unnerving as hell.

Ana stood beside A.J., her eyes fixated on the view outside the window, seemingly lost in thought.

"Is it twin day?" A.J. joked, eying Chris and Finn's matching outfits. Jeans and an army green V-neck tee.

Chris looked over his shoulder and winked. "We can be triplets if you go and cover up all that manliness."

A.J. brought his hands to his six-pack and grinned. "You're just jealous you have to work out twice as hard to keep up with this bod."

"You guys really do use humor as a survival tool." Ana's focus returned to the guys. "I like it. Makes all of this easier."

All of this. Yeah, there was a hell of a lot of "this" they still had to unpack over the next few days to wrap up the case and clear Ana's name.

"No other way to handle it," Chris said as Roman and Harper joined them in the kitchen.

"You're finally up." Harper went straight to the coffee pot, and Chris stepped aside to allow her first dibs.

"Any updates from Jessica?" Ana pinned her shoulders back as though entering "work-mode."

Harper filled the mug but handed it off to Roman, who thanked her and took a seat in the breakfast nook. "Director Mendez is being tight-lipped about whatever he may know, which means we might have to pull him in."

"That'd be a big step," Chris commented. "I don't like the idea of him knowing about us."

"And what's there to know?" Ana challenged, her lips tipping into a cute, knowing smile.

The woman already knew the answer. She got the read on them a long time ago.

"Superhero." Chris shot her a lazy grin as A.J. repositioned himself to view everyone in the kitchen.

Ana blew a strand of hair from her face. "You really are all the same."

"You have no idea." Harper filled another mug, offered it to Chris, then poured her own cup.

"I really don't want Mendez read in on what we actually do." Finn sat across from Roman at the table.

That made two of them. Well, probably all of Echo and Bravo would agree. He'd prefer Director Mendez continue to believe they were only private military contractors at Scott & Scott.

"Does this mean you don't yet have the unredacted report from the night my parents died?" Ana asked, her voice more serious.

"Not yet, and the FBI director fifteen years ago is retired, so he won't be able to comment on any classified cases he oversaw while at the Bureau." Harper went to the four-person round table and sat between Roman and Finn. She set her coffee down and tightened the knot of her ponytail. Today she'd gone with a surprisingly plain white tee to pair with her jeans.

And maybe he should get clothes on? The coffee could wait. "Gonna get dressed before we talk about stuff that might make my head spin." He reached for Ana's elbow, feeling the urge to kiss her before going off to get dressed, but then he caught himself and pulled away, given they had an audience. "Yeah, um, be back."

He grabbed his gun and went upstairs to his room. Opting not to be a triplet, he threw on a pair of jeans and a red tee before powering up his phone. More missed calls from his family. More messages.

He didn't have the heart to listen to any of them. That problem would have to wait until after the Volkov and SVR threats were put to bed. Ana's safety and national security were his priorities.

After turning off his phone and tucking his guilt away, he hurried back down the stairs to join the team.

"You're shitting me. Count Dracula isn't real," Chris was saying as A.J. returned to the kitchen, and how the hell had they gone from redacted case files to vampires in the time it took him to get dressed? "I know you're like an encyclopedia of random facts, but no, you're not gonna—"

"Dracula is based on a real man," Roman said. "Vlad the Impaler. Look it up."

Ana was sitting at the table, too, and Finn remained standing, his back to the window off to the side of the table, mug in hand. "You missed a lot, buddy," he told A.J.

"So it would seem." A.J. grabbed a coffee and set his palm to the L-shaped counter that served as the divide between the breakfast nook and where he stood. "How did Dracula get brought up?"

"It all started when Roman asked me about the two times I was in Budapest. The first time was three months before the shooting at the movie theater, and the second time was a week before the shooting," she reminded him. Her matter-of-fact voice was empty of emotion.

A.J. would have been more worried by her tone, but he recognized what she was doing. She'd distanced herself from the tragic event, and it was like she was telling the story of someone else's life. That it hadn't been her parents who'd died.

He did his best to keep his feet planted firmly in place even though he wanted to take her in his arms and comfort her. "And how does that involve Dracula?"

"Vlad the Impaler, aka Count Dracula, was allegedly tortured and imprisoned down in the labyrinth where Ana visited both times she was in Hungary. The place was once a prison and torture chamber—"

"Don't forget a Turkish harem," Finn interrupted.

"Sex and torture," Chris said with a laugh. "Sounds about right."

"Sounds like you've been doing it wrong," Finn teased.

"Define 'it,'" Chris shot back, and the boys would keep at this forever if Harper didn't stop them soon.

"Boys," Ana said at the exact moment Harper clapped twice, grinning that Ana had quickly caught on to their antics and brought them to heel like she was one of them now (and in his mind, she was).

"Anyway," Roman continued with his lesson, "the network of tunnels, or caves, whatever you want to call it, dates back to prehistoric times. They were used on and off over the centuries. But at some point, they became hidden and were rediscovered during World War One. Some of the tunnel network was unearthed by the government at the time, but there were rumors a lot more existed than just the ones open to the public. The Hungarian government allows a few tours and such down in the labyrinth during certain hours, but they're even more cautious now given they allegedly foiled a terrorist attack down there in 2011."

"And this morning, I remembered I entered that labyrinth both times I visited from an entrance not on the official tour," Ana said, her eyes lighting up this time as if the memory was fresh on her mind. "The Volkovs must have uncovered some of those other tunnels that weren't open to the public. They were extensive, too." She squeezed her lids tight for a brief moment. "I remember walking for what felt like fifteen minutes below ground to even get to the public area of the labyrinths."

"And both of those times you were there for a party, right?" A.J. asked, finally connecting the dots to "The Count," and great, now he had Sesame Street's Dracula in his head.

"Yeah. I assume the Volkovs had some government officials in their pocket to allow them into the space after hours. But I attended two masquerade birthday parties down there. The first time I was there it was for a twelve-year-old's Dracula-themed party. And the last time, was—and I can't believe I forgot this —for Grigory freaking Volkov. Not that I knew any of their last names at the time. But it was Grigory's sixteenth birthday." She visibly cringed. "The celebration was for him, of course, not me." She covered her mouth for a moment as if ashamed she'd suppressed the memory before now.

"Are you saying we should visit the labyrinths open to the public? Then once down there, try and locate the Volkovs' secret tunnel network they were once operating, hoping those tunnels lead us to wherever some of the remaining Volkovs might be hiding?" A.J. asked.

"Yes, but also . . ." Ana let go of a deep breath. "What if the night of that first birthday party, my parents used that as cover to steal the ledger and key from Adrik before attending the party? Maybe one of those tunnels was near his home, or a secret compound or something?"

"Do you remember where you first entered the tunnel system that wasn't on the official tour?" A.J. asked. "And where their tunnels connected with the public labyrinth?"

"I just remember we went in by a river one time, and then the other time was by a road. Very vague and unhelpful. I'm sorry." Her brows scrunched with apology. "But maybe one of those exterior entrances is close to where Adrik had lived." She huffed out a frustrated breath as if worried her theory would crumble before it even got wind in its sails.

"And are you suggesting your parents then hid the originals somewhere in the secret tunnels system, right under Adrik's nose? And they did that three months later, on the night of Grigory's birthday?" It was a long shot, but maybe? Why wouldn't an urban legend such as the existence of a coded ledger be in a secret tunnel network that dated to prehistoric times? *Fuuuck this is a lot to take in.*

"That's my best guess as to how a second ledger resurfaced fifteen years later. The Volkovs found it somewhere near where they may have been in hiding, which gave them the confidence to begin resurfacing." Ana peeked toward the table as if looking for an assist. How much had they discussed while he'd been asleep? All of *this* couldn't have been talked about during the three minutes he was gone to change.

"We don't even know for certain if Adrik is dead," Harper pointed out. "He may have remained in hiding since he'd always operated out of Hungary instead of in the U.S. where most of the Volkov spies were killed by the Russians."

"And Grigory is the face of the organization to protect Adrik until they have both the key and ledger," Roman elaborated on their new theory.

"And then Ana became their miracle, offering a path to the key." A.J. braced the back of his neck and squeezed the tension. He'd need a chiropractor after this mission. "But why go back and hide the ledger and key there? That's the part that still doesn't make sense," he drawled, his Southern accent deepening with his concern for Ana.

"There's one possibility." Roman stood and crossed his tanned arms as if ready to stand his ground on what he believed. As long as Dracula and harems didn't come back up, A.J. was all ears. "Ana's parents only planned on borrowing the ledger and key until copies were made, after which they'd return both to where they belonged before Adrik discovered her parents were the ones who'd taken them. Or maybe before Adrik was even aware they were missing."

"But it took them longer than they anticipated to forge the copies," Ana continued. "Knowing my parents, they wanted the book for themselves. Blackmail Russians, or more likely, the dirty American officials who'd been bribed into working for the SVR, for a huge payday."

"Maybe they wanted to remain loyal to Adrik Volkov,

while also making a few bucks on the side," Chris joined in on the theorizing, stroking his jaw in thought.

"But rumors began pointing to my parents, which meant they needed a new plan, one that would protect them from Adrik's wrath," Ana said. "So, the night of Grigory's party, they hid the ledger and key separately, in two different places, but never got a chance to anonymously tell Adrik the locations because they were killed within a week of returning home."

A.J.'s shoulders slumped. "One question." And wow, he was surprised his brain was working with only one-third of his coffee down. "Why would they risk showing their faces in Budapest, let alone go to Grigory's party, if rumors were circulating they were the thieves?"

"The rumors about who took the ledger and key—did you ever confirm them yourself, or did you learn about them from Porter?" Harper rose, her forehead tightening as if working through a problem. "You see a report or anything?"

Ana stole a look at Harper. "Porter's source, who told him about the rumors, died in prison. But no, he didn't show me his interview notes. I don't know how Porter first acquired that source or why the man ended up in prison, either. The entire Volkov case became classified after my parents died, and Porter said it had been to not only protect me but to protect any sources still working with the Bureau since it was believed there were dirty agents among them." She paused for a breath. "But why would Porter lie?"

"To explain his theory to you without confessing how he really knew your parents had the ledger and key," Roman said, his tone deepening. "We may not have the answer to that yet, as to how Porter knew . . . but we do know that your parents would never have shown up at that party a week before they died if they were aware Adrik was on to them as the thieves."

Right. A.J. had never considered that theory. But who knew what lies Porter told Ana to gain her trust? *Well, if he did lie.* There was so much speculation and theory it was coming out of his ears. Man, he was growing dizzy. No bumps on the head needed to explain it.

"I'm not prepared to accept Porter as a Russian spy." Ana turned, tearing her hands through her hair. "We need to talk to him tomorrow. And Anthony has to have answers, and I believe he'll talk to me. He was always kind. Brought me a trinket every time he visited." She smiled as if a happy memory had come to mind. "But, um, we'll know a lot more after the meeting." She slowly turned around, her eyes moving to everyone in the room before landing on A.J. last. "Either way, I'm certain the labyrinth will be where Grigory proposes we meet. Sort of brings us full circle. And then we can try and find out if Adrik is still alive."

"And if he is alive, the man would be as important, if not more valuable, to the FBI than the ledger," Roman commented. "It's possible the Russians would want him just as much as they'd want the book."

"*If* he's still alive," Harper reminded him, eyes on Roman, and the way she peered at him made A.J. feel like the two of them were having a telepathic conversation, reading each other's thoughts.

Chris lifted a hand in the air. "And meeting with a Russian mobster in a series of foreign tunnels sounds about as smart as the hot woman going down into the basement when she hears a creepy noise at night." He made a stabbing motion in the air. "No *bueno.*"

"I know it sounds crazy, but I think we can make it work if you're up to it. I promise." Ana's confidence she'd lost last night after the encounter with his brother had apparently returned. A determined woman on a mission. "You all have a lot of aces up your sleeve, is getting us on a plane to Budapest while I'm a fugitive one of them?"

"I know a guy who knows a guy," Chris teased.

"And if Porter doesn't show with Anthony tomorrow?" *There's still that giant question mark to consider.*

"We fly to Budapest either way and bait Grigory into believing we have the key," Harper answered before Ana could respond. "One way or another, we're taking down the Volkovs."

"And clearing Ana's name," A.J. added in case his team needed a reminder.

"Right," Harper said softly. "We'll go make some calls. See about that plane." Harper was already on the move.

"Maybe study the location of the safe house again," Chris added, following Harper. "There's way too much ground to cover and—"

"Wait." The blood practically drained from A.J.'s face. "I want the plan to use this meeting tomorrow as bait for The Huntsman off the table." He glared at his team now crowded by the doorframe leading to the hall. "It's the only way I go tomorrow. We can't risk something going wrong. We locate the sources another way."

"Maybe he's right," Ana said, and his shoulders dropped in relief. "One issue at a time."

"You're sure?" Harper raised a brow, and Ana nodded. "Okay, I'll loop Jessica in on the change of plans."

When his teammates were gone, he snatched Ana in his arms and pulled her tight to his chest, unable to stop himself. "How would you feel about being Echo One tomorrow?" he whispered into her ear.

She pulled back to find his face. "Isn't that team leader?"

He smiled, doing his best to lock up his nerves. "This is your mission, isn't it?"

"True." Her hardened expression loosened a touch. "You sure your people are up for tomorrow?"

He stroked her back to calm her. Hell, to calm him, too. "We do this all of the time. You wouldn't sleep at night if you knew the messes we wind up in. This is honestly a piece of cake. I mean, not that I don't want you sleeping at night from worry. But you know what I'm saying."

She pushed up on her toes and tipped her lips like an offer to kiss her, and that's exactly what he did, to hell if anyone walked in.

CHAPTER TWENTY-NINE

"Echo One, that's a good copy."

Echo One. Ana's lips would've twitched into a smile at A.J.'s use of her call sign if she weren't so nervous as to whether Porter would show with the forger, her father's old friend. When she'd worked with A.J.'s team last year, she'd been on the outside looking in, wondering what his team knew and how they knew it. It was an entirely different feeling to truly be part of his unit.

A.J.'s team was down a man, the real Echo One, and there was way too much ground to cover. They were surrounded by miles of woods in the middle of nowhere. A.J., Ana, Harper, and Roman had arrived on-site last, but Chris and Finn had spent almost the entire day at the cabin ensuring no one showed up ahead of time to set any traps.

Hopefully, The Huntsman wouldn't follow Porter to the meet. Well, assuming Porter actually escaped from him on Monday.

But no, Porter was a trained operative. He'd been in the Army nine years before joining the Bureau. She had to keep telling herself that at least.

Ana went to the window at the back of the cabin and opened the blinds a few inches. It was nine at night, and there was still a sliver of visibility outside, but the room was growing darker, and Ana needed a bit more light to see. The guys, on the other hand, had their night-vision goggles if needed.

Besides, leaving the blinds closed wasn't going to do much to keep her safe, anyway. If Ivan did show up, he'd most likely have thermal imaging to locate her inside and could take her out with a sniper rifle if that was his plan.

She moved to the front of the cabin, which was one open space. The kitchen, sitting area, and bed occupied the same room. No place other than the bathroom for anyone to hide, and she'd already checked there.

There was no one hiding beneath the floorboards, either. They'd used thermal imaging to be sure there were no heat signatures.

Chris, who Ana had learned was Echo Three, was in a tree stand on overwatch on the east side of the property. Roman, Echo Four, was in another tree stand on the west side. Finn had the north side.

A.J. was on Grant's BMX bike, well-hidden in the thickly wooded forest on the south side of the property, prepared to be mobile if needed.

Harper was in an SUV one mile out, but she was in Ana's ear on comms as well.

And Ana, well, she was the sitting duck waiting for Porter. She didn't feel that way, but A.J. was worried about her. And despite having all four directions covered, there was still a lot of land for a sharpshooter.

"He's late. Did we get all the prep work done for nothing?" She recognized the voice as Finn's.

"Oh come on, the twelve hours out here you got to spend

with me today was some good bonding time," Chris's voice came over the comms, humor in his tone. "I got to learn just how much you hate critters."

"And if you screw with me about that later, you're gonna get it," Finn returned.

"He'll be here," Ana said when the line went quiet. "Porter said ninety-six hours from Monday, but that doesn't mean it'll be to the tee." She peeked through the slit in the blinds and looked out front toward the road that led to the cabin.

Their private flight to Budapest, courtesy of the President (and yeah, that was crazy), was scheduled to leave later that night, so hopefully Porter would arrive soon since POTUS was doing them a huge favor. Was the President even aware Ana was accompanying the team on that flight? Knox may have been Bennett's son, but surely the President wouldn't risk his neck by aiding a fugitive to "escape" the country?

Well, unless. Ohhh. President Bennett wants the ledger. Of course. And from the sounds of it, people were willing to do anything and everything to get their hands on the list. Her parents had to have known the power it wielded, and yet, they'd risked stealing it . . . putting their lives, and Ana's life, on the line. And for what? Money?

"This is Three, we have incoming," Chris announced a few seconds later. "Black Jeep inbound."

"Roger," A.J. answered.

"I have eyes on the driver and passenger," Chris added. "Confirming both targets are inside the vehicle. Target two matches the description you provided."

Target two. Anthony Vincenzi. An Italian, not Russian, forger. It made sense her parents sought someone who wasn't Russian to work with over the years, she supposed. Part of her looked forward to seeing him again. One of the last people from her past still alive.

"This is Four. I have a visual. They're exiting the Jeep," Roman said over comms. "Target two's hands are tied behind his back. Blindfolded and gagged. Looks like he didn't willingly come here with Porter."

"Anthony doesn't know to trust Porter," Ana responded and stepped a few paces back from the door in preparation to see Porter and Anthony.

"At the door now," Roman alerted her as the door handle turned.

"Echo One, be safe," A.J. softly added.

"I'm here. You can enter," she called out, and then the door swung inward.

"You alone?" Porter nudged Anthony inside, and he fell to his knees as Porter shut and locked the door behind him.

"Yes," she lied because what if Porter had betrayed her, and A.J. and his team's concerns were justified?

Porter stepped around Anthony and pulled Ana in for a tight hug. She was so damn glad he'd made it, but part of her held back when he hugged her. That nagging part of her that wondered if she could trust him was preventing her from squeezing him as tightly as he clutched her.

Porter eased back and gripped on to her forearms. "I wasn't sure if you'd make it. I saw the news, but I didn't expect the media to get wind of the story about your parents. I'm so sorry."

"We both knew it was a possibility." Ana struggled to keep her voice steady. "But, Porter, your safe was empty. Someone was in the house when I got there."

"No, that can't be right," he responded, eyes going to the floor.

"Did anyone have the key to your safe?" she pressed when he kept quietly stewing.

"No, of course not." His answer sounded genuine, but . . .

The clouds of doubt thickened, slowly invading her thoughts and seeping into her pores now that she stood face-to-face with her boss. "Whoever was at your home leaked the surveillance footage of me entering your place to the media." She brought a hand to her holstered gun. "Who signed off on my undercover operation? Could he or she have gone into your home? Are they betraying us? The Bureau?"

Porter focused on Anthony, and Porter hooked his arm beneath his armpit and pulled him to a standing position, then removed the blindfold. "It's complicated." Defeat, not anger, echoed in his tone.

"Uncomplicate it for me." She inched closer to the two men, her normally steady hand beginning to shake at the idea the man who'd been a father figure to her for years may have betrayed her.

Once Porter removed the gag, Anthony asked in a soft voice, "Anastasia, is that really you?"

"Yes, it's me." She stood directly in front of Anthony but kept Porter in her sights, doubts about him still filling her mind. Anthony appeared disheveled. His plain blue button-down shirt was partially untucked from khaki pants. Dirt stains on both. Faded white slip-on shoes she doubted he would have ever worn fifteen years ago.

Anthony's brows tightened as if seeing a mirage. Plus, the visibility in the room was limited. "I tried to find you after your parents died. I looked and looked. I gave up once I learned most Volkovs were gone in the U.S., assuming the Russians got to you as well."

Her shoulders shuddered at his words, at the warmth in his eyes when framing his focus her way. He may have been a criminal, but there was concern for her in his worried expression. "I was in hiding," she whispered. "But I need your help."

"Do you trust this man?" Anthony side-eyed Porter.

Maybe I don't?

"Echo One, listen very closely," Harper abruptly announced in her ear. "I just received word from Mama Bear." Mama Bear was the call sign Chris had chosen for Jessica Scott for their mission. "She pieced together the footage from the movie theater shooting. Target One did *not* take the fatal shots."

Ana should have felt relief, but her stomach muscles clenched tight as she waited for Harper to continue.

"But he did confront your parents moments before they were killed. He was standing next to the agent who took the shots. He even exchanged a few words with your dad—I can't hear what was said, but only then did your parents raise their guns." Harper paused and Ana struggled to maintain a blank expression, to not squeeze her eyes closed. The fact Harper was no longer using code names meant the truth mattered more than anyone possibly listening in to their encrypted comms. "He lied to you, which means he may have lied about even more."

"Everything okay?" Ana jolted at Porter's question.

"No," she hissed and went for her gun. "No, I don't trust him."

Porter stepped away from Anthony, immediately drawing his Glock from a hidden holster beneath his shirt. "What are you doing?" he asked, alarmed. "Put the gun down."

"You lied," she whispered. "You were next to the man who shot my parents." Tears of more betrayal than she could stomach welled in her eyes. "What's really going on? Are you framing me? Did you send the hitman after the sources to set up the Volkovs? And me?"

"No." Porter shook his head but kept his gun on her. "I have nothing to do with that, I swear."

"Stand down. This wasn't the plan, Echo One," Roman's voice cut through the line, quickly followed by the roar of A.J.'s BMX bike flooding her ears over the comm. Most likely on his way to her.

"You walked me down the aisle at my wedding. How could you?" A part of her wanted to shoot him right there.

Anthony walked backward and planted himself against the wall and out of harm's way.

"It's not what you think. Everything I've done since I met you has been to protect you, I swear." Porter's voice was strained, pleading. "I'm going to lower my gun, and how about you lower yours?"

"I can't do that." She did her best to remain calm and firm. The FBI agent. But so much of her was the sixteen-year-old girl who lost her parents at that moment. Shaky and emotional. "You took money from the Russians to do their bidding. You still are, I assume."

Porter slowly pointed his weapon toward the ground. He took one step forward, and she took an immediate step back. No trust left. He was more than just a liar. He was an enemy of the state. The mole at the Bureau. He sold her out and set her up. Used her history and played on her emotions to get to the ledger and key. "Please, let me explain!"

"I'm on my way," A.J. rushed out over comms. "Forty-five more seconds." Panic filled his voice so loud it competed with the engine of his bike.

But no, she had to face the man who fucked up the last fifteen years of her life herself.

"We need the ledger and key to keep you safe." Porter's voice broke when he spoke. "You don't understand."

The door suddenly flung open, but instead of A.J. barging in, it was Anthony making a run for it. *Shit.* Porter peered at Ana, then tossed a look back toward Anthony.

"Don't shoot me in the back, Ana. But we can't let him get away." He bolted toward the door, leaving her wrapped in a cocoon of shock.

The snap-snap of two shots fired pulled her from her stupor, and she ran toward the open door but halted at the sight of Porter lying on the ground.

"Stay down. Stay down. Enemy fire from an unknown origin," Finn hollered over the line.

"There's movement on the south side," Chris added. "Echo Two, you have the wheels. You're our best chance at catching the shooter."

Anthony was nowhere in sight, but Ana heard the humming of the BMX closing in.

"I need to get to Ana!" A.J. insisted.

"I'm okay! Go," she pleaded as she ran toward Porter, then crouched at his side. "Target Two took off. He's somewhere in the woods. We need him!"

"Roger," Chris said. "I'll find him."

"Get back in the cabin until we find the shooter!" A.J. commanded, but she couldn't leave Porter's side until she had answers.

She lifted Porter's shirt to find a bulletproof vest, but most body armor wouldn't stop a full metal jacket steel round from a sniper rifle, and today, it hadn't. It nailed him in the abdomen. The second shot must have missed.

Porter's eyes opened and closed as he winced in agony. "I'm sorry, Ana." He slowly lifted his hand, and against her better judgment, she set her gun down and locked hold of his palm. "I never wanted to pull you back into this." His tone was fading. "I had no choice. He would have killed you. I was trying to protect-protect you. You need to get the ledger and key. It's the only way you'll survive."

"I don't understand." She squeezed his hand tighter and bent over his body to better see his face. "Please."

"You did become like a daughter to me. It should never . . . have come to this." Porter's eyes closed. "I'm so sorry."

"Please, tell me—" She let go of her words when he lost consciousness. He still had a pulse, though. "We need an ambulance now. Tell them we have a GSW in the abdomen. Male. Fifty-two. Takes blood pressure medicine," she rushed out over the radio. "Need a helo to medivac him to the hospital."

"On it," Harper responded as Ana applied pressure to the wound, not sure what else to do. "You need to get out of there, Echo One. You're in the open!"

"He may die if I leave him." Warm tears slid down her cheeks. Why was she crying? Porter betrayed her.

Her attention was quickly diverted to the woods at the sound of two more shots popping. Then a loud, crackling sound, followed by a boom. Smoke filled the air in the distance on the south side of the property. *A.J.'s bike. No, no, no!*

Three more snaps.

Static over her comm.

"A.J.?" she cried out, not giving a damn about his call sign. "You okay? What happened?"

She had no choice but to leave Porter if A.J. was in trouble. She snatched her 9mm and forced her wobbly legs to move, darting in the direction of the fire, doing her best not to stumble and fall in the dark.

"Echo Two, do you copy?" Roman's voice filled the line. He was breathing hard, running. "Echo Two, do you copy?"

"I have eyes on the bike," Finn said, his tone fatigued as well. "The bike's on fire. Ivan must've shot the gas tank."

"Any signs of Echo Two?" Harper interjected.

"I have Anthony," Chris said over the line a moment later. "What's the status on Echo Two?"

"I think I have a visual," Roman announced. "Two bodies are down near the fire."

"On my way," Finn yelled.

Please, God. Please, let him be okay. Her shoe hit a small, fallen tree, and she nearly lost her balance from running so fast without much visibility. The fire was the only light guiding her path to him.

"I'm okay, fucking hell, that hurt, though." A.J.'s words had Ana slowing, her heart shattering into a thousand fragments for a brief moment before piecing back together. "My helmet came off, and I lost my signal for a sec. Motherfucker shot my engine, and I got tossed. But I got him. He's down."

"You scared us, Two," Harper quickly said as Ana remained shocked with relief.

"Echo One . . . *Ana*, are you okay?" A.J. asked.

"Yes, and I'm almost to you," she said, her voice hoarse. "Is Ivan alive?"

"Thank God," A.J. answered, winded. "I'm dragging my ass over to Ivan now to see if he still has a pulse."

Ana was twenty feet away when she caught sight of movement on the east and west sides, flanking A.J., but her sight was impaired by the dim lighting. "A.J.!" She squinted, catching A.J. on his knees next to Ivan, the fire illuminating his location. They'd need to put out that fire before acres of forest burned down.

"We don't have much time to get out of here," Harper quickly announced. "Police and the fire department are on their way. Told them we have an assassin and an FBI agent down."

"Can someone get back to Porter and pack his wound, so he has a chance at surviving?" Ana asked over comms, and Finn responded by nodding and taking off toward the cabin.

"We got a live one!" A.J. tossed a gloved hand in the air, motioning them to his position.

Ana leaped over a log like she was an Olympic hurdle jumper and ate up the last few feet of space. She dropped to the ground next to A.J. and flung her arms around his neck. "I thought I lost you," she rasped.

He circled his arms around her and held her tight. "No way." He pressed a kiss to her temple before releasing her since they were dealing with a time-sensitive issue.

"Ivan." Ana brought her palms to the hitman's chest and clutched the vest he was wearing. A bullet had entered through his side from what she could tell based on the blood. Another bullet had struck Ivan's chest plate, not piercing flesh like it had with Porter since the ammo was from a Glock 19. "Ivan, please, talk to me."

Ivan groaned, and she pushed the night-vision goggles away from Ivan's face to see his eyes. "Why were you here? Who is calling the shots?" she asked, confused as to why he killed Porter. "Please, the SVR is secretly footing your bill. You were working for them. But who was the middleman?"

"What?" Ivan choked out, possibly more horrified by that truth than the fact he might die. "No, it cannot be."

"It's true. And I'm being set up by the Russians now, the same way they set up your brother before killing him." Maybe the hitman didn't have a soul, but he loved his brother. It was her only hope to get him to open up before he died. "What was next in the plan? Why did you kill Porter? Are the sources still alive?" she rattled off her questions, not sure if he even heard her since his eyes were closed tight.

But his hand slowly went to his side pants pocket, and she quickly snatched what he'd been directing her to—his iPhone.

"A tracker is on there. They are still alive," Ivan said, his voice even weaker this time. On the verge of losing consciousness. She brought the phone to Ivan's face for an ID, and A.J. shone a light Ivan's direction so it'd work. "I was to track Porter and wait until he met with you. Kill him, then follow you to the Volk . . ."

"Damn it," Ana said, fingers on his pulse. "We're gonna lose him if we don't do something."

Roman knelt by Ivan, removed his vest, and began compressions.

A.J. pulled Ana back and pinned her to his side as she studied the phone. "The tracker app." She showed him the screen with three blinking lights in three locations on a map of the U.S. She had to have hope that Katya and the others were alive as Ivan had said.

"The last call he received," A.J. said. "We should call the number."

Her hand trembled, the flames growing higher, not even ten feet away from where they were.

"You all need to get out of there. The sirens are closing in on you. A helo will be touching down in a field nearby to airlift Porter and Ivan to the hospital. Ana's still a fugitive," Harper alerted them.

"Shit. Ivan's dead," Roman announced a breath later. "I'm sorry."

"What's the status on Porter?" Ana sputtered.

"Still got a pulse," Finn answered. "But I've gotta leave him now."

"We need to move out to our exfil site." A.J. reached for Ana's arm, urging her to stand. "Harper, get ahold of someone you trust," he began as they stood. "We need a plausible reason for Grant's bike being here and in flames."

"Roger," Harper said.

"Come on, we gotta go." A.J. kept hold of her as they started moving fast in the dark. They followed close behind Roman and Finn since A.J.'s helmet and NVGs were broken, and he couldn't guide them out of there on their own.

She kept the phone active as they moved so it wouldn't lock again. "I need to call the number," she said as they neared the exfil site ten minutes later, and A.J. nodded in agreement. She re-dialed the last number on the "Recents" list and set the call to speakerphone.

Two rings and then an answer. "Is it done? Is he dead?"

Ana froze, her stomach sinking, and then she quickly killed the call.

"What? You recognize the voice?" A.J. asked, alarm in his tone.

Ana tightened her free hand at her side. "Yes," she whispered. "Deputy Assistant Director Winters."

CHAPTER THIRTY

A.J. QUICKLY ROSE AT THE SIGHT OF ANA BOARDING THE private plane and swatted away Finn's hand. Echo Five had ordered A.J. to the long couch on the left side of the Learjet 60 and started tending to his injuries as soon as they'd entered the plush cabin of the aircraft. There were ten more seats on the opposite side of the aisle to accommodate the team. Roman and Harper were already on board and in the cockpit talking to the pilot, and Chris was on a call with Wyatt a few seats down from where Anthony sat.

Ana walked down the narrow aisle toward A.J. "You need to see a doctor about your head when we're back," she scolded. "That's an order."

Finn secured a bandage to A.J.'s temple, hiding the gnarly cut he'd gotten when he was thrown from the BMX, and then pivoted his focus to Anthony to check for damage.

They hadn't had a chance to question the forger yet, in too big of a hurry to get away from the safe house before the fire department showed up. A.J. would feel a lot safer once their plane was in the air.

A.J. followed her down the aisle to a pair of empty seats and ushered her to the one near the window.

"Any news on Porter?" Her voice was soft yet resolute, and he was unsure whether she was feeling angry, sad, or a combination of the two regarding Porter.

"He's still in surgery. We probably won't know his status until we land in Hungary." A.J. reached for her hand and clasped it in his. They'd both changed clothes upon arrival at the private hangar west of Atlanta. Opting for comfort on the long overnight flight to Hungary.

He'd swapped his military camo fatigues for jeans and a long-sleeved, black button-down shirt, and Ana had on jeans and a scoop-neck white silk blouse.

"At least he's still alive. He was close to telling me something important, but I don't know if I'd believe anything he had to say at this point." Her shoulders collapsed, the weight of Porter's betrayal a heavy burden, and it was the last thing she needed.

"Jessica provided her contact at the FBI the three locations for the missing sources. They should be dispatching teams to find them soon," he added, hoping to offer her a glimmer of good news on such a dark night.

"Any word on Winters? What about him?" She turned her head his way, the usual sparkle in her green eyes gone, her auburn brows drawn tight.

"Natasha has people in D.C. looking for him. Winters wasn't at his home or the office. But by now, he must have heard Porter is in surgery, and Ivan is dead. I'm sure he'll take off. And with any luck, he'll hightail it to the Maldives. I assume he decided to cut Porter out of the payday." *At least Luke and Knox are there waiting.*

"Porter claimed he had nothing to do with the missing sources or hiring Ivan," Ana said, her voice still soft and subdued. "Do you really think he was trying to protect me?"

"I can understand why you'd want to believe that." A.J. squeezed her hand. "But maybe we wait and get all the facts before we determine his guilt in all of this. What do you say?"

She lightly nodded, her gaze going to the small window at her side. "I still don't get Winters's role in my parents' death."

En route to the jet, Jessica had announced she'd recovered the names of the agents in the case file from fifteen years ago. Not only was Winters not on scene that night, he wasn't even working in D.C. at the time. He was a special agent at the Bureau in New York City. Something didn't add up. "Winters will have to explain himself once Luke and Knox get their hands on him," A.J. said with a firm voice, hoping if he spoke his thoughts aloud, his words would translate to reality.

Ana pinned her back to the seat but kept her hand locked with his. "And now we know why the FBI didn't track the account to the Maldives. Winters probably blocked the agents from finding out. He wanted that payday."

"Well, POTUS will be alerting Director Mendez about the evidence we have implicating Winters as the person who not only hired The Huntsman but is most likely working with the SVR. Hopefully, once the wheels touch ground in Budapest, you'll have been removed from the fugitive list."

"Once we're wheels up, I need to talk to Anthony," Ana said as the jet taxied down the runway of the private airstrip outside of Atlanta. "I'm just afraid his answers will prompt more questions, and quite frankly, I'm tired of speculating. Too much trusting the wrong people." She peered A.J.'s way as the plane climbed into the air. "If it wasn't for you, I don't think I would have survived this."

"I got you. Don't worry." He repeated what he'd said to her the night of their first kiss in the pond.

"You do, don't you?" she whispered, and he had to read her lips when his hearing went to shit once they were in the clouds.

"I do," he mouthed and leaned in, resting his head against hers as the plane began to level off.

He wasn't sure how long they were in that position, but when he opened his eyes and pulled back, Roman was standing in the aisle.

"I think it's time to talk to Anthony." Roman cocked his head, and Ana nodded.

They unbuckled and went to the couch to sit across the aisle from Anthony's seat. He held a bottle of water, but it looked like the guy needed a gin after what he'd just gone through. Roman had given him a change of clothes before the flight since he'd been wearing the same ones for the past two days. Apparently, he'd been living in Savannah under an alias when Porter had found him.

"I'm so sorry this happened," Ana apologized, her hands falling to her jeaned thighs.

Aside from Harper, the rest of the team hung back, offering Ana some space to talk to Anthony. A.J. would never leave her side, though.

"I am so glad you're alive." His Italian accent carried through his words. "Your parents wanted you to have a good life." Anthony chanced a look at A.J. "I see you found someone you care about."

Am I that easy to read?

"I did, but, Anthony"—Ana leaned forward ever so slightly across the narrow aisle—"I need your help. You were the only friend of my parents I ever met, so I assume you were close to them."

"Your father was my best and oldest friend, yes." Anthony's blue eyes softened. "I was your godfather, but you disappeared immediately after they died."

Ana's gaze dropped to the floor. This must have been news to her. "Did you know my parents were Volkov spies?"

Anthony's chest rose with a deep inhalation before he let the breath free through his nose. His hand trembled a little. A.J. doubted it was fear. Maybe Parkinson's? He probably had trouble forging paintings and the like anymore.

"I did not know they were spies until they handed me the Daylight Ledger three months before they died, entrusting me with their secret. I was angry at first, and I did not want to help. I may be a criminal, but I love America. I moved here when I was a teenager, and I was not interested in helping to betray the country."

"So, what changed?" Ana scooted to the edge of the couch at the news Anthony might be able to unravel mysteries that had haunted her for years.

"Your parents swore they were getting out of the espionage business. They didn't want to be spies anymore. They said they'd been recently activated by the Volkovs, but by that time, they'd grown to love the U.S. and did not want to betray the country. They told me the ledger was their only way to get out."

Ana closed her eyes, and A.J. set a hand to her back, his gaze lifting to where Harper now stood silently behind Anthony's chair. Her eyes were wide with surprise. *That* was one theory the team hadn't considered.

Fuck, if it's true, then . . .

Anthony placed his bottle in the chair's cup holder and turned in his seat to face Ana. "But yes, to answer what I know you want to ask me, I made one copy of the ledger." His reply had Ana opening her eyes again. "But it took longer to acquire the specific type of leather used for the book, which was a very ancient material. Once I had that, I was able to forge a copy."

"Not the key?" Ana asked, sitting taller, but A.J. kept his hand on her back.

"No, I did not copy the key. There was no need. Your parents said the forged ledger was only meant as a distraction. A decoy if need be."

"If the Russians allegedly found the forgery thinking it was the only ledger in existence, and that it was useless without the key," Ana began, "it stands to reason the SVR felt it was safe to come down hard on the remaining Volkov spies in the U.S. even without the key."

That had been a theory the team bounced around as a possibility. The ledger and key were only valuable if someone had both.

"But is that what my parents wanted? For the Volkovs to die so they could be free of them?" Ana sounded doubtful her parents would want such bloodshed.

"No, they did not want to be Volkov spies anymore, but they didn't intend for anyone to die because of what they'd done, which is why they planned to return the original ledger and key to Adrik Volkov," Anthony explained. "Only, your parents told me something went wrong their last night there."

"What happened?" Ana asked, her voice tight.

"Your dad said he'd planned to slip the originals back into Adrik Volkov's home while everyone at Grigory's birthday, but Adrik had added several more guards, and he wouldn't safely be able to get in and out without notice."

"So, what'd he do?" Ana asked, and A.J. continued to run his hand up and down her back, hoping to help calm her in the only way he knew how.

"Your father said he and your mother hid the ledger and

key in some type of tunnel system within the labyrinth. I don't know. He said during the party, your mom went one way with the key, and he went a different way with the ledger, and they hid them. The plan was to wait a few weeks before tipping off Adrik to the locations. They thought it was best to delay for a period of time after the night of the party, concerned Adrik would quickly figure out who was behind the theft since the guest list was limited to less than a hundred close friends and family."

"So, there were never any rumors circulating that Ana's parents stole the Daylight Ledger?" A.J. asked, hoping for confirmation, another nail in Porter's coffin.

"None that they were aware of, and I doubt they would have made it out of Budapest alive after your sixteenth birthday if so, no?" Anthony looked at Ana and held both palms open as if everything were so perfectly clear.

"Why'd they tell you all of this?" Ana asked. "I know you were friends, but—"

"They had concerns that if something happened to them, you would be in danger. They wanted to make sure I could protect you, but I see the FBI hid you away." Anthony reached across the aisle. "You look so much like your mother. She would be proud of the woman you have become."

Ana flinched at his touch for a brief moment, then her body relaxed, and she reached out for him, allowing him to hold her wrist. Anthony's hand stopped trembling once he held on to Ana. "I just don't quite understand how they were going to break away from the Volkovs if the forged copy was meant as a mere distraction, and the originals were meant to go back to Adrik."

"Your father was a smart man." Anthony smiled and set his hands back in his lap. "He used the key to decode the ledger, and then he made a translated copy of the entire thing himself. He no longer needed the key or the ledger, you see. Whatever his plan was for exiting the Volkov organization must have hinged on that translated copy."

"What?" Her eyelashes fluttered in surprise. "So, what were they going to use it for? Why were my parents killed outside the movie theater? How did the SVR know they had the ledger yet the Volkovs didn't? Something doesn't add up."

"Porter knew her parents had the ledger, didn't he?" A.J. interjected. "He told you about the rumors, but if he made them up . . ." A.J. prompted, and Ana's forehead tightened when she understood what A.J. was getting at.

"Ohhh." Ana banded her forearm over her stomach. "Oh my God." She began rocking on the couch ever so slightly. "Porter and Winters knew my parents had the Daylight Ledger because they're FBI, and my parents were going to turn themselves in. Offer the ledger in exchange for immunity. But my parents wanted the Volkovs to retain possession of the original ledger and key to prevent the SVR from killing the Volkov spies living in the U.S. before the Feds rounded them up and made their arrests." She took quick breaths, and A.J.'s pulse raced as he watched Ana come to terms with the fact her parents had been trying to do the right thing. "Only, at the time, neither Porter nor Winters knew the copy at our house was a forgery."

Damn. This was another theory they'd never considered. A.J.'s head was spinning, and he doubted his now third bump on the head was the cause.

"Winters was in New York, and he had to maintain his distance, so that's how Porter came into play," Harper said, putting it all together. "Maybe even that other agent who took the shots that killed your parents was in on it, too."

"Only Porter didn't know your dad had a translated copy,

or that the originals were already hidden in Budapest. He was just told to make sure your parents didn't walk away from that theater alive," A.J. speculated, adding his thoughts on the matter.

Ana covered her face with both palms, and A.J. wanted nothing more than to wrap her in his arms.

"I assume that's why Director Mendez actually signed off on hiring you six years ago. He must have known your parents had been on the FBI's side back then," Harper said, "but since the immunity deal was never officially signed, and maintaining your safety was probably deemed more important, the media never got wind of the truth."

"This makes the most sense to me," Roman said, joining the conversation. "No one on the FBI task force who made the deal with your parents could have been at the movie theater that night—"

"They wouldn't have been able to explain how my parents ended up getting shot and killed," Ana continued Roman's theory. "And while Porter made sure my parents were killed, a team was dispatched to my house to search for the ledger and key."

"And when the Volkovs emerged five months ago, claiming they had the ledger, Winters knew he was screwed," A.J. added, the muscles in his jaw straining.

Dirty agents and corrupt politicians were about as shitty as shitty could get in A.J.'s book.

"Do you know what happened to the copy my father translated?" Ana's voice was soft, her words almost floating on a whisper.

Anthony's blue eyes twinkled, a glimmer of pride there. "If something went wrong, your father told me you would know the location. He said you would know where to find it, and it would appear right before your eyes if you wanted it to."

Ana jumped to her feet, but then the plane hit some turbulence, and she fell back onto A.J.'s lap. She glanced at A.J. before he set her back on the couch next to him. There was a spark of awareness in her eyes. She knew where the translated copy was, didn't she?

"Abracadabra," Ana said, eyes growing wide in surprise. "The magic potion he sprinkled on his special drawings to make them fade and then appear again."

CHAPTER THIRTY-ONE

BUDAPEST, HUNGARY

ANA PACED THE HOTEL ROOM, WALKING BACK AND FORTH IN front of the window, which had a view of the Danube River. The lazy, flat waterway that meandered through the city was a stark contrast to the hustle and bustle of cars and people alongside it.

Their hotel was less than 900 meters from the entrance to the Buda Labyrinth, a system of caves and passages that ran beneath Castle Hill in Budapest's historic section. So, they were within walking distance when the time came for Ana's meeting with Grigory.

The pacing probably wasn't doing wonders for her anxiety. But there was nothing to panic-clean. The hotel bedroom was spotless. And panic-sex right now would be insane, though it had crossed her mind. If Porter hadn't been in an induced coma, his recovery status unknown, and Winters wasn't MIA, she'd definitely choose panic-sex over panic-pace.

At least there'd been some good news delivered upon

their arrival in Budapest. All the missing sources had been found thanks to Ivan's tracking app. And all were alive. Katya would finally be granted the life Ana had promised, and with any luck, if the Volkovs were officially taken down tonight, Katya would be free from ever having to look over her shoulder and worry anymore.

But Ana still had to come through with the Volkovs tonight for that to happen.

In two and a half hours, she'd be facing Grigory Volkov, and there was no certainty as to how the night would end.

When she'd phoned Grigory upon arrival in Budapest, as the team planned, *she'd* been the one to offer the public labyrinths as the meeting place. The team had decided to give Grigory minimal time to prepare, but Grigory insisted the meeting location be at the "Renaissance Hall of Rocks with Wine Fountains of Mathias" in the labyrinth, which meant the entrance to the Volkovs' tunnel system was most likely close to there.

"Still nothing on Winters. He hasn't shown up at the bank in the Maldives," A.J. said while walking into the bedroom from the living room of the suite. He shut the door behind him, and she stopped pacing to face him.

He was in jeans and a gray tee, his hair wet from a recent shower. A shower she would have taken with him had his teammates not been in the neighboring room.

And now sex is back on my mind. Maybe thinking about sex was a new form of therapy to help her get through the tough times? *Therapeutic orgasms. Yeah, that makes sense*, she reasoned. The orgasm A.J. had given her yesterday before the meeting in Carrollton, when she'd had to bite into a pillow so his teammates wouldn't hear her moans while he plunged in and out of her in the bedroom, had been incredible, to say the least. She had fallen onto her back afterward murmuring that they were crazy, and he'd agreed, right before they worked up the stamina to do it again. The next time, A.J. took her from behind, and it'd been especially hot since the mirror over the dresser captured the act.

So, sex with A.J. during stressful times was, well, therapeutic. *I'm officially the girl in novels who I screamed at for having hot sex when she should have been hunting serial killers or terrorists.* Ana took back every bad thing she'd ever thought about those authors. Of course, she'd still read every word and five-starred the hell out of those books since the scenes had sizzled. None compared to what she and A.J. had together, though.

Wyatt, Owen, and even Asher had shown up an hour ago and were getting caught up on the mission details for tonight. The team needed all the boots on the ground they could get.

Which meant no picturing A.J.'s tongue darting between her thighs. No distracting thoughts. No therapeutic sex to put her mind at ease.

"Um, did you hear me?" A.J. stood in front of her, his green eyes filled with worry.

"Yes," she finally answered. "No Winters yet."

"You, uh, sure you don't want to just head out of Dodge? You and I can hop on a flight back to the U.S. and go search your storage for the translated copy and let our people here handle Grigory."

"You need me, and you know it." She rested her forearms on his shoulders. "But it's nice I'm no longer a fugitive on the FBI's Most Wanted list." That was a huge relief. "At least I can check off fugitive from my bucket list," she joked, and maybe she was getting the hang of how to roll with A.J.'s team. Humor and all. "Thank you for that, by the way." It couldn't have been easy for his team to let Director Mendez in on their "Avenger-like" lives, but they'd had no choice if they wanted to catch Winters and clear Ana's name.

"He's not my favorite person, but we'll learn to live with him. Natasha said Mendez took it better than we thought he would." He brushed his lips across her mouth as though he knew she was hungry for a kiss and needed his touch to calm her nerves. "But he's insisting we have an FBI team with us tonight," A.J. added as he pulled away, "and as much as we were against it, we may need additional support. The FBI agents will be told we're private military contractors. Mendez said he's selecting someone he trusts to run the team."

No, no, no. This is a bad idea. She stepped away from him, processing the news.

"If Grigory acts as we predict, he's not going to be happy when you tell him, contrary to what you've led him to believe, that you don't know where the key is hidden. Hopefully, when you inform him you have a translated copy of the ledger, he'll not only believe it, he'll be appeased enough to meet your conditions—you'll only hand it over once you've exited the labyrinth. We can't anticipate which exit he'll take, though. We need our bases covered." His tone was rough. Like sandpaper. He hated this more than she did, from the sounds of it. But he'd follow whatever was the safest route.

"How are we supposed to trust the agents on the team? What if there's an SVR spy? Or the Volkovs have an inside man?" First Porter. Then Winters.

"We'll try to keep as many operational details as possible to a minimum. And if there is a traitor amongst the FBI team, I guess we'll find out." He secured a hand to her waist, drawing her closer. "Although my guys can steal a boat on the Danube if needed, it'd be safer if the Feds already have one on the river and near the Széchenyi Chain Bridge if my team has to conduct a water pursuit."

And from what she'd remembered the other day, there were two secret Volkov tunnel entrances: one by the water, the other by some "random" road.

"We can't be certain where Grigory will take you, or if Adrik is still alive. But we have to be prepared for every possibility."

And maybe A.J. was right about pulling in the FBI. They were on a tight timeframe with limited resources.

"Okay." She forced a confident nod. "But I do think it's better if you don't come down in the tunnel with me to the meet tonight." She reached for his hands and laced their fingers together. "You know how Grigory will react if he sees you."

"He'll never believe you showed up alone. We stick to the plan."

"Then why did you first suggest we skip town and change the plan?" she challenged, drawing her body closer to his.

"Because your safety—"

"Is not more important than yours." She wasn't about to let him win this argument. "I just don't want you getting hurt," she said at the memory of presenting her "What Could Go Wrong" list to the team on the flight over, only to have them produce rebuttals for every item.

She still had her concerns. How could she not, when her mission risked the lives of others, especially A.J.'s?

"I have to finish what my parents started."

"They didn't want the Volkovs dead, though."

"Hopefully, it won't come to that." Her parents had wanted to protect America, and she would cling to that knowledge to help her get through tonight.

"If something goes wrong," he said, his voice deeper, "I

don't want you to blame yourself." His eyes thinned. "Do you hear me?" He unlocked their hands and caressed her cheeks in his palms.

"That won't happen." It couldn't happen.

"But if it does—"

"It won't," she said in a whisper, worried her voice would break if she spoke too loudly.

"You do whatever is necessary to stay alive. To complete the mission." He brought his face closer to hers. "But *if* something happens," he went on, and he was as stubborn as she was, "don't make me ghost your ass to tell you to move on and find happiness again." A touch of humor filled his tone like only A.J. could summon during what should've been a dark comment.

"And does that mean you think I've already found happiness?" she whispered against his lips.

"Damn right you have." He crushed his mouth over hers and walked her backward until she bumped against the window.

Urging her to wrap her legs around his hips, he deepened their kiss. They were about to go into the darkness tonight, but this hot, intense moment was all the light she'd need.

"There is one small detail I have yet to tell you about tonight," he whispered into her ear a moment later as her feet hit the ground.

"No," she said with an adamant shake of the head, crossing her arms in defiance.

"How do you know what I was going to say?"

"You can't possibly want to work with him tonight." Was he insane?

"It's not up to me, but—"

"But no." *No way!*

"You said he was overprotective. At least we know he'll

do whatever it takes to keep you safe. I saw that in his eyes on Monday night."

She'd nearly forgotten A.J. had come face-to-face with her ex-husband. Her stomach roiled. Her thoughts about panic-sex totally gone. "This is a mistake."

"Mistake or not, we don't have a choice." He checked his watch when she didn't respond, then inched closer and brought his mouth to hers, an attempt to distract her, but not even his kiss could relax her right now. "It's time to move out."

"Will we at least talk to Kyle first? I need to make sure we're on the same page."

"He doesn't want to, um, talk to you. Not right now."

"Shit, he must be upset about my parents." *Of course.* God, by-the-book Kyle Jeter probably had a mild heart attack after discovering he'd been married to the daughter of Russian spies. "He doesn't know the truth about my parents' real motives with the ledger, though, right?"

"No one aside from Mendez and Gray are aware of the truth. Not even about Winters being dirty. We don't want to scare any potential leaks into doing a disappearing act, too."

"Wait . . . Gray?"

His "oops" face said it all. "Our, uh, contact."

And now she knew why A.J. and his team were so quick to rule her unit chief out as a suspect on the potential mole list.

He squeezed her bicep and offered her a small smile. "Now, you ready to go be my wife?"

CHAPTER THIRTY-TWO

"How did you like it?" the tour guide asked as they exited The House of Houdini an hour into the tour of Castle Hill. Ana peered over at the brunette, who had given A.J. her undivided attention nearly the entire tour. Naturally, the question was directed at A.J.

He squeezed her hand, a gentle reminder he was there and everything would be okay. God, she hoped he was a fortune teller and tonight wouldn't go terribly wrong.

"We enjoyed it very much," A.J. responded and gave the tour guide one of his killer smiles. Based on the starstruck look on the woman's face, Ana thought she was going to swoon.

And how could Ana blame her? A.J. made for one gorgeous Southern hunk of a tourist. He had on those dark-washed denim jeans she loved that showed off his perfect ass. Dark sneakers since combat boots would draw attention. And a fitted black tee and black ball cap.

Of course, the heavy backpack he had on, same as Ana's, wasn't packed with tourist essentials, but what they needed for their operation.

"I'm sure if The House of Houdini had been around the last time I was in Budapest, my father would have taken me here." She stopped loving magic after her parents had died, but now maybe she could enjoy it again. And all this time, the ledger had been right under her nose. Her father, ever the illusionist, even in his death. A smile formed on her lips at the memory of her dad. It'd been so long since she'd allowed herself to smile when thinking about her parents.

Their group continued down Úri Street, then stopped outside one of the most acclaimed attractions, *Labirintus*, the famous labyrinths of Budapest.

"Who knows the story of the labyrinths? This is one of the entrances." A few in the group raised their hands. "Unfortunately, the tour is closed tonight, but—"

"I thought the government shut down the mazes in twenty eleven," one of the tourists interrupted. "A terrorist attack or something."

"We don't know the exact reason. It is all very hush-hush, but parts of the labyrinth are open again for tours," the woman explained before pointing to a sign about Dracula outside the entrance door. "In the fifteenth century, the underground system was a prison. Legend has it that Vlad the Impaler, made popular as Count Dracula, was once imprisoned and tortured here for ten years."

"I don't think so," someone with an Italian accent said. "That's a gimmick for tourists. The real Vlad was held at Visegrad Royal Palace, which is over forty kilometers away."

Ana glanced around, ignoring the rest of the woman's speech. The sun had set, and they were relying mostly on street lanterns for lighting, as well as the few handheld lanterns some of the tourists carried.

Two tourists in love. Newlyweds. That was what she and A.J. hoped to sell to everyone around them, at least. Not a hard sell. Her feelings for A.J. were intense. No acting on her part. Posing as a couple on a tour was the easiest way to get a lay of the land and be in position when the time came for the meeting.

The fact her ex-husband was prepping with an FBI assault team had her on edge, especially if someone on the six-man team was dirty. She felt as though they were playing Russian roulette. Anymore betrayal would be a knife to the chest. A sword to the stomach. A bullet to the back.

A.J. discreetly nudged Ana in the side with his elbow, and she moved closer to the golden-hued stucco of the nearby building. "Sweetheart, how about a kiss outside the labyrinth?" And A.J. was laying his accent on thick.

"Oh, what a nice idea!" the tour director exclaimed. "How about everyone share a kiss on the couples tour?"

A.J. leaned in, his hand going to the wall over her shoulder, and he set his lips to hers. Searing hot. Possessive. Bold in front of the tourists and would probably have everyone's pulse skipping at the sight.

His mouth traced a line to her ear, and he announced, "Turn on your comm. It's time." He edged back to peer into her eyes, and she reached for her other ear to power on the wireless comm she'd been provided by Harper.

"I think we might cut out early," A.J. said, which was code to his team listening in over comms now that they were about to move out. "Thank you for the tour."

The tour director fanned her face with the pamphlet she was holding, her eyes devouring every last bit of A.J. she could manage. "Have a good night, you two lovebirds." She tossed an enthusiastic hand in the air before A.J. and Ana left in the other direction.

"This is Echo Two," A.J. said once they were alone,

moving at a hurried pace to get to Lovas Street. "What's your status?"

"Outside the entrance on overwatch. Both entrances on Lovas Street have been breached, and the team is preparing to move into position," Wyatt, Echo One, answered.

Once his teammates moved underground, it'd be hit or miss if they'd be able to remain in contact with them over comms. Harper insisted they had the best of the best in communication devices, but Ana would believe it when she saw it. Well, *heard* it.

"Roger." A.J. snatched Ana's hand as they moved up a set of steps.

I can do this. I can do this. The words bounced around in her mind like the red FBI letters on her computer screensaver back at the office. Just pinging from side to side as a reminder she'd make it through the night without anyone dying. Without more betrayal.

"You good?" he threw the words out, his breathing totally freaking fine, which was kind of unfair.

She definitely needed to do more cardio once she was back home if walking at a fast pace had her out of breath. That or A.J. was just a stellar athlete compared to her. "I'm good."

She felt sweat trickling between her boobs, and as soon as they were beneath the ground, she'd probably break into a full-on sweat like she was doing hot yoga.

"I'm going to need three showers after being down here," Finn said over comms.

Well, the comms did work for the guys underground. How about that. And that meant A.J. was right, and he'd be collecting on the bet he made with Ana—to participate in an adult version of the game Seven Minutes in Heaven, whatever that was—but she assumed it involved his tongue, so she didn't think of it as a loss.

"It's dark," Finn continued, voice slightly muffled from being in the labyrinth and on the move, "dank, damp, and—"

"One more D for Dracula," Chris, the resident comedian as Ana had quickly learned after spending time with the guys in the last few days, finished for Finn.

"I was gonna go with muggy, musty, maze-y." Finn's voice was low as he spoke over comms, clearly unsure whether the team was alone down there.

"What's with you and the alliteration?" A.J. joined the conversation, still breathing normally despite their intense pace.

"Ah, such a big word for you," Chris teased A.J. "You know what that word means, brother? Leave the smart talk and big words for Echo Four, why don't ya?" If Ana hadn't gotten used to the guys and how they operated, she would've paused for a breath and questioned their sanity.

A.J. peeked at Ana as they moved faster than her feet could carry her at a "walking pace" (yeah, right).

"It's okay. Echo Three is gonna wet his pants when he hits the mannequins in masquerade costumes at his hold point," Roman said in a relaxed voice.

"This place is creepier than that Pyramiden ghost town we were in this year," Chris said. "Be prepared, Echo Two. I swear there are voices echoing off the walls."

"That'd be your loud mouth," Finn remarked, and Ana almost chuckled.

How am I smiling? Between the speed walking and the humor, she was somehow loosening up, which was probably good. Grigory would be able to read her if she showed up to the meet wound tight.

Of course, given what she knew would probably happen down there, how could she not be wound up?

Ana and A.J. slowed as they neared the sight of the *Labirintus* employee entrance, which his team had already unlocked for their entry.

They navigated behind bushes by the door and both removed their backpacks and knelt.

"This is Echo Two and Delta One," A.J. said over comms, keeping his voice low in case any straggling tourists walked by. "Waiting on the all clear to proceed."

Ana's lips twitched into a near smile at the sound of her new call sign. *Delta One.* It felt good to hear A.J. say it. It'd feel even better to hear it roll off his lips *after* their mission was successfully complete.

"This is Echo One. You're clear from my vantage point," Wyatt said from overwatch, and based on the plans they'd gone over earlier, that meant he was above the high brick wall behind the labyrinth entrance.

A.J. removed a yellow Chemlight from his bag, snapped it in half, then set it between them so they could better see what they were doing. His team had night-vision goggles, but Ana and A.J. would use the Chemlights to guide them to their final destination in the tunnels.

"This is Bravo Three. The paths are clear. No one is down here yet." That deep voice belonged to Asher. It was his first op since the twins were born.

"This is Bravo Two. We're in position. Ready for your entry, Echo Two," Owen announced as Ana and A.J. finished making preparations with their gear to go into the caves.

"Be careful. I may lose contact with you from my position soon," Harper came over the line. She was parked nearby in their mobile unit, waiting for the next steps. Not that they knew what next steps Grigory Volkov would dictate.

The assigned FBI agents were in their positions waiting for instructions as well, plus a helo and boat were on standby.

"This is Echo Two," A.J. said while strapping his gun to his back beneath his shirt, the same as Ana. "Moving into position now." A.J. peeked out from behind the bushes.

"You're clear," Wyatt noted.

"Surveillance cameras will be blind for fifteen seconds starting now," Harper alerted them.

A.J. reached back for Ana's hand, and they hugged the side of the brick wall until they reached the employee entrance door.

They were inside in a matter of seconds and used the cool, stone wall to guide their path down the steps of the dark entranceway. "We're inside," A.J. remarked.

Ana snapped their first Chemlight, which illuminated the uneven stone floor. Inside the dark bowels under the castle, she did her best to ignore what did indeed sound like voices echoing off the walls. Not to mention the staged displays of coffins, plaster gravestones, and other stone statues they passed that sent chills up her spine as they moved through the tunnel.

The darkness, the urban legends, and the sprawling winding caves were the least of her concerns, though.

"This is Bravo Two," Owen popped on the line. "I'm situated out of sight near your target location. And I now have eyes on the Volkovs' secret tunnel entrance. It's about ten feet behind those fountains where you're scheduled to meet. I guess that's why the target chose this spot. I've got two armed guards entering the area of the fountains now. No sign of our target yet."

The target—Grigory Volkov.

"We'll be okay," A.J. said softly, sensing she needed the reminder, and dropped another Chemlight. "We're past checkpoint one, Ivy Grotto," he announced to his team, and she was amazed A.J. even knew where they were given how dark it was. "One more checkpoint, then we'll be there."

The mazes were different than she remembered when there as a teenager. Of course, the tunnels had been properly illuminated back then.

"Ottoman Alley should be coming up soon," Roman told them, and each step on the uneven stone had her pulse fluttering faster at the side of her neck.

"I'm just trying to figure out why the mannequins are dressed for a ball. What happens if they get wet or we feed them after midnight?" Chris asked, and was he making a *Gremlins* reference?

Ana almost stumbled when a memory from Grigory's birthday party fifteen years ago flashed in her mind. Everyone in masks. The music. The dancing. Dominick, not Grigory, had asked Ana to dance, and she'd declined. Had he remembered her from that night?

"Checkpoint two," A.J. announced, and Ana nearly felt the history of the Turkish harem bounce off the walls and strike her as they moved. The cries of the women's voices. During Roman's history lesson, he'd explained women from the harem were often tossed like trash down wells into the belly of the earth.

Chills crashed over her skin as she raced a hand along the cold, slimy wall, an attempt to maintain her balance. It was hard to breathe down there. Stifling.

"I can hear them," Ana whispered to A.J. as they slowed their steps. "We're close."

A.J. stopped walking and faced her. He gripped her arms, leaned in, and surprised her with a quick "if something happens to me, don't blame yourself" kiss. "We've got this," he said after he pulled back, his voice deep but low. "I won't let anything happen to you," he added and then whispered more words of comfort and encouragement.

She didn't feel better, though, not when she knew what was most likely about to happen. But she drew in a breath of the thick, musty air, trying to prepare herself for the unpreparable.

"Moving in now," A.J. announced and gave her hand a quick squeeze before letting go. She maintained his pace, her heartbeat pounding in time with their slow and cautious steps.

A moment later, another memory suddenly snagged her mind as plain as day and had her jerking to a halt.

There are more passageways, her dad had told her the night of Grigory's party. *If we get split up and anything bad happens, find the Wine Fountains. There's a secret exit behind them.* His voice was in her ears now as if he'd just said the words. *Once inside, keep going until you find a fork in that tunnel. Left leads to the road near a big house. The big house is dangerous. Don't go there. Right takes you to the river. Go right. Find help.*

"I just remembered something." She grabbed A.J.'s free hand and peered at him. "When you enter the Volkovs' entrance to their tunnel system, about a few hundred meters in, there's a fork. Left should lead to Adrik's old home. Right to the Danube River."

"You're sure?"

She nodded, the memory still so clear in her mind.

A.J. tapped his ear and quietly gave the intel to his team. "You ready?" he asked, and she forced a nod. "Let's do this."

Her attention returned to the path, lit only by one tossed Chemlight ahead of them.

They rounded the corner to find the meeting space awash with a soft glow. Lanterns were scattered around the floor, circling the 4-sided fountain, which was covered in some weird greenery that couldn't possibly be natural down there.

"I'm here," Ana announced, dropping her bag down and holding her hands in the air.

Two armed men she didn't recognize stood by the fountain but quickly turned her direction when she spoke.

"Who is with you?" Ana recognized the voice as Dominick, but was Grigory with him? Adrik?

"Someone who helped me get here," she replied, her tone level. "You can trust him."

"No outsiders. If you're loyal to us, you will terminate him," Dominick stated, and she glimpsed a shadowy figure at the secret tunnel entranceway. Was that Grigory?

"No. That's not necessary." She stepped forward, but the guards raised their sidearms. "He won't say anything."

"You have my word," A.J. spoke up and set a hand to her back.

"He knows of us. Of this location," Dominick bit out. "Prove your loyalty. Now." Ana suppressed a shiver. His voice sounded like it had risen from the bottomless pits of hell.

"Please, this is—"

"Now," Dominick demanded, cutting off her desperate plea.

"I *am* on your side. He is nothing to me. My loyalty is with you." Ana's chest tightened, and she fought for a deep breath in the humid space. She pulled her gun from her back and spun away from A.J. in one quick movement.

A.J.'s hands shot in the air, and he took several steps back. "Ana, please," he murmured in protest, continuing to put space between them. "You don't need to do this. I helped get you here. You need me," he added, their one last-ditch effort to protect his life and keep him with her.

"Now," Dominick commanded, ignoring A.J.

Ana backed up several more steps until she was alongside the two armed guards. "I'm sorry," she whispered, then squeezed off a round.

But what choice did she have?

A.J. had to die.

CHAPTER THIRTY-THREE

"You good?"

A.J. groaned as Chris grabbed on to his wrist and pulled him upright from the ground. "As long as you're real and not a ghost." He missed Marcus, but he doubted that'd be the ghost haunting him down in the caves. "Damn, that hurts."

"Better than killing ya." Chris helped A.J. out of the shirt he'd changed into behind the bushes before entering the cave. He hadn't wanted to wear a bulky bulletproof vest and chest plate while faking being a tourist.

Double protection and the motherfucking round still felt like a professional baseball player had taken a bat to his abdomen, making his insides nearly shoot out of him.

"It didn't break the skin. Ana's a damn good shot. One painful bruise, but—"

"Did the plan work?" That was all A.J. cared about. Was Ana safe?

The team knew the Volkovs would require Ana to prove her loyalty. To kill in cold blood at their command. Ana had clung to the hope she wouldn't have to pull the trigger. Of course, if one of the Volkov guards had chosen to take an additional shot to ensure A.J. was down, A.J.'s people were waiting in the wings to take them out. Thankfully, that hadn't happened.

"Yeah, Dominick and Grigory, plus two guards, left with Ana. She told them she had a translated copy of the ledger, and they no longer needed to look for the key in the tunnels." Chris helped him to his feet. "We gave them a head start so they wouldn't think they were being followed. You were unconscious for a few minutes, which we didn't count on. The rest of the guys are on the move and filtering into their next positions. The FBI agents are on standby."

A.J. took the clean shirt Chris handed him once he'd discarded his protective gear, groaning with each movement. But Ana needed his help, so screw the pain.

"The Volkovs are sending a cleanup team to take care of your body. They'll be here soon." Chris reached into his backpack for a pint of blood. He busied himself with staging the scene to make it look as though A.J. had been shot, but he'd escaped. Blood on the ground. Handprints smeared on the wall.

Chris hadn't been thrilled about carting pig's blood around with him in his backpack, him being an animal lover and all. Even pigs. And yet he wasn't a vegetarian. Go figure.

"Unfortunately," Chris said while cleaning his hands and tossing the empty blood bag into his pack, "the tracking device isn't working down here. That, or Ana hasn't turned it on yet. Lost her on comms when she went deeper into the tunnel network."

They had a backup plan for their backup plan, though.

"This is Echo Two, what's Delta One's status?" he asked, hoping to link up with the team for an update. As the guys traveled farther down into the tunnels, the chances of maintaining the comms connection grew slimmer.

"Ah, glad to hear you're alive, and she didn't actually kill you," Finn popped on to the line.

"We picked up Delta's trail. Heading to the Danube," Roman announced. "Delta One gave us some breadcrumbs to follow, letting us know to go to the right."

The "crumbs" Roman referred to was a type of powder Ana had stashed in her pocket that would only show up with a special light. Another backup plan in case the tracking device didn't work.

"Bravo Two and Three are sweeping the other tunnel route to see where it leads and making sure the Volkovs don't double back," Chris explained. "Echo One and Harper are waiting for us outside the main entrance on Lovas Street. We can get to the river quicker with wheels than playing catch-up in the tunnels." Chris hooked A.J.'s arm to help him move, then used the headlight on his NVGs to guide them out of the labyrinth.

A.J. moved as quickly as he could, allowing adrenaline to push him since he was otherwise sluggish from getting shot as well as damn sore from having been thrown from the BMX last night.

"Shit, we have a problem," Harper said, her voice clear over the comms once they reached the stairs leading to their exit. "Hungarian police are patrolling the streets. But, wait."

"Annnd saved by the ex-husband," Wyatt said a moment later. "He's distracting them. Move out now while you can."

A.J. never thought he'd be happy for an assist from Ana's ex, but if Kyle was helping A.J. get to Ana and keep her safe, he'd buy the guy dinner after this was over.

Chris and A.J. hurried out the entrance and hopped into the mobile unit down the street, making a clean escape thanks to Kyle.

"Hey, brother," Wyatt said from the driver's seat. "You okay?"

Chris removed his night-vision goggles and attached headlamp and shifted the rest of the gear in the van off to the side so they could have a seat in the back.

"I'll be fine when Ana is safe, and the Volkovs are in custody," he said as Wyatt drove.

Harper clutched her laptop when they hit a bump, then peered back at A.J. "Want something for the pain?" she asked, worry flashing in her eyes.

"No." He didn't give a damn about anything other than getting to Ana. "What's the status by the water? If they take her on a boat—"

"Already on it," Harper cut him off. "We're pinpointing vessels on the river nearby. Narrowed it down to three possible yachts cruising within a half a kilometer from the Széchenyi Chain Bridge."

Two Feds were in a speedboat waiting on the water and away from any tourist cruise boats. They were told to remain near the main road, Budai alsó rkp., which ran parallel with the water, in the event A.J. and his team needed a water assist —and from the looks of it, they would.

There weren't many places for a private boat to dock, and the FBI couldn't exactly sidle up next to a "pub party" on a boat, or a romantic dinner cruise. Options were limited, which meant the situation had to be kept fluid, and they'd have to do their best not to draw the attention of nosy tourists who packed the riverbank.

A Saturday night at ten p.m., in June, in a romantic city that had its landmarks flooded with lights . . . it wasn't ideal for a covert operation, but what choice did they have?

"The FBI task force is putting up a drone over the water and using a fiber-optic listening device. We'll see what we can find out from those three vessels." Harper sounded hopeful. That was a positive sign.

"We'll get your girl. Don't worry." Wyatt caught A.J.'s eyes in the rearview mirror before they got off the roundabout, not wanting to actually cross the bridge.

"Honestly, if we didn't have the FBI assist, we would have been screwed," Harper said. "But surprisingly, thanks to Director Mendez, we have everything we could possibly need."

A.J. never thought his team would be thanking Mendez for pulling out all the stops for them, considering he'd been such a pain in the ass on their op with him last year.

"Stuck in traffic. We'll need to pull over soon," Wyatt said a minute later, and damn, the cars were bumper to bumper on the main strip by the river. Not ideal. "We lost communication with the guys in the tunnel, but once we get closer to them, we should hopefully reconnect."

A.J. had to remind himself Ana wasn't on a solo op. She wasn't alone down in those tunnels. His people were there, and she was smart. She'd make it out alive. He trusted her skills, but he didn't trust the Volkovs.

"Parking here." Wyatt swooped into a spot opposite the river when another car had backed out. "Perfect," he tossed out sarcastically. "Right in front of a church." Once parked, Wyatt scooted around on his seat to face the guys in the back, and Harper radioed the Feds their current position. A hundred feet away were three tourist boats about to unload their guests.

"Now would be the best time to move out. We can blend in with the crowd, then try and hop on board the speedboat," Chris said, eyes on the river.

"The agents are moving into position," Harper said once off the radio. "Move out. And be careful." She gave the guys a stern but loving look. "I'll be in touch when I hear more."

A.J. stepped out of the van with Chris and Wyatt and slung a bag over his shoulder. He dodged traffic to get to the river and traversed the crowd of tourists flooding the walkways as they exited the riverboats.

He abruptly halted when static filled his line.

Roman? Ana? A guy shoulder-checked him, nearly knocking his bag off as A.J. stood still, waiting to hear who was on the line in his ear.

Were those Russian words?

"It's me," he said over the line, hoping he was now in range to once again communicate with Ana over comms. "If you can hear me, I'm okay," he told her. "I'm on my way to you." He hoped to hell Ana heard him. She'd focus better knowing she hadn't actually killed him.

Wyatt turned in the crowd, searching A.J. out, then hurried back his way. "Come on," he urged, but A.J. held a hand up, begging for one second.

"A boat to get to a boat?"

Ana. Thank God. And she was giving them a clue.

"They've already exited the tunnel," A.J. said as if Wyatt hadn't also heard Ana on comms, which he had.

"They must be taking a smaller boat to get to one of the yachts," Harper chimed in. "We won't need to wait on the drone to eavesdrop. I'll have the Feds fly the drone higher in the sky and track the yacht they board."

"Roger," A.J. said, still having mixed feelings about all of this. He wished Plan A had been in play, the one where the Volkovs didn't make Ana prove her loyalty so he'd still be with her now.

"Echo Four, what's your status?" Wyatt asked as they put

eyes on their ride, a Pershing 72 speedboat. Two plainclothes agents were on board, pulling the boat up alongside one of the empty tourist docking sites so Wyatt, A.J., and Chris could quickly board before drawing attention from law enforcement. They'd prefer to keep the local cops out of this op for now.

"This is Echo Five. Sons of bitches wired the tunnel exit with explosives. We'll be a hot minute," Finn announced in A.J.'s ear a moment later.

"Lucky you all caught that before exiting," Chris rushed out.

"We'll catch another ride out to you if we have to," Finn added, a bit out of breath from whatever he was doing. Basically, ensuring he and Roman didn't die.

Another ride meant stealing a boat, probably a tourist vessel, but hopefully, it would be a quick infil and exfil tonight. Their rules of engagement, per Mendez . . . try not to kill anyone. Mendez wanted every last Volkov brought in alive if possible, which would make things trickier.

A few security guards working the tourist docks began yelling in Hungarian at the presence of their speedboat, and the FBI yelled right back at them in the same language. Adding a few hand gestures for good measure. *Just great. Gonna get into a gun battle with the local cops.*

"We gotta jet," the dark-haired agent said from behind the wheel. "Get below deck. There's dive gear down there if you need it."

A.J. and the guys stopped just before going below deck when Harper announced, "Delta One is boarding a Princess 30M yacht, and they're already moving. Heading down river," Harper reported. "Do you copy?"

"Roger," A.J. said, his heart in his throat before heading for the stateroom.

Once in the cabin, he eyed the dive gear and set his weapons bag on the bed next to it.

"They must have a frequency jammer. We lost connection with Ana," Harper said as static cut in. Reception wasn't stellar since they were rapidly moving away from her location. "The drone can't pick up sound either. You're going to . . . have to follow . . . and go in dark."

More like go in hot and fast.

"We just lost Harper," Wyatt said. "I'll go on deck and call her."

A.J. sat on the full-sized bed once Wyatt left, his stomach muscles tight and sore like he'd been punched more than once by a pro boxer. "This is gonna work, right?" he asked Chris while Echo Three slipped on his suit, minus the fins. *Since when do I have doubts?*

They had to be ready to swim, which was A.J.'s preference to the alternative—jumping from their speedboat onto the Volkovs' yacht at too fast a speed. He didn't have that much faith in the grappling hook he'd need to toss to hold his weight. He'd done a similar maneuver outside San Domingo back when Marcus was still alive, and he wasn't itching to do it again. His face had smashed against the fiberglass of the boat that night like he was a slapstick comedian, and his jaw had hurt for weeks. Marcus had laughed his ass off about it, too.

Chris leaned forward, setting a hand on A.J.'s shoulder. "Everything will be good. No worries. And nothing like a nice little swim in the Danube to cool us off, right?"

But Chris's humor was lost on him right now. Ana was surrounded by dangerous men, her status currently unknown.

The boat began to slow, and A.J. stood, throwing his arms out to the sides for balance. He caught sight of Wyatt rushing back their way, a panicked look on his face. "Get ready. Get on deck now!" he yelled, then turned and disappeared back up top.

"What the—" They picked up speed again, cutting through the water. *Shit, this can't be good.*

A.J. hurriedly got dressed into his dive gear and followed Chris to the deck as their boat passed by the lit-up Hungarian Parliament building.

"What's your status?" Wyatt had a hand to one ear to better hear out the other as he talked on the phone. "We need you now. Hijack the boat if you have to. That's an order." He ended the call, his rifle slung over his shoulder, a pistol strapped to his thigh and one at his hip. His dive gear in a pile on the couch off to his side.

The boat lights were dimmed to prevent being spotted by the Volkovs. "What's going on?" A.J. grabbed a handlebar when the boat suddenly slowed down, and he was nearly tossed overboard.

"Two more boats are joining the party." Wyatt pointed out at the water, then his gaze cut to the FBI agents at the helm. "I think it's safe to say someone on the FBI team tipped off the Russians."

CHAPTER THIRTY-FOUR

FIVE MINUTES EARLIER

"You're alive." Ana stood inside the salon on the yacht and peered at a man who'd been assumed dead for the last fifteen years. Adrik Volkov met her stony gaze with one of his own and casually crossed one leg over the other as he sat in a black leather barrel chair. "You've been in hiding for so long."

Grigory and Dominick Volkov were situated opposite Adrik, one guard was posted at the entrance to the galley, and one near the stairs leading to the top deck. And by her count, there were five more Volkov guards strategically located outside.

She didn't imagine it'd be a hard entry for A.J. and his team, but she'd need to find a way to let the guys know her position in order for them to safely board.

Ana stepped closer to Adrik, remembering him from her teenage years now that she was standing before him. He hadn't changed all that much. Gleaming brown eyes that were almost black, framed by thick, dark lashes. A pointed nose that led down to a full mustache now threaded with silver. As was his black wavy hair, pulled back into a ponytail at the base of his neck.

"Your parents stole the ledger and key from me originally, yes?" Adrik's lips twitched, his anger evident by the rigid set of his mouth and the hardness in his eyes. "My sources told me that the SVR found the ledger in the safe of your parents' home the night the FBI killed them, but I knew your father well. He would never hide something of such value in his home."

And what was she supposed to say? No sense in denying the truth.

"The forger you have been looking for, your father hired him, correct?" Grigory asked when Ana had yet to answer Adrik's question. "Did you really think we didn't know the truth all these years? That I didn't remember you and your family being down in the tunnels the night of my birthday, a week before all hell broke loose?"

She'd expected the conversation to go this way, so she reminded herself to stick to the plan and remain steadfast. "The forger only made a copy of the ledger, not the key. The originals were hidden in the tunnels, and they were meant to be returned to your family, but then my parents were murdered." She maintained an even tone, which was easier to do knowing A.J. was out there somewhere, and he'd have her back. When she heard his voice as she was being led out of the tunnel near the river, she'd done her best to hide her relief. Shooting him was the last thing she'd wanted to do, but A.J. had insisted it'd be the best way to prove her loyalty if it came to that, and he'd been right. "They never wanted your family to be slaughtered by the SVR. They only borrowed the book and key."

Adrik rested an elbow on the chair arm, his palm settling on his cheek. Eyes thoughtful as he observed her.

"I assume you found the ledger in the tunnels. I also assume you haven't found the key, or I wouldn't be here." Ana took a step forward, and out of her peripheral view, glimpsed the guards on each side of the room, bringing their hands to their holsters.

"She says her father made a translated copy of the ledger," Grigory told Adrik, his Eastern European accent thicker than when they'd spoken on the phone. Turning to Ana, he snarled, "Where is it?"

"So you can kill me?" she challenged.

Adrik suddenly rose and stood before her, towering over her petite frame. He drew the back of his hand over the curve of her cheek.

She swallowed and did her best not to flinch or recoil at his touch. To remain confident and grounded.

"I thought you were dead all these years. Needless to say, I was quite shocked when you reached out to Dominick." Adrik's tone was low and hoarse. A lifetime smoker, perhaps.

"My parents wanted out of your organization, but as I mentioned, they did not want anyone to die." She kept her chin up to try and command more confidence before him. "To protect you from the Russians, they planned to give you back the originals. But the translated copy was meant for the FBI."

"I never should have trusted your parents. I had concerns they'd been in America too long before they were activated." Adrik slid his palm from her cheek and forcefully cupped the back of her head, grabbing her hair and jerking her closer to him. His other hand gripped hold of her chin, demanding her eyes on his face. "They became petty thieves."

Maybe not so petty and small-time since they stole the "unstealable" from Adrik, but she kept that thought to herself.

"The FBI was already coming down on your organization. Surely you knew that. And the SVR would have gotten to your ledger one way or another to destroy you all. Your people would've been safer in FBI custody. Jail is better than death." In her mind, at least.

His clean-shaven jaw tightened at her comment. "Where is the copy? No time for your games. We have waited long enough." He brought his face closer, his smoke-infused breath fanning over her skin. "Fifteen years in hiding. We want our revenge."

"Against me? The SVR? Who?" she countered, maintaining her resolve.

In a quick movement, Adrik twisted the handful of hair in his grasp. Ana clenched her teeth and stifled a yelp at the sharp sting on her scalp.

A flurry of Russian words came from the armed guards a moment later, and within seconds, the familiar sound of gunshots began pelting the fiberglass exterior of the boat. No way was that A.J. or his team.

"You!" Adrik shoved Ana to the floor as the guards grabbed hold of Adrik to shield him. "You are with the SVR!"

"I'm not." She sat up but remained on the floor and kept her head low. Bullets hadn't penetrated the room yet, but a moment later—the boat took a sharp right, and their speed increased. Shit, what happened to the captain? The vessel moved wildly. "But I can help you." She shifted to her knees, eyes on Adrik now standing in the doorway of the galley. Dominick and Grigory had advanced to the steps leading to the deck but hadn't exited yet.

Round after round continued to pop-pop-pop.

"Turn off your frequency jammer so I can get word to my people. To the Feds. Let them help." A.J. and his team were on their way regardless, but if she could communicate with them, it'd be a hell of a lot safer. "Make a deal," she pleaded. "Grigory and Dominick were my age when the SVR began murdering your family. They don't need to shoulder the burden of your family's crimes. There's still a chance for them." She slowly crawled closer to where the guards remained blocking Adrik in the doorway. "Work with the FBI, and we can protect you from the SVR. Surely the Russians want you dead more than they want the ledger. Your testimony to the FBI would be damaging to them. If you willingly turn yourself over to the U.S., that'd give you your revenge against Russia. I promise." Maybe Winters and Porter had not only used Ana to get to the ledger and key, but to find Adrik as well.

Adrik's eyes thinned at her words. Contempt flashed in his gaze. But the desire to live was there, too.

"Give me my gun and turn off the fucking jammer! Let me help. We'll all die if you don't!" she yelled out when there was a lull in shots.

How many Russians were out there? A small army?

The barrage of bullets suddenly ceased its assault on the Princess, but the sound of gunfire hadn't stopped. It shifted in a different direction, away from the yacht. A.J. and his team were drawing the Russians' fire, weren't they?

Adrik hollered and cursed what sounded like orders, and she caught sight of Dominick hurrying to a switch on the wall and flipping it.

Freaking seriously? That was all she had to do to stop the jammer?

Adrik snapped out more commands, and Grigory, Dominick, and one guard ran up to the deck.

She forced herself to stand, given they weren't currently taking enemy fire. "That's my team out there holding the

Russians off. We need to get you somewhere safe," she explained, but then the boat jerked another sharp turn, moving at what felt like maximum nautical speed, and she was thrown against a floor-to-ceiling glass case, which housed the liquor.

Static filled her ear as she pushed off the glass.

My comm. "This is Delta One," she rushed out, motioning for Adrik to get a move on. "Come in, do you copy?"

Gunfire and static filled her ear.

"I want immunity," Adrik demanded, gun outstretched when she joined him and the remaining guard in the galley.

"I can't make that promise, and I won't lie to you." She braced against the fridge off to her left with both hands, trying not to lose her balance with the boat swaying hard in the water. "But protection in the U.S. has to be better than hiding out here. And if you care about your nephews, they might have a chance." It all depended on the crimes they'd committed, and how valuable they'd be to the Bureau.

Adrik's mouth tightened, but he nodded and headed for a set of stairs at the end of the galley.

Once they were below water level, in the primary stateroom, the sounds of war outside still exploded all around them, but no shots were being fired directly at their vessel.

"This is Delta One. Do you copy?" She did her best not to fall as the yacht began to slow down. Dominick or Grigory most likely got to the helm up top.

More static popped in her ear. "I need a gun." She held her palm open to the guard who'd taken away her 9mm in the tunnels. "You two stay down here. I can't get a signal. I need to move back to higher ground."

Adrik opened a door to what looked like a safe room alongside a queen-sized bed. It might protect him from bullets if they took on more fire, but he'd drown if the boat went under, wouldn't he? "Give it to her," he said with reluctance, and the guard handed over her 9mm, then joined Adrik in the steel trap. Maybe he'd pull a Houdini and escape.

"I'll be back." She shut the door to the safe room, then hurried out of the stateroom and advanced back to the salon.

"Delta One, Delta One, do you copy?"

On the second step out of the salon, she halted with relief. "Copy. This is Delta One."

"Thank fuck." It was Wyatt.

"I think you already know, but we're taking heavy fire," she replied. "And pretty sure part of the boat is in flames."

"The boys are about to dive to get to you," Wyatt informed her. "Can you get the yacht to completely stop so they can board?"

"If you can get the battery of bullets to cool off." Her gaze swung in the direction of the deck.

"Roger that. Air support is prepared to engage now."

"Is she okay?" She heard A.J.'s voice in the background, the sound of terror and relief breaking through his tone upon learning she was on comms with Wyatt.

"She's alive," Wyatt told A.J.

Ana kept her body pinned to the steps as she listened and waited for what she needed—a machine gun from overhead. The FBI helo.

A roaring blast followed, and the boat was rocked hard by what she assumed was an explosion. Maybe the Russians were down for good.

"Delta . . . do . . . copy?"

She adjusted her comm in her ear. "I'm good," she answered, breathless and prepared to go up top.

"You're clear to move on deck. There were two Russian vessels. Both have been immobilized," Wyatt said. "All guards on the deck of your boat appear to be down. Grigory is behind the helm. What's the status below deck?"

"Adrik is in a safe room with his guard. I don't think there is anyone else down here with me."

"Roger," Wyatt replied. "Be careful."

Once on deck, she nearly slipped in a pool of blood. *Oh, God.*

She peered into the night sky just as the helo was turning away, and when she returned her focus to the river, there were two medium-sized yachts on fire thirty yards away.

She did a three-sixty to search for the FBI boat where Wyatt was located, but the Princess abruptly slowed, throwing her off-balance. As Ana regained her footing, she glanced toward the helm.

Grigory, shit.

And he spotted her, too. He raised his firearm her way, and she snapped off a round while throwing her weight to the left to duck for cover from his shot.

When the yacht took a sharp turn to the right, she slid across the deck and careened into a still body. The yacht was accelerating, which wasn't the damn plan.

She pushed upright to see Grigory slumped over the wheel, and they were heading straight into the two burning boats.

There was no time to do anything else but jump.

"This is Delta One." With wobbly legs, she clutched the side railing, trying not to fall backward. "Disembarking!" she yelled just as the yacht collided with the others.

She leaped into the air, glimpsing someone in a dive suit coming up out of the water in front of her as another crackling, explosive sound filled the air, and a whoosh of heat licked her back.

Ana went in feet first, the cold water a shock as it enveloped her entire body.

She was underwater a matter of seconds before strong arms encircled her and lifted her head and shoulders above water.

A.J. kept one arm around her while ripping his mask and snorkel off. "I'm sorry I couldn't get to you sooner. Are you okay? Your head is bleeding." His brows pulled together. "I was scared I lost you," he added, his voice throaty with emotion.

"You'll never lose me," she promised. "Never."

This wasn't at all like their first kiss in the pond. They were in a river in Hungary kicking their legs to stay above water, but . . . they were alive and together, and so, she set a quick kiss to his lips before she broke the news to him they'd need to go back on that burning boat.

* * *

WYATT WRAPPED A RED BLANKET AROUND ANA'S SHOULDERS as she sat on the deck of the speedboat and eyed the *three* burning yachts fifty feet away. The fires had drawn crowds along the already busy riverbanks on each side of the Danube.

The FBI had to radio local law enforcement and alert them to stand down until they had the situation fully under control. And with any luck, they'd help push back the onlookers before the team docked.

A.J., Chris, Roman, and Finn were on board the Princess searching for survivors. Wyatt said Roman and Finn had ended up "commandeering" a small, glass-enclosed tourist vessel, probably scaring the shit out of the passengers before they kicked them out. But they'd arrived just in time for the "fireworks show" with the Russian yachts.

The buildings along the Danube were beautifully lit up, from Parliament to the Buda Castle, and then there was the illuminated chain-link bridge off in the distance from where she sat, but no one would be interested in landmarks when there was a spectacle on the river that would make national headlines.

Owen and Asher were now out of the tunnels. They located what they assumed was once Adrik Volkov's home, but from the looks of it, he hadn't lived there in fifteen years, a decision that probably kept him alive so long.

Bravo Two and Three were now with Harper in their mobile unit, parked in a lot off to the side of the main strip by the river, as they tried to pinpoint which FBI agent had fed the two Russian teams their location.

Kyle? Was it possible that her buttoned-up, by-the-book ex was taking money from the Russians? She refused to entertain the idea, but she slouched at the memory that Porter had betrayed her, so why not the man she married? She'd gotten multiple psych degrees to prevent anyone from ever taking advantage of her again, and she'd tragically failed.

Chills erupted over her skin despite the blanket as she watched the yacht burn, and every minute it appeared to slip a touch lower in the water.

Ana's pulse wasn't going to slow down until A.J. and the others were off the boat and with, at least, Adrik Volkov.

"With any luck, Adrik will still be alive," Wyatt spoke up, standing in front of her with his long gun pointed on the yacht, eye behind the scope.

"He's going to blame himself for working with the Feds." Her attention briefly skirted to the two FBI agents near the helm of the speedboat. She was on the starboard side, sitting on a couch, huddled in the cozy blanket, when she should have been on that yacht with the team.

A.J. had refused to put her in more danger, and Wyatt had agreed to stay on board with her to make sure she didn't "do anything crazy." Plus, they hadn't ruled out the two agents on board as clean.

"Mendez demanded we work with the FBI." Wyatt's tone remained matter-of-fact. "We knew there was a chance someone may be on the Russians' payroll," he added in a lower voice, so the two agents didn't hear them.

"But you know A.J.," she said softly. "He'll say he never should have taken the risk." She clutched the blanket even tighter. "I didn't expect two boats of armed gunmen to show up, though, or I wouldn't have risked your team."

He lowered his long gun for a moment and caught her eyes. "This is what we do. You're okay, and that's all that matters. Now, if something had happened to you, well, A.J. would probably burn down the city." He started to raise his gun but hesitated. "But if the man does play the blame game, I'll knock some bloody sense into him," he added, his British accent deepening.

Of course, what happened tonight was more her fault than anyone else's. She chose to go after the Volkovs tonight even though the translated ledger was safe in the storage area beneath her stairs back in D.C.

Leaving an operation unfinished made her crazy. Plus, it was time to end what began long ago once and for all. Thankfully, no one on the team had gotten hurt, so maybe Wyatt was right. *Everything will be okay.* Logically it made sense, but she couldn't help but feel they were waiting for the other shoe to drop just as she caught sight of the dark-haired agent behind the wheel breaking leather. He was drawing his gun, and shit, from the looks of it, about to take out Wyatt.

Ana abruptly stood, going for her holster but finding it

empty. Her mouth rounded in warning to Wyatt, but then a snap! sounded through the air.

The agent was hit in the arm, and he cursed and let go of his gun.

It all happened so fast, and Ana stared in shock as Wyatt and the other Fed quickly rushed the agent to the ground.

Ana twisted to find A.J. in the water, one hand gripping the boat, his rifle in the other. Thank God for his military-grade weapons ammo that allowed him to shoot a weapon after being submerged in water.

"Talk about timing," she whispered and hurried to the side of the boat to help A.J. on board.

"You were the one to tip off the Russians?" Wyatt hissed behind her toward the dirty agent.

Ana barely heard the rest of the conversation, too relieved A.J. was safe and now with her. The rest of his team were on their way in a Zodiac inflatable boat, and to her relief, Adrik was linked up—cuffed and on board.

A.J. tossed his mask and snorkel, stowed his weapon, and pulled Ana tight into his arms.

"Grigory and Dominick not make it?" she asked, her face pressed to his slick wetsuit.

"No," he said into her ear. "And Adrik and his guard attempted to escape. We had to take the guard out."

"I'm just glad you're okay. And your team," she said as tears gathered in her eyes.

"And you." He pulled back to hold her face, eyes meeting her eyes. "If anything had happened to you—"

"But it didn't." She lifted her chin. "It's over, though. It's finally over." She had no doubt Winters would be taken down at some point, and then all she wanted was to move on, and with A.J.

CHAPTER THIRTY-FIVE

ANA STARED IN A DAZE AT THE FLASHING BLUE AND RED lights off in the distance down by the riverbank of the Danube, opposite of where the Buda Castle sat perched regally on Castle Hill.

Was it really only yesterday they were in Georgia and Porter had been shot? The Huntsman killed?

Now here she was in Budapest, a gorgeous and romantic city, and just one hour ago, Russians had opened fire on the Volkov yacht, exposing yet another dirty agent.

God, she could use a break. One that involved a pond, ice cream, and fireflies—without the weight of the world on her shoulders this time.

A mix of Hungarian law enforcement and American FBI agents worked side by side as they dealt with the crime scene down below. A.J. and his team had preferred to stay out of the limelight. Too many questions they wouldn't be able to answer, so they'd moved out of sight.

She was standing in an empty parking lot that had a view of the scene. Two vehicles were parked behind her, which housed A.J.'s crew as they wrapped up mission details.

She'd changed into fresh clothes in the back of the van twenty minutes ago since she'd been covered in blood—thankfully not hers. Only a scratch on her forehead from when she'd hit the glass. So, not bad. Poor A.J. had been the one with a massive purple bruise on his chest from when she'd shot him. God, how could she ever erase that memory from her mind?

At the feel of A.J.'s arms wrapping around her waist from behind, she let go of a relaxed breath. "Hi," she whispered, grateful to be safe in his embrace. She tipped her head back to catch his eyes. "Oh, this isn't just a sweet hug, is it?" She'd learned to read the man well, and based on his tight mouth and the scowl on his face, he was upset about something.

She turned in his arms, and when she saw Kyle standing off to the side behind A.J., she knew why he was unhappy.

"Oh." She stepped back, and A.J. tore a hand through his hair. "I'm gonna go see if we've heard anything about Winters yet." He reached for her hand, checking to make sure she'd be okay, and she gave him a reassuring squeeze.

For a minute, she'd been concerned Kyle was dirty, too. Apparently, Director Mendez had sent Kyle to Hungary on special assignment to not only help with taking down Russian mobs, but to keep an eye on his fellow agents to ensure none were corrupt. And it was one reason why Mendez had trusted Kyle to lead the team tonight.

"Hi." Kyle was wearing his FBI blue raider jacket now, paired with jeans and loafers. He crossed his arms, standing in front of her as A.J. reluctantly left to climb into Harper's mobile unit.

Tucking her hands into her pockets, she took an awkward step closer to her ex. "Thank you for the assist tonight."

His mouth tightened, and his eyes fell to the ground. "I

vouched for those agents. I didn't expect one of the guys on my team to be dirty. I handpicked them," he said with disgust.

"Don't blame yourself. We've all been duped. Betrayed." And Kyle most likely felt betrayed by her, too. Her secret life. "It couldn't have been easy when you found out about my parents." She had to apologize at some point. "I'm sorry I never told you."

"I knew before the news broke the story." His gaze lifted, and the lamppost nearby threw a shadow across his face when he advanced a step closer. "I found out four months ago, actually."

Four months? "That's when you stopped calling," she whispered in understanding. He'd been phoning her while on assignment with the hope of getting back together, and then the calls just stopped. She thought he'd given up, but oh wow, he'd found out the truth. But how?

He nodded as if reading her thoughts and letting her know that yes, whatever she was thinking was true. "As I'm sure you know now, Mendez tasked me to be the eyes and ears at the attaché here, worried that corruption within the task force could easily happen, given the Feds had permission from the Hungarians to take down Russian organized crime."

"And he told you about me?" Mendez knew her history from what A.J.'s team had told her.

"I stumbled upon some old photos while looking into the Volkovs once they were rumored to have re-emerged. I couldn't believe my eyes when I saw a sixteen-year-old version of you standing in the Buda Labyrinths with two notorious Volkov spies who died fifteen years ago."

"Why didn't you tell me you found out?" Her arm went tight to her abdomen, her forearm applying pressure to cope with the moment.

"I went to Mendez with my concerns about you and was

shocked to discover he already knew and, in fact, signed off on your hire." He hissed a low breath. "He wouldn't give me the details. He said what happened to your parents was classified. And he forbade me from telling anyone, including you, that I knew your real identity."

She turned back toward the sea of officers and agents in the distance. "Is he the one that asked you to come to Headquarters when you heard about the hit against Katya?"

"Yes." Kyle's hand came down on her shoulder, urging her to face him.

"It was you in Porter's house Monday night," she said at the realization. The unnaturally colored contacts. The deep voice. It hadn't been Winters. The frame was too lean. "Why were you there?" She forced herself back around.

He brought a hand to his bearded jaw. "I had concerns Porter might have been dirty. And when we got the call about him going MIA, I was worried he may have faked his own disappearance. I wanted to check out his house. I won't get into what I knew, but—"

"You didn't leak the surveillance footage, did you? Steal the contents of the safe?" She took two worried steps backward.

"Of course not, and I never expected to bump into you that night. I was upstairs completing my check of his house when I heard someone come in. I did see the safe behind the framed photo on the wall in his office, but I couldn't access it without any tools, so I'd planned to come back before—"

"Before I surprised you."

"I didn't want to hurt you, but I wasn't sure what to think once I realized it was you," he explained. "I assume someone else was there before you and I showed up. I went to check the security footage, but it'd been wiped clean. Given the news leak, it clearly wasn't you who deleted the surveillance." His tone was a bit calmer now, though he had to be so angry with her.

"After seeing me there, and with what you knew, why'd you still believe I was innocent, that I wasn't the mole?" She remembered learning Kyle had led the "not-guilty charge" against her.

He reached out and lightly squeezed her upper arm. "I can read you like a book, Anastasia. I may not have known your secrets while we were together. But you, a dirty agent? No." He shook his head. "That I refused to believe."

"I don't know what to say."

His lips tipped into a tight but forced smile. "We weren't right for each other." He released her arm and tossed a thumb over his shoulder. "I'm guessing that Navy man is right for you, though?"

"I, um." She peered over to see A.J. stepping out of the back of the van, probably nervous to leave her alone too long. "He is," she whispered, eyes remaining on A.J.

"You know, my parents were going to turn themselves in," she admitted, needing Kyle to know the truth for some reason. Well, hear it from her first. "They'd planned on handing over the ledger to the Bureau to protect me."

"But Porter stopped them?"

"And Winters," she added, and Kyle's eyes widened in surprise. Guess he didn't know about him yet. Mendez had kept his word.

"I have a copy of the ledger. A translated copy. And between Adrik's testimony and the ledger, we'll be able to clean house," she said like a promise.

"Good." He nodded, then turned A.J.'s direction. "Ana?" He stole a look back at her. "I'm glad you found someone who makes your heart work," he said and then blinked a few times as if he hadn't quite correctly articulated what he was thinking, but she understood.

And her cold, dead heart was very much alive, thanks to A.J. "I hope you find someone, too." She smoothed her hands up and down her arms as she watched Kyle leave and A.J. come forward.

"You okay?" A.J. palmed her face and angled his head as he studied her.

"I will be once we have Winters in custody and the translated Daylight Ledger in the hands of the FBI as my parents had intended." She looked up at him and hooked her arms around the back of his neck, lacing her fingers together. "I really like you, Alexander James," she confessed, knowing her statement came out of the blue, but she'd needed to say it.

He threaded his hands through her hair, which was down over her shoulders now. "Well, I'm falling in love with you, Anastasia," he said in a tender voice, dipping in for a kiss.

She pulled back once his mouth brushed hers to catch his eyes. "I'm falling, too," she whispered, then kissed him again.

CHAPTER THIRTY-SIX

WASHINGTON, D.C., FORTY HOURS LATER

ANA'S STOMACH FELT LIKE ONE OF THOSE TIGHT SAILOR knots with all the twisty loops as the elevator ascended to her floor in the Hoover Building that Monday afternoon. It'd be her first time coming face-to-face with her unit since she'd gone on the run, and although the media had cleared her name and Mendez had formally explained the truth to everyone at Headquarters, it was still nerve-wracking to be there. She had no idea what kind of reception to expect from her co-workers.

Sweat formed between her breasts beneath her white silk blouse, and her palms were damp. She did her best not to slouch in fear, though.

She'd have felt better if A.J. could have come with her, but he wasn't exactly allowed to parade around the FBI Headquarters, even though Mendez now knew the truth about his team and their clandestine work for the President.

A.J. had opened up on the plane ride back to the U.S. and revealed the cloak-and-dagger story about how Bravo and

Echo began eight and a half years ago. Most of Ana's theories had been correct, and the fact he finally opened up to her was more than a big deal—it was a welcome into his second and secretive family, one with his brothers and sisters in arms.

As soon as they'd landed in D.C., Mendez was at the airport to personally escort her home to locate the translated ledger.

When Ana pulled the box of her childhood belongings out of the storage area beneath the stairs in her townhouse, she was overcome with emotion. It hadn't been opened since she'd packed it immediately after her parents died. She'd held back her tears in front of Mendez while digging through the items, but after handing over the stack of scroll-like papers to the FBI director, she broke down and cried in A.J.'s arms.

Thieves. Con artists. Sent to the U.S. as spies.

But she was going to choose to allow some love for them to exist in her heart once again. A.J. had revived that organ in her chest, and knowing her parents had done the right thing when it mattered was enough to offer them forgiveness in their deaths.

After she'd collected herself, she watched Mendez leave with all the papers while A.J. held her tight to his side, a nervous energy bubbling inside of her to finally be at the end of a journey she'd spent fifteen years on.

Ana had previously provided Mendez with a list of ingredients as well as the "recipe" for her father's magic trick. Well, as best as she could recall. So as soon as Mendez returned with the papers, HQ lab techs were ready to get started. With any luck, when she walked onto her floor today, she'd discover it'd been a success.

If it didn't work, well, at least they had Adrik Volkov in custody. That was a huge win, and a judge in court would most likely prefer his testimony to some handwritten pieces of paper written a decade and a half ago.

Ana steadied her hand on the frame of the elevator door as it came to a stop at her floor. She took a moment to calm herself by thinking about waking up in A.J.'s arms that morning in her bed.

They hadn't had sex after arriving in D.C. from Hungary late last night but falling asleep while he held her after such a traumatic weekend had been about as perfect as she could have ever hoped.

I can do this, she reminded herself as the doors opened.

She had no idea if she'd be allowed to stay on as an agent after today, given her identity was broadcasted all over the world, or if she even wanted to. Regardless, she needed to officially close this case that'd been open for over fifteen years.

Ana smoothed her hands over her hair, opting to wear it down to the office for the first time.

She took one step forward, her gaze on the red pumps she'd chosen to wear with her black slacks today instead of her usual dark ones. After a few more steps, she lifted her eyes from her shoes to see an agent at his cubicle rise at the sight of her, brows drawn together. Then another rose.

Dean spotted her next.

Griff.

Halle.

They all stood, and she clutched her chest when they brought their hands together to . . . *oh, God, they're clapping for me.*

Words of congratulations. Comments about taking down Adrik Volkov. Finding the ledger. Apologies for their doubt. More and more words continued to flow as she slowly walked down the pathway between the desks, numb with shock.

She stopped when she reached where Dean and Halle stood. "I'm so sorry I kept so much from you," she hurried out, still embarrassed by the secrets she'd kept.

Halle surprised her by pulling her in for a hug. And wow, she'd needed it. Tears of relief filled her eyes at the warm welcome she received but wasn't sure she deserved.

"You're one brave woman," Halle said into her ear before pulling back.

"I can't believe Porter and Winters are crooked," Dean added while standing next to her and slapping a hand to her shoulder.

"Any word on the ledger?" she asked once the rest of the floor had settled down, and the agents returned to their work.

Only Dean, Halle, and Griff remained standing with her. "Mendez was waiting for your arrival to share if there's news," Griff stated.

"Winters is still out there." Dean's brows scrunched with anger. "And Porter may never wake up."

Things had taken a tragic turn for Porter while she was en route back to the U.S., and the prognosis didn't look good, but she couldn't think about that right now. "If the Russians didn't get to Winters, he'll come for his money eventually." But how long would Luke and Knox be able to sit and wait in the Maldives? Plus, Wyatt and Natasha were marrying this month.

"Quinn."

Ana's attention snapped toward Mendez, dressed in a charcoal suit, as he stood in the doorway of a conference room. He motioned for her with a wave of the hand.

"I guess that's my cue." Ana smiled, then started

Mendez's way, still on edge and wired. She probably should have skipped the espresso earlier.

Mendez shut the door behind her, and she found herself alone in the room with him. No pictures on the wall. No warmth or comfort. Just a long, sleek metal table and a few swivel chairs. "Have a seat."

She circled the oval table and pulled out one of the navy blue chairs.

Mendez slid a gray file folder down her way.

Her hand slightly trembled as she opened it.

"We had to take photos. The ink didn't last long, and it was a hassle to keep making it reappear. Those are copies."

It worked? Her stomach did some flips at the sight of her father's recognizable handwriting. There were multiple pages arranged in various categories, from account numbers and names of judges to orchestrated hits by the Volkov spies. There was a lot of information. A lot more than she expected.

"Did my dad conveniently leave off his offenses from the list when he translated the copy?"

"I would assume so." Mendez sat across from her and clasped his hands on the table.

"Porter and Winters aren't listed, but I guess that makes sense since they weren't Volkov spies and were instead taking money from the Russian government." She flipped through another page, searching for familiar names. No one she knew personally, which was a relief. And she noticed that many names on the list had been killed shortly after her parents died at the hands of the Russians.

"The SVR only began recruiting Americans shortly before"—he cleared his throat, a fist to his mouth—"your parents were murdered."

Since the Russians never decoded the ledger, they didn't know who or how many Volkov spies to eliminate fifteen years ago, which left a lot of people for the Bureau to go after.

"There's one more page I thought you might want to keep." He opened another folder, then slid a sheet her way.

Her breath hitched at the sight of a drawing of her. Hair around her face. Palm to chin. Eyes downward. *I'll always watch out for you, my red angel. Love, Dad*, was written in cursive beneath. "Thank you," she said looking up at him, liquid coating her eyes as she tried to hold back her tears.

"Of course." He pulled his hands into his lap. "When the case is closed, I'll get you the other drawings unrelated to the case."

"I'd appreciate that."

Mendez unbuttoned his suit jacket before settling his hands on the chair arms. "I'm sorry I never told you what really happened to your parents that night."

She promptly lifted her eyes to his dark ones, curious as to where he was going with this.

"I was assigned to the task force, along with Winters, back in New York. I personally met with your parents. Your father never told our team about the forger. He just said that he was in possession of the Daylight Ledger, and it would assist in taking down a lot of corrupt people in the U.S. government, from the top and on down. He wanted safety and protection for his family. Immunity. A chance to start over somewhere in the country." From what she'd seen, Mendez was a buttoned-up guy when it came to emotions, so sharing his words probably wasn't so easy for him. "He wanted to give you a stable home life. Plant roots. He said you'd always wanted that."

She closed her eyes and drew the back of her hand over her mouth to hide the wobble in her lip. The tears just might fall if he continued.

"When your parents were killed, there was a thorough investigation to determine if there'd been a leak from my task force. We were all cleared, but evidently, not well."

She forced her gaze to return to the director and did her best to remain steady. To not let the overwhelming emotions rope her in.

"There were concerns for your safety after your parents died. The Bureau and Central Intelligence Committee decided it'd be best to keep the truth about your parents' motives hidden to prevent retaliation against you." Mendez's eyes grew soft, a look of remorse mixed with compassion on his face, letting Ana know, in his own way, that he was sorry. An apology for allowing her to believe for fifteen years her parents had died because of greed. "We're still trying to determine exactly what Winters and Porter had planned this time around, aside from a payday in the Maldives, but . . . well, if Porter doesn't make it, hopefully the team will get to Winters and force him to talk."

The team. A.J. and his people. "They'll come through." They'd never let Winters slip through the cracks. No way. "Will you keep their secret?" she asked, worried about A.J. and his team. Their truth was a fragile thing. In the wrong hands, it would be dangerous. Deadly.

"I'm still not sure how I feel about what they do, but I also don't think this case would have ended quite the way it did, had they not intervened." His answer was honest, at least. She could use a little honesty after so much betrayal. "But I'll support the team to the best of my abilities," he said as his phone began ringing. "It's Jessica Scott."

She sat taller at the news, and he surprised her by placing the call on speaker.

"Director Mendez, I'm calling to confirm our people have Winters in custody."

Ana's hand struck her chest with quick intensity, and she bowed her head.

"We were considering keeping him in the Maldives a bit longer to get answers before our guys bring him back to the U.S.," Jessica explained. "He's already talking. A bit terrified the Russians will come after him since he failed."

"Good. I want to know everything he has to say and as soon as possible." Mendez looked to Ana with a tight nod of approval.

"We'll have the money in the account here transferred to the Bureau. Be in touch soon." Jessica quickly ended the call, and Ana pushed back from the table.

Was it really over?

"Have you thought about your plans?" Mendez stowed his phone and rose as well. "You know, it might be tough to continue in Counterintelligence, but we could use your expertise at Quantico."

"Instruct?" She reached for the ruby pendant she had on, the one her dad had given her for her sixteenth birthday, and clutched it as she considered his offer.

"Maybe take some time—as long as you need—and then let me know what you think." He circled the table and offered her a hand. "Nice work, Agent Quinn. Your parents would be proud."

CHAPTER THIRTY-SEVEN

"Three months," A.J. grumbled. "I can't operate for three damn months." And how the hell did Ana manage to pull off getting him in to see a doctor so fast, especially when he didn't even live in D.C.?

"Don't be mad at me." Ana made one of those *Eek!* faces, laughter in her gorgeous green eyes. It was cute as hell.

He'd been wearing down the floors in the living room of her townhouse ever since they got back from learning the MRI results thirty minutes ago. "Concussion my ass," he muttered, tossing a hand in the air. "What will the guys do without me?"

"They managed without Asher when he was on paternity leave. Luke, too. Owen," she reminded him. "Liam." She smiled. And it was that beautiful smile that stopped him from *his* panic-pacing before he came undone. "I can keep going."

His shoulders fell, and he reached out to gently grasp her upper arms as an idea came to mind, which included a vision of their bodies tangled beneath the sheets. "Take three months off with me."

"Okay."

"I mean I know that . . ." He blinked. "Wait, 'okay'?"

She smiled, her eyes glittering with what he believed to be love. "I don't know what my plans are, and I could use a break, that's for sure. Maybe we can have a little adventure together." She pressed up on her toes and planted a kiss on his lips. "Let my hair down. Go on the run, but without anyone chasing us. Some naked times, of course."

"Okay, okay," he said with a nod. "I think I can make this three-month thing work." He roped a hand around her back and pulled her tight to his chest. "Plus, we've got my sister's wedding Sunday. Wyatt and Natasha's wedding this month too."

"About Ella's wedding." Ana pulled free of his grasp, went over to her couch, and plopped down, looking like she was about to pull the rug out from under him.

"What?" He wanted to go to her, but his body felt tethered to the ground. His nerves about to go haywire. "I told you I cleared everything up with my family." The conversation had gone over better than he'd expected, and maybe his brother was still a bit angry at him, but having the media declare Ana as innocent had helped pave the way for their talk.

It was already Wednesday, so they had just enough time to wrap up whatever they needed to do in D.C. before leaving for Alabama. He was looking forward to seeing family and slowing down for a bit. Since they'd returned from Hungary, everything had happened so fast, from Mendez sharing the translated ledger with Ana to A.J.'s doctor appointment—and the speedy MRI results from earlier that day.

But that was how they rolled ever since he'd crashed into her life. He almost broke Luke's record for falling in love with Eva, but Luke claimed A.J.'s ten-plus months of "pining" for Ana counted, so Luke remained the record holder.

Although, A.J. was fairly certain Chris fell in love at first sight with Rory, so maybe he had them all beat.

"I just don't think I should go. I know you explained everything to your parents, but Porter is still in a coma and barely hanging on, and well, I'm just worried if I'm at the wedding, I'll be a distraction from the bride and groom. There will be whispers and—"

"And nothing." He crossed the room, finally getting his feet to move to sit next to her. "I want you there. Ella Mae does, too. My family knows how happy you make me. They saw it last week. They'll love you—hell, they'll probably end up loving you more than they do me."

Her palms went to her bare thighs. She had on jean shorts and a black ribbed tank top. Her hair in a side braid. And damn did she look cute. If he hadn't just been issued the three-month mandatory break from the doc, he would've carried her upstairs to the bedroom since they STILL hadn't made love since the safe house in Georgia. It just hadn't been the right time. Not with Porter getting shot. Then the Volkov showdown. And the moment they'd returned to D.C., it'd been one work detail after another to deal with.

"Please come with me." He shifted on the couch and snatched her hands. "I can't imagine going there without you by my side." He wanted to spend every second of every day with her.

"Can I think about it? Maybe see if Porter pulls through?" She wedged her lip nervously between her teeth.

He opened his mouth to speak, but at the sound of the doorbell, they both swung their attention toward the hall. "Must be Knox and Adriana."

Knox arrived in D.C. earlier that morning from the Maldives, and he and Luke said they had news about Winters that should be shared in person.

A.J. only hoped that "news" would help put Ana's worries to rest and not make her more uneasy.

He went to the door and checked to make sure it was who they'd been expecting.

"Hey, brother," Knox said when the door opened, and he stepped in and gave him a manly one-arm hug since he hadn't seen him in weeks.

"Adriana." A.J. narrowed one eye, playing angry since she'd kept Ana's secret, but then he laughed and pulled her in for a hug.

"Sorry," Adriana whispered into his ear. "But looks like it worked out for you."

And it had, hadn't it?

"Hi." Ana greeted both Knox and Adriana, and she offered a flustered apology to Knox for asking Adriana to lie on her behalf.

"It's all good. Come in for a hug." Knox smiled and reached for Ana, taking her by surprise. They were big on forgiveness in their group. Life was too short.

Adriana went to Ana a moment later and hugged her as well. "So glad you're okay." She looked back and forth between A.J. and Ana as if assessing the new dynamics of their relationship.

"Have a seat." Ana directed Knox and Adriana to the couch, but Knox remained firm, and he leaned a shoulder against the column in the room.

"Maybe you should sit instead?" Knox's focus went from Ana to A.J.

"That bad?" That wasn't what A.J. wanted to hear, damn it.

"Just, um, it might be a lot to take in," he answered, so Ana went to the couch, and Adriana sat next to her.

A.J. stood uncomfortably, hands over his chest between

where Knox stood and the couch, mentally preparing himself for "a lot to take in."

"I asked Luke to let me be the one to come over here," Knox began, his brown eyes landing on Ana.

"You said Winters rolled over on the Russians, though," A.J. commented, growing nervous.

"He did. Between his testimony and Adrik's, plus the ledger, there will be a lot of corrupt people going down. Not to mention the fact there is a lot of intelligence in that ledger that will help the President work out some foreign relations issues with other countries," Knox explained. All good news so far.

"But?" Ana clutched a pillow to her chest and observed Knox as Adriana set a supporting hand to Ana's knee.

Knox pushed away from the column and stroked his clean-shaven jaw. "Winters did reach out to Porter and that other agent the day your family was at the movie theater. He gave them the job of making sure your parents didn't make it into custody alive. And it had to be done that night. Someone else, no longer living, tossed your house for Winters that night."

A.J. went over to sit on the arm of the couch and reached for Ana's hand. She shifted the pillow aside to clasp his palm.

"Porter was supposed to tell your parents that if they didn't give the Bureau a reason to shoot, they'd kill you," Knox said, his gaze on Ana, his tone a touch uneven, the words probably painful to say. "That's why Jessica saw Porter talking to your parents first outside the theater. He was threatening to hurt you if they didn't sacrifice themselves right there."

And that's why her parents drew their guns, "forcing" the FBI to fire.

He squeezed Ana's hand, knowing she damn well needed it. And more.

"Your parents were protecting you." Knox huffed out a breath. But there was more, wasn't there? "After the Russians found the ledger, well, what they thought was the real ledger, they wanted you dead even though you didn't know anything about it." Knox took one step closer. "From what Winters said, Porter didn't want you to die. He insisted you should be kept alive in case they ever needed you."

Ana released A.J.'s hand and stood. She had to be reeling from this news. She walked around him and the couch and went to the wall by the windows, bracing both palms against the glass.

"Apparently, over the years, Winters realized Porter had grown attached to you. And when Porter insisted you work for the Bureau, he began to suspect Porter cared more about you than his allegiance to the Russians."

"What are you saying?" she asked, tears in her voice, but she didn't face the room.

A.J. stood, trying to determine what Ana needed from him right now. Space? Comfort?

"Porter's a bad guy, but he wasn't lying when he said he was trying to protect you. When the Volkovs re-emerged, he realized Winters would want you dead. Porter offered to, um, use you to infiltrate the Volkov organization to find out if the ledger and key were still out there, as well as determine if Adrik Volkov was still alive."

Adriana was back on her feet, standing beside her husband, and A.J. took slow steps to get to Ana, not sure how to read her mood. But he wanted to be there for her.

"But Winters had concerns Porter really only cared about keeping you safe, so he made his own plan," Knox continued as Ana turned.

"Shit," A.J. said under his breath. "Winters framed Ana and the Volkovs? Hired The Huntsman. He planned to try and get the ledger back and locate Adrik, and the money in the Maldives was his safety net or backup plan, right?"

Knox nodded. When A.J. came up alongside Ana, she turned into his chest and began to sob as he held on to her tight. "Porter didn't know about Winters's plan. I think, in his own twisted way, he did care about you, and he was trying to get the ledger to prevent the Russians or Winters from hurting you."

Porter was a traitor. His actions led to the murder of her parents. And the man put Ana in danger all those years. Trying to protect her didn't undo all the wrong in A.J.'s book, but if Porter hadn't stepped in, and Winters had his way, things could've gone much differently.

It was a good thing A.J. hadn't been with Luke and Knox in the Maldives. He would've killed Winters with his bare hands.

"You okay? I'm sorry." Knox's voice was low and soft. Compassionate. Then he tossed a thumb behind him, letting A.J. know they'd leave and give them some space.

"Call you later," A.J. mouthed and thanked him before he and Adriana quietly left.

Ana unleashed more tears once the door clicked shut, then sank to her knees. He went to the floor with her, keeping her in his embrace so she could let go. Let all the pain and anger free.

"Can I kill him?" he asked when she pulled back, brushing the backs of her hands over her cheeks.

"Porter or Winters?" she whispered.

"I'm good with both," he answered in all honesty.

"I'd prefer you not go to jail before we have our three-month adventure."

"So after that," he said with a nod.

"I can't imagine what would have happened if you hadn't come into my life when you did."

He couldn't imagine either, and he never wanted to.

He brought her face closer to his, gently caressing her cheeks in his palms. "Good, don't picture it." He kissed a few stray tears on her cheek. "And I'm not going anywhere."

* * *

"By the way, you still owe me a game of Seven Minutes in Heaven for that bet you lost. You said our comms wouldn't work in the tunnels in Budapest which, obviously, was not the case." A.J. rolled to his side in Ana's bed and lowered the sheet from her chest, exposing her naked breasts. He was greedy, and he wanted every chance to soak in the sight of her before he left for Alabama soon.

He'd only be gone for two days, but right now, that was two days too long. Maybe if Porter hadn't died on Thursday morning, he would have been able to convince Ana to go with him to the wedding, but he didn't want to push since she was still emotionally recovering from a damn tough week.

It was Saturday morning, the day of Ella's dress rehearsal, and one week since Ana was on a yacht on the Danube with the Russians shooting at her . . .

He'd originally planned on going to Alabama last night, but then he and Ana had made love for the first time since the safe house in Georgia, and he hadn't been able to get out of bed. He just might have the same problem this morning.

Leaving her would not be easy. The idea of Ana being alone after what she'd been through made him crazy.

"I think the twenty-plus minutes you spent with your

mouth between my legs earlier, and afterward when I returned the favor, is a lot better than Seven—"

He cut her off, needing to taste her. Kiss those sweet lips. She moaned against his mouth and intensified the kiss when her tongue met his.

He palmed her breast before trailing his hand along the curve of her hip and down around to her ass cheek. "This is heaven," he murmured, growing harder than hard. "I really don't want to leave."

"Your family will hate me, and you'll hate yourself, if you miss Ella's wedding." She gently placed a hand to his abdomen, a look of distress on her face when she touched the bruise as though angry at herself for shooting him.

Thank God the woman was a damn fine shot, though.

"You could make me the happiest man in the world and board that plane with me in ninety minutes." He had, maybe, twenty minutes before he needed to leave for the airport. And twenty minutes out of the next forty-eight hours was not nearly enough time with Ana.

"I just don't think I can. I'm an emotional basket case. I'll get better, I promise. But this has been . . ."

"I know." And he understood. He didn't think most people would be able to function after what Ana had gone through, but she was strong. Brave and determined. A force of nature. And a woman he wanted to spend the rest of his life with.

"You'll have some of the guys there with you, right?"

"Unfortunately, while you were sleeping earlier, I got a call from Wyatt. Echo Team is spinning back up. Should be a quick op in Vancouver, but Luke is filling in for Wyatt just in case the op turns into something longer. Can't have Wyatt missing his wedding this month."

"Who is filling in for you?" She softly circled her nail over the shape of the bruise on his stomach.

"Knox offered." And A.J. wanted to hate that he wouldn't be serving as Echo Two for the next three months, but getting to spend all that time alongside Ana was more than he could hope for.

"So, no one is coming with you to Ella's wedding, then?" she asked, her voice soft as if sad for him.

"It's fine. No one really wants to see Ella marry Brian. Me included," he grumbled. "Of course, Chris was probably the most sour-faced. He'd wanted to come with me."

"Right. He has the hots for Jesse's sister, huh?"

"Looks that way, but it's probably better if he doesn't see her again anytime soon. Even if Rory decides to settle down in New Orleans, I just don't want that big teddy bear to get his heart broken." A.J. squeezed her ass cheek, then brought his hand over her hip and to her center. He crooked a finger between her legs.

"You know, I thought we were having panic-sex last week, but that's not what it was," she said after drawing her lip between her teeth and bucking her hips against his palm while he touched her. "Not distraction-sex, either."

"And what would you call it?" he asked, his voice husky, laced with love.

"Exactly what I need," she rasped, eyes connecting with his. "Just you and nothing between us."

"Is that so?" He scooted closer and slid his finger deep inside her, and she parted her legs, a request for a lot more of him than just his hand, and he'd be happy to oblige.

"You know, I've got a list running in my head right now," he said while positioning her onto her back before he lowered himself over her, framing her body between his muscular thighs.

"Oh do you now?" Her eyes glinted with passion. "Taking after me, I see."

"I think this is a list you'll like." He brought himself closer to her, positioning his tip near her wet pussy. "But I'd rather show you than tell you."

She smiled, her white teeth flashing. "Now, Alexander James, I like the way you think."

CHAPTER THIRTY-EIGHT

JUST OUTSIDE BIRMINGHAM, ALABAMA

"I can't believe you blew up Black Beauty," Grant grumbled for the tenth time in as many minutes. "I mean . . . my truck, I wouldn't care, but damn, A.J." Grant leaned against his truck, the one A.J. borrowed last week, and shook his head. The poor guy did look upset. "And you really can't tell me how my bike got destroyed?"

They were standing in the driveway of the main house at his parents' ranch waiting to head over to Ella and Brian's rehearsal dinner, and A.J. was feeling the heat. In more ways than one.

He squeezed the back of his neck as Grant removed his aviator shades and pinned him with dark brown eyes, trying to get a read on him. "Yeah, so there was this guy, uh, shooting at me, and well, shit, you know how fast those kinds of situations can go south," he rambled and peered at his buddy with what he hoped was a look of apology.

Grant leaned forward and set a hand to his shoulder. "Rather have my bike full of holes than you, brother." He slipped his sunglasses back on. "Ella really planning on marrying Brian tomorrow?" He directed his focus on the house. "I mean, I'm not gonna lie, I don't like the guy."

"No one does," A.J. muttered and faced his parents' two-story home, taking in the wraparound porch with a new perspective ever since Ana had declared how much she loved it and wanted one someday.

Leaving her earlier that day had been hard, but he kept reminding himself he would see her back in D.C. on Monday. He'd gotten used to spending every day with her, and he was looking forward to their time together that wouldn't involve getting shot at.

"Maybe you should go talk to her one more time? Feel her out." Grant lifted his chin toward the house where Ella was inside getting ready with Rory.

"And have her hate me again? Surely the guys told you about the aftermath of the bachelor party." He winced at the memory.

Ella was moving to Mobile, and . . .

Shit, maybe Grant was right. "Okay." He slapped his palms together. "One more shot."

"I'll wait in the truck with the engine running in case you need to make a run for it." Grant opened the door to the driver's side.

"Thanks for the vote of confidence." He smirked, then started for the house. It was hot as blazes out there in his jeans, black boots, and long-sleeved black "dress shirt" his mother had insisted he wear for dinner. Thirty-eight, and his mom still wanted to dress him.

He made a beeline for the stairs, worried he'd lose his nerve if he didn't head straight for Ella's room. He knocked on the door and waited for a beat before calling out, "You decent?"

"Come in," Ella answered, her tone so soft he nearly missed her words.

Ella's eyes moved to catch him in the mirror of the vanity as he entered the room, but her body remained stiff as she sat facing forward in the chair beneath an arched window that overlooked the front of the property. Their mom had kept their rooms exactly how they left them when they'd each moved out. Ella's walls were still covered with pictures of her childhood crushes alongside of her very first fashion sketches pinned to a bulletin board.

"Almost done." Rory garbled around the bobby pins clenched between her teeth as she worked to put Ella's hair into some fancy updo.

Rory was wearing a pale pink, sleeveless dress that went to her knees, her blonde hair down over her shoulders, while his sister was in a fitted dark wrap dress that made him feel like they were going to a funeral instead of a rehearsal dinner the night before what was supposed to be the happiest day of her life.

Based on the way Ella eyed him in the mirror, A.J. must have been giving off the *Are you sure?* vibe all over his face

"Can I just have one minute?" He removed his black cowboy hat and set it against his thigh.

Rory secured two more pins in Ella's hair and then smiled. "Done. You look gorgeous." She whirled around and stole a look at A.J., shooting him a glare that read, *Don't break her heart.* "One minute." She held up a finger. "That's all you get. Or I'll send Brooke in here, and I know she's one bridesmaid you'd prefer to avoid."

"I don't need to avoid her, but—"

"A.J.'s a taken man now, didn't you hear?" Ella smiled. The first real one he'd seen since arriving a few hours ago.

Oh, he was sure Rory had heard. All of Alabama had to

have heard that A.J. was dating Ana, the FBI agent whose face had been all over the international news recently.

"Well, it's too bad your friend Chris didn't come with you." Rory started past him. "Surely Brooke would've left you alone if she'd set eyes on that man."

"Ha." He shook his head. "Like *you* would have been okay if Brooke threw herself at Chris?"

Rory's mouth twisted, and she stuck her nose in the air. *Uh-huh, just what I thought.* A.J. gave her a smirk.

"I'll give you that minute," she said in a haughty tone.

A.J. waited for Rory to leave, then sat on Ella's childhood bed. "I'm surprised you didn't design your wedding gown yourself." His gaze moved to the dress hanging on the back of her closet door.

Ella peered his way, and he saw pain in her eyes. "Yeah, well, you know . . ." She trailed off, looking back to the mirror. "And, um, it's too bad Ana couldn't come with you this weekend. Despite all the crazy Russian espionage stuff, and Beckett originally blowing a fuse about it, she fit in down here. I hope you don't screw things up with her." She stood and snatched her black, strappy wedge sandals and slipped them on.

"I won't screw things up," he muttered in protest, then tightened his hand on the brim of his hat as he held it on his lap. *Way to turn the conversation, Ella.* "I have every intention of marrying that woman. No doubt in my mind." And he had no qualms about admitting it, either. "But, Ella Mae, do you have doubts about tomorrow?" And there, he said it. What choice did he have?

A.J. focused on Ella's reflection in the mirror, her eyes revealing the truth that yes, she did have doubts. He'd seen his sister with Brian enough times to know that she'd never once looked like a woman in love when they were together because now, thanks to Ana, he was very familiar with that look. Ana's love for him shined through her eyes and melted his heart every time they gazed at each other.

"Please, don't do this. I already got an earful from Shep and Caleb. And a few grumpy warnings from Beckett last night, too." She clutched the skirt of her dress. "I don't know why you're all so against my happiness."

"Don't you get it? We're concerned you're *not* happy." He stood and circled a hand around her wrist. "Just tell me why you want to marry him. Tell me what the rest of your life would be like without him."

Her eyes dropped closed, and her lower lip trembled.

"You know that horrible, empty feeling as though your soul has left your body, and you can't breathe? Can't eat. Everything hurts on the inside, and your heart is just . . . gone?" He took a shaky breath himself, finding a lump in his throat. "That's how I feel when I imagine what my life would be like without Anastasia. And I just want to know if you have that same gut-wrenching, painful feeling when you imagine your life without Brian. Just think about it." He released her and turned, then froze, worried he was seeing things again.

His heart was in his throat. His pulse racing. About every other emotion imaginable washed over him the second he saw Ana backing up, her beautiful face tinged pink as if embarrassed to have interrupted his conversation, but—

"Ana," he breathed out, dropping his hat. "You're here." Once the shock wore off, he hurried to the door.

"I'm sorry to interrupt. Grant told me you'd be upstairs," she said as he scooped her in his arms like he hadn't seen her in months instead of just hours.

"What are you doing here? How did ya even get here?" He set her down, still utterly surprised by her presence.

"I know a guy who knows a guy." She smiled, then pointed to the window.

Ella was already on her way to the window. Curious, A.J. followed his sister to get a view of the "guy" Ana knew.

Owen was outside talking to both Beckett and Grant, standing in front of Beckett's sheriff's truck. "What . . .?" He raced a hand over his hair before reaching for his hat on the floor.

"Your brother called me right after I dropped you off at the airport, and he convinced me to get my head out of my ass—his words—and get on the first plane down here." She lifted both shoulders. "There were no flights, so Adriana suggested Owen fly me here. You know, since he has a pilot's license."

"Right." He shook his head, still in disbelief.

"I'm so glad our plan worked." Ella approached Ana and pulled her in for a hug. "When we heard you weren't coming with A.J., well, we decided to have Beckett call and guilt-trip you into coming down here."

"Well, I gotta say I'm surprised. But grateful." And now he felt guiltier than ever for pushing Ella about her wedding tomorrow, and all the while, she'd been going behind his back to make sure he was happy. "Thank you, Sis." He swallowed. "I guess we have a dress rehearsal dinner to get to, then."

Ella smiled. Damn it. It wasn't a real one. "Meet you there?"

A.J. leaned in and pressed a kiss to his sister's temple, then reached for Ana's hand. "See you there."

"Howdy, stranger," Ana said once they were alone in the hall.

He spun her around and pinned her against the wall, nearly knocking a collage of family photos to the floor.

"Thank you for coming," he said, bringing his mouth close to hers. "Did you happen to hear what I was saying just before I saw you in the doorway?"

She arched a brow and set her palms to his chest as he leaned in closer, setting his hand on the wall. "I did," she whispered, lifting her chin. "And I feel the same, which is why it didn't take any convincing to get me here when your brother called. In fact, I was already in the middle of packing, prepared to hijack Air Force One if need be to get down to you."

He lifted a brow and smiled. "Oh, really?" He caught her lower lip between his teeth, then swept his tongue into her mouth.

"Young love," his mom called out in her booming voice, startling A.J. into breaking the kiss. Deb Hawkins was grinning from ear to ear as she strode their way.

He brought his forehead to Ana's and laughed. "Sounds about right," he said before kissing her again, and no one would be stopping him this time.

"ARE WE REALLY DOING THIS?" A.J. EYED HIS BROTHERS, trying to wrap his head around what happened last night, and what was about to happen now.

"Ella is insisting, so yeah, I mean—it's the Fourth and all, and everyone in town was planning on being here today, anyway." Caleb braced a hand on the mantle in the living room as Shep paced back and forth on the wood floors, the click of his cowboy boots in A.J.'s ears.

"But she called off the wedding in the middle of the rehearsal dinner last night." A.J. peered out the window, searching for Ana.

The two hundred folks on Ella's guest list were slowly filtering in for the "Fourth of July party." The backyard had been transformed for the wedding reception, and it was now being repurposed for America's birthday.

There was a large platform beyond the pool for a band and dancing. An open tent with enough tables and chairs to accommodate half the town. Catering trucks had already arrived. Champagne flutes were being filled. Kids were running around with sparklers and laughing.

But no wedding had taken place at the church today.

And A.J. knew why. Hell, everyone knew why, but no one was talking about it.

Brian hightailed it back to Mobile with his appalled friends and family last night after Ella announced she wouldn't be marrying him.

But Independence Day was a huge event in his town, so Ella declared the party was still on.

And it was the damndest thing, but A.J. was fairly certain it was the first time Ella looked happy since agreeing to marry Not-So-Perfect Brian. There hadn't been tears when she broke things off with Brian, much to A.J.'s surprise. He might have felt a little guilty about that, but he'd get over it.

"I still can't believe she called it off," Caleb said as A.J. faced the room again.

Beckett stood in front of Shep, effectively putting a halt to his pacing.

A.J. thought back to dinner last night. Jesse had been staring intently at Ella all evening, looking as though his dog had died. Hell, worse than that. And then he'd abruptly stood from the table, and the room they'd rented at the restaurant fell silent. Jesse's jaw was clenched, and his eyes were pinned Ella's way. "I'm sorry, but I can't do this," he'd rasped. "Brian ain't right for you, and I can't watch you marry him tomorrow." And then he tossed his linen napkin on his plate and took off.

No one had been able to reach him since he'd gone God knew where last night. A.J. left him message after message after Ella had called off the wedding thirty minutes later. But knowing Jesse, he was off-grid now.

"Ella say anything to you? You think she's got feelings for Jesse? Is that why she finally ended the charade of marrying Brian?" Shep went to the window alongside A.J.

A.J. shut his eyes, thinking back to what Ella had told him last night.

That soul-leaving-your-body feeling, Ella had said to him outside their parents' house. *I know what that's like. But I don't get that when thinking about not being with Brian.* She'd squeezed his arm. *Thank you for finally putting some sense into me.*

A.J. was fairly certain Jesse standing before her and declaring he refused to watch her marry Brian was what actually set her mind right, but he had no idea what would come of the two of them. They were both stubborn as all hell, and he had no clue why they'd held back for so long.

"She wants a party." A.J. folded his arms. "So, we give her a party."

"Throwing her reception without the wedding, ain't that gonna be a reminder that shit went sideways?" Shep turned toward his brothers. "I don't want her suffering."

"It's what she wants, and you know how Hawkins women can be. You don't stand in the way of what they want," Caleb reminded him.

"Okay, fine." Shep adjusted his tan Stetson. "I guess we can all breathe a little easier since we didn't have to put on those monkey suits and watch our little sis marry that guy."

"Let's go help her get through today." Beckett motioned

toward the backyard, signaling for them to get a move on, but A.J. stopped Beckett from following Shep and Caleb outside.

"I wanted to thank you," A.J. told him, hand on his arm. "I didn't get a chance."

Beckett removed his black cowboy hat and brought it to his side. "It's clear how you feel about Ana. Clear as day. No doubt in my mind like I'd had with Ella and Brian."

"Well, thank you. I wouldn't want anything coming between us." He reached for his brother's hand. "You've always been there for me, even when I didn't think I needed you. So, thank you."

Beckett eyed his hand for a moment. "This is Alabama, boy. You give me a hug." He pulled A.J. in and slapped his back twice, and A.J.'s throat thickened with emotions.

Once they were outside, A.J. navigated through the crowd already in full swing as the sun set—dancing, eating, and drinking—to try and find Ana.

And, jackpot.

Ana was laughing at something Grant was saying while they danced. She had on a soft yellow wrap dress that hugged her curves and fanned out when Grant spun her. But it was the cowboy boots paired with that dress that was his favorite accessory on her. They must have been Ella's. God, she was gorgeous.

"A.J.?"

He blinked and turned at the sound of Savanna's voice. "Hey, you came. I wasn't sure if you would." He pulled Marcus's widow into his arms for a hug. "Been too long."

"I know, I'm sorry. Things have been hectic in the city. I started my own little bakery and coffee shop this year," she announced when he released her.

"That's great. Congrats. Marcus would be so damn proud of you."

She drew a hand to her chest and smiled. "Is it strange that I can still feel him here? Like he's watching us right now?"

He tilted his face to the sky and closed his eyes. "I know exactly what you mean."

"I heard you and the pretty Federal agent are together," she said with a smile. "Marcus would want you to be happy."

He gently gripped her arm. "He'd want you to be happy, too, you know."

"Is that you? Hot damn, Savanna! So good to see you!" Shep charged their way and scooped Savanna into his arms, and she laughed. "Girl, you better come out here and dance with me."

"How about we teach Ana a little two-step?" Savanna suggested once Shep finally put her down.

"What makes you think she doesn't already know it?" A.J. teased, but hell, he was pretty sure Ana wouldn't have a clue. "Nah, you're right." He went to the small raised stage above the dance area and put in a request for "The Git Up" by Blanco Brown, and then a more romantic song by Clint Black for another round of two-step after.

He made his way to Ana, the anticipation of pulling her into his arms and dancing lighting a fire inside of him. "Mind if I cut in?"

Grant kissed Ana on the cheek, then allowed A.J. to take over.

"I've been patiently waiting for you," she murmured.

"Hopefully you don't change your mind after this." He set his hat on her head, then snatched her hand and spun her once the band leader began playing his first song request.

"What are we doing?" Ana asked with a chuckle when the guests began dancing in synchronized fashion.

"A little two-step boogie." He grinned. "Directions are

right in the song," he promised, and his smile stretched when she held the hat on her head and surprised him by letting loose, following along with the crowd.

She swayed her hips, rolled her shoulders, and took it down.

And damn he was in love.

"Get it, girl." Ella came to stand in front of Ana and danced with her, and even Ella was laughing. She hadn't married Brian, and this was her wedding reception, but . . . everything happened for a reason. And maybe the next time she planned on marrying it'd be to the right man.

A.J. went still when he lifted his gaze and saw Jesse coming down the hill from where the cars were parked out in a field.

Ana looked up as well and slowed her movements at the sight.

So, Jesse finally got his messages. About damn time.

When the band switched to singing a Clint Black song, A.J. stole Ana into his arms, prepared to teach her the next moves himself. He wanted her as close to him as possible. "Later," he whispered into her ear, "when the sun sets, how about we go into the back of my old truck and—"

"Make love?" she mouthed seductively.

"I was gonna say check out the stars," he said with a grin and leaned in closer, bringing his mouth to hers. "But I like the way you think." He kissed her, then surprised her with a spin.

When he caught her in his arms, he chanced a look Ella's way, happy to see her dancing with Jesse, and from the looks of it, tonight was going exactly the way it was supposed to go.

Shep had Savanna laughing and dancing.

Caleb had McKenna on his shoulders as she swayed her arms from side to side to the crooning of the music.

Even Owen had stayed for the party, and A.J.'s mom was teaching him a few two-step moves.

With Ana in his arms in his hometown . . . yeah, it was about as perfect as perfect could get. And there wasn't a place in the world he'd rather be. Hell, now he sounded like a living country song.

"Sing for me?" she asked as if reading his thoughts.

"Oh?" He tightened his hold of her waist, drawing her closer. "And what would the lady like to request?"

She teasingly worked her lip between her teeth for a moment. "'Somebody Like You' by Keith Urban."

"That I can do." His hand drifted down to her ass cheek, and he squeezed, the material so thin he practically felt her skin, and was she wearing panties? He'd have to do an inspection later. "I love you, woman." He snatched his hat back from her and set it on his head. "But I gotta get you your own hat."

"I don't know," she said, drawing her eyes down the front of his jeans when he stepped back. "I think it looks pretty good on me, especially when that's all I have on."

Tease. Temptress. He ran through a list in his head of words to describe her. And his favorites, *all mine.*

EPILOGUE

JUST OUTSIDE BIRMINGHAM, ALABAMA - TWO AND A HALF MONTHS LATER

"You're not peeking through that blindfold, are you?" A.J. waved a hand in front of Ana's face as he walked backward.

"No." She reached out in front of her to find her balance as she walked. "But if you don't plan on making love to me with this thing on—your reasons for blindfolding me better be good."

"What makes you think we're not going to have sex?" he teased while reaching for her forearms to stop her from walking any farther.

"Because you're my husband, and I know you." Her lips twitched into an adorable smile.

"Say that one more time." He closed his eyes, relishing in how the word rolled from her tongue.

She made a show of wetting her lips. "Husband," she purred with a lift of her chin.

And even after a three-week honeymoon of traveling to

different romantic spots along the Mediterranean, where he'd had her say the word over and over again, he doubted he'd ever grow tired of hearing it.

Now they just had to find a time to tell their friends and family that they'd eloped. But hell, they had followed Asher and Jessica's lead. When Jessica had dropped the bombshell on everyone at Wyatt and Natasha's wedding in July that she and Asher had secretly eloped, well, Luke almost had a stroke. Surely the blowback for his and Ana's wedding wouldn't cause as big of a shock with his team. His parents and siblings on the other hand . . .

But he and Ana had been eager to make it official. To give Ana a last name she'd never have to change again.

"Anastasia Hawkins." Damn did he love saying it. He went behind her, preparing to untie the blindfold. "That was the name you were meant to have."

"And when your parents find out about us?" She reached out, searching for him.

"They'll force us to have a big party to celebrate." And they were planning on telling them tomorrow at his father's birthday party. A "Happy Birthday, We're Married" surprise. He'd just have to hide his mom's gun, so she didn't shoot him in the ass for eloping. "Okay, you ready for the surprise?"

"Will my surprise be you in jeans and chaps and nothing else? I'm still waiting on that fantasy to come true." Desire floated through her tone. A sexy drawl as she teased out the words to purposefully turn him on.

And yeah, sex would be happening today. But first . . .

He untied the blindfold and tossed it over his shoulder before stepping around her.

They were standing inside an old barn filled with rusty equipment equally as old. He'd strung Christmas lights overhead and placed a soft, red cashmere blanket on the ground on top of some hay for padding. A picnic basket and a woman's cowgirl hat were on top of the blanket.

"This is adorable and romantic. And," she said while turning into his arms, "we are having sex, then?" She lifted one arm and tipped up his Stetson. "That cowgirl hat mine? Will that be all I wear today?" She dragged her tongue along her lower lip. "Any leather chaps in here?" A teasing smile met her eyes.

"Oh, there will be plenty of romancing you soon enough." He closed one eye. "And maybe I will even fulfill that jeans and chaps fantasy of yours."

"But first?" She stepped back, now sensing they were in that barn for a lot more than a good time.

"I was, um." He sucked in a sharp, nervous breath.

They'd talked about their plans for weeks. Hell, the last two-plus months. But there was one question he'd yet to officially ask her, and he wasn't sure why he was so nervous, but he was.

"This is your wedding gift."

"The picnic and sex?" Oh, she knew. The woman was too smart not to know what he was getting at, but she looooved to give him a hard time.

He closed the space between them and drew the back of his hand down her cheek. "Two acres of land. A house where this barn is sitting." He swallowed. "A wraparound porch."

She draped her arms over his shoulders. "Mmmm. Tell me more."

"Right here where we're standing could be your office. You know, while you write that book you've been plotting." She'd decided she wanted to share the pages of her story while also helping others cope and move on with their lives in the face of tragedy or betrayal. "I know you'll be teaching a few courses at Quantico a couple times a year in between your writing, but—"

"But nothing." She brought her mouth to his. "I'd love to make a home here if that's what you're trying to ask."

He lowered his forehead to hers and wrapped his arms around her waist, then released a shaky, emotional breath. "You would?" he whispered against her ear.

"More than anything." She leaned back and captured his eyes with her intense focus, one that had his world spinning in just the right direction.

"My family can be a lot, and I'll be starting to spin back up in two weeks, but I think it'd be nice if we set down some roots. Build a home together."

"Will your mom help me design it?" She teased his lower lip between her teeth before inching her face back, eyes on him again.

"If that's what you want."

"I do," she murmured. "And I want roots. And a family. And all the things." Her smile stretched. "I want you."

"And you want me in jeans and chaps?" he asked as she swooped his hat off his head and set it on her own, her golden-red hair down over her shoulders. She looked relaxed and sexy in ripped-up jeans and a white ribbed tank top.

"Oh," she said with a nod, "I really, really do."

He snatched his hat from her and stepped back. "You got your own hat now, woman," he said with a grin. "But I think I just might have some brown leather chaps here somewhere. I mean, I gotta make my wife happy."

She peeled her tank top over her head, revealing her sheer, white lace bra. Then unbuttoned the top of her jeans.

Ana was officially a relaxed woman. No more panic-anything had been needed in months.

Just lots and lots of making love. Enjoying life.

He turned to find where he hid the chaps for her viewing pleasure, but then halted at the sound of his ringing phone. "It's Chris," he grumbled.

"You think they're pulling you in early? You better take it if they need you."

He slowly faced her, but there wasn't disappointment in her eyes. Just love.

"I knew the man I was marrying, and I happen to love that man." She pointed to his phone in his palm. "My fantasy can wait." *But* she went ahead and removed her boots before unzipping her jeans.

Wait? Yeah, right. "It's me," he nearly croaked upon answering. "What's up?" He swallowed when Ana shimmied her jeans down her hips before they fell to her ankles, and she kicked them off.

Oh, Anastasia the erotic dancer was coming out to play. *Hot damn.* He bit down on his back teeth when his wife circled her hands around one of the wood pillars and arched her back, offering him a show.

"Say that again." A.J. missed whatever Chris had said when he cocked his head to the side and watched while Ana bent over and set a hand to the ground, then shook her ass in a seductive but adorably comical fashion. And he loved every second of it.

"A canine," Chris announced, probably for the second or third time. "I officially rescued one for the team, but I can't decide on a name," he rambled, and A.J. barely focused on what Echo Three had said when his wife lost her bra and panties. "You think Rory can train him since you said she's starting her own business in New Orleans?"

"A canine," A.J. repeated. "Great. Rory, yeah," he added while Ana placed her new cowgirl hat on her head and lifted one shoulder, then seductively set her hands over her breasts and squeezed. "So, I'm not spinning up right now?" he confirmed, his throat and chest tight as desire took over him.

"No, I—"

"Then I'll call you back." A.J. tossed his phone and lunged for his wife, pulling the little vixen tight in his arms. "You're naughty."

"Oh," she said softly, "just how you like me in bed."

His dick grew so damn hard he'd barely be able to contain it in his pants.

"Now the chaps," she urged, then stepped away and flicked a commanding finger.

"As you wish, sugar." He pressed a quick kiss to her lips and turned to find the chaps.

He'd do anything and everything to fulfill her every wish.

And he knew when the time was right, she'd give him a few wishes of his own—babies.

He went into one of the old stalls and retrieved the chaps where he'd hidden them. After tossing his shirt, he unbuttoned the top of his jeans, secured the leather chaps in place, then fixed his hat before facing her.

She had her thumbnail between her teeth, standing beautifully naked on top of the cashmere blanket. "My sexy cowboy," she whispered as he strode closer.

"And I'm all yours." He took her into his arms, guided her chin up, and set a hot kiss to her lips. "Forever and ever," he added. "And now let's act out this little fantasy of yours, shall we?"

MORE STEALTH OPS & ALABAMA SERIES

Want more of the Stealth Ops team? Chris's book, ***Chasing Fortune,*** releases October 8th, 2020. Stay up-to-date on releases by heading over to Brittneysahin.com.

If you missed the latest <u>bonus scene</u>, Stealth Ops #6, which features **Asher & Jessica's twins** plus more **Liam & Emily** . . . the bonus scene is now available for download on my website. (Be sure to bookmark the page or join my newsletter so you don't miss out on the next scenes!)

Curious about the conversation between Natasha and Wyatt when they stepped out in the hall in chapter 5 - find it on my website - brittneysahin.com/bonus-content.

* * *

ALABAMA SERIES
Don't worry - I'd never leave you hanging about what might happen with Ella and Jesse ...

Plus, we have a whole cast of characters from Alabama that need a happy ending!

This new series starring A.J.'s family and friends launches in 2021.

Series title and release information to be revealed first in the Stealth Ops Spoiler Room and Brittney's Book Babes FB groups.

* * *

Stealth Ops Team Members

Team leaders: Luke & Jessica Scott / Intelligence team member (joined in 2019): Harper Brooks

Bravo Team:
Bravo One - Luke
Bravo Two - Owen
Bravo Three - Asher
Bravo Four - Liam
Bravo Five - Knox (Charlie "Knox" Bennett)

Echo Team:
Echo One - Wyatt
Echo Two - A.J. (Alexander James)
Echo Three - Chris
Echo Four - Roman
Echo Five - Finn (Dalton "Finn" Finnegan)

Stealth Ops World Guide

Stealth Ops Timeline
Stealth Ops FB Spoiler Room
Reading Guide
Pinterest Muse/Inspiration Board

PLAYLIST

Lil Nas X, *Old Town Road* (Chapter 2)

Brett Young - *In Case You Didn't Know* (Chapter 7)

Blake Shelton and Gwen Stefani - *Nobody But You* (Chapter 12)

P!nk, Khalid - *Hurts 2B Human* (Chapter 19)

Thomas Rhett, Reba McEntire - *Be A Light* (Chapter 21)

The Avett Brothers - *Ain't No Man* (Chapter 23-24)

Luke Bryan - *What She Wants Tonight* (Chapter 25)

Blake Shelton - *Hell Right* (Chapter 25)

Lee Brice - *I don't Dance* (Chapter 25)

Regard - *Ride It* (Chapter 26)

Kelly Clarkson - *I Dare You* (Chapter 33)

Andra Day - *Rise Up* (Chapter 36)

Blanco Brown - *The Git Up* (Chapter 38)

Keith Urban - *Somebody Like You* (Chapter 38)

Luke Bryan - *Knockin' Boots* (Epilogue)

Spotify Playlist - Chasing Daylight, Brittney Sahin

READING GUIDE

Get the latest news from my newsletter/website and/or Dublin Nights Spoiler Room / Brittney's Book Babes / the Stealth Ops Spoiler Room.

* * *

A Stealth Ops World Guide is available on my website, which features more information about the team, character muses, and SEAL lingo.

Also, check out this handy **reading guide**.

Stealth Ops Series: Bravo Team

Finding His Mark - Book 1 - Luke & Eva

Finding Justice - Book 2 - Owen & Samantha

Finding the Fight - Book 3 - Asher & Jessica

Finding Her Chance - Book 4 - Liam & Emily

Finding the Way Back - Book 5 -Knox & Adriana

Stealth Ops Series: Echo Team

Chasing the Knight - Book 6 -Wyatt & Natasha

Chasing Daylight - Book 7 - A.J. & Ana

Chasing Fortune - Book 8, Chris & Rory

Book 9 - Harper & Roman (2021)

Book 10 - Finn (2021)

Becoming Us: *connection to the Stealth Ops Series (books take place between the prologue and chapter 1 of Finding His Mark)*

Someone Like You - A former Navy SEAL. A father. And off-limits. (Noah Dalton)

My Every Breath - A sizzling and suspenseful romance. Businessman Cade King has fallen for the wrong woman. She's the daughter of a hitman - and he's the target.

Dublin Nights

On the Edge - Travel to Dublin and get swept up in this romantic suspense starring an Irish businessman by day…and fighter by night.

On the Line - novella

The Real Deal - This mysterious billionaire businessman has finally met his match.

The Inside Man - Cole McGregor & Alessia Romano

Dublin Nights 5 (title pending) - Sean and Emilia

Stand-alone (with a connection to *On the Edge*):

The Story of Us– Sports columnist Maggie Lane has 1 rule: never fall for a player. One mistaken kiss with Italian soccer star Marco Valenti changes everything…

Hidden Truths

The Safe Bet – Begin the series with the Man-of-Steel lookalike Michael Maddox.

Beyond the Chase - Fall for the sexy Irishman, Aiden O'Connor, in this romantic suspense.

The Hard Truth – Read Connor Matthews' story in this second-chance romantic suspense novel.

Surviving the Fall – Jake Summers loses the last 12 years of his life in this action-packed romantic thriller.

The Final Goodbye - Friends-to-lovers romantic mystery

WHERE ELSE TO FIND ME

Thank you for reading A.J. and Ana's story. If you don't mind taking a minute to leave a short review, I would greatly appreciate it. Reviews are incredibly helpful to keeping the series going. Thank you!

www.brittneysahin.com
brittneysahin@emkomedia.net
FB Reader Group - Brittney's Book Babes
Stealth Ops Spoiler Room
Pinterest Muse/Inspiration Board